"One book you don't want to read on a plane. . . . Heart-stopping descriptions of what happens after a plane crash. . . . The NTSB ought to give Thayer an award for showing what a tough job its investigators have."
—*Orlando Sentinel* (FL)

"Gripping. . . . A page-turner and a fascinatingly well-researched look inside an NTSB crash investigation."
—*Tribune-Review* (Pittsburgh)

"A thrilling 'Event' . . . with high-voltage suspense . . . that's difficult to put down."
—*Naples Daily News* (FL)

"Thayer scores again . . . [and] gives readers their money's worth with a bang-up, surprise ending."
—*The Pilot* (Southern Pines, NC)

"A fascinating thriller . . . a genuinely engrossing novel, which contains a twist that few, if any, readers will see coming."
—*Booklist*

"A riveting detective story. . . . There are perhaps a dozen blind alleys that the investigators must go down, and the story follows all of them . . . until a seemingly insignificant fact leads to the solution."
—*Drood Review of Mystery*

FIVE PAST MIDNIGHT

"As fast and straightforward as a punch in the jaw. . . . Fans of Jack Higgins will devour this fast-paced thriller."
—*Publishers Weekly*

"Fast-moving and entertaining."
—*Kirkus Reviews*

"One of the best war stories of the Nineties. . . . Great work from the leader of suspense thrillers."
—*BookBrowser*

WHITE STAR

"[Thayer's] writing is smooth and clear. Deceptively simple, it wastes no words, and it has a rhythm that only confident stylists achieve."
—*The New York Times Book Review*

"A cram course in the art of killing. The best against the best in a compelling yet thoughtful thriller that draws you through a labyrinth of deceptions until the explosive climax."
—*Clive Cussler*

"A gripping espionage tale. . . . entertaining, fast-paced, even educational. . . . Thayer's prose is clear and clean, and the small details of a professional sniper's life are fascinating. . . . *WHITE STAR* is a winner."
—*Seattle Times*

NOVELS BY JAMES THAYER

Terminal Event

Man of the Century

Five Past Midnight

White Star

S-Day: A Memoir of the Invasion of England

Ringer

Pursuit

The Earhart Betrayal

The Stettin Secret

The Hess Cross

TERMINAL
—EVENT—

a novel

JAMES THAYER

POCKET BOOKS

New York   London   Toronto   Sydney   Singapore

POCKET BOOKS, a division of Simon & Schuster, Inc.
1230 Avenue of the Americas, New York, NY 10020

Copyright © 1999 by James Stewart Thayer

Originally published in hardcover in 1999 by
Simon & Schuster, Inc.

ISBN: 0-671-01371-8

First Pocket Books printing March 2001

10 9 8 7 6 5 4 3 2 1

POCKET and colophon are registered trademarks of Simon & Schuster, Inc.

Front cover illustration by PM Workshop

Printed in the U.S.A.

To my brother,
John L. Thayer, M.D.,
and his wife, Kathleen Polley Thayer,
and their children,
Carolyn May Thayer, James Lewis Thayer,
and John Henry Thayer

My heartfelt thanks to Don Bagley;
Mark Coates; Tom Cypher; Carl Dennhardt;
Doug Duncan; J. T. Elder; Dick Foort; Berne Indahl;
Pam Indahl; June McAdams; Keith McGuire;
Mike Moran; Ann Nornes; Bud Pangan;
John D. Reagh III; Judy Rice; Mike Sanchez;
Greg Smith; Fred Sparhawk; Michael Stockhill;
John L. Thayer, M.D.; Mike Walker;
Doug Wanamaker; and my wonderful wife,
Patricia Wallace Thayer.

The aeroplane has unveiled for us
the true face of the earth.

—Antoine de Saint-Exupéry

ONE

A face caught on my shoe. A human face, with a seal brown mustache and a keyboard of strong yellow teeth, was snagged by the toe of my brogan. The eyes were open and the jaw was slack, a startled expression, which was understandable since the back of the head was missing and my shoe had sunk into gore behind an ear.

My hand found a tree trunk, made soft by moss, and I braced myself to scrape the face off my shoe, trying to be respectful of the dead, yet determined to loosen the face so I wouldn't have to walk with it clinging to me like an errant piece of tape. The nausea would come later. It always did.

The face finally dropped off my shoe, and I started again for the cones of sterile white light, glimpsed through the trunks of Douglas fir and ponderosa pine. The spring melt was well underway, but the night's ice crust had formed on the remaining snow, and my shoes cracked through it with each step. I hadn't had time to dress for the mountains. Under the shelter of trees and on stone outcroppings, the snow was gone, and I could move quickly, but some drifts were up to my knees, and I had to high-step, the snow crawling up my pants. I breathed the chilled air in huge gulps.

The light ahead was broken by stabs of red and blue, quick strobe pulses that cut the night. A generator's rumble reached me, made deeper by the long echo from steep slopes all around. Shouted orders were carried in the sough of the wind in the trees. I pushed through a bank of licorice ferns and stepped over a rotted log. These woods had been clear-cut long ago, and old, crumbling stumps marked my way. A canopy of boughs from newer trees blocked most of the moonlight, and cast the snow in dappled blue-black shadows. The cold air held the elemental scents of red cedar and Pacific yew, and of aviation fuel.

I climbed toward the light, sidestepping a rangy wild rhododendron. The wail of sirens came from down the hill, from the way I had come. My foot slipped on a skunk cabbage and I skidded downhill. I grabbed a juniper branch to steady myself, then moved up again, the snow to my calves. I had no gloves, and my fingers were aching from the cold.

I should have thought this through, realized the dangers of my destination, and found some mountain clothing and maybe snowshoes, but there had been no time. Dread had pushed away useful thoughts. I had rushed into the mountains unprepared for the snow and for everything else I knew I would find. My stomach was sour, and only some of my trembling was from the cold.

The Forest Service road off Interstate 5 had taken me several miles south of the highway, and then to a narrow logging road a mile or two farther. Snow had been compressed by snowmobiles and cross-country skis, and my four-wheel-drive Explorer had no trouble, but I had taken a wrong turn somewhere. I had seen the glow of the white lights, but couldn't find the way there in my rig. So I had abandoned the Explorer and had taken off on foot, thinking the light only two or three hundred yards up the forested hill. And now I was tramping through snow, wet to my knees, sweat running down my back, realizing my estimate had been off by about a thousand yards. I plowed through the snow, but the pool of eerie white light seemed to recede ahead of me.

The cold was as sharp as flint. Frozen breath drifting over my shoulder, I passed a copse of lodgepole pine—the trunks are so straight that settlers could make cabins from them—and walked around a chokecherry, and in the darkness almost bumped into a man and woman sitting in chairs in a patch of blue wildrye that had poked through the snow. The couple was wearing matching ski sweaters, and she was gripping a purse on her lap. Their legs ended in bloody stumps at the knees, and the snow under their seats had wicked away their blood. Safety belts had kept them in their chairs.

A few more steps brought me to a lower leg lying across a box elder. The leg had been ripped from the body at the knee. A running shoe was on the foot. Hanging from the shoelace was a silver charm, a tiny pair of crossed skis. Maybe the leg belonged to the woman in the ski sweater, but maybe not. A shrill cry drifted with the wind from the south. A hair-raising *yip, yip, yip*. Probably a coyote. I prayed it was a coyote. I pushed ahead, toward the light.

I stepped on a piece of flat metal I hadn't seen, and it slipped from under my foot like a sled. I caught myself, sinking to a knee. Struggling uphill, I skirted a poison hemlock and approached a propeller, rising out of the snow as if it had been growing there. I am one of the few people alive who can recognize a Hamilton Standard 14SF-11 four-blade propeller at twenty yards on a dark night on the side of a snowy mountain. The blades were bent only slightly rearward, perhaps indicating the engine was generating little or no power at impact, and that the propeller had been windmilling.

I instinctively reached for the kit strapped to my waist, but found only my belt buckle. A year ago I buried my kit in a basement trunk and swore I would never put it back on.

Next came luggage, thrown among the trees and littering the slope. Suitcases had burst like popcorn kernels, spewing out their contents. Pants and a ski parka hung from hemlock boughs. Crystal perfume bottles were here and there, and a cloying cosmetics-counter odor mixed with the winter scents of the mountain. I almost tripped over a package of three JCPenney T-shirts, still in their store wrapping.

Several boughs lay on the snow, torn from pine trees by a turboprop engine. I tried to step around a half-dozen fractured skis and snowboards without disturbing their location, which would be mapped soon enough, along with everything else larger than a pin on this grisly field. I approached an engine, a Pratt & Whitney Canada. The cowling had been ripped away, and the machinery lay exposed. The engine had slid down the hill a few yards, pushing snow in front of it, exposing mountain heather and chickweed.

At a granite outcropping, I grabbed the rough trunk of a Scotch broom to pull myself up. A man was peeking over a rock ledge above, staring down at me. I climbed higher, and saw he was missing both arms. A laptop computer lay next to him, its CD-ROM slot open. Bicycle playing cards lay all around. I moved through hemlock trees toward the white light.

A new scent turned my head. Then I heard a low crackling. A brake of Alaska cedar hid a fire off to my left, I was sure of it. I pushed toward it, ducking boughs and crunching through the snow. I crawled uphill over English ivy, partly covered with snow and as slippery as an ice fall, wound through a labyrinth of cedar trunks, and came to part of the fuselage. Fire worked on the wall panels, and the six passengers still strapped to their chairs were burned to black and resembled beef jerky. This portion of the fuselage was fairly large, indicating the plane had not been flying at a high altitude or great speed when it came apart. Wind picked up black ash and my jaw involuntarily opened at the odor of charred flesh. I had smelled it before, many times. I bit my lower lip hard enough to taste blood, trying to keep my dinner in my stomach. I had never been able to adjust to the carnage, and it had cost me my career.

I stumbled away from the fire. Above me a woman hung upside down, her ankle caught in the fork of a tree, her skirt hiding her face, like Mussolini's mistress. When I came to a patch of bare rock, my shoes scattered rivets, dozens of them, popped from the skin of the plane. Thousands more would be found. I slipped on clubmoss, and slid sideways into a snowdrift, almost bumping into landing gear. The Dunlop wheel was still attached, the tire still holding air. I used juniper boughs to pull myself from the deep snow. A few more steps uphill through the snow—my knees rising almost to my breastbone—brought me to the crest of the plateau, where the rescue operation lay before me.

There was likely no one to rescue, of course, but the Kittitas County sheriff and his deputies knew their first duty was to look for the living. Their cars—bubble tops throwing shafts of blue and red light—lined the logging road I had been unable to find. A dozen fire trucks had also arrived, different colors from different jurisdictions, some pulling into the field to make way for more vehicles. Two trailers with portable generators and klieg lights on telescoping poles were already in place. The kliegs produced the clinical white light I had seen from afar. Everything was in stark white and black, robbing the field of dimension, and making the scene even more nightmarish than it would be in daylight. The tortured ground looked like a garbage dump, and was covered with shreds of cloth, strips of insulation, wiring, torn sheets of aluminum, and flesh and viscera.

Two television vans had arrived, and technicians were aiming the cab-top satellite dishes. A reporter was getting ready for his broadcast, preening himself in front of a mirror held up by his soundman. One truck had KITTITAS COUNTY EMERGENCY SERVICES painted on its side panel. Police and firefighters roamed the site, many looking dazed.

A wing and more of the fuselage and other parts of the plane had fallen onto this small plateau. Bodies were flung across the place, some whole, some in pieces. This flat area looked as if it had been graded at one time, and had been a logging staging area, where line skidders, log loaders, donkey engines, and logging trucks went about their business. The hill began its steep climb again just west of the logging site.

The severed cockpit had also landed here. On its nose was *Sacajawea,* painted in blue. The cockpit's interior was visible, like a cutaway drawing. Instruments glowed eerily green and red, still powered by the backup system. The copilot was in his seat but the pilot and his seat were missing. Firemen poured water from a pumper onto another chunk of the fuselage. Steam hissed away from the wreckage. Near the cockpit was a woman, leaning back against a fir trunk, sitting as if at a picnic, except that she was dead and naked, her clothing having been sucked off her. Cops were cordoning off the area with yellow tape.

A deputy carried a piece of the plane—one of the black boxes—toward his boss, the county sheriff. I caught up with him, stepping over a Fatbob snowboard and a backpack.

"Where'd you get that?" I asked.

The fellow had tears running down his face. He turned away quickly to wipe them, then demanded gruffly to compensate, "Who are you?" He was wearing a peaked cap and a plastic yellow vest with SHERIFF stamped on the back.

"I'm from the National Transportation Safety Board." A small lie. "I need to know where you picked up the black box."

Planes contain two such boxes, the cockpit voice recorder and the flight data recorder, each about the size of a fisherman's tackle box. *Black box* is a misnomer, as this one—and almost all of them—was Day-Glo orange. FLIGHT DATA RECORDER DO NOT OPEN was printed on the box in English and Spanish.

"Back there." He nodded toward the east. "Near some trees."

I held up a hand like a traffic cop, a gesture he would appreciate. "Look, I want you to give me the box, then retrace your steps and try to discover where you found it. It'll be important."

"Sure." He handed it over. "There was a man back there, lying near the box, in a ski sweater. He had a piece of metal stuck through him. A lot of blood. I can find the place again, and I'll . . ." His voice broke and he walked away, back the way he had come, his shoulders hunched protectively.

I had seen this before. Cops and firemen, no matter how tough and street smart, just aren't ready for their first big crash site. NTSB investigators call these sites *majors*. I had seen quite a few majors, and I was never ready, either.

A deputy sheriff was piling up metal pieces of the fuselage, stacking them like cordwood. Carrying the black box, I rushed over, as quickly as the calf-deep snow allowed.

"Don't do that," I ordered. "Leave the pieces where they fell."

"Shouldn't we be cleaning up?" His voice was distant and vague. He inhaled a huge draught of air. "I mean, I should do something. I should help." He cringed, as if I might tell him to collect body parts.

"Search for survivors."

He moved his hand in a small way. "Nobody could live through this."

"Search anyway. Let's make sure nobody lucky enough to survive the crash freezes to death in these mountains."

I left him there, and headed toward the sheriff, who was holding a cell phone to his ear and a map in his other hand. A deputy was standing at his shoulder and pointing a flashlight for him. The sheriff wiped his mouth and looked around. His face flashed blue and red from his car lights.

I crunched over the snow to the sheriff. "Has anybody been found who needs medical attention?"

He looked up. "No. Not likely, either."

"Have you found any more pieces of the plane that are still burning?"

"We've put out as many fires as we've found." He looked closely at my face, as if peering through a misted window. "And we're still finding them."

"Who have you notified?" I asked.

"Who the hell are you?"

"Joe Durant. Senior investigator for the NTSB." My name was truthful. The rest was another small lie.

"You got any ID?" he demanded.

Cops at a wreckage site always feel better if they can see a badge, and that's the only reason NTSB investigators carry them.

"It's at home on my dresser, right next to my reading glasses." Another lie. If you don't turn in your badge your last day on the job, you don't get your last paycheck. "You want some help or not?"

The sheriff hesitated, then allowed a trace of relief to cross his face. He introduced himself as Don Kingman, Kittitas County sheriff, elected just this year. "I received the call from the FAA. They said they were notifying the NTSB and the Red Cross and the FBI. I've called our county services. I'll have some experienced people here soon, medical and rescue folks, and dogs."

"Your deputies' safety is paramount, and the firemen's. Sometimes radioactive isotopes and other dangerous materials are in a cargo bay. Have you found anything like that?"

He shook his head.

"Or any gas containers or flammable solids or organic peroxides or corrosive materials? Or lab specimens? They could all be dangerous."

"Nothing like that yet."

More vehicles arrived. Another television station truck and a flatbed carrying a winch and generator.

I said, "Tell your men to treat this area as a crime scene."

It was a phrase cops understood, and it galvanized the sheriff. He turned to his deputies and began issuing orders to leave the wreckage where it lay and to preserve any fleeting evidence, such as soot deposits, by photography or notation, and to leave as little indication of their passage as possible. And he ordered his deputies to try to detect the scent of explosives, which would blow away quickly. He was well aware of a psychological factor that would affect those early at the site, the irresistible urge to act, even when lives were not at stake. He had to slow them down, to preserve the evidence. After a halting start, the sheriff was proving himself.

Standing near a prowl car's bumper, a deputy spoke into another cell phone, relaying the readout from a handheld global positioning system. We were three or four miles from Snoqualmie Pass, the east-west route through the Cascade Mountains, and were sixty or so miles east of Seattle. To the northwest I could see the reflection of the lights illuminating Snoqualmie Pass ski runs.

The deputy turned to the sheriff and asked, "What kind of plane was it?"

The sheriff looked at me.

"An Aero Transport France 94, a twin turboprop," I said. "Emerald Airlines, en route from Hailey, Idaho, to Seattle. The plane was called *Sacajawea*." Emerald Airlines named all its planes after northwest explorers and pioneers.

The sheriff had an aggressive jaw, stuck out into the air. He rubbed it ruefully, then stepped closer, out of earshot of his subordinates. "You're the investigator. What else do I do now?" His lips were thin and bloodless, and he pressed them together. He loathed having to ask for help.

"Secure the area against the curious, who'll show up in an hour or two, so they don't move things around. And against looters." Over thirty people were charged with stealing from the Lockerbie site.

"What else?"

"Check everyone's credentials. Don't let any lawyers on the site, no matter what they say."

He smiled sourly. "Do I look like a dunce?"

"And insurance representatives. Keep them away."

Firemen were trying to hack their way to a point higher on the mountain where part of the fuselage had fallen. An orange glow could be seen through the trees and undergrowth above us. Left untended, a fire in an airplane section might burn for hours. Ash settled on the snow, speckling it.

Two ambulances arrived, but had to remain a hundred yards down the narrow logging road due to the congestion. A driver tried his siren for a moment, but the Red Cross truck in front of the ambulance had nowhere to go. The hollow pounding of a helicopter came from the west.

A man in a red parka approached us, holding up identification.

"I know who you are, Frank," the sheriff said with acid sweetness. "You can put your ID away."

I was introduced to the county hazardous materials coordinator. Frank Jessup had the clipped diction of an officious bank clerk. He said, "I'm ready to declare this place a biological hazard, Sheriff. Do you agree?"

The sheriff looked at me. Having the site declared a hazard would complicate the investigation, and it would be hard on the investigators' bladders because they would rather hold their pee than perform all the scrubbing and clothes changing required to leave and return to the site. But here there was no choice.

When I nodded almost imperceptibly, the sheriff said, "Agreed."

"I'll start bringing in my equipment." Jessup walked away.

The sheriff commented, "Jessup is the biggest pain in the ass in the entire goddamn world."

"You've never worked with me, that's clear." My banter was an attempt to keep my stomach under control. I was losing the fight.

The sheriff grinned narrowly. "The bodies make this a bio hazard? Blood-borne pathogens?"

I swallowed several times. My mouth under my tongue was tingling, and I was salivating heavily. I was all too familiar with these precursors. My shirt was stuck to my back with sweat that had begun to chill me. I said, "It'll be slower up here in the mountains, with the cold, but even so the bodies will quickly become dangerous."

Sheriff Kingman indicated me with his thumb and ordered a deputy, "Get this man some gloves and a better coat."

The helicopter loomed overhead. I couldn't make out its markings. The effect of its nose spotlight was lost in the kliegs. The copter slowly moved south, illuminating the logging road. Landing areas were scarce in the mountains.

My quick visual survey of the site indicated half or two-thirds of the plane had landed on this small plateau. The remainder would be strewn across the forest east of here, a wreckage trail that might be five miles long. Above me to the east, just at the upper cusp of the light thrown by the kliegs, several trees had been chopped off, their tops lying in the snow. The plane had clipped the trees on its way in.

Two men entered the site from between fire trucks. I had worked with them before. They were father and son, and almost identical in appearance, a generation apart. Charles Ray was the founder and chairman of Emerald Airlines. His son Wayne was the chief executive officer. They crossed the snow, Charles's hand on his son's arm, the son supporting the father. Charles was as bald as a peeled egg while his son had a full head of dark hair, carefully coiffed, even in his distress. Charles blinked rapidly, one hand delicately on his temple as if exploring it for a bruise. They gathered in the horrifying scene, their faces open and undefended, and slowly crossed the snow toward the sheriff. Their days ahead would be dreadful.

A deputy wearing a Kevlar vest handed me gloves and a parka with SHERIFF on the back, then drew Kingman away to confer. The sheriff's brisk efficiency had been an antidote to my nausea, but when he stepped away the sickness returned. No single body organ should be able to hold a person hostage for years, but my weak stomach had done it. I desperately looked around for a discreet place, my gaze sweeping over the butchery, my bile rising.

And my grief returning. This time—on this wreckage site—there was the grief. At least, I think it was grief. Hard to tell, with the chaos of rubble and corpses all around, and my churning stomach. Perhaps bereavement should have immobilized me. But right now I needed to find an out-of-the-way place, and quickly.

I moved around a knot of tossed luggage and clothing, and found a suitable stump near some rock brake at the edge of the clearing. The loggers had left a length of skid cable here, still shiny and curled like a snake. I swallowed repeatedly, breathing huge quaffs of air. I put the black box on the stump. The klieg lights made my new sheriff's coat glow a soft green. After a moment, my innards subsided a bit. Maybe I was getting tougher in middle age. After a few more long, even breaths, I took a step back toward the sheriff.

Then I saw a doll lying on the snow. A little girl's doll, with pudgy hands, a gingham dress, a tiny red ribbon in curly hair, and an eternal, dimpled smile. I folded like a jackknife and vomited.

I heaved and heaved, gripping the edge of the rotting stump, bent over, spilling my dinner onto the snow, some of it on my shoes, none of this for the first time, goddamn it. Finally I was empty, and could lever myself upright. I wiped my mouth with the back of a glove.

The governor of the State of Washington had arrived. A gun muzzle at his temple wouldn't make him miss a photo op. He must have been in the helicopter. The governor removed his cap to run his fingers through his sparse blond hair, readying himself for the television interviews. He was as silky as politicians come. And now running awkwardly in old-fashioned galoshes into the klieg light was Allen Chapman, head of the pilots' union, who worked for Alaska Airlines and was based in Seattle. And then came a Red Cross official whose face I remembered but not her name. She and Chapman walked across the snow toward the governor. Also arriving was the Kittitas County coroner, who had no reason to be here. She'd see the bodies soon enough without a visit. She too had been unable to find the logging road, and had come in following my path, her pants damp to her thighs.

I lifted a handful of snow, made sure it was clean, then chewed on it to clear my mouth. A National Guard Hummer drove along the side of the road, bypassing police trucks. Another helicopter appeared, this from Seattle's KOMO television station.

My legs wobbled as I stepped around a flight attendant's cart, a few peanut packages still in an open tray.

"Joe," someone called. "Joe Durant."

I recognized the voice. Richard Dahlberg, NTSB regional director.

He padded his way over the snow toward me. "I'm surprised to see you here, Joe."

"I'm surprised to be here."

Dahlberg probably wasn't on this week's Go Team, but his job would be to establish NTSB control of the site, handle the press, and provide the initial stakedown, to administer site security pending the team's arrival.

He said, "I saw someone tossing a meal over by a tree stump and figured it must be you."

I smiled weakly. "You've seen me puke more often than you'd care to, I'd imagine."

Dahlberg chewed on his lip a moment, indecision on his face. He should have been stitched taut, full of disapproval at my presence, but as a friend for a decade he was going to give me the benefit of the doubt. Dahlberg's face was seamed with harsh angles, and his eyes were always narrowed, as if he were looking into the sun. He had been a navy pilot, and still looked it. He was carrying his field kit, hadn't yet strapped it on.

He said, not unkindly, "Last I heard, Joe, you don't work for me anymore."

"No. I don't suppose I do."

"You aren't employed by the NTSB. Aren't an investigator anymore."

I rubbed my chin with a glove. "No, Dick. I'm not."

"Why are you out here, then?"

"My wife."

"Janie?"

"Yeah." I drew in a sharp breath. "She was on this flight."

TWO

I live in Ballard, a Seattle neighborhood first populated by Scandinavian fishermen and boatbuilders. The place has been gentrified, but it's still possible to buy a gelatinous, lye-soaked fish called *lutefisk* and potato dumplings called *komle* in delicatessens where the customers have Eric the Red accents. Ballard celebrates Norwegian independence day every May 17 with a lively parade down Market Street, which the king of Norway has attended. I parked the car in my driveway.

The hardest thing I would ever have to do was just ahead. I sat in the car a moment, the radio off. The house's first-floor lights were still on, seen through rhododendron branches I'd let go too long. I pinched the bridge of my nose. Death and hell, I didn't want to go into my house.

But I did, of course. I locked my car and activated the alarm. Descendants of the Vikings will sometimes steal a car. It's their genetic inheritance, same type of thing their forefathers did to the Norman coast. I climbed the steps. My shoes were caked with mud and my pants were damp and creaseless. I had forgotten to return the sheriff's jacket. Vomit had caught the edge of the fabric, but it blended in with the green just fine. Heather along the walkway still wore its winter pink bloom, lit poorly by the porch light. I pushed the key into the lock and opened the door.

"Sarah, it's me," I called out.

Hanging across our entryway, a banner generated by our computer read WELCOME, MOM, replete with cheery representations of balloons and hearts along the borders. Sarah's first banner had said, WELCOME HOME, MOM, but she later thought it too forward, and had balled it up and thrown it into the wastebasket.

Rarely is a father happy to find his daughter watching television at two o'clock in the morning, but now I was vastly relieved. She would already know. I wouldn't have to tell her. The idiot box had broken the news for me.

Sarah was sitting on the den floor, leaning against a couch in front of the television, puffy-eyed and breathing in little hiccups. She was cried out, at least for now. I lowered myself to the floor next to her. She didn't look away from the screen.

Dick Dahlberg had pushed the television crews far away from the wreckage, and nothing was on the screen but trees backlit by the distant klieg lights, and several deputy sheriffs who were keeping the TV crews right where they were. A reporter was speaking into the camera, frequently glancing at his notes and then off screen, hoping the anchor in Seattle would relieve him of the burden of ad-libbing. An Emerald Air turboprop flying from Sun Valley to Seattle had gone down. The reporter had almost nothing else to say. Dahlberg would have seen to that.

I put my arm around Sarah but she flinched as if I had burned her. She angrily moved away, sliding along the rug to the other end of the couch and wiping her cheeks with her sleeve. Her voice carried unconcealed wrath. "Mom is dead, isn't she?"

"She was on the plane, Sarah. I'm so sorry. For you and for me." I scooted sideways and this time she let me hold her. She began crying again, bucking in my arms, her face turned away.

"Your mom loved you, Sarah."

She shook her head so violently that her gold-brown hair whipped across my neck and cheek. Her words were ragged. "No, she didn't. She never did."

My eyes were damp. And I was angry, once again. Goddamn my wife. Maybe I deserved it, but not my little girl.

"She didn't leave you, Sarah," I said in a low voice, as measured as I could make it. I didn't want to break down in front of her.

"We've already talked all about this." She pulled a pillow off the couch to dab at her face. "I know everything you're going to say. You've said it a hundred times before. And it's all a lie."

She tried to move away, but I gently held her, and she finally slumped into me, sobbing.

"Your mom didn't leave you, Sarah. She left me."

"As if that makes any difference. She left."

I held her. The television switched to a shot of Wayne Ray, Emerald Air's CEO. His name appeared at the bottom of the screen, next to the station's logo. Wayne was trying to say something without saying anything. Camera lights lit his face like a tropical sun, and his pupils were pinpricks. He knew better than to try to shade his eyes from the glare, which would make him look like a gangster being arrested. Ray looked ghastly.

A Replogle globe and an old upright Clarendon piano and the TV crowded our den. Janie had known I liked maps, and so had given me the globe as an anniversary present years ago. It had been manufactured during that brief time after Vietnam had been reunited but before the Soviet Union had been disbanded. On the walls were framed old maps of cities I had visited. Most places I go, I seek out old map shops.

Sarah quieted to a soft burbling. She was my only child. I had been promising her for three years that she could get her driver's license on her sixteenth birthday, and not one day later. She had circled the date in huge red circles on our kitchen's Norman Rockwell calendar, lest I forget, as if there were any chance of that. She didn't know that I had purchased a nine-year-old Volvo for her. Silver, an automatic, with a hundred and ten thousand miles, but built like a tank, and no rust. It was parked in my brother's garage over in Bellevue. I was going to tie a big red ribbon around it. I have tried over the years not to indulge my only child but this—her sixteenth birthday—was too much, and I hadn't been able to resist.

Sarah resembles her mother, and as I liked to say—at least before her mother did to me what she did—that I didn't marry a beautiful woman to have my daughter look like me. Sarah's eyes are the blue color of smoke. Her teeth are flashy white and perfect, for which I transferred to an orthodontist most of my income for two years. She doesn't like her nose, because it has a little bump on the bridge, the tiniest thing on the planet, I swear. When she's grumpy she likes to argue about this bump. She says it makes her look like a boxer, and I'll reply that there have been some cute boxers over the years, like Leon Spinks. Or she'll say it's the size of a potato, and I'll say it's smaller than most molecules. Then she'll say it looks like a horse chestnut, and I'll counter that it's smaller than a neutrino. I think she is angling for plastic surgery, but she doesn't need it, and in any event I've scarcely recovered from the orthodontist. She has her mother's mouth, and it is inviting and saucy and voluptuous, terms that shouldn't be used describing a fifteen-year-old, but they fit nevertheless. At 5'10", Sarah is only a few inches shorter than me.

She railed against her height until the captain of the Ballard High basketball team started squiring her around. Now she stands straight and tall, and still only comes up to his breast-bone. Sarah is a point guard on the varsity girls' team, and Sarah and her boyfriend are cute together, except that he is dumber than a mushroom.

"You thought Mom was a tramp," she said, almost under her breath.

I sighed heavily. "Sarah, that thought never occurred to me. Not once, not ever."

Well, I was spending the entire night lying, it was turning out. That thought—that Janie had been a tramp—in fact, unfortunately, and with some regret, had entered my mind. More than once.

"I don't think she was a tramp," she said around another gush of sobs. "I loved her."

"I did, too." Sort of.

"I think she was on her way back to us."

"Me, too."

"We could've talked her into staying." Sarah didn't have any Kleenex, so she sniffed hugely. "I don't think she would have ever gone back to Idaho."

"Me neither."

How to confess my great humiliation? A year ago Janie and her sister Eva traveled to Sun Valley for their annual four days of skiing, the tenth or eleventh anniversary of this event, their big yearly get-together. Eva would fly into Hailey from San Francisco the same time as Janie. They'd rent a car, and drive the ten miles north to Ketchum and Sun Valley. I don't ski. Journeying to the mountains in the middle of winter to put bed slats on your feet has never made sense to me. Janie and Eva would ski the hell out of Mount Baldie and close down the Pioneer Saloon a few times, and then Janie would return to Seattle.

But a year ago I went out to SeaTac airport to collect her after her ski holiday, and she wasn't on the plane. When I telephoned the condo she and Eva had rented, Janie calmly announced she wasn't coming back, that she was going to live in Sun Valley and ski. It took her about as long to tell me as it does for me to tell you. She didn't offer an explanation.

Not one goddamn reason why she would desert her husband and daughter. She just did.

There is, of course, more to it than that, but it has been up to me to figure it out, largely by examining my own character, something I normally don't find profitable or enjoyable. My conclusion was that there was something wrong with me. There must have been. No other explanation exists. But try as I might—and Lord knows, I'm not perfect—I couldn't figure out what. I had been summarily terminated as a husband, without even the courtesy of a drumhead court-martial.

One defect in my personality is suggested by my surprise. I'm blind. I didn't see it coming. Something had been appallingly wrong with our marriage, and I had missed it.

Over the phone I had begged Eva—who had returned from the skiing trip to her plumbing-contractor husband in San Francisco—for some clue as to why Janie would leave me, and Eva stammered around awhile, said she didn't really know, and then volunteered that maybe it was because I was boring. "Hell, Joe," she said, "you're an engineer, and they are all boring." Not like goddamn plumbing contractors. And I wanted to protest that there had been more to my life than being an engineer, but I just put down the phone.

"She was coming home to stay, don't you think, Daddy?" Sarah seldom called me Daddy anymore.

"Maybe so, Sarah." Or maybe to retrieve the rest of her things, like her exercise treadmill and her tennis rackets.

"Were you going to talk with Mom?"

"I was going to say we loved her, and wanted her home with us, that we wanted her here with us very much."

Silent sobs now, a gentle bucking in my arms. On my way to pick up Janie at SeaTac, I had heard an initial report on my car radio. With my cell phone I had called a friend, a senior supervisor at SeaTac Operations, who said that Emerald Air 37, coming in from Hailey, had disappeared from radar screens. He told me the location, as best they could surmise at the time. I had also called Sarah, saying vaguely that I was going to be later than I had thought, and then had headed up Interstate 90 toward Snoqualmie Pass, calling SeaTac Operations twice more for updates on the location as it became known with more precision.

Sarah snuffled. I brushed tears from her cheeks. The television showed Dick Dahlberg, fifteen microphones and cassette recorders shoved at his face, who was saying that a Go Team had been launched from Washington accompanied by a member of the NTSB, and that until their arrival the site had been closed to preserve evidence, and that no press access would be granted until the Go Team was on-site. Dahlberg was stalling the press, straight from the manual.

"Maybe Mom is alive. Do you think there's a chance?"

"No, sweetie."

"But you don't know for sure."

"I've seen a lot of these, Sarah. There's not much chance. No chance, really."

After a long moment, she asked, "Are you glad she's dead?"

It was a cattle prod of a question, and it came not from my daughter, but from her vast pool of pain and anger and confusion. I gently turned her shoulders so she had to look at me. "Sarah, I love you more than life itself. Almost sixteen years ago your mother gave you to me. For that alone, I will always love her."

She started up again, huge wails. I hugged her, hard this time, pressing her into me, trying to help her.

Then my eyes got leaky. I blinked the moisture away but they filled up again, and my breath came in long, serrated sighs. I didn't know whether I was weeping for Janie or for Sarah or for me. My daughter and I held each other and cried, our tears mixing together on our cheeks.

THREE

I returned to the site the following afternoon. Before leaving my car I spread Vicks VapoRub on my upper lip, more out of habit than necessity. Perhaps the bodies hadn't yet begun to putrefy in the cold. It is little known among the public that victims aren't taken away from a crash site until after much of the evidence has been gathered, so the corpses lie around awhile, maybe as long as three days. Then it might take ten days to remove all the remains. I walked toward the first barricade, wondering how I'd bluff my way in. First I'd have to push through a mob.

A National Park Service gravel lot—usually used by weekend rock climbers and hikers—was one of the holding areas for the press and public. Hundreds of people and dozens of vehicles filled the area. Mourners were gathered in knots, and a pitiful keening came from all corners of the lot. They huddled together, leaning against each other, bracing themselves, and casting fearful glances north, where the main wreckage site lay. They were dressed in dark coats and pants, even dark scarves and hats. The only white among the mourners were the handkerchiefs, and there were many of those, all crumpled and damp.

At the west end of the gravel lot under a camouflage green and brown National Guard tent, a team of social workers and clergy had established a triage site. A generator hummed next to the tent. Quiet conversations, with gentle hands on shaking shoulders, were occurring around a table that held a metal coffee urn and plastic cups. Red Cross workers were carrying doughnuts and sandwiches from their truck into the tent. Other volunteers were setting up a telephone bank, ten phones in portable booths to be used by relatives, linked to Airtouch Cellular by antennas on the Red Cross vehicle. Television vans lined one side of the site like circus trucks, all with satellite dishes aimed south, their technicians sitting in the truck cabs, chatting away and eating lunch, their jobs done. A technician had been called away for some reason and had left his lunch on the hood of his truck, and black-and-white birds called Clark's nutcrackers were tearing at the Baggies and wax paper to get to the sandwich and cookies.

Reporters and cameramen and soundmen had found suitable backdrops for their airtime. The press was here in vast numbers. The news organizations lucky enough to have arrived first—Seattle television stations—clogged this site. Others filled a second parking lot with vans and trucks and trailers half a mile down the road.

Don Kingman was standing near a sheriff's car behind the barricades. His deputies were manning the barriers, shaking their heads sympathetically when heartsick relatives of the dead asked them questions. The deputies knew as little as the onlookers. Kingman walked over when he saw me. He was wearing a badge allowing him to enter the site.

I said, "You've been demoted to perimeter patrol, looks like."

"And you've been demoted off the site, looks like." He

smiled. "Telling me you were with the NTSB. Shame on you."

"Well, it was only a little fib."

"An outright fabrication told to police authorities," he said.

"Stalin was worse, everything considered."

"I'm sorry about your wife. Dahlberg told me. Jesus, that's tough."

"Can you let me back onto the site? I want to talk to the IIC."

Most others would have given me a long-winded explanation about civilians and crime scenes because sheriffs are, after all, bureaucrats, but Kingman quickly said, "Sure," and pushed aside an orange-and-white barricade. The crowd abruptly turned their moist gazes to me, instantly suspecting I wasn't a civilian, and that I might have something to tell them, but Kingman escorted me away at a quick pace, perhaps glad to get away from the grieving relatives.

"You look beat," I said. "Up all night?"

"I don't normally pull all-nighters, except Ellensburg High School prom nights." Ellensburg is the Kittitas County seat. "Dahlberg told me a few things about you."

"Great."

"Says you were a legend at the NTSB."

"We're all legends. Anybody who can work a crash site automatically becomes a legend. It's a nice benefit of the job."

"Dahlberg said you were so good, you could stick your nose into the air like a wolf, take a few big sniffs, and pretty much determine why a plane went down."

"Being a legend, you get the best seats in restaurants, never near the kitchen or the door to the toilet."

The sheriff wouldn't be deterred. "He says that in your career, you and your teams never failed, not once, to find the probable cause for a crash."

"Yeah, well . . ." Only four majors in NTSB history have not been assigned a probable cause.

The wreckage site was a quarter mile up the road. We walked in ruts where tires had crushed snow to slush then mixed it with mud. I was wearing rubber Sorel boots and a parka.

The sheriff asked, "You been listening to the news reports?"

"Some."

"Reporters are having a surge of creativity, each trying to invent the name that will stick in the national consciousness."

"Yeah?"

"NBC is calling him the Cascade Bomber. CNN weighs in with the Sky Bomber, and ABC is trying out the Ski-to-Sky Bomber."

"That's not bad."

We walked through a tunnel of pine and spruce, and came to the wreckage site. Decontamination trailers were already in place. We were each handed a plastic bag containing a white protective suit, rubberized booties, and a mask. I knew to use one of the nearby Porta-Potties before putting on the suit. Don Kingman pinned his site badge to the outside of the suit. Wearing white, with snow all around, we looked like First Mountain Division troopers.

The hazardous materials coordinator Frank Jessup had that morning trained several volunteers—they looked like high school students—who taped over the seams between our suits and the gloves and boots. Another volunteer stood by with a laptop computer on a card table set up on the snow, ready to note any worker's exposure to potential biohazards. We would undergo a bleach-and-water shower on leaving the area. Guards surrounding the site made sure that workers entering and leaving passed through this decontamination facility.

At another edge of the site, tucked in against a precipitous granite rise of the mountain behind, was the NTSB's command trailer. A dish was already on top. Next to the trailer was a generator hut. Nearby were three refrigerator trucks that read SNOHOMISH POULTRY PROCESSORS, rented by the NTSB to transport the bodies to a morgue. The company's name would be covered over before the trucks left. Next to one of the trucks was a box of red body bags, still flat and empty, some large for intact corpses, some smaller for the partial remains. Only one fire truck remained, but other vehicles had been brought in, including three cherry pickers, a backhoe, and an industrial vacuum truck, to pump out snowmelt from impact craters. A guard at the site entrance—a National Guardsman with an M16 over his shoulder—glanced at Kingman's badge and didn't object when the sheriff escorted me through the police line.

The field of corpses and wreckage had been made almost cheerful by a forest of red flags, each at the end of a three-foot-long numbered stake planted near remains. As we skirted the site, looking for the investigator-in-charge, a search-team member called out from down the hill that he needed a photographer. After the body was photographed from several angles, it would be put into one of the red plastic bags, and then left where it had been found. Also dotting the ground were yellow flags marking off the area into grids. The locations of bodies and airplane parts would be entered into computers using a CAD-like program.

A team of searchers—maybe fifty people, all deputized by the county coroner that morning, and all in white bio suits—was spread evenly in a line across the site, moving slowly, often bending over, looking like rice planters. The air smelled of the forest. This was the brief time after the odor of fuel had dissipated but before the onset of rot. The smell of human body decay—once experienced, never forgotten—would be the single most vivid memory for most of these volunteers.

Several Go Team members were near the severed cockpit, wearing white bio suits and blue dozer caps with NTSB on them. I knew all of them, recognized them even in their masks, by the way they gestured and walked. Also on-site were FBI and ATF agents, and I recognized the special-agent-in-charge of the Seattle FBI office, Cal Guthrie, and the FBI's executive assistant director, Frederick Yamashita, who investigates terrorism against United States citizens and property. The head of the FAA's Aviation Explosives Security Unit was speaking with three engineers from Air Transport France, who had flown in from Paris overnight, and with the pilots' union representative. I had worked with them all before.

Two NTSB investigators from the structures group were taking photographs and talking into microphones pinned to their bio suits. Dick Dahlberg pointed at a gauge in front of the copilot, who still hung there in his seat. Only a superficial examination of the plane's parts would be made in the field. Eventually about fifty NTSB investigators would be on-site. I spotted the investigator-in-charge, as he was dispensing that morning's plan to a dozen people surrounding him. I crossed the field to him, trying not to look at the bodies littering the snow, all the torn tissue and broken bones and staring faces, but once again my old friend nausea began its rise.

The IIC saw me coming and greeted me with a tentative grin. His name was Richard Shrader, who was based in Washington, D.C., and who had probably taken an FAA Gulfstream out to SeaTac that morning along with a member of the NTSB, though I hadn't seen the board member yet. Sheriff Kingman found a state patrol captain to talk to.

Shrader left the group of investigators and stepped toward

me. The snow was shiny from that day's melt. "God, I'm sorry, Joe."

I nodded. Rich Shrader was incapable of saying anything he didn't mean, which made him instantly likable. I'd worked with him on and off for a decade. He probably didn't know anything about my troubles with Janie. Rather, her troubles with me. Shrader's black eyebrows were visible just above his spectacles. His eyes had only lately begun to collect a few wrinkles.

He would excuse my failure to trade pleasantries. "I'd like to be assigned to the job, Rich."

His latex-gloved hand pulled at his earlobe. "Dick told me you were here last night, and I figured you'd be back today."

"Can you take me on?"

"Joe, you know I can't hire you out in the goddamn field. There are procedures to go through. And I don't hire people anyway. That's done by the human resources division."

"Well, think of something." I was calling on our friendship.

My offer to join his team could not be dismissed out of hand. Two years ago I had been IIC on an ATF 94—a turbo-prop identical to *Sacajawea*—that had gone down on a flight from Green Bay to Minneapolis. The Central Airlines ATF 94 was on a repositioning red-eye flight, and the plane was mostly empty. Five people had died. We had assigned proba-ble cause to ground crew error: the plane's wings had not been deiced sufficiently close to takeoff. So I was an expert on ATF 94s. Shrader looked around the site, to the mangled metal and bodies.

"Think out loud," I insisted.

"The best I can do is check with Washington. I'll strongly recommend that you be employed in some capacity for this investigation."

"Where'll you let me in?"

He sucked on a tooth. "I've already filled my group spots, including your specialty, the structures group."

A major investigation was conducted by specialist groups, including the power plant group, the human factors group, the systems group (hydraulics, flight controls, landing gear, and the like), the maintenance records group, the flight recorder group, the weather group, the air traffic services group, and others, each with an NTSB investigator chairing the group, and often including non-NTSB scientists and engineers. Because each group submits findings, the group method prevents early pet theories and predispositions from being weighed too heavily.

"None of the group chairs would take it lightly were I to dump them for you," Shrader continued.

"Sure."

"And you are sort of a pain in the ass to work with anyway."

"I've been told that before."

"But credibility is the NTSB's main weapon, and if I turn aside your offer to help, I may be criticized for not doing all I can to find probable cause." He paused, again surveying the site with broad sweeps of his eyes. "The FBI."

"Yes?"

"They've already concluded an explosion brought down Emerald 37 last night." He snapped a glove cuff several times. "They're going to try to take over the investigation right away, and not let it run its full course with us."

"Well, that's standard procedure for them."

"I want you to deal with the FBI."

"Ah, hell."

"That's my offer," Shrader said. "I'll talk to Washington today, and with their okay, I'll get you a badge letting you onto the site and everywhere else the investigation takes us, but you will have to liaison with the FBI."

I smiled my thanks at him, then remembered he couldn't see it because of the mask. "This was easier than I'd feared, Rich."

"No, it wasn't. I wasn't going to turn down your offer, and you knew it. The NTSB doesn't turn aside expertise. If I'm going to have to deal with a bunch of damned Frenchmen from ATF who want to tell me my job, I might as well deal with you, too." He stepped closer. "A surgeon doesn't operate on his own family members. Are you going to be able to work on the incident that killed your wife?"

"Have you found her body?"

"We aren't at that stage yet, not officially, not of IDing the bodies. But all the NTSB people here know Janie was on the flight, and some of them knew her, and would have told me if her body had been found. It hasn't."

I touched the corner of my eye. Shrader may have thought I was wiping away a tear, because he stepped closer and put a hand on my elbow by way of comforting me. Actually, I had been chasing away a fly. Even in the high-mountain conditions, the site was already flyblown. Flies begin laying eggs in a corpse's mouth within two minutes of death. Forensic scientists often use the development of the fly eggs in the mouth as a rough indicator of the time of death.

Shrader said in a quiet voice, "You quit our outfit because you couldn't take it. Those're the words you used. Couldn't take it. How is it going to be different this time, especially when your wife was onboard?"

"I'll make it different." Not yet, I wasn't. I was breathing in small bursts, trying to settle my stomach. "How do you handle the carnage, Rich?"

"You know well enough all the ways we do it. They just don't work for you."

"I know, but how do you do it? You, personally. How do you keep yourself from getting sick?"

"I look, but I don't see." He started toward the command trailer and I followed, walking around a fur coat. "I examine the tiny details, all the little engineering problems presented by each piece of evidence, and I try not to see anything human. I wear blinders, and they keep my vision tightly focused. That's how I do it. Others, like Dick Dahlberg, don't have to go through any mental gymnastics. The slaughter just doesn't bother him. Ask him, and he'll counter with, 'Do you get sick when you enter a butcher shop?'"

We walked around a body wearing athletic sweats and big Nike shoes, lying facedown and spread eagle, like a free-falling parachutist, except that his head was turned sideways and something, maybe a raven or a rat, had eaten the eyeballs, leaving the sockets hollow. We skirted three empty aircraft seats facing each other as if at a tea party, then reached the command trailer.

Shrader took a long breath. "I know Janie was on that plane, and I know you are busting to get to work, but don't do anything until you hear from me, until I get clearance from Washington."

I nodded.

Shrader climbed the steps and said just before entering the trailer, "Two years ago, on that Central Air ATF 94, you were the IIC. This year, on *Sacajawea*, I'm the IIC."

"I won't forget the chain of command."

FOUR

My gig that night was at the Longliner, and I didn't see any reason to miss it, not while Rich Shrader was trying to get me hired on and I couldn't return to the site until then. Maybe grief should have prevented me from appearing at the tavern, but I simply didn't feel it, not that pure, immobilizing sadness my daughter was suffering. My sorrow was mixed with rekindled humiliation and anger, leaving me with some nameless alloyed emotion. Whatever it was, the blues seemed the perfect antidote.

I backed through the Longliner's door, trying not to bang my amplifiers on the frame. One of these days maybe the band will be able to afford a roadie, but until then I lug my own amps. The drummer was already there, setting up his kit on the stage, which was so small that I was always banging his hi-hat with my elbows, not that the drummer would notice because he always flailed away in a mad trance.

The owner was doing his own bartending, and he lifted his rag at me as I sidestepped through the tables, trying not to splash his patrons' beer. By word or deed, the owner never let us forget he was doing us a favor letting us play here. He never paid us, but he allowed us to pass the hat, and fifty dollars at the end of the night meant the fish were running. The Longliner Tavern is in Ballard, where hundreds of purse seiners, longliners, crabbers, and factory trawlers crowd the piers. Many of the vessels are over fifty years old, with lovely vertical prows and curved wheelhouses. Their crews come to the Longliner to drink beer, and plenty of it, and not to listen to a blues band, and there've been times when I've had to wrestle with some fisherman who switched on the big-screen TV during one of our sets. Between sets, I don't mind. Some fishermen were at the back of the bar playing pool and pinball. Others were carrying pitchers between the bar and their tables. Two customers sat at the bar in front of the pull-tab jar, and a pile of discarded tabs lay on the floor around their stools.

I said hello to the drummer. His name is Johnny Moore, I think. One time he said it was Johnny Maloney. He's a white guy, but he wears Rastafarian dreadlocks, blond velvet ropes of hair. He always peels off his shirt after a song or two, to reveal a tattoo along his collarbone that reads LIVE FREE OR DYE, but I never supposed they could spell in prison. With his shirt off, drumming crazily, he flings perspiration like a sprinkler, and my back will be sodden with his sweat by the end of the first set, so I'll sit between sets getting chilled. When he's drumming, his eyes resemble Rasputin's, piercing and insane. When he's idle, they glaze over as if coated with paint. The guy lives to bang on his hides, and he insists on two solos a night. A drum solo is like a sneeze. You can feel it coming, but there's nothing you can do about it.

On the stage our bass player, Will Worthington, was running up and down his chords. Worthington works for a megabank downtown, making his living tossing pensioners out of their homes for failing to pay their mortgages. He plays a fretless Fender bass, and he can lay down a groove. Worthington is African American, and once each performance he will shout into the microphone, "Lord, I'm playing the blues with a bunch of white guys. What did I do, Lord? What did I do to deserve this?"

The lead guitarist, Mike Dunham, is a lawyer having a midlife crisis, and who as a teenager learned the guitar by memorizing everything Herman's Hermits ever recorded. He'll occasionally sneak in a lick from "Mrs. Brown You've Got a Lovely Daughter," which is the only thing the fishermen ever applaud.

I'm the frontman and harmonica player. Many people hear *harmonica* and think "Oh! Susannah." But my band plays up-tempo Chicago electric blues, in the style of Buddy Guy, Muddy Waters, and Freddy King, though I don't say their hallowed names and ours in the same breath. Our band's name is the Longliners, after the tavern that gives us most of our gigs. A longliner is a commercial fishing boat that trolls for fish with lines—many hooks on each line—rather than using nets. I carried a stool from the bar to the stage, and laid on it my old metal flute case in which I carry my harmonicas. I plugged my bullet microphone into my amp, and my singing mike into another amp, did a couple of sound checks, and I was ready to get down with the blues.

But the college basketball game on the tavern's big screen hadn't ended, so we couldn't go on yet. The owner had purchased a satellite system, and was determined to get his money's worth from it. I lowered myself into a chair next to the stage, and a waitress brought me a Coke, circling a bit to keep away from the drummer. Worthington and Dunham also sat at the table. Worthington had ordered a hamburger, and it arrived, the lower bun damp from the pickle next to it.

I had asked Sarah to join me tonight. The bartender

wouldn't card her, I knew, and she could have sat in a corner and had a burger while we played. But she wanted to stay home, and when I volunteered to stay home with her, she replied that I didn't need to. She was still angry with me, even after I had exhausted all my parental stratagems, the transparency of which children realize long before adults do. She was so anxious to get rid of me that she lugged both my amps out to the Explorer. She wanted to be alone, and she meant it, so I drove down to the Longliner, and we didn't have to cancel our performance.

I timed my last sip of Coke for the end of the basketball game, but then the damned thing went into overtime. I was about to protest to the bartender—a useless bumping of my gums, as I well knew—when a woman approached our table wearing a business suit and clutching her purse like a fullback. She walked right up to us, instinctively knowing we weren't the fishing-crew patrons.

"Are you Joe Durant?" she asked loudly over the noise of the TV and the guffawing and slurping of the patrons and the cracks of billiard balls and the whistles and clangs of the pinball machines.

"I am if you're a drummer looking for a job."

Worthington and Dunham chuckled dutifully, but she only stared at me. "I'm looking for Joe Durant. I was told he was in a tavern playing a harmonica, which I could scarcely credit."

I rose to push back a captain's chair for her. "Who are you?"

"Special Agent Linda Dillon." She lowered herself into the chair.

Worthington said, "I knew Moore crossed state lines at some point."

"He's up there." Dunham pointed to the stage. "Don't get near his mouth when you cuff him."

"Why would an FBI agent be looking for me," I asked.

"You haven't talked with the investigator-in-charge?"

"Rich Shrader and I spoke last when I was at the site, earlier today."

"His office in Washington has given him permission to take you on," she said. "Your position is as liaison to the FBI. I'm the FBI's liaison with the NTSB."

"All my liaising is going to be one way, me to the FBI. I don't need any liaising from the FBI to me."

She wiped the table with her hand before placing her purse on it. The purse landed solidly. It contained her handgun. "My agent-in-charge told me if I didn't like being the liaison, I could do something else for a living," she said, shaking her head at the waitress who had come by for her order. "And now I'm in a rundown bar with a guy who plays a harmonica, instead of out at the crash site."

I spread my arms and lied, "This place isn't so bad." Distract her from the harmonica. People don't understand the harmonica. Blues players call them harps.

She reached across the table for Will Worthington's paper napkin, wadded it up, and threw it onto the floor in a corner. "That napkin will still be there two months from now. Want to bet?"

Her blond hair was cropped fairly short, and maybe highlighted with a rinse; I couldn't tell in the garish light from the neon beer signs on the windows. Her eyes were straight and blue and untamed. Her lips were full and peaked, but were pressed together in a pedagogic, disapproving line. She was in her thirties, maybe late thirties, with a few tiny wrinkles at the corners of her eyes. She wore no jewelry, except for a wedding ring. She was too slender, rather wiry. Her blouse was buttoned to the neck.

"How does a navy fighter jock end up blowing a harmonica?" she asked.

"You were in the navy?" Worthington asked me around a French fry. "Do you have to learn to swim to join the navy?"

"I was a second-seater, running the electronics on a Prowler, most of the time out of Hawaii, then Whidbey Island." I pointed north, as if she could see Whidbey Island, twenty miles north of Seattle. Almost all NTSB investigators have flying backgrounds. "I couldn't get into the pilot's seat with any regularity so I left the navy."

"Liaising involves confiding." When she reached for a French fry from Worthington's plate, he began eating them at a faster pace. "You confide in me, I'll confide in you. Where'd you pick up the know-how to join the NTSB?"

"I received an M.S. in aerodynamics engineering while in the navy. From the University of Washington. Then I joined the NTSB." I paused. "Now, you confide in me."

"These French fries are soggy."

When she volunteered nothing more, I said, "That's not really a checkout counter tabloid confession."

"That's all you'll get from me." A trace of acid was in her smile. "And you've been working at Boeing since you left the NTSB?"

I nodded. I'm a stress analysis engineer. I analyze airframe structure to support design and repair activities on 757s, specializing in fatigue, damage tolerance, and finite element analysis methods. Boeing hired me after I left the NTSB. It's an important job at a company I'm proud to work for. I'm bored beyond tears.

She was relentless. "An agent-friend of mine told me you vomit at crash sites."

Canisius won the basketball game, and the bartender flicked off the TV with his remote.

"We're on." I rose from the chair, followed by my bass and guitar players.

We positioned ourselves on stage. Moore tapped his snare rim three times and we cut into Willie Dixon's "I'm Ready." Two-bar harp intro, then my singing. I have a pretty fair blues voice for someone who has never smoked cigarettes.

"I'm ready, ready as anybody can be." A powerful, throaty first line. Even a pinball player looked.

The waitress carried a platter containing three sloshing pitchers to a table of fishermen, all wearing plaid Eddie Bauer knockoff shirts. They laughed at some joke.

"I'm ready for you, I hope you're ready for me."

We were tight. We played a forty-five-minute set, and I blew out a reed on my C-key Marine Band and had to reach for another. We only had one heckler, some fisherman wearing a T-shirt with a photo of Pol Pot on it, who yelled, "You know what's the difference between your band and the *Titanic*? The *Titanic* had a band."

After several numbers I forgot the FBI agent was in the room. The blues are meant to soothe the heart, and I played the blues for my daughter even though she wasn't there, and then for my wife, though she hadn't been there, and now would never be. We actually received a smattering of applause along the way. We ended the set with Sonny Boy Williamson's "Don't Start Me Talkin'."

As she rose from the table, Linda Dillon smiled at me. Or maybe at the drummer. I couldn't see much because of the ceiling spotlight on my face. I was unaccountably pleased she had waited until the end of the first set to leave the tavern. I might puke at a crash site, but I can sure play the harmonica.

FIVE

On my NTSB identification card was a ten-year-old photograph of me, as there were no rules as to how often we had to get a new photo. Some of my friends at the bureau have photos that show them in Beatles haircuts, wide polyester lapels, and ties with knots as big as a fist, from back when disco was turning our minds to mush. My photograph is more recent, but not by much.

Some resemblance remains between my old photo and the current me. My forehead is higher now but I still have most of my hair, and it's dark, almost black. The hair on my chest started turning gray last year, lightening so quickly that when I'm shaving in the morning it'll catch my eye like a flag and startle me. This gray is spreading in a pernicious, concentric ring but hasn't yet reached my head.

My eyes are gray in some light and blue in others. I broke my nose during navy parachute training, and the navy more readily breaks a nose than fixes the resultant bump. At least my reading glasses don't slide down my nose, so the knob there has proven of modest use. The reading glasses are new last year, after I tired of playing the trombone with reading material. My wife, Janie, always said my best feature was my feet and too bad they were hidden by shoes most of the time. She also allowed that the small notch on my chin, and my ears—tight against my head and without fleshy, dangling lobes—were above average, if not cute. Janie never called anything cute, and certainly not me. I'm tall enough—just over six feet—so that no navy cockpit was comfortable.

So I'm a decade older now than when my NTSB photo was taken, and that decade has done peculiar things to my body. I'm sagging here and there. The skin under my eyes, my chin, my belly, my enthusiasm. "You're not a disaster zone yet, Dad," Sarah has said graciously. "Not like some of my friends' fathers." Little solace there.

I've tried to tighten things up, watch what I put in my mouth. Now I only eat red meat once a day but, given this sacrifice, it has to be real red meat, like bacon or pepperoni. Once a week I'll eat something green, such as pesto on a pizza or an olive from a martini. I take vitamin supplements, though in all likelihood they are a scam and do nothing but make my urine expensive.

I watch my weight. That is, I've watched it increase. I simply cannot endure those curious measures—such as spinning your feet on a $2,000 stationary bicycle while wearing shrink-wrap tights and staring at a digital pulse monitor—that my fellow baby boomers swear by. My basement resembles the Star Chamber, with a stationary bike, Nautilus machines, free weights, a treadmill, and a step machine. I never touched them. For an hour, Janie would rush from one machine to another as if a drill instructor were barking at her—lifting, twirling, bending, running, grunting—then she would come upstairs and sweat and glow near me while I was trying to eat my nachos, fully loaded, with double sour cream, extra cheese, and *grande* jalapeños, all in all enough BTUs to fuel a *Nimitz*-class carrier for a week.

We are not going to live forever, a fact of some consequence that has escaped many of my friends. The few days I could tack on to the end of my life by eating oat bran like a goat or hopping up and down to those bubbly exercise videos or running through my neighborhood like a fugitive, I'll forgo. At the end of my time on this earth, I'll probably be in a wheelchair, living off intravenous fluids, with a blanket over my lap, my eyes yellow, spit at the corners of my mouth, and I don't see any point working now to prolong that then.

So I am falling apart, but it's a gratifyingly slow process, and the knacker's cart won't come for me for quite a few years. The mirror doesn't wail in agony when I stand in front of it. I'm still presentable. At my age, that's enough.

"Okay, run it." I leaned toward the screen.

Kent Brausitch pointed. "The splat comes in up here, but Seattle Center hasn't handed it over to me."

A splat is a blip on the radar screen that isn't yet accompanied by a data box, usually because it is outside the controller's airspace. Two dozen other targets on the screen were accompanied by data boxes, just below the blips. The first line of the data block is the plane's call sign. The second line is a time share, alternately showing destination and type of airplane and the ground speed. The small letter to the left of the data block shows which controller is working the plane. Kent Brausitch's letter that day was *E*, so the blips in the upper right of the screen had little *E*'s next to them. He was working approach control, and had been bringing planes into SeaTac in the northwest quadrant that day.

Brausitch said, "Emerald 37 was seen on radar at Boise, at Salt Lake Center, and Mountain Home Air Force Base." His hand was on a mouse on the ledge between him and the screen. He could move an indicator to light up and identify any target. "But right now," he repeated with some emphasis, "Seattle Center still has it. ARTS hasn't recognized it." ARTS was the acronym for the radar system.

We were in the TRACON room at Seattle-Tacoma International Airport. TRACON is located just below air traffic control, in the same tower. While air traffic control has huge windows on all sides, TRACON is so dark that when I entered the room I had to wait a moment for my eyes to adjust. A dozen controllers sat in front of radar screens on two sides of the room. TRACON hands off a plane to the controller upstairs when the plane is about three miles from landing. With its amber screens, red and blue indicator lights, and low, purposeful chatter, the place resembled an aircraft carrier's weapons room. Brausitch had a professor's gray goatee and was wearing a golf shirt. He had on his headset, though he wasn't on duty at the time. Standing at my shoulder was Brausitch's supervisor, who had already seen the tape several times.

Next to me was Linda Dillon, who had been waiting for me downstairs in the operations office when I arrived that morning at six. I made the mistake—well, it was sort of a mistake—of calling her my assistant, and she reminded me that she was packing. She leaned close to the screen. She smelled of lilacs. The NTSB regional director, Dick Dahlberg, stood near her. Rich Shrader had put him on the structures group. Two other NTSB investigators watched the screen, one from the human factors group and another from the air traffic services group.

Next to TRACON was a computer room, with big humming machines lining the walls. A magnetic disk keeps on file for fourteen days everything seen and heard at TRACON. The disk which captured the last moments of Emerald 37 had been flown to the NTSB lab in Washington, where the raw data had been used to re-create the images as they had appeared on the radar screen. Now the tape was being played.

"This is tough," Brausitch said under his breath. "Jesus, this is tough."

"What's happening," demanded Linda Dillon.

"Now I've got the data block on Emerald 37, *Sacajawea*." Brausitch pointed. "You can see it here. Now, watch. The block changes from Emerald's call sign to a flashing *EM*."

"The pilot or copilot has dialed 7700 into his transponder," I said. "EM. Emergency."

"And then, look," Brausitch said unnecessarily. Sweat had formed on his forehead. "The target on my screen breaks into three little targets, then four targets."

The plane breaking up.

"And now," he went on, narrating the replay for us, "the data block begins to coast."

"What's that mean?" Linda Dillon asked.

"Our radar system isn't correlating with anything. It happens sometimes when a navy fighter gains altitude so fast that the computer can't accommodate it. The second line of the data block suddenly reads *CST*, for coast. And now you see each of the little spots blink out as they fall under the radar."

"ARTS didn't recognize the plane coming apart," Dahlberg said, "and so it put it on the coast list."

"What's the time span between when you get the 7700 signal and when ARTS labels it as a coast?" I asked.

"Ten point two seconds," Brausitch answered.

That was all Ken Brausitch could tell us. We left TRA-CON, squinting mightily as we emerged into the daylight. The other investigators took their van back toward Seattle.

Linda Dillon said, "The pilot had time to dial the emergency number into the transponder."

I nodded.

"So he had time to understand they were in trouble."

I don't open car doors for people carrying weapons, generally. She opened the passenger door and got in next to me.

"God," she said. "The pilot and copilot probably lived to see their plane come apart. Maybe saw blue sky through the seams."

I nodded again.

"And heard the wind all around."

The car was still warm from our drive out to SeaTac but she shivered. And when she thought I wasn't looking, she rubbed down the goose bumps on her arms. I was backing the car out of the parking slot, hands on the steering wheel, and so couldn't rub down mine.

Multiple anatomical separations due to high-velocity impact due to aircraft accident. The Kittitas County coroner would enter the phrase on sixty-three death certificates. The remains were being brought to a temporary morgue in a National Guard armory, where portable refrigeration units were keeping the place chilled.

With FBI Special Agent Linda Dillon stuck to me like some growth, I passed row after row of tables, each containing a body or a body part in a red bag. The Kittitas County coroner was escorting us toward the back of the building, and she was walking too slowly for my taste, lingering too long amid the bodies.

When she learned I had worked majors before, Dr. Susan Halsey lowered her professional mask. "All these dead people, laid out in an armory. God. I had a chance to become a dermatologist."

Linda Dillon looked at her sideways, and Dr. Halsey added briskly, "I've asked the Washington Mortuary Association to come in with some help, and the X-ray equipment is being installed in the garage in back. The doors to the X-ray room are wide enough for the litters."

Dr. Halsey's hair was in a bun under her cap. She was wearing a white lab coat and carrying a clipboard. She was a tall woman, and had played basketball at Washington State. She was taking us in the direction of a row of boxes against the back wall, a box for each victim, to contain personal effects that could be determined to have belonged to that person.

Wayne Ray was sitting in the middle of the room on a folding chair, next to a red bag. His head was in his hands. The armory was a brick building built in the 1920s, and gloomy in every aspect, with barred windows, a low ceiling, and, at one end of the room, circular rifle racks and four World War I howitzers with spoked wheels. The garish overhead fluorescent lights did nothing to dispel the room's morbidity. The place had begun to stink. Somehow—and I don't know why—body bags can keep everything in but the smell. And so intractable was the odor that the refrigerated poultry trailers that brought the bodies here would later be destroyed.

The coroner said, "Forensic examiners from Seattle will be helping me."

"What'll you be looking for?" Linda Dillon asked.

"I know it's too early to jump to conclusions, but I'm going to look for blast effects on eardrums, damage to lungs due to overpressure, and traumatic injuries not usually associated with an aircraft's impact with the ground."

"You mean," Linda asked, "damage occurring while the plane was still in the air, like from a bomb detonation?"

Dr. Halsey nodded. "We'll also be examining the skin for hot penetrations, for peppering and flash burns, that sort of thing. And all body parts will be X-rayed for shrapnel and bomb parts."

Most of the victims' relatives resided in Seattle, but Dr. Halsey and IIC Rich Shrader had agreed to use the armory here in Kittitas County to avoid problems of jurisdiction. State law said the county coroner—in Kittitas County it was Dr. Halsey—was responsible for a site on which fatalities occurred. She and Rich Shrader had earlier in the day agreed on an Incident Command System which divided tasks into manageable categories. Dr. Halsey would be in a shared command, along with the NTSB, the county hazardous materials coordinator Frank Jessup, and the Washington State Patrol. She was directly responsible for the temporary morgue, for identification of the bodies, and for providing a certificate of death for each body. She would also have authority over final arrangements for remains not identified.

Dr. Halsey saw Linda Dillon looking at the sixty-three pine caskets lining the west wall. The caskets were a dreadful sight in a dreadful room.

The coroner said, "It's important to the families of the dead that we find something for every casket. Those poor people—the brand-new widows and widowers and orphans and bereaved parents—won't find much to help their peace of mind, but having a casket that contains even a portion of their loved one will help some."

Extraordinary lengths would be taken to find something for each casket. Identifications would be made from photographs provided by family members, from fingerprints and tattoos and dental records, or from old medical procedures on the remains, such as screws and plates from orthopedic repairs or a stainless-steel wire around the sternum of someone who had undergone open heart surgery. DNA tests might be helpful identifying some remains but no reliable control samples would exist for most victims. No casket would be released to any family until all remains had been processed.

The coroner asked me, "Am I to run toxicology tests on the pilot and copilot? What'd be the point?"

She knew the answer, of course. Such tests would show whether the pilot and copilot had been using alcohol or drugs, and were performed as a matter of course.

"Don't jump to conclusions about what brought that plane down, Doc."

"Come on, Joe. Nobody's fooling anybody about *Sacajawea*. A blast brought down *Sacajawea*. I already know it."

Concluding anything about probable cause so early in an investigation was against all my training. I wouldn't commit, not to her, not to myself. "How do you know it?"

She led me toward a body bag, checking her clipboard against the tag on the bag. She tugged it open, revealing two bare legs.

Dr. Halsey asked, "Do you see the fractures?"

"I see burns, and the legs seem crooked, sort of loose-jointed."

"The tibia and fibula on both this woman's legs are broken. Of the bodies brought in here so far, more than sixty percent of them suffer a fracture of the lower leg or ankle or foot. It's my guess that these injuries occurred before the . . . what do you call it if you are too tentative to call it an explosion at this point?"

"The initial event," I replied.

"These fractures resulted from the initial event—an explosion, I'll say it, even if you won't—and not due to subsequent impact with the ground."

"You sure?" Linda asked.

Dr. Halsey closed the bag. "No, but I will be in a day or

two. I haven't even started my tests, and bodies are still coming in."

The crash site was slowly being cleaned up. Any crumpled part of the plane that might contain a body would also be brought to the morgue, to be pried apart to determine if a victim was inside. Some bodies were being found two miles from the main crash site.

"Give me a moment, will you?" I left Linda Dillon with Dr. Halsey, picked up a metal folding chair from a rack on wheels, and walked along a row of red bags toward Wayne Ray. I loudly unfolded the chair to announce I was coming. He lifted his head from his hands. I sat down in my chair next to him.

He looked away, maybe to compose his face. In the bag next to him was his wife, identified easily because she landed whole. The crash had devastated Emerald Air families. Not only had the pilot, copilot, and two flight attendants died, but four other employees had been deadheading on the flight, and four more employees had been flying on passes with their families, returning from ski vacations. Wayne's wife, Charlotte, had spent several days skiing with her sister, and had been flying on a pass home to Seattle on *Sacajawea*.

I didn't say anything, just sat there next to Wayne. He looked back around. His eyes weren't damp, but he looked old, with ochre crescents under his eyes and a malarial cast to his skin. Emerald's founder, Charles Ray, was in a protracted process of retiring, and had largely stepped aside at Emerald in favor of his son Wayne. So Wayne had the double burden of his own sorrow and representing the corporation as it tried to help grieving families of dead employees. I had heard that even his flight attendants liked working for him, which said a lot.

"I'm an engineer, Wayne," I said finally. "I don't know what to say to people. They don't teach that at engineer school. All I know are numbers."

Blank eyed, he stared at a howitzer. "A masters in business doesn't do much good for me along those lines either." He turned his eyes to me. "I'm sorry about Janie, Joe."

"Yeah. I know."

"I heard about her going to Sun Valley, leaving you. It was none of my business, but I heard anyway. I'm sorry about that, too."

"Yeah."

"I met Charlotte over there, in Sun Valley, I ever tell you?" he asked.

I shook my head.

He chuckled, an entirely forced sound. "Charlotte always wanted me to tell people we met on the slopes, that we spotted each other skiing, and fell in love instantly. She thought that was the most romantic notion in the world."

"Didn't happen that way?"

"Her father owns a restaurant over there, called Saltwater. Fifteen years ago Charlotte's father had this nutty notion that he could get rich by opening a fresh seafood restaurant in central Idaho. Most places that catered to skiers over in Sun Valley were serving steaks and potatoes. Well, he started selling fresh salmon and scallops, had a big oyster bar."

"Sounds like he had a good idea," I said.

"It was an instant hit. I met Charlotte there one evening while she was working the cash register." He laughed again. "Not on the ski slopes. I went back the next night to the restaurant just to see her. And we were married three months later. She moved to Seattle. Her old man would drive me crazy, knowing I was with Emerald, calling me up in the middle of the evening from his restaurant, asking me to ship oysters or clams or something to him from Seattle because he was running out."

I smiled along with him. "He had you confused with a fish broker."

"I obliged a couple of times—Charlotte teasing me all the while about having to accommodate in-laws—driving down to Fisherman's Terminal and buying whatever he'd ordered and shipping it to him on the next Emerald flight. But after the third or fourth time I told him just that. I'm not a goddamn fish broker." He tried another laugh, but it faded to nothing. "God, I'm going to miss her."

We were silent a moment. Then I asked gently, "What are you going to do, Wayne?"

He took a long breath. "Soldier on. Keep going. Running an airline is the only thing I know how to do." His voice broke, but he caught himself. "I don't know if Emerald can survive, but I owe it to my father and our employees to try to save the company."

I nodded.

"And maybe," he added, "I can lose myself in work. Maybe I can work so hard I won't remember this body bag. And maybe Charlotte will fade a bit for me."

I was going to bawl if I sat there any longer. So I rose from the chair, gripped his shoulder a few seconds, then left him.

Dr. Halsey had gone elsewhere in the armory, but Linda was waiting for me. She asked, "You okay?"

"Never better."

"Go ahead and wipe your eyes. I won't hold it against you." So I did.

She asked, "There aren't a lot of laughs on this job, are there?"

"Not like the FBI, no."

"You know why I've been assigned to you?"

"To spy."

"My supervisor thinks that because of your reputation and expertise, you'll end up running the investigation, if not in name then in fact. So I'm to funnel whatever you learn to him."

I started toward the back room, where the X-ray equipment was being noisily installed.

"Are you going to make my job easy?" she asked.

"Nah."

"Yes, you are. We can work together. I'm pretty good."

"On the firing range and lifting fingerprints, maybe. Those things don't have a lot to do with an NTSB investigation."

She walked quickly, trying to keep up with me as we passed row after row of shiny body bags. But I outpaced her. I said over my shoulder, "I don't like spies. I have enough to think about."

"Joe, you're stuck with me," she called. "Get used to it."

SIX

I told my supervisor at Boeing I needed a six-month sabbatical, and was nonplussed when he granted it so quickly. IIC Rich Shrader had asked that in addition to working with the FBI I be the point man with Boeing regarding their laboratories and specialists. When I asked Boeing if the NTSB could use their labs, the company quickly agreed.

Linda Dillon, Holly Langtree, and I were gathered around a tape machine. The IIC had appointed Holly Langtree chair of the flight recorder group. She had been a navy C-130 Hercules pilot before a stint teaching at Annapolis, then moving to the NTSB. Dick Dahlberg, two other NTSB investigators from the flight recorder group, and Wayne Ray were in the small room. We were all leaning forward in our chairs, listening to the last sound on the tape, a half a crunch, a short grinding sound that ended abruptly and was followed only by soft sibilance. On the transcript of the cockpit voice recorder, the NTSB usually transcribes the sound of the crash as "Loud crunchy sound." The NTSB wouldn't be releasing a transcript for another sixty days or so.

Holly switched off the machine. The cockpit voice recorder had been sent to the NTSB audio lab in Washington,

D.C., and this was a duplicate of it. Holly and her investigators had listened to it a dozen times already, but this had been Linda's and my first time through. Holly's playback machine was built by Samsung, with a fifteen-band graphic equalizer that could be used to suppress sounds in specific ranges.

Linda Dillon's face had grayed during the playback. I'm sure my face matched hers. This was one of the goddamn reasons I had left the NTSB, having to listen to the last words said in a cockpit. Especially in a case like this, when the pilot and copilot knew they were in mortal danger, and had time to talk about it.

Holly didn't seem bothered by the contents of the tape. She said, "The voice recorder was a Fairchild model A-100A. The exterior received minor structural damage, just several small dents on the outer casing. The interior, including the magnetic tape, was intact, and didn't sustain impact or heat damage."

"How many channels?" Dahlberg asked.

"Three," she said, rewinding the tape. Holly's eyes were jackdaw blue and her large chin had a cleft. Her brown hair fell to her shoulders and was tucked in. She had either just returned from the tropics or had joined a tanning salon because her skin was the color of copper, darker than the last time I had worked with her. She wore a Scandinavian wool sweater. Her eyeglasses were low on her nose. "One channel covered the cockpit microphone audio signal. The other two channels held the captain and first officer's audio panel signals."

"What are all those sounds early in the tape, the bumps?" Linda asked.

Holly replied, "The pilot and copilot hear only airborne sounds, but a voice recorder also picks up sounds transmitted through the plane's structure."

"Like a bomb detonating?"

"Well . . ." Holly hesitated, glancing at Dahlberg, then me. "Yes, in certain circumstances."

"In certain circumstances?" Linda smiled narrowly. "You folks sure are tidy engineers, aren't you? You can't even say the word *bomb* yet."

Holly said stiffly, "When twenty-five tons of disintegrated and burned debris are spread over many square miles, evidence is rarely clear early in an investigation." She cleared her throat. "The CVR picks up switches being activated, aural warning signals, engine noise, cockpit sounds indicating changes in airspeed, flap and landing gear selectors being operated, all sorts of things."

Dahlberg added, "But *oh, shit*, are the most common last words on a tape."

"I hear them time and time again," Holly said quietly. "*Oh, shit*. Then nothing."

Linda looked stricken. She glanced at me. She regretted being acerbic with Holly Langtree, I could tell. Listening to the tapes did get to Holly, after all.

Commercial planes contain two recorders: the cockpit voice recorder and the flight data recorder. Both must survive extremes of penetration, compression, and inertia, and both are usually placed in the plane's tail cone section because it is the most survivable area. Sometimes they can't survive stupidity, though. On one of my investigations a helpful policeman located a missing flight data recorder using a mine detector, which erased all the data.

The cockpit voice recorder performed a thirty-minute continuous loop, the recorder erasing and recording over the old recording every half hour. Holly's investigation would involve three areas: the readout/transcription of the tape, the timing functions, and the correlation with the flight data recorder.

I asked, "Have you heard anything from the lab about the flight data recorder? Anything preliminary?" The FDR's readout and evaluation would take weeks, maybe months.

"The flight recorder was a Loral/Fairchild model F800," Holly said.

This F800 was capable of recording 115 parameters, with a twenty-five-hour loop. Some planes in the United States were flying with older FDRs, recording only eleven parameters. Recording the plane's every burp and creak, the F800 would give *Sacajawea*'s investigators an enormous head start.

She went on, "The lab told me there's no spikes at the end of the FDR. Nothing that leaps out at them, anyway."

Spikes might have meant a detonation on board. Sudden cessation of the recorded data, often accompanied by wild diversion of traces, is usually due to the power being cut off because electric cables are ruptured. Which often happens when a bomb detonates.

"Anything yet about the *G* record?" I asked.

"Too early to hear."

A flight data recorder that ceases abruptly following an apparently normal flight, with the *G* record diverging suddenly off the plus and minus scales, often indicates that a violent and sudden disaster occurred while the plane was still in the air.

Wayne Ray said, "I couldn't make out some of Captain Pritchard's words on the tape, just before the emergency starts."

"Me neither." Holly fiddled with the tape player. "The lab is going to eliminate static and isolate certain sounds and words by computer, but we don't have those results yet. I decreased bass response to listen to the tape. That cut out some engine noise and some of the bass in the captain's voice. It didn't help me, but maybe it will for you. He's got some words there that don't come through, just before it all breaks loose."

A gentle knock came from the door, and I opened it. Captain Barry Pritchard's wife stood there, wearing a dress she might have lived in for the past three days, her face collapsed entirely. I recognized her—sort of—from a photo I had been shown. Her auburn hair hung loosely around her face. Her eyes were red-rimmed and puffy. She tried a smile, but it wavered and disappeared. Wayne Ray moved quickly to help her into the room.

She held his hand a moment, and said in a tremulous voice, "That was awfully good of you to visit us yesterday. It helped me, and the boys, too. Thank you, Wayne."

"It helped me, too, Gwen."

"You shouldn't have come out, not on a workday. You're too busy."

"Not anymore," he said with a small grin. "Emerald is almost shut down."

"The FAA closed your airline?"

"Lack of passengers closed it. We can't sell a seat. Over at Spawn of Satan, they're so full they're strapping passengers under the wings like Sidewinder missiles."

Gwen managed a laugh, and rolled her eyes at Wayne to tell him he was trying a little too hard. Spawn of Satan was Emerald corporate-speak for its main rival, Horizon Airlines.

Wayne Ray introduced her around. Gwen Pritchard was left with two boys, ages six and three.

Holly Langtree helped her into a chair in front of the tape machine. Holly said, "Mrs. Pritchard, this is going to be painful."

"I've prepared myself. I want to help."

"We are looking for anything that'll assist us in understanding what happened to the plane. Your husband says a couple things on the tape that we can't make out. I've discovered that a spouse, who is familiar with the pilot's speech patterns, often can detect words I can't."

"I'll help if I can."

Wayne Ray reached again for her hand as Holly pressed the button to start the recorder.

Holly said, "Both your husband and the copilot were wearing boom microphones rather than handheld mikes, so we can hear them clearly, even when they turn their heads. But there's a few words I just can't get. We'll listen starting seventeen eleven hundred. That's eleven minutes after five in the afternoon for you civilians." She smiled at Mrs. Pritchard, who only stared at the speaker, waiting for her husband.

Over the speaker came a voice: "That's the key to flying in the Pacific Northwest, knowing where Mount Rainier is."

"That's Barry," Mrs. Pritchard almost yelled.

After the sound of a chuckle from the speakers, Holly said, "That's First Officer Aurelio Lopez."

Still holding her hand, Wayne Ray said, "Take it from this airline executive, Gwen, one of a first officer's jobs is to laugh at the pilot's jokes."

He was trying to help, but she stared with unceasing eyes at the main speaker, as if she could see her husband's face in it.

The speaker: "Emerald 37, descend to eleven. Heading two-eight-oh."

Holly said, "That's Seattle Center."

The speaker: "Emerald 37, descending to eleven. Heading two-eight-oh."

"That's the first officer," Holly said.

"Where'd you get the name *Aurelio*, Aurelio?" from the speaker.

"That's my husband Barry speaking," Gwen Pritchard said.

From the speaker: "I'm Mexican American, man." With a

Cheech accent, "Can't you tell from my 'stache? And we don't give no stinking names like Jim or John or Joe or Jay. Or Barry. We give proud names like *Aurelio*."

The pilot said, "But *Aurelio*'s a pretty odd name, even for someone whose first introduction to the United States was climbing over razor wire."

Lopez said, "My father told me I was named *Aurelio* because it was the only name with all the vowels."

"That's cool," the pilot said. "My father could come up with only one vowel. In Barry."

The copilot: "*Y* is sometimes a vowel. Didn't you go to school? A-E-I-O-U and sometimes Y. So you got two vowels, Barry."

"Well, I feel better, with two vowels now."

With distress and embarrassment on her face, Gwen Pritchard looked at Holly Langtree, then at me.

I said, "Mrs. Pritchard, pilots and copilots chat just like everyone else, sometimes to relieve tension, sometimes to relieve boredom. They don't sit up there and invent the calculus or chart the motion of the stars."

Gwen Pritchard smiled her thanks.

A slight, quick click.

When Holly didn't offer an explanation, Mrs. Pritchard asked, "What was that noise?"

"Probably nothing. There's lots of noise on a cockpit voice recording. Most of it doesn't mean anything."

From the speaker: "SeaTac reports clear, visibility eight, temperature forty-two, wind light and variable, altimeter 3001."

Holly explained, "That's Flight Watch, the weather service."

"What's that new noise?" Linda Dillon asked. "An alarm?"

"Captain Pritchard is whistling," Holly replied.

"Sounds like Bonnie Raitt," Dahlberg said.

"It isn't," Mrs. Pritchard said. "It's Raffi."

"Raffi?" Holly asked.

"The children's singer. We have several Raffi tapes, full of cute songs, some nonsense songs, some old standby kids' songs. Our youngest boy loves them."

Holly said, "Now here's the words we can't understand, Mrs. Pritchard. They're coming now."

From the speaker: "Yassaluu. Yassaluu. Yassaluu."

Holly quickly turned off the tape, not wanting the pilot's wife to hear more than necessary. "Any idea what your husband is saying?"

"Sure. He's saying, 'Yassaluu. Yassaluu. Yassaluu.' "

"Well, I know that." Holly smiled. "But what does it mean?"

"It's from the Raffi song. It doesn't mean anything. Our three-year-old, Steven, marches around the house saying, 'Yassaluu. Yassaluu. Yassaluu,' imitating Raffi. And so does Barry, once in a while, having fun with Steven. They go around the house with each other, laughing and saying 'Yassaluu.' To see them doing that is . . . is cuter than I can make it sound."

Mrs. Pritchard was still referring to her husband in the present tense. It would take a while.

Holly looked at me, then asked, "You mean, it's baby talk?"

"Words from a Raffi song, is all." Mrs. Pritchard's face, so abused with grief in recent days, began to cloud. "You mean, it isn't helpful to know that? I can't be of any help?"

"You were a great help, Gwen," Ray said quickly.

"We needed to know what those words meant, Mrs. Pritchard," I added.

Holly said, "That his words meant nothing is very important to us. It keeps us from going down a dead end. It saves my group much, much time, believe me."

The two other members of the flight recorder group nodded vigorously, trying to make her feel better.

Holly rose from her chair and began her polite dismissal. "Mrs. Pritchard, I can't tell you how much I appreciate you coming in."

Gwen Pritchard said bluntly, "I want to hear the rest of the tape."

Holly glanced at me, then at Dick Dahlberg. Then she said, just as bluntly, "No, you don't, ma'am."

"I want to hear my husband's last words."

Wayne Ray now took both her hands. "Gwen, there's nothing to know on the remaining part of the tape. Nothing that'll tell you anything new about Barry. Nothing to offer you any comfort."

"Let me hear it," she demanded. "I came all the way down here to help you, and now you help me."

"Mrs. Pritchard, you will be listening to a nightmare," I said firmly. "It'll be the worst thing you'll ever hear in your life."

She tossed aside Ray's hands to stand and glare at me. "Three days ago I heard my husband was dead. That's the worst thing I'll ever hear. Let me hear the tape." She softened. "My husband . . . I don't want others knowing what he said without me knowing. It's like keeping a secret from me. Please."

I looked at Holly. It was her call. She chewed on her lower lip, then sat down to reach for the recorder's control buttons.

Gwen Pritchard returned to her chair. Wayne Ray again reached for her hand, patting it with another. At fifty years of age, Ray may still attend all University of Washington pre–football game tailgate parties in the stadium parking lot, wearing a purple and gold sweatshirt, and drinking Husky Highballs, but I was beginning to understand why Emerald's employees liked working for him. A Husky Highball is 150-

proof tequila mixed with 100-proof tequila. Get a slice of lime anywhere near and it is ruined.

Holly hit the REWIND dial for an instant, then the PLAY button.

The speaker: "Yassaluu. Yassaluu. Yassaluu."

Then a dull thump, and a short tearing noise. Nothing of any consequence in any other situation.

Captain Pritchard asked, "The hell was that?"

Aurelio Lopez: "Goddamn, the wheel damn near yanked out of my hands."

Pritchard: "The hell?"

A long beep. Holly said, "That's the low-pressure alarm."

From the speaker: "Jesus, Barry, what the . . ."

Pritchard: "Punch in 7700."

A muffled yell.

Holly said, "That's a flight attendant, I think. And then that noise sounds like a latch, maybe the hatch to the cabin. I'm not sure."

Pritchard: "Cut out auto."

A searing grind, and a hollow *whoompf*.

Then repetitive rapid triple chirps.

Holly said, "That's the autopilot disconnect warning."

Lopez: "No response on that."

"Goddamn, Aurelio."

More ripping. Sounding like a dress tearing.

Sounds of labored breathing.

Pritchard: "Mellow it out. Mellow it out."

A wailing sound.

"That's the pitch trim alarm," Holly said.

"Nice and easy." Pritchard. "Mellow it out. There we go. Mellow it out."

"No lift," Lopez said. "Six thousand, falling."

"Starboard. Starboard." Pritchard. "Now, we can take it . . . Ah, goddamn."

Mrs. Pritchard's hand flew to her face to cover her mouth. Her eyes were locked on the main speaker.

Holly moved to turn off the tape. Mrs. Pritchard caught her hand, squeezing it so hard Mrs. Pritchard's knuckles whitened.

A series of thumping.

"Aahh." Either Pritchard or Lopez.

"I can't . . . I can't . . ." Lopez.

Repeated beeps.

Holly said, "That's the overspeed warning."

Pritchard: "Aw, goddamn it."

A long, grinding noise. Then muffled but terrible screams from the cabin.

A horn sounded. *Whoop whoop whoop whoop*, as evil a sound as exists.

Holly said, "That's the altitude alert signal."

More screams.

"Oh, shit," from Lopez.

Sound of intermittent heavy breathing. Screams from the cabin.

Pritchard: "Good-bye, dear God. Good-bye."

Loud crunchy noise.

Hissing. End of tape.

Mrs. Pritchard released Holly's hand. Ray helped her from the chair. Her face was now oddly serene. Perhaps she had spent every last emotion, and had nothing else inside her. She was utterly empty.

Ray guided the widow to the door.

"Mrs. Pritchard," I said, stopping her. "I've investigated a lot of plane crashes, including eight majors. And it's way too early to make any conclusions, but from everything I now know, your husband couldn't have done anything to save his plane."

She slowly shook her head. "No."

"After that first loud sound we heard on the tape—that loud bump—your husband and the first officer became passengers on *Sacajawea*. The plane was lost to them."

"Passengers?"

"Just like everybody else on the plane. All they could do was ride it down."

I don't know if that helped, but she touched my arm, thanked Holly, and left us. Wayne Ray offered to drive her home, but she said she could do it on her own.

Dahlberg and Ray stayed behind to listen to the tape again. Maybe there was something we had all missed. Holly walked me and my personal FBI agent toward the elevators.

Linda said, "I snipped at you in there, Holly. About tidy engineers. Sorry."

"That's okay. It gets tense, listening to those tapes."

"They have a special class in it at the academy," Linda said. "It's called *How to Say Dumb Things*."

"That's all right, really. Listening to those tapes makes you do strange things. I've done some myself."

Linda brightened. "Like what?"

We stopped at the elevator. "After I listen to them again and again, I start to feel like I know the pilot and copilot. Know how they think, what they'll say. Know their sense of humor. Sometimes you hear snippets about families back home, that sort of thing."

"Yes?"

"Several times, as the awful moment is about to arrive on a tape, I've shouted out a warning to the crew."

I pressed the elevator button.

"Shouted?" Linda asked.

"Loud and clear, right at the tape machine," Holly said. "Trying to save my new friends on the doomed plane."

Linda said glumly, "I thought you were going to tell me something funny, some humorous story from the trenches."

Just as the elevator doors closed, we heard Holly say, "I don't laugh a lot in my job. Not much at all."

SEVEN

Linda and I were in the wheelhouse of the *Sally M,* a fifty-year-old fishing boat owned by a first-generation Norwegian American. The vessel was a longliner, used mainly for catching salmon that were destined for restaurants and for market displays, salmon that needed to look handsome for the consumer, not beat up from a net. She was sixty feet long, her hull made of plank-laid oak. Except for the radar and antennas mounted on top of the wheelhouse, the exterior of the vessel looked as it had for five decades. The pilothouse had a rounded front. A dozen small windows arrayed in a curved row provided the master's view out over the prow. The prow rose almost to the master's eye level, designed to split blue water waves and ride up over them.

Linda's hands were around a coffee cup, and she was watching the activity at Fisherman's Terminal, where hundreds of commercial fishing boats cluttered the skyline with rigging. We had met the *Sally M* 's owner here, and had also interviewed a fish broker, trying to determine how an explosive device might have been put into an empty fish crate. Fresh fish was sent to the ski resort daily, packed in ice. Empty fish crates returned daily. Emerald Air carried almost as many salmon as passengers on each trip east, usually in the forward hold. Could a bomb have been placed into a crate with the fish in Seattle and somehow remained in the empty crate on the return flight, when it detonated? The theory was a stretch, but nobody had a better one. We had learned nothing useful, and the *Sally M*'s master had made coffee for us before he had gone below to argue with a manufacturer's service representative about his Detroit Diesel engine.

"Maria Lopez called me last night," she said. Maria was the wife of *Sacajawea*'s copilot. "Gwen Pritchard had telephoned Maria to let her know what she had heard on *Sacajawea*'s voice recorder. Then Maria phoned me to ask if she might be able to listen to the tape, too."

"What'd you say?"

Linda sighed. "Well, Maria got more than she bargained for when she called me, I'm afraid."

"What do you mean?"

"I sort of fell apart." Linda turned her cup slowly, rotating it on the table precisely an eighth of a turn each twist. "When she phoned me, Maria was trying to be steady, but I could tell she was struggling to hold in her grief. She wanted to know if she could bear hearing her husband Aurelio's last words."

"And so what happened?"

"I spoke to her for a moment, my voice professional and supportive, telling her that her husband had been brave to the very end but that listening to his last words would be very hard for her, and then . . ." She turned her cup. "And then I started to cry."

"You? Not Maria?"

She nodded. "Big gulping sobs, all of a sudden, right into the telephone. A huge gusher, everything I'd been holding in. I couldn't stop. And suddenly the copilot's widow is having to comfort me on the phone, telling me that it'll be okay and that she knows I have a tough job, having to listen to the cockpit tapes and going to the morgue and things like that. And all the time Maria is saying these nice things, I'm bawling my eyes out." Her gaze was still down on her cup.

I wanted to say something helpful, but all I could think of was, "Crash investigation is tough, Linda."

"I thought I was handling it, putting all of it into a nice corner of my brain where I could visit it when I had to, detached and clinical, but it isn't like that, is it?"

"Not for me. Never has been."

"Finally, when I could stammer something out around all my sobbing, I said I was sorry and hung up. Then, when I stopped crying, I was mortified, the professional investigator, the FBI agent, weeping uncontrollably in front of a new widow, rather than vice versa. My phone rang a moment later, but I couldn't answer it. I know it was Maria, calling me again, trying to see if I was all right."

I asked gently, "Are you going to be all right?"

Linda finally looked up. "I think about those sixty-three people a lot. And their families, like Maria and her children." Moisture glistened at the corners of her eyes. "Every night I think about them, lying there awake."

She blinked away the tears. We were silent a moment. I wanted to reach for her hand, but I didn't. We both searched for something to say, some other topic.

Finally she asked, "Are you from Seattle?"

"Almira, two hundred miles east of here."

"Never heard of it."

"It's between Govan and Hartline," I announced, as if that would place the town for her. "Almira has four hundred ten people or four hundred twelve people, depending on whether you enter from east or west on Highway 2. It's wheat country. Dry-land farming."

"Your dad was a farmer?"

"He owned a grain elevator."

"What's that? A wheat warehouse?"

"How is it possible you don't know what a grain elevator is?" I cast my face in astonishment.

"Well, what is it?"

"A wheat warehouse." I sipped the coffee, which tasted like the master polished brightwork with it. We were sitting at the chart table, which had a wood ridge around it so cups wouldn't fall off in heavy seas. *Sally M*'s hull might have been laid down half a century ago but the wheelhouse was filled with silicon chips. Icom SSB and Simrad VHF radios were hung over the wheel, their handset cords hanging down. Monitors for the Furuno radar and the Raytheon fish-finder and a plotter for an Apelco global positioning system were mounted next to the wheel. An Autohelm instrument system was near a bank of toggle switches and the throttle levers.

She waited for something more, tapping her cup.

"That's an interrogator's trick," I accused her. "Offering only silence, hoping the suspect will fill it with chatter."

She waited more, staring right at me. The boat lifted with the wake of a passing vessel.

"I worked at the elevator when I was a kid," I said after a moment, defeated. "The worst duty was cleaning the boot after a long winter."

"The boot?"

"Farmers' trucks come into the elevator, and dump their wheat through a grate into a funnel-shaped bin. At the bottom of the bin are buckets on a long motor-driven belt. The buckets take the wheat to the headhouse, ten stories up, where the wheat is directed by chutes into the storage tower."

She sipped her coffee and said nothing, so I went on, "Snowmelt and rain collect in the boot, along with wheat and wheat dust. Wheat sprouts in the moisture, but then dies for lack of light down there. And it rots, emitting a sulfur odor. And dead rats are down there, smelling away, maggot ridden. I'd puke two or three times every time I cleaned the boot. I decided the elevator business wasn't for me."

She asked, "How does a grain elevator boot lead to the navy?"

"Down there in the boot, gasping and heaving, I determined that the farthest away from that smell I could get was up in the sky in a navy plane. It was an odd notion, but so compelling that it never left me. I marched from my college graduation ceremony straight to a recruiter's office. Now it's your turn."

"We aren't taking turns. I am the interrogator and you are the victim."

"How did you come to the FBI?"

She thought a moment, lifting her cup, then lowering it without drinking. The horn for the Ballard Bridge sounded, a long, soulful blare. The bridge was about to rise so a boat could pass beneath it.

"Six servants," she said finally, then offered no more, as if those two words explained everything.

"You are deliberately being obscure to compensate for your appalling lack of knowledge about grain elevators."

"My parents' home has six servants, not counting the gardeners. Thirty-two rooms, including a solarium and indoor swimming pool and a carriage house. My father made his fortune in the trucking business."

"He owned a trucking line?"

"Transcon Trucking."

"My Lord." I despise it when my mouth falls open. "The red and yellow trucks all over North America?"

"My father is retired now, but he still owns most of the Transcon stock, except for the eighty or ninety thousand shares he's given me over the years as part of his estate planning."

"I've been buying Cokes for someone who owns ninety thousand shares of Transcon Trucking?"

"When I was twenty-five I decided that the spa life—the life my mother has studied assiduously and now excels at—wasn't for me, so I went back to college, earned an accounting degree, became a CPA, then joined the bureau."

"I am bathing in the rays of your nobility."

"Not all that noble. Once a year, in January, I spend a month with my parents at their home in Aspen. I am pampered morning to night as Mom tries to show me the error of my ways. Mom and I ski, sit in the hot tub, work out with a personal trainer named Julianne, shop for boots made from endangered species, eat five-star meals, and generally act the part of the degenerate rich."

"That sounds fun to this poor working stiff."

"One month of utter worthlessness. I love it. And it takes me those thirty days to once again become repelled by the life, and I return to my FBI cubicle with renewed purpose."

"Your husband goes along to Aspen, I imagine."

She abruptly sat back, and a shadow crossed her face. "Sometimes he does, yes."

An incomplete and awkward answer.

She rallied. "He and my father smoke cigars in the library. Brandy and cigars. Their little ritual."

"They get along? Your husband and your father?"

She hesitated. "Some of the time. Dad is quite fond of Kevin, sometimes. So, tell me how you met Janie."

"You have changed the subject about as subtly as a fullback charges the line."

"Yeah, well, my husband is none of your business. How's that for subtle?" Before I could react, she reached across for my wrist. "Joe, I'm sorry. You don't deserve to be snapped at." She smiled tentatively. "At least not today you don't."

"No need to talk to me about anything you don't want to, Linda."

"My husband is a complicated subject for me, that's all." She pushed the cup away from her in a motion of exaggerated disgust. "This coffee has reduced my life expectancy by five years. Let's go."

"Where now?"

"Assistant Director Yamashita gave us a list of fifteen people to interview. The fisherman was only number four."

I followed her out of the wheelhouse, along the gangway to the stern. I could hear the service rep and the *Sally M*'s owner down in the engine compartment banging away on something, the owner cursing. Linda leaped over the rail onto the dock, holding her heavy purse against her ribs. I jumped after her, clumsily, catching my foot between the bumper and the dock, and yanking it free only on the second try.

We walked up the dock toward the parking area. I glanced sideways at her, trying not to be obvious. I admit to having spent some time thinking about Linda Dillon that the government was paying me to think about *Sacajawea*. I'd like to know more about her husband, but I wasn't going to ask her, that was for damned sure.

• • •

Matthew Ripley spread the documents in front of Linda and me. IIC Rich Shrader had already seen them, but he attended the meeting, wanting my take on them. We were in the command trailer at the wreckage site. Ripley was chairman of the maintenance records group. A space heater hummed.

"Any problem getting the records?" I asked.

"Emerald sent the disks over before I had even asked, and I printed them out." Ripley wore a perpetual frown. His bifocals were thick, and I don't think I'd ever seen him when he wasn't bent over a table studying documents, as if the weight of his spectacles had permanently bent down his neck. His hair was burr cut, so he either was fond of the 1950s or had just taken up the electric guitar. He had flown in from Dallas. "You know the wiring on ATF 94s better than me, Joe, what with you working on Green Bay."

"What are these?" Linda asked, thumbing through the stack of documents.

"Every time a mechanic does something to the plane, the work is recorded." I moved a table lamp closer to the maintenance records. Outside the trailer, a truck-mounted vacuum pump started a low wail. Water was going to be removed from an impact crater. A raven croaked angrily, and again and again as it flew away.

Ripley said, "I've flagged the ones I want you to look at with yellow Post-its."

I picked up the first sheet. "Last September, a worker had to jiggle a fuel-valve switch every three or four seconds, changing it from normal power to battery power, to get readings on *Sacajawea*'s center tank."

Ripley nodded. "A short in the wiring, maybe."

"Or just a bad switch, more likely," Shrader said.

I brought up another document and summarized it. "In

December, *Sacajawea*'s fuel-flow transmitter was replaced, and the problem disappeared." I lifted another flagged record. "Then last February 10, a circuit breaker that overrides the fueling shutdown was removed, in order to fuel the plane." And yet another record. "And then ten days later, all the fuel valves shut down during fueling, and couldn't be reopened electrically."

"So replacing the fuel-flow transmitter didn't fix the problem," Linda said.

"Then on April 4—that'd be five days before *Sacajawea* went down—two fuel pumps, including the scavenger pump, were replaced." I shifted the records. There were no more yellow flags. "Those fuel pumps were the last fuel-related repairs on *Sacajawea,* looks like."

Ripley nodded.

I scratched my ear, the repair records in front of me. "You interviewed the mechanics yet?"

"I'm leaving for Boise on a noon flight. I'll talk to them at the Emerald hangar. Wayne Ray has arranged for one of *Sacajawea*'s sister planes to be there, so the mechanics can walk me through what they did. One of the mechanics asked if he needed a lawyer, and I told him no."

Linda asked, "The Green Bay ATF 94, did it have similar switch and breaker problems?"

"Nothing on the maintenance records." I took a deep breath, and could smell diesel exhaust from the generator outside the trailer. "This stuff with the fueling means something, Matt." I looked up at him, then at Rich Shrader. "But I don't know what."

I followed Linda into the holding room. The prisoner sat at a small table, and a forest ranger on a metal folding chair leaned against the wall. The ranger rose and smiled politely at Linda. The prisoner sat there, hands folded in front of him. A large green plastic bag was on the table with a manila tag at one end. Several lines of condensation had formed along the plastic folds. It had been recently removed from a freezer.

Linda showed her badge. "May we speak with him alone?"

The ranger left the room.

"I'm a little late," she said to the hunter. "Sorry."

We sat in chairs around the table. Linda's handbag was on her lap. She had checked her pistol on the first floor, the first time I had seen her handgun.

The prisoner's walnut brown hair was to his shoulders, and still had several twigs caught in it. His beard was unkempt, and went all the way down his face and under his chin to disappear beneath his denim shirt. His eyes were sad and guileless, bloodhound eyes. Gold showed on an incisor. His fingers were stained with tobacco.

"Can't smoke in jail anymore," Linda said. "It's tough."

He didn't say anything.

"You talked to your lawyer?" she asked.

"I don't got a lawyer." The prisoner's voice was barely discernible above the hiss from ventilation pipes. In jail, the pipes are always narrower than the smallest of persons' shoulders. "Can't afford a lawyer."

"I can get you one, right away. Court appointed. You need one. I shouldn't be talking at all to you until a lawyer is here." She reached into her handbag. "Here. Something that'll take the edge off a long day." She handed the prisoner a tin of Copenhagen.

He couldn't keep the gratitude off his face. He tapped the can's top, opened it, and put a pinch behind his lower lip.

"We need to talk about what you saw out in the forest."

He held out the tobacco tin to her, but she waved it away. "You can keep it."

"I know what you're doing." The prisoner slipped the tin into his shirt pocket. "I've been arrested before."

"You know what I'm doing?" Linda grinned at him.

"You're being nice and all, but it's just to get me to talk."

"Well, I thought that's why you wanted to chat with us," she said. "It was your idea."

"Yeah, but I'm not going to talk about any bears." The prisoner cracked his knuckles, sounding like gunshots.

"All right. You're too smart for me, that's for sure." There was heavy invention in her voice, probably lost on the prisoner. She brought out a dictating machine from her purse. "You mind if I tape our little talk? My penmanship is bad." She paused. "Penmanship. You know, writing."

"I don't give a damn," he said. "Tape or no."

"I'm advising you of your right to a lawyer. I'll stop right now if you want a lawyer here."

"Nah. I've met one or two. They're all bloodsuckers."

Linda said her name and the date for the benefit of the tape recorder, then added that I was also in the room. She looked down at the clipboard. "Your name is Thaddeus Wilson."

"I go by Thad."

"What do we have in the bag, Thad?" She opened it and dumped out four bear paws onto the table.

The paws were about nine inches long and half that wide. Huge claws, five on each foot. Fur above the paws was the color of cinnamon. The feet had been sawed off the animal quickly and with little care. The tissue was ragged.

"You're a poacher, looks like," Linda said. "Caught red-handed."

He shrugged.

"I'll bet this isn't the first bear you've shot, is it? Just the first you've been caught with."

"Second I've been caught with," he corrected. "Just got probation, first time. First time was a grizzly. This here's a black bear. You probably don't even know the difference."

"That all you been arrested for?" she asked.

"Couple other small things that don't much count."

"This time you weren't expecting the forest to be crawling with policemen and state patrol and National Guardsmen looking for bodies from a plane crash. You were out there, minding your own business, trying to kill a bear. And some cop steps out from behind a bush and asks what's in your backpack. Before you know it, you're hearing your Miranda rights."

The prisoner pushed his chew around in his mouth. "You got anywhere I can spit. I got some friends who can swallow the juice, but I can't."

"Poaching." She shook her head. "Aren't you ashamed?"

"Out in the woods, it's me versus the bears, I figure."

"No. It's you and a 30-06 and a scope and four hundred yards versus the bears. And now you tell the cops that you've got something important to reveal about Emerald 37, *Sacajawea*."

"That's right."

Linda continued, "But you won't say anything unless you are granted immunity from prosecution for the poaching."

"Right again."

"What do you do with those bear paws?" I asked.

Linda clicked her tongue. I had spoken. Broken her rhythm. "I don't do nothing with them. I ain't a poacher, not really."

"You sell them to some middleman who visits your trailer

in the middle of the night, and the paws eventually end up in Hong Kong," Linda said. "Am I right? You would've cut other parts out of the bear—his spleen and his testicles and whatever else those idiots over there use to get their peckers up— but the cops tripped over you out in the woods. And now you are looking at five years at the Walls."

The state penitentiary at Walla Walla.

Linda made a show of shivering and looking at me. "The Walls. You wouldn't believe the things I hear about that place. Maybe you'll be lucky, Thad, and be some big guy's girlfriend. That way you'll have some protection inside."

"A boyfriend?"

"A big mushy, inviting face like yours, with a beard that looks just—and I mean absolutely just—like pubic hair."

He touched his beard. "My beard ain't like no pubic hair."

"I've got some, so I know," Linda said. "You're going to be a hot commodity at the Walls, unless you get a boyfriend who'll take care of you."

"That's sick. You're sick."

"Of course, you'll have to be his sweetheart. Give him little kisses, that sort of thing."

"Have we got a deal?" A trace of whine was in the poacher's voice. He glanced at me.

She snapped, "Thad, don't look at him for help. He's just my assistant. He brings me beakers and chemicals and once in a while I let him throw the laboratory's big red switch."

The poacher clenched his fists.

Linda said gravely, in the tone of a judge announcing a criminal's sentence, "Your deal just doesn't work for me, Thad. It just isn't a go."

"It ain't?"

"It ain't."

"But I've got something good to tell you," the poacher pleaded. "Something real good. You won't be sorry."

"How good?"

"I know what happened to that plane, but I ain't saying nothing until you promise me about the poacher charge."

She said, "Nobody grants immunity to the guy who murdered Smoky the Bear."

"Then I'm not going to say nothing."

"But we can do a softer deal, Thad."

"Yeah?"

"I'll tell the prosecutor that you were helpful in the *Sacajawea* investigation. The plane crash is a big, big event around here. Much bigger than a dead bear. And my word to the prosecutor might help you. Might help a lot."

He looked at her, then at the table, weighing his prospects. Then he announced, "I saw a rocket bring that plane down."

My shoulders slumped. Damn it to hell. I'd had enough rocket reports, what with TWA 800 and the goofy conspiracy buffs who claim a U.S. Navy missile brought down the plane over Long Island Sound.

The poacher must've read my reaction. He said with heat, "I saw it. Saw it come up from the ground."

"You're inventing some crazy story about a missile, is that it?" Linda sighed loudly. "Hoping to profit from my sweet nature?"

"It's no story," the poacher persisted. "I saw it, I swear."

"Tell me what you saw," she ordered.

"I saw a rocket shoot straight up."

I asked, "What do you mean, a rocket?"

"A long string of light, shooting from the ground, almost straight up. Maybe at a little slant, but mostly straight up."

"What time was this?" I asked.

"Little after five in the afternoon, the day the plane came down."

"Where were you at the time?"

"Near the headwater of Rocky Creek."

That put the poacher somewhere under the plane.

He said, "The rocket trail looked to be a mile away. Somewhere around a mile."

"Did you see the plane?" Linda asked.

The poacher shook his head. "Never saw it. Didn't hear nothing, either. Just saw the light shooting up. It was bright daylight. I could see it plain as day. But I didn't know anything had happened to no plane until I heard about it on the radio."

Linda said, "And you put two and two together, and figured this rocket brought down the plane?"

"That's right."

"Well, that's just crapola."

"I swear, lady."

Linda breathed deeply. She looked at me again before asking, "You willing to be hooked up to a machine?"

"A machine," the poacher asked. "What kind of machine?"

"A goddamn brain implant machine. What do you think?"

The poacher still didn't know what she was talking about.

"A lie detector." Linda's tone was one of vast patience. "You willing to talk to a lie detector?"

I was startled, and so was she, when the poacher immediately exclaimed, "Sure."

"Yes?"

"Anytime, any day," the poacher said, tapping the table. "Right now, if you want."

She rose from the chair. "I'll arrange it. Probably for later in the day. You can get your story straight in your cell until then."

The last thing the poacher said as we left the holding cell was, "I need somewhere to spit. I ain't used to this snuff."

We had retrieved her pistol, and Linda and I were in my car again before she asked, "What if that moron is telling the truth, that he saw a missile or rocket fire up from the ground? What if he green lights the lie detector test?"

"You ever heard of the Farnborough Air Show?" I asked.

"I'm not sure."

"It's Great Britain's big air show. A huge international event. In 1952, a de Havilland 110 fighter came apart just in front of the grandstand, killing the pilot and second-seater. An engine flew into the crowd, killing thirty people and injuring another sixty."

"My God."

"Over a hundred thousand people saw it happen. The director of the Royal Aircraft Establishment appealed to witnesses for statements. Thousands and thousands of letters came in, and hundreds of witnesses were later interviewed by British investigators. Every single one of the interviewed witnesses got it wrong, got the plane's second-by-second break-up sequence backwards."

"How was that determined?"

"The witnesses said that fragments detached from the tail before the aircraft reared up, and therefore the tail must have caused the accident. Subsequent research on the plane's pieces proved them wrong, and showed the compression buckles on the starboard wing split near the leading edge, initiating the disintegration. The witnesses' imaginations had filled in much of the break-up sequence."

She asked, "So you think Thad the Poacher is telling us the truth?"

"The truth as he knows it, maybe."

"But you don't think a missile brought down Emerald 37, do you?"

"Thad thinks so, and he's the only witness we've found," I replied. A bike messenger was in front of the car, taking his time. I resisted the urge to bump him with my fender. "And Thad is willing to take a lie detector test. I'm not going to dismiss what he says, but I remind myself about Farnborough. And about other mistakes made by witnesses to airplane incidents."

"Like what?"

"The disintegration of a high-speed turbine disc can produce an explosive noise, and has been confused in the past with a bomb. And a main wing spar failure can produce a sound like a cannon. Kerosene clouds escaping from the tanks are sometimes confused with smoke. That sort of thing. Aircrash witnesses are notoriously unreliable."

We were silent awhile.

Then I said, "Nice going with the Copenhagen. Do you always have a tin of it in your bag?"

"For interrogations, yes. You'd be amazed at how it loosens up the nicotine fiends."

"And that's some handgun you carry. What is it?"

"A Sig Sauer 10 millimeter." She tapped her handbag affectionately. We rode along a moment, then she added, "I can field strip it in eight seconds."

I replied, "Somehow I already knew that."

EIGHT

"Ed, I'm slipping into a coma here." Rich Shrader's words rattled back and forth in the conference room, made metallic by the cheap public-address system. "Can you cut to the chase?"

"Too many multisyllable words for all you ex–navy and air force pilots?" Edwin Murdoch was sitting next to Shrader at the head table. Murdoch was a forensic chemist with the FAA's Aviation Explosives Security Unit. "Here it is then: by magnifying several pieces of metal 1,500 times with an electron microscope, I found extensive cratering."

Excitement spread across the room like a wave on water. Cratering was the single most conclusive evidence of a blast. An explosion is caused by the extremely rapid conversion of a solid or liquid into gases having a much greater volume than the substance from which they are generated. This is called detonation, and it produces temperatures of several thousand degrees and very high-velocity shock pressure waves. The distinctive signature of a detonation is high-velocity penetration.

The conference room had been rented from a Snoqualmie Pass lodge. About 150 people were in the room, sitting in rows of chairs as if at a theater, facing the investigator-in-charge and several others sitting at the front table. Above and behind the IIC were several white projection screens, and on a board on the west wall was a wreckage distribution polar diagram. On another wall was a reconstruction of *Sacajawea*'s flight path derived from radar images. The path ended on the side of a mountain.

We were at the daily progress meeting, which usually occurred at eight in the evening, after most everybody in the room had already worked sixteen hours. The meetings were held to disseminate information, discuss investigative efforts, review progress, and to introduce people new to the investigation. The room contained photocopy machines, tabletop computers and printers, and a telephone message board for anybody who didn't have an e-mail address, which was almost nobody.

"What else?" Shrader prompted the chemist.

Edwin Murdoch waved at assistants at a projector and at the room's light dimmer. The room darkened, and a photo appeared on a screen. Dr. Murdoch wore circular tortoiseshell glasses. I'd never seen him without a pencil behind his ear, which I'd never seen him use. A laptop computer was open in front of him.

"My lab is still doing radiophotography and X-ray diffraction analysis for molecular species identification, and chromatographic tests for chemical identification of the explosive. And we're not done with the infrared spectrophotometry."

"The chase, Ed. The chase."

"So everything I say is preliminary," Murdoch said. "This is a photo of a piece of aluminum in one of *Sacajawea*'s flooring supports. Notice the gas-wash effect on the metal. It's surface melting, sort of an orange peel effect. I've got lots more photos of the same thing on different pieces of the airplane, pieces from the structure just behind the cockpit."

People at the back of the room stood to better see the screen. A dozen or more organizations were represented here. The FBI and ATF and NTSB, of course. And the Washington State Patrol and the Kittitas and King County sheriff's departments, several county coroner's offices, the airline pilots' union, Air Transport France and the French Directorate General for Civil Aviation, Emerald Airlines, and numerous other groups. The room was searched for electronic eavesdropping equipment before each meeting, and Washington State patrolmen carefully studied badges—which had photographs on them—before allowing anyone into the room.

The director of the FBI, William Henley, leaned against the wall, conspicuous in a business suit. His dark hair had a bold, peculiar white streak through it, front to back, and he was sometimes called Indira, but never to his face. Near him was Boeing's CEO, who was welcomed at the meeting because the NTSB was using Boeing's Seattle-area resources extensively. The Boeing CEO was attending tonight because the FBI director was a golfing buddy.

When Murdoch nodded to his assistant, a second photograph replaced the first on the screen. "Here's a photo of rolled edges on a metal piece, again from behind the cockpit. Indicative of a detonation. We've got lots of photos of these. And on this next photo"—the screen blinked to a new image—"you can clearly see surface spalling."

Yet another photo appeared. Murdoch explained, "This piece of nylon was taken from a ski parka. We can see explosive heat fractures—this flash melting—at the fiber ends."

I was sitting next to Wayne Ray. On the other side of him was his father, Charles. I had saved a seat for Linda Dillon, but she hadn't arrived yet from the King County jail. Many people in the room had sandwiches and chips on their laps, sold to them by a vending truck outside the building. Because of the extensive delays involved in leaving and reentering the site due to the bio safety procedures, many investigators were staying all day on the site, not bothering to eat until the end of the day. Another photograph was brought up.

Ed Murdoch said, "And here's my favorite. A nice little piece of work by yours truly. This is a snip of polyester taken from the lining of a piece of luggage. You'll see that red fibers have been forced through the undamaged fabric and appear on the opposite face of the polyester weave. Virtually certain evidence of a detonation."

"Any twinning?" The questioner had an English accent, and I knew him, an investigator from the Royal Armaments Research and Development Establishment at Fort Halstead, northeast of London. He had beaten fifty other people in the room with the question.

"Can't find any yet," the chemist replied, smiling, knowing the import of what he had just said.

A long pause ensued. With that short answer, the room had been presented with a puzzle. Two items of evidence were now directly in conflict.

"I'll be the dummy," Sheriff Kingman said loudly. He was sitting on the other side of Charles Ray. "What's twinning?"

"Parallel lines or cracks cutting across crystals of metals such as copper, iron, and steel," Murdoch replied. "They usually occur only if the specimen has undergone extreme shock, say, about 8,000 meters per second. For twinning to occur, the specimen must have been near the seat of the explosion and"—he paused dramatically—"it must have been a military type of explosive."

Everyone in the room knew of poacher Thaddeus Wilson's report of a missile. The payload of modern missiles contains a high explosive such as RDC or USA/C4, with detonations in the 8,000 meters per second range. Old-fashioned gunpowder and commercial explosives such as blasting gelignites and low-strength dynamites detonate at more like 1,000 meters a second.

So the poacher—the only living witness to anything—claimed he saw a missile. Yet all the evidence of a detonation—and there was plenty of it—indicated that the force of the detonation was much less than that caused by RDC or other military explosives. There was no other trace of a missile, but that meant little at this point. Evidence of a missile would not normally be found in the main debris field. The missile's extreme velocity could have caused the incriminating debris to be blasted miles from the main wreckage.

"Did you get the Revlon ladies over?" asked a man with a heavy Scandinavian accent. He was from the Säkerhetspolis, the Swedish security agency, known as SAPO.

He was asking about Semtex, the high-explosive manufactured at Pardubice, sixty miles east of Prague. The Czechs now put a detectable odor in the explosive, but much pre-odor Semtex is still available. Revlon and other cosmetics manufacturers employ people—usually women—with freakishly acute senses of smell to quantify the effectiveness of their deodorants and for other scent testing. They spend much of their workday with their noses in men's armpits. They are also good at detecting small traces of odorized Semtex.

"We did," Rich Shrader answered. "We let them smell the control detonated Semtex samples, and they went to work on pieces of *Sacajawea*. None of the Revlon testers detected Semtex."

Someone asked, "Is it too early to tell where the bomb was planted?"

Sitting on a bench along the wall, the structures group

chair, Bruce Hereford, replied, "We've started trajectory plotting, but our best information at this time comes from the seat damage chart you see on the wall. Julie, you're on."

Julie Halstrom chaired the cabin interior documentation group. Her brown hair was in a ponytail, and she stepped to the chart, a cutaway drawing of *Sacajawea*'s cabin. "All seats we have found are represented here, back in their place on the plane. Different colors indicate different conditions for the seats. Light blue means minimal damage. The seat—the seat legs, seat, pan, seat back, armrest, and belt-restraint system—was intact. Dark blue means moderate damage, meaning minor deformation to one or more components."

She stepped along the chart, indicating with her hand. "Green means the seat suffered a fracture or deformation in one of its parts. Yellow seats had two fractured or missing parts. And red means three component parts of the seat were destroyed or missing."

Julie Halstrom didn't need to say more. A rainbow of colors from fiery red to peaceful blue spread front to aft. Those seats forward in the cabin had been substantially destroyed, while those farther back were less damaged, and those near the rear of the cabin were intact.

Hereford summed up. "So the detonation came from behind the cockpit, forward of the wing, roughly. We'll be more precise in the days to come."

The structures group would study the mode of breakup and the sequence of failure. Damage due to an explosion is without the logic of normal aerodynamic overstressing.

An FBI agent couldn't help himself. He called out, "That goober of a poacher is lying his ass off. No other evidence of a missile exists. The guy thinks we're going to believe his Darth Vader theory, for God's sake. All your evidence points to a low-velocity detonation, such as that provided by gunpowder, the old pipe-bomb standby."

FBI agents around the room nodded. Rich Shrader ignored the comment. Crime in the sky has gone through three distinct phases. Until the intercontinental jet arrived in about 1960, most attacks on civil aircraft were suicide or murder attempts. A second stage was common in the 1960s: the hijack attempt. Then, after tighter airport security was installed, hijackings declined and a third stage began, and was still underway: the bomb on board. An airplane wants to fly. Bringing it down against the pilot's will is difficult. A bomb is the technically easiest, least demanding way to do so.

I rose from my chair. "So we clearly have a detonation, but we can't automatically assign it to an explosive device planted on *Sacajawea*. You're using the word *bomb*, and it's too early to do so. You're jumping to conclusions."

I meant, of course, the FBI and ATF agents were jumping to conclusions. Evidence of a bomb squarely put *Sacajawea* in their realm, and human and organizational nature was such that a momentum was developing to steer the investigation the FBI's way.

Two rows behind me, Matt Ripley stood to lend me support.

I said, "We've discovered that an electrical problem existed on *Sacajawea*."

Someone asked, "Something that might have caused a blast?"

"We don't know yet," Ripley answered. He took sixty seconds to outline the switch-breaker-pump repairs that had been made to *Sacajawea*. He concluded by saying that his interviews with the Emerald mechanics in Boise had produced little beyond the written maintenance records.

FBI Director Henley asked, "So given there was an explosion, what do you think exploded?"

"It's too early to assign a probable cause," I replied.

He smiled, sort of. "Don't give me that NTSB-engineer-speak. What are you looking at?"

"The blast pattern and our initial evidence might point to a problem with *Sacajawea*'s center fuel tank."

Disappointment in the room was suddenly thick, with a souring of expressions and the slumping of shoulders, at least on the FBI side. I sat down, FBI agents looking at me like I was Typhoid Mary.

I concluded lamely, "We'll know more in a few days."

Shrader said, "Last piece of business tonight. Any new offers of wealth this past twenty-four hours?"

A young woman at a computer terminal at the side of the room quickly raised her hand. She had been waiting for her moment. When Shrader nodded toward her, she rose to say, "Twenty-five thousand pounds from a newspaper called *The World Today*."

Someone said, "It's one of those yellow tabloids that usually has something like Bobby the Three-Headed Goat-Boy on the cover."

Some tired laughter. News crews had been camped outside the hotel, shoving microphones into the faces of anybody who didn't sprint away from the building at the end of the meetings. Offers from tabloid TV and newspapers were being made daily. Huge sums were being waved about by seedy news organizations that wanted to be the first to break the story of a confirmation of a bomb aboard *Sacajawea*.

With a smile, Shrader asked, "Well, Debbie, are you going to accept the offer?"

"I'm still negotiating," she replied. "Do you think I need an agent?"

Some appreciative laughter.

Shrader said, "We'll meet again at seven o'clock tomorrow evening."

People reached for coats. Chairs began to scrape.

I hadn't seen Linda Dillon arrive. She appeared at the elbow of Dr. Murdoch's assistant to hand him a slide.

She waited until the new photograph appeared on the screen, then announced loudly enough to still everyone, "This is Thad Wilson, the poacher."

Groans from around the room. Wilson's hairy, hapless, hangdog face floated on the wall above Shrader and Murdoch. The IIC grimaced at Wilson's proximity.

Someone called out, "Grizzly Adams with a lobotomy."

Linda Dillon said, "I've just returned from the King County jail, where polygraph tests were administered to Wilson." She paused, letting the room wait a moment. There wasn't a sound. Even the FBI director had caught his breath. Then she grandly announced, "The poacher is telling the truth."

The room erupted. That is, as much as engineers, scientists, and policemen ever erupt, which isn't exactly a Brazilian soccer riot, but still quite a sight, all that education and all that seniority, talking out of turn, calling out questions, whistling at the news.

Rich Shrader tried waving us to silence.

A medical examiner called out, "The guy's a gomer." *Gomer* stands for *Get Out of My Emergency Room*.

"Are we going to believe anything this moron says?" someone else asked loudly. "I've read his sheet. And look at him, for God's sake."

An FBI agent said, "We can't turn our investigation on the word of a convicted felon."

Someone else put in, "Give me a Valium, and I could beat a lie detector test even if I was guiltier than Ted Bundy."

"Who administered the test?" Cal Guthrie asked. Guthrie was the special agent in charge of the Seattle FBI office.

"Eric Thorberg," Linda replied with satisfaction.

That quieted the room. Thorberg had flown in from D.C. for the test. No one was infallible with a polygraph, but Thorberg was close.

Then an FBI agent sitting up front said, "I still think you've been suckered by this backwoodsman, Linda. You're way off the mark."

She gibed, "Dan, you've always been daunted by my intellect."

That brought some hoots from FBI agents.

The agent named Dan replied, "Quota female."

"Dan, let me refer to the FBI manual on coworker relations." Her tone was mild. "Shut up."

Rich Shrader again addressed the room. "I know of the pressure on everyone in this room. The public demands an answer. They believe—not without some justification, it may turn out—that an airplane bomber is loose out there. Tonight I'm going to announce to the press our preliminary finding that a detonation of some sort may have brought down *Sacajawea*. It'll get out anyway if I don't, and this news should come from me." He glanced at his wristwatch. "We'll meet again here in twenty-three hours."

Linda Dillon met me at the door. We joined a stream of investigators leaving the building, forming a flying wedge to push through the media. The reporters jumped up and down, jammed things in our faces, yelled out questions, blinded us with flashes, and generally acted like the horses' butts they are.

At least I wasn't the IIC. Rich Shrader was taking a beating from these people, who didn't understand a finesse-filled nonanswer when they heard one. The press would be stampeding for their cell phones and modem-equipped laptops and satellite uplinks when Shrader made his announcement that preliminary tests indicated a possible detonation. Under no circumstances would Shrader use the terms *explosive device* or *bomb,* but those words were going to be flashed around the world in about ten minutes.

We broke free of the mob, and walked across the slushy parking lot toward my rig. This was a Friday evening, and the runs at Snoqualmie Pass were filled with skiers and boarders.

"Did you talk to your boss?" I asked. "Did he commute my sentence?"

"You're still stuck with me. Good thing, too. I can teach you a lot, and there's plenty you need to know, believe me."

Linda Dillon and I were having lunch in the federal building cafeteria when a legend walked in, turning the heads of the NTSB folks there who knew anything about the history of air warfare or the history of commercial aviation. Aero Transport France was founded by Pierre Lemercier, and the moment he entered the cafeteria, Rich Shrader rose from his table to greet the Frenchman, energetically pumping his hand, then passing him coffee in a Styrofoam cup. Dick Dahlberg joined them, taking Lemercier's hand and only reluctantly letting it go, smiling all the while like an adoring fan.

Pierre Lemercier as an eighteen-year-old became the first Frenchman to shoot down a Luftwaffe fighter, notable because Lemercier was flying a Morane-Saulnier, a plane known both for its inability to take punishment and its inability to give it. Fueled by rage at his country's plight, he brought down two more German planes before a Junkers nose gun separated his Morane-Saulnier's tail from its cockpit so that there was air between the two, and both halves fluttered from the sky, round and round like maple seedlings. Lemercier parachuted into the English Channel to be plucked out by a patrolling Royal Navy motor torpedo boat.

French pilots who made it to England early in the war flew in the Royal Air Force. Lemercier pestered the RAF to loan him a Spitfire. *Loan* was Lemercier's term, and no one at the RAF believed they would ever see the plane again, except when Lemercier appeared briefly at bases in Kent begging for fuel. His anger undiminished, Lemercier brought down four Messerschmitts and two Stukas in his first month, before losing his ride over a pasture near South Foreland, sixty or seventy bullet holes through the fuselage.

When he appeared yet again at Fighter Command, hat in hand, he was of course loaned another Spitfire, which, after bringing down five more Luftwaffe planes, he lost over the Channel again. A German tracer shell had ricocheted around inside the cockpit, setting everything on fire, including Lemercier's flight suit, and he parachuted into the Channel—not for the first time—smoking like a flare.

Pierre Lemercier went through seven RAF fighters before the end of the war, but in the process inflicted hellish damage on the Luftwaffe. He was awarded the Croix de Guerre, the Legion of Honor, and more medals from Great Britain than he could lift, as well as the coveted Médaille de la Résistance directly from de Gaulle. I had read about his exploits when I was a boy, shaking my head in wonderment, and laughing aloud when I learned that he carried a baguette and a cheese roll in his flare pouch on every flight.

When the war ended, Lemercier borrowed fifty pounds from his wing commander and purchased a shot-through and rusted Avro York off an airplane cemetery near Tunbridge Wells. The plane was missing a propeller, the pilot's seat, most of its gauges, its rudder, and dozens of other parts, so Lemercier pirated replacements from other planes at the cemetery. He flew the patched-together Avro York on freight runs between Marseille and Paris for a year, before realizing that it wasn't the flying he enjoyed so much, it was the killing of Germans.

He sold the plane for a profit, and purchased three surplus planes in assorted states of disrepair, again from the Tunbridge Wells cemetery. These he remade into passenger planes, borrowing against the planes to purchase the one item he could not find at the plane cemetery: passenger seats. He sold all three planes to the new Air Argentina, and by then Pierre Lemercier had determined that building airplanes was his life's work. Even after Lemercier could hire dozens, then hundreds of employees, he liked to say that he worked a wrench on each plane his plant produced.

In the 1960s, Lemercier Manufacturing became Air Transport France, made a successful public stock offering, and opened a huge fabrication facility between Paris and Rouen. By 1980, ATF was producing two aircraft a week, and Pierre Lemercier lived on a 400-acre estate near Paris that had once belonged to Etienne de Silhouette, Louis XIV's finance minister, about whom it was said that when Silhouette was finished taxing you, only your shadow remained. ATF planes were renowned for safety and durability, Lemercier believing that any plane he built should be able to survive a Messerschmitt attack, and so he instructed his engineers.

Pierre Lemercier had retired from management of ATF but he still sat on the board, and he still took offense when one of his planes was blown from the sky. His was an august, revered presence, and he lent his calming and benevolent influence to any investigation involving one of his planes.

He came over to me, walking with a cane. There aren't many people in the world I would feel compelled to rise to my feet for and remain there when they entered a room. Maybe the United States president, maybe the pope, but surely Pierre Lemercier. I resisted saluting him. His hair was shock white and his chin sharp and his smile full of white teeth. He still looked the part of the dashing fighter pilot, even with the cane.

He spoke as if I had just seen him that morning, rather than two years ago on the Green Bay ATF 94 investigation. "I wish I could blame this lame leg on a Luftwaffe shell. But it's the effects of time and too many women." His English was gnarled with a strong accent.

"It's good to see you again, sir."

He gripped my elbow. "You find the bastard who blew up my plane."

I particularly dislike having to parse my sentences and hum and haw in front of someone like Pierre Lemercier. "Well, sir, we know it was a detonation, but we can't say yet it was a bomb."

"Then what was it?" His gaze alone could have brought down a Messerschmitt, and it was aimed right at me.

"We don't have all the facts yet, sir, is all I'm saying." I was fairly stammering.

"My planes do not explode on their own." His words had the percussion of a machine gun. "I tell you that there was a bomb on board *Sacajawea*."

"Then that's more her department, Mr. Lemercier. She's an FBI agent." What a craven dodge.

The old man surveyed her, up and down in the French way. "Do you carry a weapon, young lady?"

She nodded.

"When you find the *saland* who brought down *Sacajawea,* you put a bullet into him."

Linda laughed. "I'm a law officer, not a lynch mob. I don't know about France, but in America we have courts of law. Our criminal justice system is one of the foundations of our republic."

"You put a bullet into him," Lemercier said, "and I'll pay you one million dollars."

She stuck out her hand. "You've got yourself a deal."

I think they were both fooling, but I wasn't going to take the chance. I intercepted their deal-striking handshake, smiled a quick good-bye to the Frenchman, and led Linda away.

NINE

At the north end of downtown Seattle is one of the oddest structures ever to grace a city: the Space Needle, which was designed by the same folks who brought us the Jetsons. About in the middle of downtown is the federal building, which even architects who dislike skyscrapers admit is a lovely structure, with sandstone-like textured surfaces and a brick plaza. The FBI's Seattle offices are in the building, and I was in its offices.

So was every FBI agent in the country, it seemed. The place was jammed with them, filling every chair, leaning against the walls, hanging over cubicle dividers, everyone waiting for the news. The FBI director had canceled his flight back to Washington, D.C., and was sitting in a carrel speaking with Cal Guthrie, local SAC.

Also in the room were Dick Dahlberg and others from the NTSB, and operatives from the State Department's Office for Combating Terrorism—which is called SCT, though no one I've ever spoken to about it knows why—and the State Department's Division of Intelligence and Research. CIA agents were probably in these offices, too, but they weren't about to identify themselves to me, I suppose. FBI special agents are known for their staid professionalism. Even so, tension rippled through the offices. We were all waiting for the results of tests on a letter the Seattle office had received the day before.

Linda Dillon and I were sitting around a desktop computer, leaning forward to study the monitor. Bridget Thompson, a special agent with the FBI's Terrorism Research Analytical Center, rested her fingers on the keyboard. To the side of the desk was a printer. An FBI agent was bracing himself against the printer stand, speaking in low tones to three others.

Bridget Thompson spoke with a soft, southern accent. "This unit is connected to a system we call *Desist*, the world's most comprehensive database on terrorists. Desist terminals are mostly in Washington, D.C., at the CIA, FBI, Pentagon, State Department, and NSA, and now here."

She tapped the keys. She was a slight woman, probably no more than a hundred pounds. She wore a helmet of thick black hair, with gray at her temples. Her features were outsized for her small face, with a wide mouth and eyes that seemed to stretch from ear to ear. She was chewing gum furiously, snapping it every few seconds, maybe a smoker in a nonsmoking building. Linda Dillon had worked with Thompson before, and had told me Thompson had served in the navy for six years, was a graduate of the U.S. Naval Explosive Ordnance Disposal School, and had a master's degree in forensic science from George Washington University.

"The communications system is called *Flashboard*," she said. "It's manned around the clock. Some guy likes gunpowder, we've got him in here. Flashboard is like the web, except it's private."

"My daughter has booby-trapped our web browser on my computer at home," I said. "Every time I try to search for something, I end up at the Carpal Tunnel Syndrome home page."

"Give me a date and a time of day."

Linda thought for a moment, then said, "March 5, 1997, three-fifteen in the afternoon."

Bridget Thompson's fingers tapped out a few commands. "I'll break the request into ten-minute blocks, beginning at three-fifteen on that day. All times local, so it's the middle of the afternoon wherever we find ourselves."

Some colorblind programmer had given the screen a puce background with green letters. In the corner of the screen was a cartoon representation of one of those anarchists' bombs that resembles a bowling ball. Every few seconds the fuse burned down, and the cartoon bomb exploded, raining debris across the screen, which disappeared after a second or two, and then a new bomb would materialize. I found it distracting.

Thompson said, "At that exact time, Estevan San Martin, a member of the Tupac Amaru, set off in a dory powered by a Johnson nine-horsepower engine from the Oreto Fruit Company dock at Callao, just west of Lima, heading toward a Liberian-registered tramper named *Tigre*. He returned to the dock ninety-three minutes later. We don't know what San Martin was doing on the *Tigre*, making arrangements, probably, because two crates of Chinese-manufactured AK-47s were offloaded from the ship that night."

She entered a few more commands, bringing up another segment. "At three-seventeen that same afternoon, a meeting began at the Continental Hotel in Damascus between representatives of the Popular Front for the Liberation of Palestine—George Habash's group—and the Movement for the National Liberation of Palestine, known as Fatah." She brought up an emblem. "Note that Fatah's seal is a grenade and crossed rifles superimposed on a map of Israel, a clear indication of their purpose." She worked the keyboard again. "Here's a list of attendees at that meeting." Then more key-strokes. "And here's a transcript of what was said there, trans-lated to English." The transcript slowly rolled up the screen.

Linda said, "Quite a few of the words are marked 'obscured.'"

"The microphone was in the heel of a shoe, so it missed a few things."

I admitted, "I'm impressed."

A buzz went through the room. The FBI agents and every-one else straightened from their leaning and slouching to respectful stances. Heads popped up from carrels, and agents flowed into the office from other rooms. Frederick Yamashita made his way into the room, carrying a sheaf of papers in both hands as if they were fragile. He was the FBI executive assistant director in charge of terrorism investigations. I had last seen him on the *Sacajawea* site. Yamashita parted his hair in the middle and wore wire-rim glasses. He was thin, and his clothes hung on him as if from a hanger. He had served with the U.S. Marine Corps' First Force Reconnaissance Company, and he still looked tough, even with the John Lennon spectacles.

The Kittitas County coroner, Dr. Susan Halsey, followed Yamashita into the room. She was carrying the same clipboard I'd never seen her without.

Yamashita positioned himself in the middle of the room, Dr. Halsey next to him. He said, "Most of you know about the letter we received yesterday afternoon. It was flown overnight to our labs in Washington, and I've just been noti-fied of the initial results. The letter read, and I quote, 'Another plane will come down in ten days.'"

Yamashita paused to let the words, and the puzzle, sink in.

Finally someone asked, "Or what?"

"Or nothing," Yamashita said.

Linda Dillon had turned in her chair away from the monitor. She asked, "But, where's the demand for a million dollars? Or the demand that the British get out of Northern Ireland? Or that Israel leave the Gaza Strip or that we stop cutting down redwoods or quit experimenting on lab rabbits?"

"The letter contained eight words," Yamashita replied. "I just read every one of them."

"Any other communication from the sender?" Bridget Thompson asked. "Any other letters or phone calls?"

"Nothing. And no prints on the letter or envelope or stamp. No dried saliva on the stamp or envelope. No hair, no dander, no dried mucus, no flakes of skin. A big zero."

Someone asked, "The paper? The ink?"

"Eaton twenty pound, twenty-five percent cotton, the same stuff that's in ten million offices in North America. And the printing was made by an HP LaserJet, we think. But that's only a guess, and we can't trace it further. There's millions of HPs out there."

By unspoken but clearly understood rules, the million-dollar question was reserved for someone at the top of the chart. So the FBI director asked, "What about the signature?"

He was referring to a piece of metal that had been inside the envelope with the letter. That's all most of us knew at this point. A piece of metal.

"The signature contained in the letter was a nail," Fred Yamashita said. "The lab tells me it is an asphalt shingle nail, designed to secure asphalt and sometimes fiberglass shingles to solid sheeting. The nail was one and seven-eighths inches long with a seven-sixteenths-inch head, which is a large head for a nail but not for a shingle nail. The nail had a spiral shank, sort of a twist, that secures it to softer substances such as asphalt. It was coated in molten zinc, as a preservative."

"Where was it manufactured?" the FBI director asked.

"Leeds, England, by the Sure-Secure Manufacturing Company. Sure-Secure is one of the world's largest manufacturers of nails, all sorts of nails. Shake nails, copper slating nails, insulation roof-deck nails, rubber washer nails, the works. Last year Sure-Secure exported forty tons of their product to the United States, including three tons of these asphalt nails. The nails were sold sometimes under the Sure-Roof name, but mostly under hardware retailers' names. Sure-Secure nails are available in all fifty states. TrueValue and Ace and Home Depot sell a lot of them, and wholesalers sell them directly to builders."

"Any batch markings?" someone asked.

"No. This particular nail"—Yamashita pantomimed holding up a nail, as the signature nail was still at the lab—"could have been purchased anywhere in the country, anytime in the past four years. And this nail was examined, of course. No prints. Nothing."

"Why four years?" the director asked.

"Sure-Secure reports that they began double-dipping, rather than single dipping, their asphalt nails in zinc four years ago. Our lab says the signature nail clearly has two coats of zinc. So we know it was manufactured within the last four years."

"But your signature nail doesn't mean anything, does it?" I asked. "Someone writes a letter claiming he brought down *Sacajawea,* and puts a nail into the envelope to accompany the letter, and mails it to the FBI. What does that mean?"

Yamashita turned to me, and all the others in the room did, too. I felt the weight of their gazes. I was a foreigner in these FBI offices.

I asked, "Dr. Halsey, have you found any of these shingle nails in *Sacajawea*'s victims? Nails as shrapnel?"

"I've examined nineteen bodies so far. No nails."

"How about the bodies of those sitting near the source of the detonation?" I asked. "Michael Palmer was in seat 2A. Have you examined him?" I tried not to sound like a cross-examiner.

She flipped up pages on her clipboard. She studied a moment, then said, "Michael Palmer died of massive and instantaneous trauma. He suffered numerous burns, penetrations, fractures, and separations. I removed about half a pound of assorted metal, plastic, and fabric fragments from his body. No nails, though."

"How about the person sitting in 2B? And 2C and D? They'd be most likely to have nails, of anybody, sitting closest to the bulkhead."

"None in the body in 2B," Dr. Halsey replied. "We haven't identified the people who were in 2C and D yet."

I said, "And I know from our debris charts that no nails have been found at the site. So how does the nail in your letter constitute a credible signature from a bomber?"

Yamashita replied, "I'm well aware that treating the nail as a signature is premature. But two things. First, people who make false claims to having committed a criminal act rarely provide a fake signature, some little piece of phony evidence they hope will intrigue us. They don't want to send us something that our labs can readily prove is a fraud. So imposter-bombers almost never send pretend signatures, but real bombers sometimes send real signatures."

I cleared my throat. I had been unaware of this bomber psychology.

"And second," he continued, "much of *Sacajawea* is still

out there in the mountains, especially the little pieces. There's a four-mile debris trail, you told me yourself, Joe. And shrapnel is often found farthest from the wreckage. That we haven't found a nail yet doesn't mean we won't."

"Yeah, well . . ."

"Joe, I know you're hot for some bad-wiring theory. Some airplane self-immolation notion. That's fine."

"I'm not hot for any theory," I said angrily.

"Let's just say, then, that you are trying to develop a theory about the plane's wiring, something to do with the fuel-gauge wires, and—"

My voice rose unprofessionally. "I don't have a goddamn vested interest in how *Sacajawea* came down. I just want to make sure that we don't focus so tightly on one aspect of the investigation that everything else is pushed to the periphery."

"I'm a cop, Joe. This room is full of cops. We look for criminals. When you convince us that *Sacajawea* was not destroyed as the result of a criminal act, then all us FBI agents will go on a holiday. Until then, we'll take the nail and the letter seriously."

I was about to protest that I wasn't asking them not to treat the nail seriously—that that wasn't my point at all—but Linda cut me off. "Nails—presuming we find out the nail is a real signature—rule out that poacher's story about a missile, don't they? Even though he passed the polygraph test?"

"Not necessarily." The speaker was Hank Lewis, from the State Department's office for combating terrorism. "Missiles are often taken apart for smuggling, which makes them harder to detect on a truck or a ship or a camel. The missile's nose cone explosive can be repacked with anything for shrapnel, any bits of metal, including nails. I once saw a Hizballah missile, captured by the Israelis before it could be used, that had several brass hookah handles in the warhead."

The FBI director rose from his chair. He spoke as he walked toward the door. "Three tons of nails each year for four years, sold all over the country. We haven't limited our search much, have we?"

Silence in the room.

"Tomorrow morning I have another press conference about *Sacajawea*. At this stage in the investigation the threatening letter and the nail will be confidential. But I need to report some progress. I haven't heard of much yet."

The director paused at the door. His voice was dark. "The nail means the letter's threat may be"—he glanced at me—"*may* be credible." He stepped through the door, but added over his shoulder, entirely unnecessarily, "And it means we have ten days."

Boeing had lent me a lab at their Renton 737 plant, and had offered the services of five quality-control technicians. Structures group chair Bruce Hereford had also sent three NTSB engineers. All of us sat at benches in front of microscopes. Linda Dillon brought the lengths of wire to us, carefully checking them off against the inventory on a laptop computer. Each length of wire and each wire fragment and each harnessed wire bundle had been tagged with the location where it had been found on the mountain.

We had been at it for over five hours. My back and neck ached. My eyes were having trouble focusing. In front of me was a Wang BioMedical stereo microscope, used by Boeing for quality control in many areas. The microscope had a zoom feature, with a ratio of one to six, and a beginning magnification of 7X. Two of the microscope's tubes were for my eyes, and the third tube was for a camera. The image I saw through the Wang could be run through composite-imaging software, designed to overcome a microscope's inadequate depth of field when viewing three-dimensional specimens, such as wire. The composite was a perfectly focused image achieved by combining a series of images focused at different heights on the specimen. I hadn't taken any computer-enhanced photos yet. I hadn't found anything worth photographing.

Much of *Sacajawea*'s wiring was a type known as Poly-X. When subjected to stresses, such as a tight bend radii, Poly-X was known to crack. The plane had been built eight years ago, and so some of the electrical wiring was eight years old, though not all of it because of periodic upgrades and repairs. I looked around, wondering where a pop machine might be. Linda was at the north end of the room, lifting a harness that appeared to have six or eight wires through it. She read the tag, then carried the electrical harness to her computer, on the table next to my microscope. I bent back to the microscope's eyepiece.

"Joe, take a look at this."

I scooted off my stool and around the table to a Boeing technician. I had just met her a few hours ago, and had to glance at her security tag. Emily Anderson. She wore a white coat, a hair net, and a hopeful smile. She moved aside so I could bend over her microscope. Linda came over to stand at her shoulder.

I asked, "What am I looking for?"

"This length of wire—it's a scrap, really; just more than half a meter long, was found inside the fuselage, loose, detached from a bundle or mounting. See the hot stamp?"

"Sure. Number 1288."

"What's a hot stamp?" Linda asked.

Emily Anderson replied, "A brand burned into the wire's insulation by the manufacturer to identify the wires in the plane."

Emily Anderson smelled of talcum powder. She said, "Look at the number one."

I looked, glanced up at her to mouth the word *wow*, then bent to look again. "It looks like the Grand Canyon under this microscope, doesn't it?"

"What?" Linda exclaimed. "Goddamn it, Joe. Tell me."

"There's a crack below the fissure of the hot-stamped number one."

Emily said, "The crack goes all the way down to the core, through all three layers of insulation, which was probably degraded by time. I've only found this one, but in that big pile of wire we have yet to examine, I'll bet there's a lot more of these failures."

"So the insulation had failed on this part of the wire." I stood again, feeling vindicated, even though tiny cracks in electrical wiring in all likelihood meant nothing. Still, finding a crack in the insulation—and surely there were more of them because the older Poly-X wires on the plane, installed when *Sacajawea* was manufactured, would have degraded at about the same rate—opened up the investigation, and might—just might—suggest an explanation for *Sacajawea*'s destruction other than a bomb.

Beaming, Emily Anderson said, "And we all know what can happen when wires aren't fully insulated."

"We sure do," I replied. "Sparks."

TEN

"See the wire?" Linda Dillon asked. "It's a booby trap. Don't touch it."

"I wouldn't think of it." The backpack was rubbing my shoulders raw. When I shifted its weight, the snowshoes strapped to the pack bounced against my ear.

She stepped across the snow to the side of the rutted road, following the wire's route toward a thicket of kinnikinnick. Overhead was a canopy of white fir and lodgepole pine boughs. A feathering of snow had fallen that night, and now the melt fell in sprays when wind nudged the branches. The wire was iridescent in the sun, maybe fishing line, and it was taut across the road, about an inch above the snow.

I walked to the other edge of the road. The wire disappeared into a patch of serviceberry. I pushed leaves aside, and discovered the end of the wire was tied to an elm sapling. This end of the wire, at least, was harmless. I returned to the center of the road, my boots pressing down snow with each step.

"It's an alarm, not a spring gun," she said, rustling around at the side of the road. She was hidden by bracken. "The wire is connected to this transmitter, which is strapped to a tree.

The radio will broadcast our presence to the cabin ahead. Go ahead and set it off."

"Trip it?"

"We want this guy to know we're coming, believe me. It'd be dangerous to startle him."

With my boot I pushed the fishing line forward. It became taut, but didn't snap. I didn't hear an alarm. The line sprang back when I released it.

Linda emerged from the bushes. She was wearing a cornflower blue ski jacket and gray gloves. On her shoulders was a camouflaged backpack. Our packs carried thermos bottles, a first-aid kit, a bird identification book, and sandwiches. Binoculars hung from a strap around her neck. We were supposed to look like hikers out for a day walk. A crow high in a tree clacked his bill together repeatedly, an eerie staccato. Linda's cheeks were pink from the cold. She grabbed her shoulder straps for somewhere to hang her hands, and took off again, up the road. She was in good shape, moving easily over the unsteady landscape. I had to work to keep up with her.

We had flown into Hailey an hour ago, rented a car, and had driven north through Ketchum and Sun Valley toward the Galena Pass in the Sawtooth mountains in central Idaho. The pass is so steep that in the days of ore wagons, logs were roped to the rigs and trailed behind them on the descent to keep the wagons from slipping their brakes and running away. Our road crested a hill, and we could see the mountains all around, blocked only by a few larch trees that must have been 250 feet tall. Granite peaks—the Sawtooths—were in the distance. They were jagged masses, with glacial gouges and cirques that spoke of their unrelenting harshness. During the summer months the lower slopes would be blanketed with wheatgrass and Idaho fescue, and blue and yellow lichen would color the stone near the peaks. But snow still lay over the range, almost blinding, reflecting the high-altitude sunlight. When a cloud passed over, the peaks grayed quickly, then burst forth in the sun again, golden and glittering.

Even these foothills where we marched were tough country, filled with sharp ridges and peaks and the narrow defiles of river canyons. Like Meriwether Lewis, Linda led with confident strides. I struggled along, my boots too loose and rubbing my heels. There aren't enough chairs in the mountains, is one of the problems. For someone from Seattle to admit he doesn't favor the mountains is apostasy, I realize. The city is framed by showy mountains, the Olympics to the west and the Cascades to the east. Forty-five minutes from Seattle, the mountains are so wild that I expect to see Raquel Welch dressed in ragged fur every time I pass through them.

The citizens of Seattle are endless in their excuses to journey into the Olympics and Cascades: mountain climbing, white-water rafting, downhill and cross-country skiing, rock climbing, orienteering, backpacking, bungee jumping from old railroad bridges, and numerous other ways to kill yourself recreationally. When they can't get to the wilderness, they go to the new REI store to study crampons, or they browse through the Eddie Bauer catalogue searching for that perfect fleece liner. They dream of Nepal.

I hasten to add that I am not a wimp. Try playing harmonica at the Sasquatch Tavern in Goldbar, where every once in a while Will or Mike has to yell "Incoming" like we were in Vietnam, and where the owner won't erect chicken wire between the band and the drunk loggers because he claims it would destroy the tavern's ambience, pronounced to rhyme with *pants*. It's just that I prefer the horizontal, a place where if you fall, you won't keep on falling. I prefer a place where wolves and bears and other predators can't roam freely, where I'm at the top of the great food chain—like in a grocery store—not somewhere in the middle.

Boot prints showed on the snow, coming from a deer trail to our left, then heading in our same direction. They were large prints, made by a big man.

"Red on the snow." Linda pointed.

Blood accompanied the prints, a small splash every few paces. The blood's warmth had melted into the crust of snow.

"Who left that blood?" I asked, breathing hard from negotiating the snow. Puddles had formed in tire ruts. I could smell the bitter scent of yarrow, which the Shoshone and Nez Percé had used to make soap.

"Something dead or dying, most likely, knowing Billy."

"It doesn't worry you, this blood on the snow?"

She replied, "I'd be more worried if it were my blood."

I was having trouble keeping up with Linda. She had long legs. We passed a row of white birch, then several bent and knobby crabapple trees. The sides of the road were lined with dog rose and banks of wild raspberry.

"I don't like walking in the woods," I complained. "Not enough cigarette smoke and pinball noises. Not enough surly waitresses, or peanut shells and pull tabs on the floor."

"If I can dig around a pile of aircraft wiring all day until my back is killing me, you can accompany me on a little nature walk." She glanced at me. "You think we are wasting our time out here. You think you've got *Sacajawea* figured out."

"I've made no such claim to you or Rich Shrader or Fred Yamashita or anyone else, not even to myself. That the probable cause might be the disintegrated insulation on *Sacajawea*'s Poly-X wiring is only a theory, one of many."

"We're out in the Idaho woods on a theory, too. And I

think we're much closer to the mark here than we were in your lab staring through the microscope."

When we were about two miles from our car, I heard a dog bark. Not some lap dog. This animal was a huge, muscled, sharp-fanged piece of business, I could tell just from its bark. I could feel the hairs on the back of my neck rise against the parka. I don't like dogs much. The French allow dogs in their restaurants, lying under the tables among the patrons' feet, and we wonder how the Panzer divisions could dash unimpeded through France.

"Nice touch." Linda nodded down the road.

A human skull was atop a post, inside a wrought-iron gibbet resembling a birdcage that hung by a short chain from a crossbeam on a post. The skull's hollow black sockets stared at us, more startled than malevolent, its long teeth a perfect row. The head was sparkling white, and across the bare cranium was inked the word TRESPASSER. Nailed to the post under the cage was a shingle on which were the crudely painted words NATION OF JEFFERSON, and below that on another shingle, BEWARE OF DOG.

A few more steps, and we came to another sign, red paint on two cedar shingles nailed to a post: SMILE. U ARE BEING WATCHED THRU A RIFLE SCOPE.

"You sure you know what you're doing?" I tried not to sound nervous. "If this isn't the right place, we're in serious trouble."

A sharp noise came from my left, maybe a foot snapping a branch, sounding somehow deliberate. We picked up our pace. Linda carried her pistol under her coat. It didn't seem enough.

We passed a few freshly logged tree stumps, and a pile of scrub limbs, ready for burning. Another loud footfall came from the brush. We were being trailed. We rounded a stand of Norway maple, and came to an opening in the forest. A dog was behind a gated fence, guarding a shack and several outbuildings.

This was the dog from hell, a brindle and white pit bull that must have weighed eighty pounds, most of it in his shoulders and fangs. His eyes were slits under low brows. His front legs were off the ground and his back legs were churning, and his muzzle was pressed against the fence, bowing it outward. I swear that damned animal's eyes were red, and glowing from within, like burning coals. He growled and barked and hissed, sounding like a locomotive. He wanted at us, frantic to do some damage. I shuddered.

The flat crack of a rifle shot came from the bushes to our west—so loud it seemed to slap me—and at the same instant a piece of bark from a pine tree at the edge of the road three feet from me ripped away from the trunk. Then I heard a bolt work, the sinister clank and snap of a bullet being pushed into a chamber.

A voice came from our left. "Better state your business." A male voice, laconic and knowing, and filled with the backwoods, even in those few words.

I turned toward the voice, but could see only bull thistle and mulberry in front of a glade of blue spruce. The dog continued its dervish prancing, straining at the fence, its teeth glittering.

"We're being shot at," I said under my breath. "Shouldn't you pull out your gun, or whatever you're trained to do?"

Linda Dillon said loudly to the brush, "We're out looking for birds. And not just any birds."

"There aren't any birds." From the brush. "Not around here."

I took this as a code, because it was nonsense. These Idaho

woods were filled with birds even in winter. Spruce boughs began to wag, and a man stepped from behind the trees, walking toward us, his deer rifle leading the way. I had a dog muzzle pointed at me from one direction, and a rifle muzzle from another. I'd have been hard-pressed if given the choice which to take on. The smell of spent gunpowder drifted across the road.

The man walked toward us, slowly, keeping the rifle up and ready. "Show me something. Do it real slow."

Linda moved her hand into her parka and brought out her badge. She held it up. It winked in the sunlight.

The man stepped closer, lifting his legs high to clear a snowdrift. He was wearing buckskin, one of those fringed coats so corny not even dance-hall cowboys wear them, the kind that Buffalo Bill Cody used to wear, just hoping some poor fool would pick a fight with him. But as the man with the rifle approached, I could see that the coat was handmade, with irregular length strips of hide hanging from everywhere, and intricate beadwork over much of the rest. The beads flashed and opalesced in the light, and the rawhide swished and twisted, giving the man the transient quality of a mirage, ruined only by the unyielding rifle.

He hadn't been near a razor in months, and black hair like a schnauzer's was curled tightly against his face. When he came closer I could see his pants were also made of buckskin. His boots looked homemade, and came up almost to his knees with white wool liner showing at the top. A knife the size of my forearm hung in a sheath next to an ammunition pouch. He closed on us.

"Anybody else here?" Linda asked, just loud enough for the mountain man to hear.

"I'm alone." His furry face split into a huge grin. One of

his front teeth was a black stump. He lowered the rifle. "Hi, Linda."

She returned the broad smile. "Billy, you've taken some hard shots since last time I saw you."

He stepped around a clump of bull thistle, lifting his legs high to negotiate the snow.

Linda was beaming at the fellow, and stepped forward to hug him. It was more than a friendly hug, and spoke of a history between them.

"What happened to your mouth?" she asked, leading him toward me, arm in arm. "You used to have a beautiful smile."

"My tooth was knocked out by a marble when I was ten. The tooth you knew was a cap, which was removed as part of my cover. Nice teeth are a dead giveaway."

She ran her finger along a puckered ridge of skin on his jawline. "And this?"

"Did it myself with a knife. A little more camouflage. Same with this." He shouldered his rifle to pull off a glove. He held up his left hand. On the webbing of the thumb was a design resembling a trident, except that the trident's prongs were lightning bolts, the kind on SS collar tabs. The tattoo was poorly done, in Bic blue, and was already leaching into the surrounding skin. A prison tattoo.

"You always took your job seriously, Billy."

Linda introduced him as Special Agent Bill Fitzpatrick. She had taken courses with him at the academy.

"What are you doing here?" he asked, suddenly all business.

"You don't have a phone."

"We kooks don't trust phones. The phone company is trying to take over America."

"How do you get messages?" she asked.

"I go into town twice a week."

I asked, "The FBI doesn't have small radios, something you can hide, so you can call out?"

"Two years ago an agent working undercover along the Rogue River in Oregon was found at the bottom of a ravine, dead." Fitzpatrick led us toward the gate. "He had such a radio, a state-of-the-art digital number that sent its signal directly to a satellite. It was never found. He might have fallen, but more likely he was pushed off the cliff and into the ravine after someone found the radio. So it's too dangerous to have them around."

The pit bull stared at me as if I were a flank steak. This dog made a Doberman pinscher look like the Pillsbury doughboy. The shack was constructed of railroad ties, laid out in the pattern of a log cabin. A stovepipe chimney rose above the roof. The shack was squat and sturdy, resembling something from the Maginot line, with tiny windows and a narrow, low door. I wondered why he needed two mail slots, until I realized they were gun ports. I didn't see any power lines into the shack.

A chicken shed was behind it, near a roofed woodshed. A log splitter sat on a stump next to the shed. A ten-year-old Ford pickup truck was parked to the south of the cabin, with four inches of snow on the cab and hood. It hadn't been used in a while. A bumper sticker on the fender read REMEMBER LITTLE BIGHORN. Suspended from a crosspiece between two elms was a dressed-out mule deer, hanging there to allow the blood to drip away, too high for coyotes to reach.

Fitzpatrick opened the gate. Near the truck was a pile of sandbags, a shovel, and a wood box of empty burlap bags. Many sandbags had been placed against the cabin's north side, a wall of them, reaching to the roof line.

"How about killing that dog before I come in," I suggested.

"His name is Hawkins. He won't hurt you, as long as you keep your hands in plain sight, and don't look him in the eyes."

Hawkins was a coiled spring, shivering with eagerness to lunge at me, looking for the subtlest indication that his master might agree to this course of action. I followed the FBI agents toward the cabin, trying not to climb up Linda Dillon's back in my eagerness to get away from Hawkins. The pit bull's hot breath warmed the backs of my knees.

"Your tree is on fire." Linda indicated a maple trunk. The tree was old, with a rotted core, and had been cut off at a point twelve feet above the ground. Wisps of smoke came from the top of the trunk. A plug was in the tree's bark waist high.

Fitzpatrick said, "I'm jerking some beef. I don't have an all-spice tree, but that maple will do."

"There's blood on your road," she said.

"I was working my trap line just before you arrived. Caught me a bunny. I'm going to skin him out and line some gloves I'm making."

"This your latrine?" I indicated a trench that ran from a corner of the house toward the pickup truck. I felt braver now that Hawkins was slacking off, giving me two feet of room.

"It's a slit trench, just like at the Somme."

"Why is it crooked?" Linda asked. The trench was about five feet across, forty feet long, and it zigzagged left and right.

"If a shell lands in it, shrapnel can't tear along the entire length of it."

She looked at him. "How much of this is an act, Billy? You sound a little too sincere."

He smiled. "Randy Weaver's biggest problem is that he didn't have a slit trench up there on Ruby Ridge."

He pushed open the door, but not without effort. It too was made of railroad ties, held together by horizontal rods, amateur carpentry done without any nod to appearance. The place was a fortress.

Inside was one room, with a bunk against one wall and a long table built of two-by-fours against another. On the table was a shortwave receiver and an AM radio, and boxes of three-by-five-inch index cards next to a stack of periodicals. The room smelled of creosote, and was poorly lit, with the small windows. A gun rack against one wall contained a dozen deer rifles, assault rifles, and shotguns. Below each window was a wall-mounted rack containing a rifle. Hanging near the bunk bed was a framed copy of the Constitution, on yellow and aged paper, made to look like the original. Next to it was a planed and stained board that had been intricately worked with a wood-burning set. Inside patterns resembling grape leaves was: *A well regulated militia being necessary to the security of a free State, the right of the people to keep and bear arms, shall not be infringed.*

In a corner was a wood-burning stove. No plumbing was evident. A bucket of water stood next to the stove. The chair at the desk was made of twisting and curling deer antlers. A lamp with an electric bulb was on the desk, so a generator must have been out back, but oil lamps were all around, hung from the walls on holders made from tin cans. A small white cloth bag and pack of papers indicated Fitzpatrick rolled his own.

"This isn't how I thought your life would work out." Linda removed her pack and tried out the antler chair, arranging herself several times before she found a comfortable position. "How long have you been here, Billy?"

"Eleven months." Fitzpatrick leaned against the door.

The mountain clothes had given him bulk and height. He was wiry up close. The room had only one chair, so I stood also. He didn't get many visitors, looked like.

He added, "Eleven months up here, and this after a month in jail."

Linda smiled. "Jail doesn't surprise me, knowing you."

Again she was trading on a shared memory. I noted it, and wasn't sure if I liked it.

He said, "It was in Missoula, so I could acquire the jailbird look and mannerisms. They're hard to fake otherwise. I'm all new, from my last name to my history. Up here I go by Perkins."

"Hawkins and Perkins have gone to ground, that's for sure," she said, surveying the cabin. "What's that smell? You?"

"You always had a way with words, Linda."

"Smells like someone died in here."

"You try bathing yourself with a bucket."

"Any luck yet, up here?"

He placed his rifle in the rack. "I've been invited to some gatherings, more social than anything else. These people are paranoid as hell. They haven't talked business with me yet."

"Are they checking you out?" Linda asked.

"If they do, they'll discover I was raised in Tracy, California, and that some folks on Emerson Street still remember me, and that some teachers at the high school still recall me, though I dropped out after my sophomore year. There's even several old annuals at the school library that've been altered to show my face in the class photos and in the Auto Mechanics Club. And they'll find out I was in the army, and that I worked in ordnance at Fort Lewis near Tacoma. My sergeant will still remember me. And they'll discover that for my second arrest for owning a machine gun I was sent to jail in Missoula. And all of it is fake, except the jail time."

"Who're you trying to connect with?" I asked. "The local militia?"

"Not the militia, nor the skinheads nor the Identify nor

the Klan nor the Posse Comitatus nor the Freemen. I'm trying to connect with a new group, five or six, maybe seven fellows—I'm not sure at this point—who broke away from the militia two years because of the zip code controversy."

I shook my head.

Fitzpatrick said, "These folks believe that the government uses the zip code to monitor its citizens, and that the federal government is in cahoots with all the states' departments of motor vehicles. The feds and the DMVs provide the information about people's locations to creditors. So this group refuses to use zip codes, and that's why they broke away from the militia, after loud and long arguments."

"They arrange their lives according to a zip code controversy?" Linda moved her legs again, still trying to get comfortable on the antler seat. "They sound too far gone to be much of a threat."

"Wrong," Fitzpatrick said bluntly. "We're pretty sure that three of these guys robbed a bank in Boise fifteen months ago, and another in Twin Falls three weeks later. Like they were trying to bankroll themselves."

"What do you have on that?" she asked.

"A month ago I was having a few beers with them, and one of them let something slip—a joke about orange dye—something only an insider would know. He was immediately stared down by the others, and maybe they don't think I picked up on it."

"Did the dye pack explode during one of the robberies?" she asked.

"At Boise. The bank reports its dye was orange. The dyes vary in color. The robbers made off with seven thousand dollars. So kooks, maybe, but they rob banks, more than likely."

"You don't have enough to arrest them for the bank robbery?" I asked.

"Beer talk—a half a sentence worth—about orange dye is nowhere near enough, I'm told by the federal prosecutors."

"This breakaway group have a name?" I asked.

"The Idaho Resisters."

"Are they recruiting you?" Linda asked.

"They'll have a couple of drinks with me, three times so far, once at the Sawtooth Tavern in Stanley and two times at their leader's house. We talk about hunting, talk about the Second Amendment, and about the runaway federal government, but they don't quite trust me yet. I'm coy with them. I don't trust them either, and they like that. I'm a loner, and I didn't accept their invitation the first time. They liked that, too."

"You tell them you've been to military ordnance school?" Linda asked.

He smiled narrowly. "They love to chat about explosives and weapons. I fill their ears about mortars and Claymores. One of them—their informal leader, Ed Fahey—brags that he was a navy SEAL, even has the SEAL Budweiser tattooed on his arm."

"He was a SEAL?" I asked.

"Fahey was rugged enough to make it through SEAL training, and that's plenty rugged. But he didn't have the discipline, at least when he went off base. The first tavern fight he got into, the navy put him into the brig for a week. The second was at the Silver Strand Tavern, where off-duty cops hang out, near the navy base in San Diego. The melee lasted five minutes, him against about five San Diego cops, and much of the tavern's interior was destroyed. Fahey wouldn't quit, and had to be beaten into unconsciousness."

"What happened to him?"

"A general discharge, and Fahey has been bitter about it ever since. Somehow the navy was out to get him, he figures. The brass. The big shots. Fahey despises big shots, a term he uses in every conversation. Fahey is suspicious and cunning. He likes to give the impression he's hiding something from you, and gets a lot of his authority from his secrets."

"We're here about *Sacajawea*," Linda said.

"I figured that."

"Fred Yamashita is running the show, and he wants you to speed it up."

"What's that mean?"

I said, "Whoever destroyed *Sacajawea* has sent a letter saying they're going to bring down another plane nine days from now." I told him about the tests on the letter, and its shingle nail signature.

"We need to know if the Idaho Resisters have equipment like the stuff that brought down *Sacajawea*," Linda said.

"You mean toss their houses? That'll really bollix up my work."

"We've got nine days, Billy," she reminded him.

"I've spent most of a year up here"—he waved at the index cards on the table—"jotting down my notes about the grand conspiracy whenever I hear fragments of it on the radio, cleaning my rifles, setting traps and eating roots, and memorizing the Constitution and all the other paranoid crapola, all to work my way in with these bastards. And a month in jail, and some bad tattoos. Now you want me to throw it all away?"

"Nine days and counting," I said.

We were quiet a moment, then I suggested, "Maybe the searches can be done so the Resisters don't discover them."

"Can't be done," she said. "It's always discovered. But maybe it won't matter if the Resisters know their places have been searched."

"It'll matter to me," Fitzpatrick said. "They'll go into hyperparanoia, and close me out. I'll have wasted my year."

"This is more important than your year in the boonies," Linda said. "We need to find out what they've got."

"It's unlikely they'd keep explosives or other evidence such as those nails on their premises," Fitzpatrick argued.

"Then maybe we'll find something else to charge them with," I said. "At least they'll be behind bars nine days from now."

He studied his boots a moment, then said, "I'll go in, do the search of Fahey's house. I know the layout because I've been there a couple of times. Are the Resisters the only group you are looking at?"

"Three others in central Idaho," Linda replied. "Every paranoid, well-armed group within driving distance of the Hailey airport."

He chewed on his lip a moment. "This Ed Fahey. You haven't been around people like him, maybe. He's a goof, but he's a scary goof."

She nodded.

Fitzpatrick added softly, "I'm afraid of him."

"You?" She laughed. "The guy who broke our hand-to-hand instructor's kneecap at the academy?"

He wouldn't even smile. "You haven't met Ed Fahey. I'll go into the house, but I want you behind me, with the trigger half pulled back on your handgun."

She studied his grave expression, then said, "To hell with the pistol. I'll be carrying an automatic shotgun."

ELEVEN

For the *Sacajawea* investigation, the federal government rented floor space near the Hailey airport. Hailey is ten miles south of Ketchum. The lovely Big Wood River runs between the towns, and the river valley is filled with horse farms. The Hailey airport is used by skiers coming into Sun Valley, right next to Ketchum, and during the season the road between Hailey and Ketchum carries mostly shuttle buses and rental cars with ski racks. In the off season, it's hay trucks.

Workstations had been brought into the place, which had been an outlet store before it failed. The NTSB, FBI, ATF, and other organizations were all on the ground floor. Space was tight, and Linda Dillon and I shared a carrel and a computer. After our visit in the wilderness, we had stopped for sandwiches in Ketchum. At Terry's Takeout she had ordered the Heart Attack Pastrami, which the chalkboard menu had guaranteed would have a minimum 3,000 calories. We sat at the carrel—two chairs in one space, our knees not quite touching—and unwrapped our lunch, hers on her lap. On our desk was her Jolt Cola, all the sugar and twice the caffeine.

I logged on to the computer. She dabbed at the corner of

her mouth with a finger. She was leaning forward so anything that dropped from the sandwich would miss her lap.

"You're eating like a marine," I said.

"Someday, if you are ever lucky enough to see me at a candlelit dinner, I'll eat like Queen Elizabeth, but right now I've got to get this nutrition down my throat. The backwoods made me hungry."

I took a bite of my sandwich, then clicked the mouse several times to check my message box at the NTSB. I had new e-mail, of course. I had been getting over a hundred messages a day since the investigation began. I left most of them for later, then came to a return address I didn't know, so I opened the message.

I abruptly leaned toward the screen. "Read this."

She scooted her chair toward the desk, and swallowed several times before she could read aloud, "'Mr. Durant: I must speak with you about a passenger on *Sacajawea*. He was not who he appeared to be. I am a prisoner, but I will contact you when I can.'"

I looked at her. "You're the cop. Tell me what this message means."

"It's a joke. A prank."

"It's not funny enough to be a joke."

"What's the e-mail address of the sender?"

I turned again to the screen. "Glasgow Anon. Never heard of it."

"It's a remailer."

I shook my head.

"A guy in Scotland has a computer and some phone lines, and he operates a forwarding service. He strips incoming e-mail of its identifier, then sends it to its destination, allowing anonymous e-mails."

"Why does he do that?"

"Because he can, I guess. There are quite a few remailers around the world. What I'm wondering is, how'd the sender get your e-mail address?"

"On the NTSB web site. We post investigators' e-mail addresses, department addresses, everybody, hoping to get tips."

"And why you? Why not the IIC?"

"Maybe because I've been on TV some, caught by reporters who keep asking about *Sacajawea* and the threatening letter. I don't know, other than that."

We chewed a moment.

Then I asked, "So I'm going to be waylaid by some convict?"

"Sounds like it."

"I'd better run this by the IIC. I don't like it. I'm no commando. I thought you had SWAT teams for this kind of thing."

"You've got me." She smiled. "That'll be enough."

Linda Dillon's fingers were on her laptop's keyboard. A cell phone was clipped onto the machine, and she was connected to the FBI computer in Washington, D.C. We were in the Warm Springs lodge, at the base of the Sun Valley ski runs. I could look right up the face of Mount Baldy, covered with snow and skiers.

The view offered an appalling contrast to the last snow-covered mountain I had been on, *Sacajawea*'s crash site. Here at Sun Valley, rather than blood and gore and twisted metal littering the slope, the mountain was pristine, with lovely expanses of white snow patterned with evergreens, and was being used as God intended: so rich Californians could do stem christies down the mountain, each on ski equipment that cost more than some cars.

I lowered my coffee cup. "I told you my dad was a grain warehouseman in eastern Washington."

She didn't look up from the screen. "Why are you telling me this again?"

"My father taught me two great lessons. The first was to never take anything for granted. Sometimes a crop would fail. A whole field would turn yellow before it was mature, and the farmer would get ten bushels of wheat an acre rather than thirty-five. Sometimes it was lack of rain. Or maybe a late freeze. Sometimes it was too much anhydrous ammonia fertilizer. My father was both suspicious and deliberate. The first answer isn't always the real answer, is what he taught me."

"So what's your point?" She didn't look up this time either.

"Those militia goobers. They're too easy an answer. On the one hand, they are paranoid and violent and, on the other hand, a plane came down. That connection is all we've got."

"But we don't have anything else, except your spark theory. And you've got just as big a gap in your reasoning. A few cracks in wire insulation and an explosion. Where's the connection there?" She tapped the keyboard a few times, then asked, "Have you talked to your daughter today?"

"She wasn't home when I called."

"Do you feel bad, leaving her in Seattle like that? I mean, it's a tough time for her."

"What was my alternative?" I sounded too defensive.

"Did Sarah say she didn't want you to leave?"

"No."

Linda finally brought up her eyes from the screen. "She didn't say anything?"

"She waved good-bye and turned back to her homework. I went over to hug her, but she just kept on staring at her algebra text."

"What'd you do?"

"You can't make someone hug you good-bye against their will." My voice was full and bitter. "I picked up my suitcase and left."

"Joe, she just lost her mother. Not everything Sarah does is going to be rational."

"It bothers the hell out of me. Sarah acted as if it didn't matter, one way or the other, if I left."

She returned to her work on the computer, but after a moment she said, "You said there were two great lessons your father taught you. What was the other one?"

"Never walk the lead-off batter."

The lodge at Warm Springs has high ceilings and vast windows. The building was made to resemble a log cabin, but airy and bright. A hundred people were enjoying after-ski beer and wine, not a care in the world, except maybe how to get back home, now that an Emerald plane had been bombed out of the sky. On the patio, a Seattle band, the Nightsticks, was playing up-tempo blues. The harmonica player—a good one—used an old-style crystal microphone I'd never seen before. I'd ask him about it after the set. When he put his harp away and picked up a saxophone for the next song, I lost interest and turned back to Linda.

Maybe it was her FBI training that got me talking. "After my wife ditched us, I watched Sarah try to build a wall between herself and her mother, try to make her mother matter less to her. Sarah would invent all these reasons why her mother never really loved her and why she never really loved her mother."

My personal FBI agent looked up again. I had her full attention now. Her laptop seemed forgotten and she was weighing my words. It made me want to tell her more, which was odd because I hardly knew her and because I'm uncomfortable revealing things about myself. My father told me those two great lessons of life, but he never told me he loved me. I never doubted it, but he just never said it, and he never said a lot of other things. I learned his way, keeping my own counsel. I don't tell other people my hopes and problems and I'm grateful when they keep theirs to themselves. My wife once called me callous, and said I never opened up to her. I tried, sort of, but so much of what rattles around in one's head is unformed and juvenile, and rather than force it into some presentable sentences, it's easier to keep it inside. I told Janie this, and she said I was rationalizing.

"Sarah tried to build a wall?"

"Maybe that's what she's trying to do now, between me and her."

"Why would she do that?" Linda asked.

"She blames me for her mother's death. I took her mother away, somehow, so Sarah is going to take herself away from me."

"You never call your dead wife by her name, do you know that? You call her your ex-wife or Sarah's mother."

I fiddled with the coffee cup.

"You've stripped her of her name," Linda said. "It's part of your effort to excise her from your memory."

"She deserves it."

The bright sun through the high windows lightened Linda's hair, making it look like straw. She rested her chin on her fist. "You still love her, I can tell."

"That's ridiculous."

"Sure you do."

"After what she did to me and Sarah, that's absurd."

"You struggle every day with your love for her."

I searched for some response, her staring knowingly at me. I couldn't come up with anything.

She said, "So let me tell you how you should think about your wife."

"*You* tell *me*? You hardly know me, and you never knew her."

"What was her name again?"

I was silent, feeling like a child.

"Come on," she said with a small smile. "Say it."

"Janie."

"You should treat Janie as having been two people. The person you loved, and the person who left you. Something weird happened to the first Janie, turning her into the second Janie. A Dr. Jekyll and Mr. Hyde transformation. Something changed her entirely. You can continue to love the early Janie."

"That's just mental gymnastics."

"It works." After a moment, she added, "Believe me, I know."

My words were chopped with anger. "My wife's leaving us has almost destroyed Sarah."

"That's the second Janie, the one you don't love anymore, and don't need to feel guilty about."

I waved my hand, shooing away her reasoning. I felt snippy and aggrieved, and didn't want to feel better, not at the moment, not with me also feeling terrible about leaving Sarah in Seattle. Maybe I should have ditched the *Sacajawea* investigation instead of my daughter. Carrying a tray of plastic cups of wine, a blond and tanned skier in a shiny jumpsuit brushed by me, her suit belted tightly to show off her tush. You'd think with all the money she spent on her ski outfit, she could have done her dark roots.

"Joe, you are really having a problem," Linda said. "I think you need to seek some therapy."

"What do you think this is?" I opened my wallet to show her a snapshot of Sarah.

She smiled. "You aren't a lot of help with our work, sitting over there worried about your daughter."

I pinched the bridge of my nose. "I failed in my marriage. I want to do one goddamn thing right in my life, just one. And that's to raise my daughter the right way."

"You—"

I cut her off, my voice rising like a wind. "After my wife ditched me, that's the one damned thing left to me to do right. My daughter."

"Joe—"

"And I don't know how. Goddamn it, I'm blowing it." I was almost yelling, creating one of these little restaurant scenes I despise. I bit down in rage, stopping the flow of words.

"Quite a few of these pretty skiers are looking at you," Linda said. "I brought you out to this lodge to cheer you up, get you away from our carrel. It's not working."

In a calmer voice, gained only by struggle, I said, "I want to help my daughter get through this."

"You've read too much into Sarah's anger, Joe. She'll get over it."

I passed my palm across my forehead, my eyes closed tightly for a moment. "What if something has snapped between my girl and me? Something irreversible. It happens, you know. The bell is rung and it can't be unrung. Something is said that can't ever be unsaid."

She reached across the table to pat my arm. "You're letting your thoughts about Sarah run away from you, is my point."

"I'm wasting my goddamn time here," I said. "It's an FBI show now, out here in Idaho. I'm going back to Seattle to my daughter." I made to rise.

Someone over by the lobby caught Linda's eyes. Linda stretched her backbone to see over skiers' heads, then she grinned. "You don't need to go home to Sarah. She has come to you."

I wheeled up and out of my chair. Smiling shyly, Sarah was picking her way through the tables toward us. She was wearing a ski parka, and was carrying the maroon Nike bag she used as an overnighter.

When she reached our table I gave her a mighty hug and then introduced Linda.

Sarah said, "I called the Hailey office when I arrived, and they said you were at the Warm Springs lodge. I thought you were working in Idaho, but all I see are a bunch of skiers having a good time."

"I'm glad to see you." I tried to keep the emotion from my voice. "More than you know."

She looked at me. "Not more than I know, Dad."

Gallic rage shimmered in the room, quieting all of us around the table. We were in a makeshift conference room adjacent to the room filled with carrels, in Hailey. Three headless mannequins were in a corner next to a box of plastic clothes hangers. We were as still as those mannequins, watching and waiting. The only evidence of the anger was a slight tick above Pierre Lemercier's right eye. His hands were on the table, the palms open to show his understanding and forgiveness, a papal gesture. Yet the flickering muscle above his eye was a telltale.

His voice was just above a whisper. "Mr. Durant, even Orville and Wilbur Wright understood the dangers of stuffing a narrow airborne hull with electric wiring."

Lemercier's stare was piercing my eyeball sockets, drilling

through my skull, and probably burning through the wall behind me.

He said, "You are not suggesting that my engineers are unaware of the devastating effect of an electric spark on fuel vapor."

"Of course not." The back of my shirt was suddenly damp. The great man was grilling me.

"So that you are not inferring we French aircraft designers do not understand the principles of the spark plug."

"Sir, I'm only saying—"

"It has occurred to you perhaps that we as aircraft builders might go to great lengths to ensure that electricity gets nowhere near vapors inside a fuel tank."

"But electricity is deliberately introduced into a fuel tank, sir." I held up a block of black plastic called a fuel terminal.

Boeing had loaned me this one, manufactured by Honeywell and used on 737s. Terminal blocks in ATF 94s were made by the German company RDS. The search teams had not yet found the block from *Sacajawea*'s center tank.

I trod lightly. "You of course know that metal probes are introduced into the fuel tank through this block. These probes use tiny electric currents to measure the amount of fuel in the tank."

Claude Dumond was Aero Transport France's senior electrical engineer. He had flown in from Paris for this meeting. He said, "It is a low-voltage current, and perfectly safe. It is a minuscule current, which runs through the probes, then to cockpit gauges. The current is far too weak to create a spark. Almost every commercial and military aircraft uses this same system to measure fuel."

His English was knotty but readily understandable. Also around the table were IIC Rich Shrader, and Bruce Hereford, whose face was adorned with a professorial white goatee and half-spectacles that were low on his nose. I knew him well, had eaten dinner at his house more than once. Linda Dillon and Fred Yamashita represented the FBI. They were only too happy to let me be on the receiving end of this French punishment.

I rallied. "But the low-voltage wires are bundled tightly with as many as 300 other wires. And some of those carry as much as 192 volts. That's anything but low voltage."

"You are suggesting that current jumped from a high-voltage line to a low-voltage line?"

"We have found several cracks in the Poly-X wire," I replied. "And studies show that only one-quarter of a milli-joule is required to ignite fuel vapor."

A millijoule is a unit of energy equivalent to the energy absorbed when a dime is dropped from a height of two inches.

"We are well aware," Dumond said, "that thirteen civilian and thirteen military aircraft have blown up since 1959 due to fuel-tank explosions. We attempt—entirely successfully, we believe—to eliminate high-voltage electric discharges near or in the fuel tank. Yours is not an unknown concern."

Lemercier added, "But we do not have any evidence of your voltage-jumping hypothesis."

"We understand that eight months ago Aero Transport France experimented with an inerting gas," I countered.

Lemercier leaned back in his chair, a rigid movement. "Perhaps it is only my poor English, but is there a note of accusation in your question?"

Lemercier spoke English as well as I did.

ATF's Dumond said, "We experimented with injecting nonexplosive gas into fuel tanks to decrease the system's volatility. The problem is that inerting gases are toxic, and potentially lethal. We decided that the risks of the inerting gas outweighed the benefit."

"You mean that the risks *and the costs* outweighed the benefit," Linda said. "What did the inerting gas units cost?"

"Two hundred thousand U.S. for each plane," Dumond answered. "Which is an amount we could easily have accommodated in the ATF 94 pricing structure, had we thought the inerting gas system was warranted."

"Let me assure you"—Lemercier's gaze began with me, then went to Rich Shrader and Linda Dillon and Fred Yamashita, a scythe felling fragile wheat stalks—"our decision regarding the inerting gas units had nothing to do with cost. The plane's fuel systems are safer without the gas than with the gas. It is as simple as that."

I asked, "Do you have records—?"

My childhood hero cut me off. "If this preposterous notion—that my company sacrificed passenger safety to save a few francs—were to become public, the effects on Aero Transport France would be devastating."

"I'd like to see—"

"You have no basis for your spark plug fancy." Lemercier's words were brittle. "You admit to having found only five microscopic cracks in the four miles of wiring you have examined so far. You would find this many cracks in four miles of any airplane's wiring."

Dumond ganged up on me. "This rate of failure is well within the norm, if these minuscule cracks can indeed be called a failure."

"So you are trying to make something from nothing," Lemercier said. "And to make such an accusation—that we have created the equivalent of a spark plug in our fuel system—is shameless." He tapped the table with a knuckle, syncopating with his words. "Simply shameless."

With an effort that made me tremble as if I were doing a

bench press, I looked Lemercier in the eyes. "I am requesting that ATF provide worldwide repair summaries."

Every time an airline made a repair—however minor—to an ATF plane, the information was reported to the manufacturer in Paris. Monthly summaries were generated which revealed failure trends. ATF issued replacement and repair directives to its customers based on the probability of future failures. I wanted to see if fuel gauge and fuel switch repairs were isolated and sporadic, or whether a pattern of electrical failure had become apparent in ATF 94s. And—unspoken but well understood by all sitting around the table—I wanted to know if a failure pattern had precipitated ATF's inert gas system tests. Why had ATF begun time-consuming and expensive tests on making fuel vapor less ignitable? What had they known?

I had expected resistance to my request for records, at least some lawyerly talk about the overly broad nature of my request and the enormous efforts that would be required to gather the documents.

So I was startled when Lemercier said, "We can have them to you within twenty-four hours." He glanced at Dumond, who had no choice but to nod his agreement.

Then Lemercier asked grandly, "Anything else?"

"Reports from your wiring lab. Results of tests you may have run that show the effects of extreme temperature variations, age, and other variables on Poly-X wire."

"Also within twenty-four hours," Lemercier assured us. "But I must ask a service of you."

I stared at him, fearing an incriminating proposition from the legend.

"I will help in every way I can to ensure the truth comes out about *Sacajawea,* but until a credible theory has developed, there is no point in turning the traveling public against ATF planes based on these preliminary requests for information."

I glanced at Rich Shrader. His expression said it was my call.

"Okay," I said. "Nothing will come from us about an inquiry into ATF 94 electrical and fuel systems at this time. And I will alert you, Mr. Lemercier, when we believe we can no longer prevent the release of the information."

Pierre Lemercier rose from the table, moving like a man half a century younger. The cane was an unneeded accessory. Maybe it disguised a sword. Dumond followed as ATF's founder stepped to the conference-room door.

Lemercier turned back to me. "My philosophy has always been to keep potential ignition sources outside the fuel system." This was a joke by way of understatement. "Look as hard and as long as you want, Joe. You won't find fault in our planes. *Sacajawea* was not brought down by design or manufacturing error."

After the Frenchmen disappeared through the door, Rich Shrader clucked his tongue in relief, and rose to go to the water cooler. Yamashita joined him. Linda opened her laptop and switched it on.

I stared at my hands. Pierre Lemercier had been a larger-than-life figure to me during my young years. He had been a call to courage and self-sacrifice. Now I was suddenly cast as the great man's enemy. I was chagrined and sorrowful. I sighed heavily and scowled.

I didn't think anyone else in the room noticed my bout of self-recrimination, until I looked up to find Linda Dillon looking at me, slowly shaking her head and smiling in a reassuring way, trying to comfort me.

It worked. I suddenly felt stronger. With her staring at me, I was abruptly ready to take on Lemercier and his minions.

TWELVE

"Don't say nothing you don't want read back to you in a trial." The voice was guttural, more a series of croaks, but made airy and slightly metallic by the FBI's equipment.

"Thought you had a bug sweeper, Ed. You said you could find anything with that wand of yours." This was a second voice, younger, with a touch of carefully measured insolence.

The first voice replied, "Then you put your goddamn life on the line, Doug. Not me. Those bastards are listening, five'll get you ten."

"You think so?"

"I don't give a flyer if they are."

Billy Fitzpatrick said, "That's Ed Fahey, the one who wouldn't give a flyer. The other one—the kid's voice—is Doug Dietz."

Fahey and Dietz's voices were being amplified by four speakers lining a wall, near the mannequins in the conference room. An FBI technician hovered over a control panel that resembled a high-end mixing board that I wished the Long-liners could afford. Next to the board was a CPU and monitor. About thirty people were in the room. Everyone was rumpled and glum. More sounds came from the speaker, some scraping, like a chair being pushed back.

The technician at the board was wearing a pea coat and jeans. He looked fifteen years old, but was a decade older. His hair had been cut with a No. 1 shear, giving him the popular chemotherapy look. His name was Jeff Rose.

He said, "I can eliminate most of the static, and add bass to the voices, making them sound almost human, but I can't eliminate the hillbilly twang."

A sharp pop and hiss came from the speakers.

Jeff Rose explained, "A beer can being opened."

"You know that for sure?" I asked.

He tapped his CPU affectionately. "I'm running Sound Vet five point one, which recognizes fifteen thousand sounds. The noises in Fahey's house are being fed through Sound Vet at the same time they come over the speaker. The program almost immediately labels the sound. It's a rare one it doesn't nail."

Linda Dillon wasn't impressed. "Anybody can recognize a beer can being opened. It's not like beating Kasparov."

From the speaker: "Make sure the furniture is pointing at me, not the end with the hole in it."

Fitzpatrick said, "'Furniture' is the wood stock of a rifle or shotgun."

"Do you have a transmitter inside the place?" I asked.

"Nothing inside," Rose said. "A laser gun is pointed at one of Fahey's windows. The gun measures the precise distance between itself and the window a thousand times a second. The window acts as the tympanic membrane, like an eardrum. These measurements are digitized, then transmitted by a radio to a dish, sent to D.C., then here."

A snap and jangle came from the speaker.

"That's a rifle bolt being opened and closed," the technician announced.

"Still not impressed," Linda said. "A slide rule could recognize a rifle bolt."

Jeff Rose's face creased into a triumphant grin. "Sound Vet says it's a Browning automatic rifle Grade 1 gas-operated semi-automatic, side-ejecting, hammerless 7 millimeter magnum."

Amid laughter, all eyes turned to Linda.

She said, "I'm sorry for you, Jeff, trying so hard to compensate for your suspect masculinity. And me, being of the weaker sex."

Laughter was followed by a couple of people calling out, "Weaker? You?"

One asked loudly, "What about the mouse?"

Another FBI agent laughed. "Yeah, the mouse."

More laughter followed. I didn't know what they were talking about. Linda grinned. These people liked her, and she knew it.

"I hear Smith's truck." This from the speakers. "I hope that idiot brought the stuff."

At the word *stuff* all eyes snapped back to the speakers.

Except Fitzpatrick's. "Don't get your hopes up. *Stuff* usually means alcohol. They like to use the word to make it sound illicit."

"Does their stuff always have tax stamps on it?" an ATF agent asked. "Maybe we could get them that way."

"It's legal, far as I know," Fitzpatrick replied. "Bottom-shelf hooch usually used to preserve biology class frogs. That'll be Runny Smith entering the house."

The sound from the speaker was of a door opening, no knock. A new voice, "You guys haven't been pre-functioning, have you?"

"*Pre-functioning* is a college term," the agent on the other side of Linda said. "This Smith ever been to college?"

"You can't get into college if you never were in high school," Fitzpatrick said.

"Well, maybe he read it somewhere," the agent said.

"You can't read it somewhere if you can't read. Smith is illiterate. He stops at an intersection not because he can read the sign but because he recognizes its shape and color." Fitzpatrick turned to the technician. "Let's see these guys, Jeff."

"About time, goddamn it." Fahey's voice.

"Had to jump my truck." The voice belonged to Runny Smith.

Fahey: "You buy a rig on the goddamn reservation, what do you expect?"

Rose stepped to a projector. A hole in the wall seemed to suddenly open, showing the street outside. A man in cowboy boots and a straw hat walked along a boardwalk in front of a saloon. He had a vast chest, pylon arms, and a belly that hung only a little over his belt. He passed an iron hitching post. It could have been a hundred years ago.

Fitzpatrick said, "This is Ed Fahey, taken last summer from our van, over in Stanley. Fahey is forty-eight years old. He took over his parents' dairy farm when he left the navy, and ran it down to nothing over the next ten years, borrowed on it, then was foreclosed. He became a welder."

From the speakers: "This tastes like horse piss. What is it?" Runny Smith's voice.

"When's the last time you ever bitched about any drink I bought?"

Smith and Dietz laughed, and one of them, I couldn't tell, ended by coughing, more a choke, ending in a rattling clearing of the throat.

Fitzpatrick went on, "In the early nineties, Fahey spent twenty months at Lompoc on a weapons charge. Seems he had a British Vickers machine gun and a U.S. Army bazooka—both World War II models—in the back of his pickup under a tarp. He claimed he was a collector, and the judge said he could do his collecting in prison."

"Was there a proffer?" someone in the room asked.

The video on the wall ended after Fahey spit onto the dirt street, then turned into the tavern.

Fitzpatrick replied, "The prosecutor said he would recommend a sentence on the low end of the guidelines if Fahey would reveal where he purchased the weapons, but Fahey wouldn't make a deal. Here's a close-up."

Ed Fahey's mug shot appeared on the wall. He had a bulldog's face, with a wide, turned-down mouth and a flat nose. His chin was forward. The front of his head was bald, but tufts of hair grew at his crown. His eyes were sunk deeply. Even in the washed-out flatness of the photo, Fahey had an assertive, brawler's presence.

A momentum was in this conference room. I was swept along by the FBI agents' professionalism and confidence and enthusiasm. They wanted a villain, and maybe Ed Fahey was their man. The agents' job was to catch someone, not to listen to nascent theories about sparks. I sat there quietly.

Fahey said through the speakers, "Did I tell you about the time my diving buddy bet me he could eat a beer mug?"

Fitzpatrick interrupted. "Turn it down a bit, Jeff. I've heard this lie. His diving buddy, as in SEAL diving partner. Runny and Doug just lap this crap up. Fahey despises his boss, the owner of the welding shop. Thinks he has it out for him. He despises the Ketchum Ace Hardware owner. Thinks he cheats him when he weighs nails. He despises the school board because they allow pornography in public libraries. He despises—"

Linda cut him off. "We get the picture."

"He owns twenty-three semiautomatic weapons. He commemorates Waco every year with a religious fervor, flies a flag that has crossed lightning bolts on it, big fireworks displays he invites all his friends to, barbecued chicken and corn on the cob, and he passes out his twenty-five-page treatise on what he'd do if he were king of America. Ed Fahey believes millions of Americans are ready to rise up against their government. He's cocked and loaded, ready for the uprising."

Fahey blinked off, and was replaced by another man's face, impassive and moonlike, with loose, wet lips and radar-dish ears.

"This is Runny Smith," Fitzpatrick said. "Real name is Gerald. The man is a moron, pure and simple."

Smith had blank, puzzled eyes, and wide, spatulate cheeks. His Beatles bangs made him appear younger than he was, mid-thirties, I'd guess.

"What kind of name is Runny?" asked an FBI agent wearing a T-shirt with LEGALIZE PUBLIC BREAST-FEEDING printed on it, I suppose to make sure J. Edgar Hoover was really dead.

"He had a chronic sinus infection when he was a kid. Maybe it pickled his brains. Runny never heard a bad idea he didn't think was a good idea. One time when he was thirteen years old, a friend suggested they could make a Molotov cocktail, and they did, and it worked just fine when they lobbed it into a Lutheran minister's car."

"What'd he get?" Linda asked.

"Eleven months in juvie. Then when he was fifteen, his older brother Wiley suggested that Runny steal a red Chevy Malibu the older brother had taken a fancy to. So Runny managed to open the Malibu's door with a slim jim made from a hacksaw blade, and he got the engine going, and he revved the engine and popped the clutch to make his getaway. Only trouble was, the gear was in reverse, and the tires laid rubber, backwards, and the Malibu crashed into a fire hydrant, ripping the hydrant out of the ground. The Malibu's engine died, and water shot up from the exposed pipe like Old Faithful. That's where the Ketchum police found Runny, still in the dead Malibu, water still gushing all around. He's done one stupid thing after another all his life, usually ending up in jail. He's only thirty years old, if you don't count the six years he has spent in assorted jails and prisons."

"Any violent crimes?" an FBI agent asked.

"Nothing he's been caught for. He likes to plink bottles with a .22. Fahey loans him the rifle and gives him a box of shells. Let's see Dietz."

Runny Smith was replaced by a face resembling a gnawed bone. Doug Dietz's nose had been broken and badly set, and had an off-kilter knob. A scar on his forehead looked like it had been stitched together with fishing line, reminding me of the legendary Chicago harmonica player Little Walter's scar. Dietz's eyes were shallow and close together, and his brows were heavy, with a permanent tuck of suspicion. He wore a buzz cut that made him look like a skateboarder. His ears were close against his head and the size of buttons. He wore a short blond goatee, only a week's growth or so. He had no neck, just sloping muscle from his ears down to his shoulders. Dietz looked tough.

"Doug Dietz wrestled for the local high school, four years on the varsity. During those four years, he broke five bones of five different opponents. He was state champion in his weight class, which was 134."

"He looks 234," Linda said.

"You can't tell from this picture, but Dietz is as wide as he is tall. He's only five-four. To make his high school wrestling team, he started injecting himself with anabolic steroids at age thirteen, which gave him muscles but sealed his bone plates, and he stopped growing. That also explains the blocky look to his face. He usually wears facial hair to hide small scars on his chin. The steroids made his chin get larger and larger, and finally the bone began pushing through his skin. A plastic surgeon shaved off bone there, though you can see his chin is still big."

An FBI agent said, "He looks like he lifts weights."

"Dietz enters bodybuilding contests, four or five a year, and so still shoots steroids. Two years ago he placed second in the Mr. Idaho competition, the division for shorter men. Once, when he and I and the others were having a few drinks, Dietz began railing against the people who withheld from him the information that steroids can make you stop growing. The drunker he got, the angrier he got. I sat there, nodding my head again and again, and he took this as encouragement. He believes some sort of conspiracy kept the information about steroids from him."

"A conspiracy to make him short?" I asked.

"Exactly."

A couple of people laughed.

"And he still takes steroids?" Linda asked.

"He knows it'll crystallize his innards, but Dietz is twenty-eight, and no twenty-eight-year-old worries about that."

An ATF agent said, "Doesn't sound like he's got enough brains to keep his ears apart."

Fitzpatrick said, "But Dietz is serious. All his adult life, he has been mad about the conspiracy to make him a runt, and his anger is renewed each time he has to buy jeans off the kids' rack."

"Who is Dietz mad at?" Linda asked.

"I'm not sure he knows, but he spends much of his life in a 'roid rage."

I asked, "Are these guys Luddites?"

"They don't object to modern technology unless it's being used to monitor them."

The U.S. attorney for Idaho picked up my thought. "Then what would be their motive to bring down an airplane, and to threaten another one?"

Fitzpatrick replied, "To strike a blow for freedom, maybe. A strike against the tyranny of the United States government."

"That's it?" the attorney asked. "That's not much motive to bring before a jury."

"Well, I'm going into Ed Fahey's house tonight to see if we can bring something more substantial before your jury." He looked around the room. "I don't have anything more. Let's break into teams and get ready."

We began to rise and gather our things.

Linda leaned back in her chair. "You do have something more, Billy."

He looked up from the keyboard. "What would that be?"

"You told me you were afraid of Ed Fahey."

Bill Fitzpatrick must have been a hard customer because the room was abruptly still. The agents looked at Linda and Bill, back and forth, as if Linda had just challenged him to a duel.

She said, "The more we know about him, the better prepared we'll be."

Fitzpatrick pursed his lips, then said, "Two months ago Fahey and Dietz invited me to have a couple beers and shoot some eight ball with them. Runny Smith wasn't with us. Three bikers showed up, from the Lewiston Demon Deacons, fat guys on Harley-Davidsons, wearing colors and pill helmets, thinking they're kings of the road, hopped up on something and looking for a little action."

"Where was this?" Linda asked.

"Over in Stanley, at that same tavern you saw in the video. I was in the head minding my own business and didn't see how it started, but when I came out these three bikers were standing near the pool table, telling Fahey and Dietz to get the hell away from their table. Faced with these two bikers, Fahey looked suitably afraid and meek. He said, 'Sure. You can have the table, just don't cause no trouble.' Fahey stepped to the rack, as if to put his cue away, but then pirouetted around and came out swinging with the cue."

"He doesn't look like the kind of guy who does pirouettes," I said.

"When Ed Fahey went into action, he was transformed from a pot-bellied, bowlegged hick into a vicious machine. He chopped at those two guys with the pool cue, aiming at their heads, jabbing and slashing. And Doug Dietz launched himself at the nearest biker and slammed the biker's head into the table."

"The bikers didn't put up a fight?" someone asked.

"They didn't have the time. One instant they were standing there giving orders, and the next they were laid out on the floor, blood all over them. Then Fahey shoved a billiard ball into each of their mouths."

"A billiard ball doesn't fit into a mouth," Linda said. "I know. I've tried."

"It does if you break off all the front teeth, which is what Fahey did. Bottom and top teeth on all three bikers, just smashed them into chips, leaving nothing but broken stumps, and pushed the balls into their traps. Then he and Dietz and I finished our beers and left."

"Did this get reported to the authorities?" the U.S. attorney asked.

"No biker tattles to the cops." Fitzpatrick signaled to Jeff Rose, who doused the projections. The room seemed safer without Dietz on the wall. Fitzpatrick said, "So, yeah, I'm afraid of Ed Fahey. He's ferocious and stupid and cunning, and he loves firearms. A dangerous combination."

I reached for my coat.

Fitzpatrick added, "He also thinks he's a funny guy."

"Yeah?" Linda said.

"As we left the tavern, Fahey said to the comatose bikers, 'Next time you want the pool table, put a quarter on the bumper.'"

THIRTEEN

The panel truck was parked a quarter mile from Ed Fahey's home. CENTRAL IDAHO PLUMBING CONTRACTORS was painted on the exterior. I was squeezed between banks of electronics. The trailer was called a C3, for command, control, and communications. The interior was filled with twelve huge monitors mounted on the walls. The screens were large and close, and pressed in on me, throwing harsh light. The rare vertical surfaces not covered by screens were busy with blinking red and green lights, dials, knobs, switches, and digital readouts. I sat on a metal milking stool. Faint static came from a dozen speakers.

The Boise FBI SAC was at a metal table next to an agent who had one hand on a joystick that controlled a moving eyeball on a tiny CCD camera, which was mounted on Bill Fitzpatrick's helmet. Another FBI agent worked Linda's camera. Some monitors displayed Fitzpatrick's point of view and others showed Linda's. The team leader—an FBI agent named Jamie Suarez—stood behind the SAC, his gaze going back and forth between POVs.

Around us were audio and video recorders, a data acquisition and registration system, a cell phone scrambler, a dialed-number decoder, VHF and FM receivers, digital electronic countermeasures, and other surveillance devices. A panel of eight four-inch color LCD monitors was on the table in front of the SAC, some monitors with the feed from Fitzpatrick's camera, others from Linda's. The thermostat was broken, and heat poured into the trailer. Beads of sweat formed across my lip and forehead.

The Boise SAC's name was Rob Winsor. Both he and Suarez were wearing headsets, the microphones at their mouths. The SAC had on a tie and a white shirt, with damp crescents under his armpits. His dark hair was combed carefully, with gray showing at the temples. His face was carefully composed.

Jamie Suarez wore a T-shirt with a photo of Che Guevara's bullet-riddled body on it, above the text, THANK YOU, BOLIVIA. Suarez also wore a Groucho Marx mustache. He asked, "Do you get an IR reading?"

"Nothing yet." Linda's voice came from a speaker. She was also wearing a headset, this one mounted on a helmet, standing fifty yards from Ed Fahey's home near Ketchum.

"I've got the IR feed in front of me," Suarez said. "I don't see anything either."

Linda was pointing an infrared gun at the house. An LCD readout was at the back of the gun, and the data was also being relayed to a monitor inside the van. The screen glowed with bright colors, waves of green and blue and red and orange and yellow. Heat showed as blue.

His voice tinny in the van, Bill Fitzpatrick said, "There's a slit of light from shades over the front window."

Suarez said, "There's nobody in the house. The only heat source I see is a lamp in the front room. I don't even get any readings from heat ducts, so the heat is off in the house."

On the screen, the lamp resembled a suspended blue ball.

We knew Ed Fahey and his wife weren't in the house. Fahey was drinking beer at the Farmer John Saloon in Ketchum with Doug Dietz, and Fahey's wife was in Boise at a bowling tournament, staying overnight at the Mountain West Motel. Both were being followed by FBI agents, who were reporting their whereabouts to the van.

"You hearing anything on the dishes?" Fitzpatrick asked. His point-of-view monitor showed the house getting bigger as he approached. Linda's POV monitor showed Fitzpatrick's back.

Suarez replied over the radio, "Nothing but the rustling of trees."

The FBI had set up parabolic listening dishes in several locations around Ed Fahey's residence, lest anybody come tromping through the woods, I suppose. I thought all this was overkill. How many computer chips does it take to search a house?

I could hear Fitzpatrick breathing through the speakers, sounding like Lloyd Bridges. The image of Fahey's house rose and fell on the monitors with each of Fitzpatrick's and Linda's steps, and so many screens carried the jerky image that it seemed as if the trailer were rising and falling. When Fitzpatrick looked over his shoulder at Linda, the trailer seemed to spin. In the close and hot trailer, I was feeling the first rumble of motion sickness.

Linda said, "This damned Kevlar vest was made for Kate Moss, not for real women. It's one more tiny piece of the FBI's glass ceiling."

Suarez and the others laughed, but not the Boise SAC.

Fahey's residence—bouncing on all the monitors—was a house as drawn by a child, with a door in the middle and one window on each side, a house-as-a-face. Part of the foundation had been dug up, and concrete blocks were supporting the northwest corner. Nearby, a shovel was stuck into a mound of dirt. It looked like Ed had begun some project, then winter froze the ground on him. Miners' lamps were attached to the agents' headsets, and they threw a beam smaller than the video projection, so the trailer's screens had dark edges.

"You'd think this dork would put pavers in his front yard," Linda said. Although Sun Valley's slopes still had snow, much of it man-made, in the lowlands mud was everywhere.

SAC Rob Winsor said into his microphone, "Cut the chatter, Dillon."

Her voice filled the trailer. "What'd you do to get assigned to Boise, SAC? Flunk Wichita Falls?"

The SAC covered his microphone with a fingertip and looked at Jamie Suarez. "Is she always this way with her superiors?"

"I'm stepping onto the porch," Fitzpatrick said over the speakers.

"This isn't the moon landing," the SAC said into his mike, maybe to compensate for Linda roughing him up. "We can see what you're doing well enough."

When Fitzpatrick sank to his knees, Ed Fahey's front door rose on the monitors as if we were in an elevator. Fitzpatrick pulled a pick from a fabric kit, and inserted it into the keyhole. Linda's POV camera showed Fitzpatrick's back and his headgear. The blur in the foreground was her shotgun, the barrel pointed at the sky.

"Got it," Fitzpatrick said.

"Go slow now." Linda's voice had dropped to a whisper, so Jamie Suarez turned up the volume.

From his belt Fitzpatrick pulled a slim jim, bent on one end to form a handle. He slowly pushed open the door, but only a fraction.

"Easy does it," Linda said under her breath, words that

filled the van. She looked left and right, at the windows, then back to Fitzpatrick. She stepped onto the small porch so she could watch him maneuver the slim jim. Her POV monitors showed Fitzpatrick's hands.

"What's he doing?" I asked.

Suarez said, "Checking for booby traps. A string tied to a doorknob, that sort of thing. These guys love booby traps. Fahey even subscribes to a newsletter about them."

"I don't feel anything." Fitzpatrick pulled the slim jim back. "Hand me the camera."

Linda's POV wiggled, then showed her hand passing something that resembled a snake to Fitzpatrick, who was still on his knees.

"That's a gooseneck camera," Suarez explained. "Much like an arthroscope the surgeons use."

Linda's monitors showed Fitzpatrick slipping the camera through the crack in the door.

"Bring it up," Suarez ordered.

When a technician tapped his keyboard, Ed Fahey's living room appeared on one of the monitors, the image sent from the camera through the gooseneck, then through a feed to Fitzpatrick's backpack, where a shotgun transmitter sent it to a relay dish on an FBI truck parked 200 yards from Fahey's house. When Fitzpatrick moved the gooseneck, the image in our van leaped. From Linda's POV, I could see him press a flat button on the side of the goggles.

"I've got it on the heads-up." Fitzpatrick was viewing an image of the Faheys' living room on the glass of his goggles. His helmet was a modification of the Honeywell integrated helmet and display sight system (abbreviated by the army to IHADDAS and pronounced *I-hads*) worn by the crews of Apache helicopters. "You see anything?"

In the van we all leaned toward the monitor. A couch and a huge TV, a basket with magazines in it, a telephone and a lamp on an end table. Above the couch was framed needlework, a representation of grape leaves twined together as the border and in the middle old English letters that read *An Armed Society Is a Polite Society.*

The SAC said, "Turn it more to your right, get the corner."

"Let's make damned sure," Fitzpatrick said. "It's my ass going in there."

"Now up at the ceiling," Suarez ordered.

The image lifted, then swung left and right, panning the ceiling.

"Nothing," Suarez said.

"Me, neither," Fitzpatrick's voice stuttered with static.

The image dropped.

He asked, "Anything on the floor? A mat that's wired, maybe?"

The carpet was wall-to-wall shag. A teddy bear the size of a cement sack sat in a corner, a big ribbon at its neck.

"Nothing there," the SAC said.

"I don't see anything either." Fitzpatrick pulled the gooseneck camera from the room, and the image jumped around on the monitor. Then that monitor went black for a moment before the technician filled it with Linda's point of view again.

She looked over her shoulder, the images on the monitors spinning. Carrying assault rifles, two more FBI agents were on the road near a mailbox. An FBI evidence van was parked on the road, and an agent had begun to unload a tool cart. Fitzpatrick pushed open Ed Fahey's door. Linda hustled in after him.

"Check every room before you start looking for evidence of a crime," the Boise SAC said.

Linda replied, "Thank you, Colonel Klink."

The SAC looked at Suarez, who shrugged and said, "She doesn't like to be told her job."

All monitors showed the living room sweeping back and forth. Then the dining room appeared on Fitzpatrick's screens. A copy machine was on the table. Fitzpatrick picked up a brochure from near the machine and held it up to the camera. It read "Republic of Idaho Press Release."

"You there, Joe Durant?" Linda asked.

Jamie Suarez handed me a microphone. "I'm here."

In the C3 van, surrounded by FBI agents and their equipment, I felt as useless as tits on a goat. She knew it, and she was sticking me.

"This is more fun than your spark theory, you've got to admit," she said.

On her screens, Fitzpatrick swept out of sight, and the door frame to the kitchen grew, then disappeared to the sides as she stepped into the kitchen. Fitzpatrick's monitors still showed the brochure, and I read the next line: Idaho Resisters announce contest to design Republic of Idaho currency.

"A meat loaf is on the counter." Linda's voice had picked up low-level background static.

The static became a little louder. Linda's monitors showed a print over the stove that read *Remember the Alamo,* and under that: *The Alamo had a back door. 173 men chose not to use it.* The kitchen-door window was covered with blinds. To one side was a cat scratching post. She opened a closet door and flicked on a light.

"Fahey is expecting a long siege, looks like," Linda said, her voice crackling in the van.

The door was to a walk-in pantry crammed floor to ceiling with sacks and canned goods, leaving too little space to step inside.

For some reason the technician was adjusting the volume control, and Fitzpatrick's voice rose and fell. "Let's give the bedrooms the once-over, then get the evidence guys in here."

Rob Winsor said into the radio, "I want you to find something to bust Fahey, Bill. We want this guy out of action."

Fitzpatrick's voice came from the speakers all around, as if his voice were in my head. "You are preaching to the choir, SAC. If anything's here, we'll find it."

Both agents in the house turned at once to leave the kitchen, and our van once again spun as if we were a centrifuge. Fitzpatrick led the way to a back bedroom, Linda's monitor showing his back. Her shotgun was still at the ready, its nose an out-of-focus smudge at the bottom of her video screens.

"Ed Fahey is too stupid to be clean," Fitzpatrick said. "We'll find something."

"Where're all his firearms he brags about?" Suarez asked. "Fahey will have converted semiautomatic rifles to automatics with mail-order kits, is my guess. That'll be enough to bring him in."

Fitzpatrick entered a bedroom. Another teddy bear was propped between two pillows against the bed's headboard. This one was dressed in denim overalls with a red farmer's scarf at its neck. Another bear was on a dresser next to a comb set.

"Is it Ed or his wife who likes teddy bears?" Linda asked.

Fitzpatrick pulled open a closet door.

His monitors instantly blinked out. The van filled with sound so loud that it distorted the speakers, and I couldn't tell what it was. A bell ringing or a car crash or an anvil dropping. Linda's monitor showed Bill Fitzpatrick pitching back toward her. His head was an odd shape, no longer oval, but ragged and pulpy. He disappeared from Linda's screen toward the floor. The image was blurry, something on the camera lens.

Linda gasped, "Oh God. Oh God."

Suarez yelled, "Linda. Get out."

Her monitors lifted, showing the bedroom's ceiling. Then she spun to the teddy bear, then back to Fitzpatrick, who lay on the floor with half his head missing and blood puddling under the remaining half.

Suarez tried again. "Linda, can you hear me?"

"Oh God," she said, her voice suddenly far away. "No, no, no."

Her hand came up to the camera, and it was covered in blood.

Then the image lowered slowly to the floor, to show Fitzpatrick's back. Linda was sitting down or kneeling.

"Ah, no. I'm hit."

Her monitor showed the floor coming up, and then we could see the shag of the carpet, and one of Fitzpatrick's ears sitting by itself on the rug. Linda groaned, ending in a long sigh, and then her monitors went black.

FOURTEEN

The wretched remains of the airplane filled the hangar, blackened and gaping, and floating above the floor. Much of *Sacajawea* had been found, had been trucked down the mountain and was being reassembled around a wire and wood frame. Parts that had yet to be attached lay on the floor. Boeing had rented space at its Renton plant to the NTSB for a nominal fee. Each ragged, displaced chunk of the plane was being meticulously subjected to a range of tests and catalogued.

When the pieces arrived at the hangar, they were laid on a grid corresponding to ATF's longitudinal fuselage station designation system. Other areas of the floor had grids for wing structure, wing center section, and body fairings. The engines and landing gear had their own areas.

Parts that could not be associated with a specific position on the airplane were sorted according to type of structure. And parts that could not be identified at all were sorted according to where they were found in the debris field.

Now the piecing together of the fuselage was well underway. Because the plane had come apart in the air with pieces floating down, rather than being driven into the ground as was the USAir 737 that had cratered the field outside Pittsburgh in 1994, the ATF 94 was in fairly large pieces, and was coming back together at a quick pace. The USAir 737 was a DNA event. *Sacajawea* was only a dental records event.

I lay on a platform of two-by-twelves that was part of a scaffold constructed inside the fuselage so investigators could navigate through the plane without falling through gaps to the hangar's floor. Bruce Hereford was on his belly next to me. Below us, on another level of planks, one of his investigators stood where the deck to the cargo hold should have been.

"*Sacajawea* was decapitated," Hereford said. He was holding a thin fiberglass rod resembling a fishing pole. "The blast originated from behind the cockpit, roughly where Paul is standing. You can see the football."

On the planks below, Paul Lorent attached a rod to a football that represented the estimated location of the detonation. A dozen rods radiated from the football like cartoon sun rays. Next to Lorent was a tackle box containing the low-tech tools of crater searching: a magnet, cotton swabs, collection bottles, and a magnifying glass.

"You can see the keel beam box, Joe." Hereford pointed to the lower end of the center wing front spar. "It broke into three large sections. There is considerable sooting on all the pieces. And take a look at the vertical web attachments and the lower keel chords." He inched forward to gesture in the right direction. "And look at the bulkhead frames."

Bulkhead frames redistribute loads between the fuselage, wing, and landing gear assemblies. They were broken and twisted. Hereford spoke for a few more moments, pointing out the bends and fractures associated with an abrupt and cataclysmic event.

I asked, "But your location of the football is only an estimate, right?"

"The bomb was—"

"Bruce, don't buy into the bomb talk just yet. There are other scenarios out there."

"The poacher's missile? You believe that guy?"

"More scenarios than that."

"Ah, yes. Your theory, the mysterious spark."

"You need to withhold judgment. That's one of our main tasks as NTSB investigators."

"You sound like the manual." He smiled, his goatee moving around on his face. "You're right, of course. What shall I call the initial event? An overpressure?"

"At this point you can't tell exactly where on *Sacajawea* the detonation occurred. There's too much damage to pinpoint it."

"The explosion destroyed most of its immediate environment. So our football's location is only an educated guess, the rough center of the destruction. The actual point of detonation could be six or eight feet in any direction of where we've placed it."

"So it could be lower than where you've placed the football."

"At the center fuel tank, you mean, down where Paul is standing. Yes, that could very well be the location of the overpressure. Or it could be in the nearby baggage holds, or it could be somewhere on the flight deck behind the pilots, near the bulkhead."

A helmet resembling a welder's mask covered Lorent's head. A large magnifying glass on the faceplate made his eyes seem the size of fried eggs. He sounded like he was speaking into a bucket. "The detonation took out the electrical substation attached to the bulkhead behind the nosewheel bay."

I said, "So the plane's nerve center was destroyed."

"Instantly, yes." Hereford reached down to help Lorent

place a rod. "And in that same instant, passengers were subjected to 250-mile-an-hour winds. Loose items in the cabin became shrapnel."

On the hangar's concrete floor was an NTSB specialist at a workstation who entered data into a computer as Hereford called it out. The specialist's monitor showed a three-dimensional image of a portion of *Sacajawea,* its skin represented in light blue, various systems such as fuel, braking, flight controls, and landing gears in different shades of blue, gray, and black. The suspected location of the detonation—the football—glowed red on the screen, while the rods—the known paths of projectiles—were rendered in orange. Projectiles found thus far had been tentatively identified as pieces of the plane, bits of structure ripped off the plane and shot outward by the detonation. No shrapnel from an explosive device—whether bomb or missile—had been recognized.

Hereford noticed me glancing at the monitor through a gap in the fuselage. "I get some comfort knowing the bloody computer can't entirely replace putting the actual pieces back together. Look at this."

He and I rose to our feet. He pointed to one of the orange rods, this one emanating from the area of the football and passing between us as it gradually rose. He slowly led me along the catwalk. This rod went through the back of a passenger seat, meaning that whatever object the rod represented surely passed through a passenger because Emerald 37 was full. The back of the seat was stained dark with the blood of the victim.

I walked back along the reconstructed aisle. Most of the seats had been found, but a few were still missing, making the cabin look gap-toothed. Breaches in the fuselage allowed glimpses of the rest of the hangar, where NTSB investigators were sitting at computers. Structures and power plant group members stood in circles, analyzing parts of the aircraft that had yet to be placed. Tables near each group were covered with ATF 94 documentation, scores of loose-leaf binders.

I had seen fuselages that were much more mangled than this one. An explosion superheats metal as it blows outward. When the detonation occurs at an altitude higher than 30,000 feet, where temperatures are below freezing, the metal often remains in its bomb-contorted position, and the reconstructed fuselage resembles a cheese grater, more hole than surface. *Sacajawea* was at about 11,000 feet when it came apart, and the forces of the wind and temperature had not been as powerful as, say, over Lockerbie. Large pieces of *Sacajawea* had come down in factory condition. Even so, the reassembled fuselage was broken and punctured, allowing views of the rest of the hangar.

Snowmelt had darkened much of the fabric and wall paneling inside the fuselage. Most of the seats toward the rear of the passenger compartment were intact. Even a slight tear in the aircraft's skin—metal that is less than a twentieth of an inch thick—results in the aircraft blowing apart because of the slipstream and almost instant depressurization. *Sacajawea* had suffered high stresses, differential pressure, locally applied force, or a combination of these, and had broken up.

Wires hung from the ceiling. The place smelled of mildew and cordite. I followed Hereford and the rod, passing rows of seats.

"Up here." He pointed. "We haven't found this roof panel or the skin here, and so the wing strut is showing."

Sacajawea's wings had been above the fuselage, but the structures group had found no point in reattaching them, and the wings, largely reassembled, lay on supports at the south end of the hangar. They were being examined for possible fire and explosion of a fuel tank, perhaps caused by lightning. Wing tips are a favorite location for lightning strikes, which usually cause no damage, but there have been instances of lightning causing an explosion if fuel is vented near the wing tips. The wings were being searched for evidence of electrical discharge entry or exit. Nobody believed it was lightning, not on a sunny day, but nothing was being ruled out.

Hereford pointed to an exposed steel flange, part of the assembly that had attached the wing to the body.

He said, "This is wing assembly part 402AR, ATF book six, manufactured by the Vosges Machine Plant in Strasbourg, under a contract with ATF. Note the pock, right here."

The crater in the flange was the size of a grain of rice.

I guessed. "You think it's some kind of a timing device?" Bomb parts were often found jammed into the structure. It's called high-speed particle penetration.

"Piece of a battery, we think." Hereford was grinning, exultant at the discovery. "A grocery store battery, something you'd put into a flashlight. We just found it this morning, pulled it out with tweezers, and sent it to the lab. We'll know shortly what it is, but I think it's a bit of a battery jacket." He chuckled. "Vosges Machine Plant has assured us that scraps of battery are not normally found embedded in their flanges."

I was ready for him. "Allen Boyd, in seat 4A—right near the detonation—had purchased a Sony boom box at the Radio Shack in Ketchum, the FBI found out. His daughter in Bremerton thinks he was taking it home to his grandson as a gift. This model boom box contains six D batteries. Maybe Allen Boyd carried the boom box onto *Sacajawea,* so it wouldn't be jostled around with the rest of the luggage in the hold. This little piece of battery you've found could've come from that boom box."

"That's a stretch, Joe."

"Follow me." I led him through a hole in the fuselage that no aviation engineer had ever designed. A workstation had been lent to me, and I sat behind the computer monitor. He stationed himself at my shoulder while I called up a document.

"Take a look," I said. "This is the debris summary from Pan Am 103, all the stuff found on the ground near Lockerbie when *Maid of the Seas* came down." I tapped in several commands. "Now I break out the debris into type, and it shows that eighty-two commercial batteries—Duracell, Fuji, Eveready, and others—were found on the debris trail." Again I entered a command. "And six different batteries were found in some state of penetration into the structure, driven there by the blast or sudden depressurization of the cabin or the impact with the ground. Sure, one or two of these might've been powering the timer on the bomb that brought down *Maid of the Seas,* but not all of them."

"Your point is that a passenger plane is full of batteries."

"The piece of battery you found isn't conclusive proof of a bomb, Bruce. Maybe it's part of a timing device, and maybe it isn't."

He scratched his ear. He knew I was right.

"Well, we all have moments of enthusiasm," he said. "But I'm beginning to lay my bets with our FBI friends."

He returned to the ladder and climbed back up into the fuselage. I lifted the phone and pressed the redial button and in a moment said, "Room 308, please."

The operator at St. Luke's Medical Center in Boise told me that room 308 was vacant, so I asked for the nurses' station on the third floor.

I said into the phone, "I'm looking for Linda Dillon, who was a patient in room 308."

"She's not here." The nurse's voice was testy.

"She was released? I thought she was going to be there for several days for observation."

"She released herself," the nurse said. "She showed her badge, and when I still objected, she showed me the handle of her pistol, and pushed right by me. So she's gone." The tone implied good riddance.

I punched in the number for her desk at the outlet store field headquarters in Hailey, and there she was. She tried to bark, "Special Agent Dillon," giving it authority, but it came out windy and weak.

"What are you doing?" I asked.

"What I'm paid for. Working."

"You sound like you need a respirator."

"I'll live." She breathed through her teeth, probably from pain.

"What about the hole in your neck?"

"Nothing's leaking." I heard her tap her keyboard.

Buckshot had soared into her throat just above the body armor. It hadn't hit anything critical, the doctors told me, but it was still a deep pit where there shouldn't be one. She had also been hit in the left hand, the lead shot going clean through her flesh into the wood of her shotgun.

Bill Fitzpatrick was in a drawer at the Ada County morgue in Boise. Most of the shotgun's load had hit him in the face. Ed Fahey had rigged a spring gun in his closet where he kept his arsenal. Fahey had designed a release, hidden above the door frame, so that he could disarm the spring gun when he wanted to stroke one of his rifles. Ed Fahey had somehow given the FBI the slip, and now every law enforcement official in six states was looking for him.

"Linda, you need to be in the hospital. You still need some care."

"Are you at the reconstruction hangar?" she asked.

"Yeah."

"Pretty bleak place, I'll bet."

"Yes, but worse is the gate outside, where relatives of the dead are hanging around, asking us questions every time we come and go. They have posted a vigil. They want to know what happened to their loved ones, who is responsible. They are grieving and angry at the same time."

"You online?" she asked.

"Sure." I had an ISDN connection, so my computer was always connected to the NTSB and FBI.

"Get to our page. Do you have the new code?" The access code was changed daily.

I typed it in.

Linda said, "Go to 48BD, insurance coverage."

When I did, a list of *Sacajawea*'s passengers appeared. Next to each name was the name of one or more insurance companies, and the types of insurance and the amount of proceeds due upon that person's death.

I whistled. "The insurance industry took a hit, didn't they?"

She breathed quickly, small yips.

"Linda, do you have any pain medication? You're sitting there in agony."

"Pain is just part of life's rich tapestry." She inhaled hugely. "This document is new, just posted. With some of the companies, a polite request worked, with others we had to threaten them with subpoenas. It took a long time to get this. What is Plastore Corporation?"

"A maker of plastic component parts, based in Tacoma. It has contracts with Ford and John Deere and Boeing and others."

"So Allen O'Neil, the CEO of Plastore Corporation, had a ten million dollar term insurance policy on his life?"

"That's not unusual, not for someone making a million a year."

"How about Windward Design Corporation?"

"A marine architecture firm. Has its offices not too far from the Longliner Tavern, near Fisherman's Terminal."

"Says here that its founder and president, Peter Crabtree, was insured for eight and a half million. I guess I should've been a marine architect."

"Crabtree is one of the timber Crabtrees. If you build a house around here, the wood usually has a big *C* stamped on it. He inherited a ton of money, and didn't want anything to do with the family business, which his brothers run. He designs boats for fun. He doesn't need to work. That's not an inordinate amount of insurance for him, either."

"And his wife was insured for five million?"

"The rich live differently than you and me. A photo of him in the newspaper two or three years ago showed him in front of his eighteen-car garage on Mercer Island. He collects old cars. He's got a Dusenberg worth more than I've earned in the nineties. Any insurance company would write that amount on those people."

"Wayne Ray's wife had a policy on her for three million?" Her voice was husky with exertion.

"She wasn't the only heavily insured Emerald Airlines spouse on that trip." I pointed at the screen, as if she could see me, sitting five hundred miles away. "Emerald Airlines Captain Phyllis Thorpe was deadheading on the trip, sitting in first class. She was insured for a million, and her husband Ronald, a software engineer and one of the Microsoft millionaires, was sitting next to her, and he was insured for four million."

"Still, three million is a lot of money. And Wayne's wife, Charlotte, died on *Sacajawea*."

"You are looking for a motive?"

"Always."

"No motive here, though. Wayne's father, Charles, the founder of Emerald Air, has been giving Wayne stock in Emerald Airlines over the years, and Wayne has also been earning hefty stock options as part of his salary. Before *Sacajawea* came down, Wayne owned Emerald stock worth about six million dollars. Now, with the stock taking the *Sacajawea* hit, Wayne's stock is worth a little more than four million. So Wayne lost a bundle when *Sacajawea* came apart. *Sacajawea* was the worst thing that could have happened to his net worth."

"Well, nuts." She was struggling to get the words out.

"Linda, you okay?"

She gasped, then tried to hide a whimper of pain. "Damn, you wouldn't think a couple of small holes would . . . would hurt so much."

"You need to get back to the hospital." Silence at the other end of the line. "Linda, you listening?"

"There was over twenty-five million dollars in insurance coverage on the passengers and crew on that plane, an extraordinarily high amount." She seemed stronger. "I'm trying to follow the money."

"Lots of well-off folks were returning from expensive ski vacations," I pointed out. "The amount doesn't surprise me."

"I . . . I think that . . ." Her voice faded.

"Linda?"

"Follow the money . . . is the first thing they teach you."

"Will you please ask somebody to drive you back to the hospital?"

Silence from her end.

After a few more seconds, I said, "Linda, say something."

When I heard the phone handset drop onto her desk or the floor, I punched up another line and number.

I heard, "FBI Hailey field office, Special Agent Suarez."

"Take a look over your shoulder, Jamie. I think Linda Dillon is on the floor, at her carrel."

After two seconds, Suarez blurted, "Ah, hell," and dropped the phone, and I could hear his footsteps as he ran toward her.

FIFTEEN

Black was everywhere, with only a few dashes of color, mostly on scarves. Many women wore hats. Handkerchiefs dabbed at faces. The coffin was about to begin its slow descent into the ground. A second coffin was nearby, still on its drapery-covered blocks. The coffins were pearl-colored metal with brass handles and decorative brass loops and swirls.

The Evergreen-Washelli cemetery in north Seattle was the last resting place of Emerald Airlines Captain Phyllis Thorpe and her husband, Ronald. The Thorpes had been traveling on an Emerald pass, returning from a few days of skiing. The Thorpes' two teenage children stood by the grave, each holding the hand of a grandparent, Phyllis Thorpe's parents. The children were openly sobbing, the girl with her head tucked into her grandfather's shoulder. Gray clouds slipped by overhead, and graveyard trees rustled and bent with the breeze. A Bible in one hand, a minister in a black cassock with a white tippet around his neck stood near the children.

Over 200 people were at graveside. Two hundred and twelve, to be precise. Friends and family, many from Emerald Air and Microsoft. The Thorpes must have been well liked, because the crowd—even in the back rows—showed more grief than mere relief at an obligation almost fulfilled. When the Evergreen-Washelli representative operated the levers, the hydraulic machine began lowering the coffin into the hole. The Thorpes' daughter managed to toss her bouquet onto the coffin before turning back to her grandfather. The old man's cheeks were shiny with tears. His wife's face was behind a veil. She was bent low in her grief, as if she were being pummeled. The coffin sank into the ground.

This was my second grim event of the day. My wife's memorial service had been held at our church that morning. Her body had been found a quarter mile from the main crash site. "She looked almost alive," the coroner Susan Halsey had told me, but with a look that begged me not to inquire further. During the service, Sarah had been stronger than me, squeezing my hand the entire time, glancing at me regularly, telling me with her eyes that she was all right, and that I could use whatever strength I had for myself. Afterwards, I was exhausted and limp.

"Freeze it there," Fred Yamashita ordered.

The graveside tableau jerked once, then came to a standstill.

"Bring up the names," he said.

Jeff Rose entered a few keystrokes. Black data boxes opened near most faces at the graveside service.

"We're still missing a few names," Bridget Thompson said. She was the agent from the Terrorism Research Analytical Center. "Take a look, Joe. Recognize anybody who doesn't have a computer tag?"

I knew many of the people up on the screen. The NTSB had sent a delegation, and Dick Dahlberg and his assistant Tom LaLonde were several rows behind the deceaseds' family. They had already been tagged. Charles Ray was next to his son Wayne. The elder Ray's cheeks were damp and glistening in the sunlight. Wayne's head was turned, and he was speaking with a fellow I didn't know, but whose data block identified as Dwight Vaughn.

"Who is Dwight Vaughn?" I asked.

"Wayne Ray's wife died on *Sacajawea*, as you know. That's Charlotte's brother. Lives in Hawaii."

"They don't like each other, looks like," Fred Yamashita said. Dwight Vaughn appeared to be snarling at Wayne Ray.

"Wayne is being yelled at all the time by grieving relatives who don't have anywhere else to vent," I said. "He's taking a beating, but he views it as part of his job to help the relatives of the dead, even if it means being their target." I leaned toward the screen. At least five of the people gathered around the casket were labeled FBI. I recognized Jamie Suarez.

Yamashita replied, "The FBI attends funerals. The perpetrator often can't keep away. We have profiles we look for."

Seattle's mayor was labeled, as was his press secretary. Washington State's lieutenant governor was also there, as was Allen Chapman, head of the pilots' union, a union button on his lapel. Aurelio Lopez had been the first officer on *Sacajawea*, and his widow, Maria, stood next to Chapman. She would attend her husband's funeral the day after this one. She was rigid with grief, her hands at her sides as if at attention. She had been unable to save her tears for her husband's service, and they coursed down her cheeks unattended. Two Seattle *Times* reporters were tagged, as were those from Seattle television stations. Gwen Pritchard, the widow of *Sacajawea*'s pilot, was also graveside.

When Jeff Rose clicked his keyboard, an arrow appeared in the sky over the coffin. When he moved the mouse, the arrow descended to a blond man wearing a gray sports coat who was frozen while scratching his chin.

"Who is that?" Bridget Thompson asked.

"Bad News Barnes," I replied. "He's the NTSB director of field operations. His real name is Franklin Barnes. The FAA usually gets the first news of an accident, and they alert Barnes via a red telephone on Barnes's desk. Then Barnes dispatches the Go Team. When Barnes calls, it's bad news."

When Rose typed in his name, a data box opened next to Barnes.

"Why did he attend this funeral?" Yamashita asked.

"Same reason Dick Dahlberg did and the mayor did. Respect for the dead."

"Jeff, let's get the reverse angle," Yamashita said.

The scene blinked out, and was replaced by a new set of mourners, who were looking at the casket from the other side. Behind them, visible through the trees, traffic passed on Aurora Avenue. More Thorpe family members were identified, and family friends, and many Emerald pilots and flight attendants. The FBI agent with the video camera who had taken the first angle was also labeled, his face hidden behind the camera.

Bridget Thompson asked me if I knew the identity of several more people who were so far without tags, and I knew the name of only one more, Michael Bagley, a reporter for an alternative weekly newspaper who had come to the Longliner for one of our gigs. Bagley had apparently been at the tavern to drink beer rather than work, because he never wrote anything about the band in his piece of dirt newspaper. Jeff Rose filled in a data box for him.

Repair and test records from Aero Transport France had been received, more recent ones on disk, older ones in boxes flown into Seattle on an ATF corporate jet. Pierre Lemercier could have insisted we retrieve them, but he was living up to his reputation by sending them to us immediately and at his considerable expense. The records were in French, of course. IIC Rich Shrader had requested ten Foreign Service translators to work on the records, and they had arrived from Washington, D.C. I had nothing to do except my liaising, which Shrader insisted on. He wanted to know what the FBI was doing. And the FBI thought I might be able to identify mourners. So I sat here watching a funeral. I don't like funerals, and in particular I'm not looking forward to the last one I'll attend.

"Jeff, unpause it," Yamashita said.

The video panned left, and as more guests at the service came into view, data boxes popped up next to most of them.

"Freeze it now. Highlight the lady in the veil, Bridget."

The arrow settled next to a woman in a broad-brimmed Sophia Loren–style hat. A translucent veil hung from the brim. She was wearing a black pleated dress and a gray blouse under a square-shouldered wool coat that was open and hung to her ankles. A necklace glinted in the light. Her lips moved, whispering to herself.

"Is there a chance you know who this is?" Yamashita asked.

I shook my head.

"Jeff, bring up another photo of her."

A still photograph of the same woman appeared on the screen next to the video projection. The 35mm camera had been to the woman's right, so the photo showed her right side from her waist up. Her face was obscured by the veil and the shade under the hat's brim. Her hair hung over her ears and was gathered at the back of her neck by a clasp. Her hair was as dark as a raven's wing.

"Enlarge the photo, Jeff, and remove the veil from her face."

The woman seemed to jump at us as her face abruptly became four times larger. An instant later the diaphanous fabric over her face vanished. Her eyes and nose were now visible. Her nose was hooked nicely, and lent her face intelligence and authority. Her cheekbones were pronounced, and her chin was fine-boned. Her face was now slightly more blurry than were her hat and shoulders.

I asked, "You have a computer program that eliminates veils?"

"I programmed it myself," Jeff Rose crowed. "The computer accents the second layer—her face—and eliminates the first layer, which is the cross-hatching of the veil. Then it fills in the eliminated area by extending lines and planes of the face."

"I still don't recognize her," I said.

"Notice that she is standing a little apart from everyone else, as if she doesn't know anybody else there," Yamashita pointed out. "And she has put herself in the back of the crowd, as if she doesn't want to be noticed."

Bridget added, "We've had her jewelry analyzed. She has a three-carat diamond on her left ring finger. Her necklace contains a row of one-carat emeralds set in white gold, and is worth more than most Seattle homes. Her coat is made by Langres, the Parisian couturier, and is available only in France and Switzerland. For the price of the coat, your Seattle house could have a swimming pool."

"This same woman attended Captain Pritchard's funeral the day before this one," Rose said.

"There are five other people we have yet to ID, not counting this one." Yamashita removed his glasses to wipe the lenses on his tie. "I don't doubt we'll find out who the others are because they all look like they should attend this funeral. They look like Pacific Northwesterners, people grieving, looking like

Emerald Air families, looking like they belong. This woman doesn't fit in. No one knows who she is, and she apparently didn't know anybody at the funeral, at least not well enough to stand next to anyone and make small talk. No one offered this lady condolences, and she offered none to anyone."

Bridget added, "She showed up, stood a little apart from everyone else, then left. That's peculiar behavior at a funeral, where people use each others' shoulders."

"Why didn't you follow her when she left the cemetery?" I asked.

"We hadn't analyzed the photos yet, and didn't know she had also been at Captain Pritchard's graveside service."

"Did she appear the next day at Aurelio Lopez's funeral or at the cemetery?"

"No cemetery for him because he was cremated. But she wasn't at the Lopez memorial service at St. Mark's."

"She's not the dead man's—Ronald Thorpe's—extramarital girlfriend, is she?" I asked. "The great secret and happiness of his life?"

"Little chance of that," Bridget replied. "Thorpe was a straight arrow, a devoted family man. We've been fooled before, but we've studied him and his family closely, and it doesn't seem likely."

"Besides, look at her." Yamashita returned his glasses to his nose, then pointed as if I couldn't find her on the screen. "She isn't the type who has dalliances with us working stiffs. She is pedigreed, moneyed, and so would be any boyfriend she ever had. She just doesn't fit in here."

I asked, "Is there any possibility—the remotest of possibilities—that she has anything to do with those goobers over in Idaho? Or the poacher who saw the missile?"

Yamashita's face turned as cold as a carving. "Those goobers, as you call them, are murderers. At least Ed Fahey is. You kill someone with a spring gun, even inside your own house, you are a murderer. An FBI agent is dead."

I spread my hands, an apology. "I mean, those are your only other leads, Ed Fahey and the other Idaho Resisters, and the poacher's missile."

Bridget Thompson said; "It's unthinkable that this woman would have anything to do with Ed Fahey or Doug Dietz or Runny Smith or the Idaho Resisters. And even less thinkable she even knows Thad the Poacher. She is about two million years later in human evolution."

"Maybe she's one of those folks who attends funerals for fun," I suggested.

"She doesn't have that look," Yamashita said.

"They have a look?"

"Yes, and she's not one of them, though there were quite a few funeral fans at these Emerald services."

Bridget said, "We've IDed all of them already."

"I want to find out who this woman is." Yamashita was talking more to himself now. "I think she's important but I don't know why."

"Some of you FBI agents are rolling your eyes at my so-called spark theory," I said, trying to keep the satisfaction in my voice to a minimum. "But here you are, snooping around at funerals. So who is working on better leads, you or me?"

Yamashita stared unpleasantly at me.

The telephone rang. Bridget held the receiver to her ear, then announced, "Linda Dillon is trying to break out of the hospital again. And, Joe, this time your daughter Sarah is helping her."

I didn't say anything, just pushed myself out of the chair and hurried for the door.

SIXTEEN

I found Linda Dillon in the surgery theater at St. Luke's. I had left my daughter in the waiting area, and had gotten past the desk by flashing my NTSB badge, which is big and gold, but other than that won't get you a cup of coffee anywhere if anybody looks closely at it. I stared at Linda through the window in the surgery's door.

Linda was on an operating table, her wounded arm supported by a table extension on which was a disposable armrest. Two lights were over the table. A surgeon was bent over her arm, and an anesthesiologist was behind his machine near the headrest. Near the table was an IV pole. Two garbage bags on wheels were near the table, one for cloth, one for paper. A scrub nurse was doing something at her small desk on which was a computer monitor. On the wall above her was a marking board, where she logged in what was in the field, such as sponges, so they wouldn't be left anywhere inappropriate, such as inside the patient. Also noted on the board was when the tourniquet went up. Near the board was a needle-and-sharp-instrument drop box. An X-ray view box was on another wall, with four slots above and four below. Linda's eyes were open.

When a nurse passed me in the hall, I asked for a mask.

"Who are you?" she demanded.

Again I held up my badge. She hesitated, then produced a mask and a cap from cupboards near a nurses' workstation. I clumsily put them on, then pushed through the double doors into the surgery.

The surgeon looked up. "Who are you?"

I knew I was pushing my luck with the badge, but I held it up anyway. "Joe Durant."

He squinted at the badge. "The National Transportation Safety Board?"

I nodded, feeling ridiculous. Linda smiled up at me. Her wrist was laid open, bloody sinew looking like a red rose.

"How'd you get in here?" The surgeon didn't wait for an answer. "Get the hell out of my operating room."

"Linda, you look terrible," I said nicely.

"You can be quite a comfort, Joe." Her voice was faraway. She licked her lips. "They've got me on some happy juice. Putting it into my veins."

The anesthesiologist asked, "Linda, this isn't your husband you were telling us about, is it?"

"Of all the goddamn gall." The surgeon's mask was billowing with his words. "A federal bureaucrat posing as a cop enters my surgery. Get out."

I hadn't seen anybody following me, but a man dressed in a banker's suit entered the room. He was holding the mask to his face so I didn't recognize him on my first glance. Then I saw the hair. The badger's streak of white in his hair was a political cartoonist's dream.

The surgeon was wearing a hood that covered his forehead and sides of his face, resembling a child's ski hat. Its strings were crisscrossed under his chin and tied at the nape of his neck. He yelled, "What in the goddamn hell is going on?"

The scrub nurse lifted the wall telephone and spoke into it, nervously eyeing the other intruder and me. Near her was a Mayo stand for sterile instruments.

When the man held up a wallet, the surgeon said, "Another fake cop?"

The man in the suit said, "I'm William Henley, director of the FBI."

"Yeah, and I'm Mr. Bojangles."

Director Henley lowered his hand, holding the mask, revealing his face just long enough for the surgeon to recognize him.

The surgeon hesitated, glanced at the anesthesiologist, then asked in a humble tone, "This isn't about my taxes, is it? My lawyer said he had cleared up that little misunderstanding."

"I'd get up and salute, sir," Linda said, "but they've got me strapped to the table."

Director Henley patted her shoulder.

"What are you doing here, sir," she asked.

"If one of my agents is injured, I have to visit her. It's in the manual."

"Is that a joke, sir? I can't tell due to the Valium they have me on."

"It's a joke." He nodded at me. "I saw Joe Durant enter the operating room, and I figured if they let him in, they'd let anybody in."

I was gratified Director Henley remembered my name. Three days ago he had granted me three minutes to brief him about the possibility of sparks igniting fuel vapor in *Sacajawea*'s center fuel tank. At the end of it, he had said only, "That's clever." Director Henley wanted a bomber as much as any of his subordinates.

The anesthesiologist said, "It isn't Valium. It's Versed, a cousin of Valium. Linda will act appropriately during this operation, will answer questions, can talk just fine, and she won't remember a single thing after it's done, not anything."

The director asked, "She won't remember my visit?"

"Sure I will," Linda insisted.

The anesthesiologist shook his head. "With Versed on board, she'll have no memory of it, sir."

The director smiled. "I'm here to buck you up, Linda, but I guess if you won't remember my visit, I'm wasting my time."

"Sarah's out in the waiting room," Linda said. "She's so sweet. She visited me in my hospital room, and when I asked her to help me break out, she didn't hesitate."

"What are you doing?" the FBI director asked the surgeon.

The surgeon struggled with his control, evident in the chewing motion behind the mask. In one gloved hand was a scalpel and in the other a bulb-tipped syringe. He finally said, "I'm debriding the wound. In the first procedure, I left the buckshot in. But it must have dragged in some bacteria."

"Why didn't you take the buckshot out in the first procedure?" I asked.

"A small piece of metal can usually be safely left in a wound, if taking it out means tearing up a lot of tissue. But it didn't work. The wound pussed out. So now I'm doing an I and D on the abscess."

"Irrigation and debridement," the anesthesiologist helped.

"Now that it has become infected, I have to get the buckshot out because otherwise it'll become a nidus for infection, like a sliver. So I'm opening the hole up, taking the shot out, irrigating the wound, and cutting out any dead tissue. I'll close it partly, but I won't stitch it all the way up. I'll put a Penrose drain in it so any further fluid can drain out."

The door was flung open. Wayne Ray rushed in. He hadn't bothered with a mask. "Director Henley, may I have a word with you?"

"I am trying to perform a surgical procedure here." The surgeon's forehead had gained a cheery rose hue.

"Whatever you want to tell me can wait, Mr. Ray, I'm sure. Well, Linda, I'm going to recommend you for the FBI valor medal."

"That's great, sir."

"But if I change my mind, you won't remember it anyway."

"Please." The surgeon's hand—the one with the blade— was shaking with anger. "I simply cannot work in this environment. We have an open wound in this room. It needs attention."

The nurse handed Wayne Ray a mask. He tied it awkwardly, trying mightily not to muss his hair. "Director Henley, I've been trying for several days to get ahold of you, without any luck."

The director said to me, "I have a good secretary."

Ray said through the mask, "Emerald Airlines is failing. We are headed to bankruptcy. Ever since *Sacajawea* went down, and ever since word got out about the letter threatening an Emerald plane, we haven't generated any revenue. Our expenses remain high, with gate rental and salaries and hangar overhead. Operating losses are running at three hundred fifty thousand dollars per day, and are accelerating."

"You've come to the wrong place for advice on running an airline," Director Henley said dryly.

When the surgeon motioned to the back tray, the nurse brought him a power lavage, with a small electric motor on it, that both blew water into the wound and sucked the water and blood and pus out. She took away the bulb syringe. The surgeon leaned over Linda's arm and went back to work. I averted my eyes from her arm.

"You have enough evidence to announce you have determined who brought down *Sacajawea*," Ray said.

"I've been assured by the U.S. attorney that we don't."

Ray fairly yelled, "There were two Redeye missiles in Ed Fahey's closet, behind the shotgun that brought down your agents. Two surface-to-air missiles and a goddamn machine gun."

The missiles that had been in Ed Fahey's closet were antiques. The first Redeye missiles had been delivered to the U.S. Army in 1964, and had been largely replaced by the Stinger. The Redeye was a soldier's nightmare. He had to wait until the target aircraft passed him—often allowing the target time to drop its payload—then aim the missile on a pursuit course, wait for the infrared lock-on buzzer, and finally fire the missile. Each seeker cell required a cooling unit, and three were packed with each missile tube. The Redeye struck me as being beyond Ed Fahey. The FBI had yet to determine how he had come to possess them.

Director Henley said, "We have warrants out on Ed Fahey for murder and for unlawful weapons possession."

"That doesn't help Emerald Air in the slightest." Perhaps Wayne Ray had seen the director in the parking lot, and had run after him into the hospital, because Ray brought his hand across his head, wiping away perspiration. "I won't be able to convince customers to fly us until you announce the terrorists have been caught. Emerald has become a pariah, and it's going to stay that way until the bastards have been arrested."

"There is no provable connection between Ed Fahey and the downing of your airplane, Mr. Ray."

Veins pulsed along Ray's temple. "The man had anti-aircraft missiles in his closet. What more do you want?"

The director's correctness grew on him. He was no longer having fun. "We'd be laughed out of court, Mr. Ray."

"But there's eyewitness testimony of a missile blast. And Ed Fahey has Redeye missiles in his goddamn home. Isn't that enough?"

I said, "While the NTSB can't as yet rule out a missile, it's more likely that the overpressure occurred as a result of an incident entirely inside the plane."

Ray inhaled deeply, a crater in his mask. He looked away, looked at a tiled wall. "I've got twelve hundred employees who are going to lose their jobs. What about them and their families? What do I tell them? What about Emerald stockholders who have seen their investments in Emerald shrink and shrink?" He paused, then said in a low voice, "I'm losing my father's business."

"We'll find whoever was responsible," Director Henley said.

"He built it up, I'm tearing it down."

The director added in a kinder tone, "Hang on—you and your airline—until we find them, Mr. Ray. We'll catch them."

Wayne Ray turned for the door. "Emerald Air might not be around to celebrate it." He pushed his way out of the surgery.

Director Henley looked down at Linda. "Give yourself a rest when you get out of here, Linda. We'll be able to carry on for a while without you."

She smiled vacantly.

I followed Henley toward the swinging door, me nodding to the anesthesiologist. The surgeon said something, some parting shot, but he didn't have the nerve to say it loud enough for us to hear clearly.

Henley said good-bye and left me for the elevator. I found Sarah in the waiting room.

"Linda is in good hands. She's awake, and wisecracking full

steam. They'll be done with her shortly. We can visit her this evening."

"I saw the way you barged into the operating room." She looked at me. "That was way cool."

Funny how a little throwaway comment can make you feel so good.

Director Henley's elevator had already come and gone. Sarah punched the button. She looked at me again. I had the impression she was reevaluating her old dad.

She said it again. "That was way cool."

More torn and twisted sections of *Sacajawea*'s wings had been arriving at the hangar every day. Strips of the metal skin and the spars were curled unnaturally and folded at odd angles, a collection of grotesqueries. Chalk marks on the concrete indicated sorting areas, where portions of the wings were arranged in rough approximation of a completed structure. Bruce Hereford and his crew had tagged every piece with a bar code.

Hereford and I and Ardis Tower, a mechanic on loan from Boeing, were working on a section of *Sacajawea*'s port wing. We wore surgical gloves. A tool belt was around Tower's waist, and he was clearly in his element, ordering us to lift this way and pull that way. Tower must have been a linebacker before he came to Boeing. His sleeves were tight over his biceps, and the pants around his muscular thighs appeared to have been painted on. The fuel tank had been wadded up like paper bound for the wastebasket. Tower worked with a hydraulic spreader. An air hose lay at his feet, and it snaked away to a compressor near the wall. He could plug the hose into an array of tools on the rolling tool carriage behind him, including an air impact wrench and a power cutter. We were untangling the tank to look at the terminal block.

Search teams on the mountain had not found the central fuel tank's terminal block, nor had they found any portion of that tank. It was either the nexus of the explosion, or had been very near it, and the tank was probably in a thousand pieces scattered over five square miles.

We worked until we were perspiring, and then could finally reach the block, which resembled a plug in the tank. This tank—from the port wing—had been ripped open during the crash, but the fuel had not ignited, unlike at the starboard wing. Many of that wing's components had been charred black.

"Try not to scuff the block when you pull it out, will you, Ardis?" I asked. "I need it in original condition, if possible."

The mechanic looked at me like I might be a moron. Then he used the power wrench on three bolts. Next came an impact tool, resembling a miniature jackhammer. He broke through several soldered joints.

"It's ready," he said. "The seal will give you some resistance."

Wires that had connected the fuel probes to cockpit gauges were missing, lost in the impact. I gripped the plastic block, my fingers finding only narrow purchase. Hereford helped, while Tower braced the tank. We inched the block out of its slot.

I held it up. The terminal block was the size of a one-pound butter package. On one side were the tiny metal probes. On the other were electric contacts.

I ran my fingers along the corners of the block, and tried to suppress rising excitement. "These edges are rough."

Hereford took the block from me. Ardis Tower pulled a flashlight from his belt, and pointed the beam at the block.

"Doesn't look like any sort of decomposition," Hereford

said. "Probably done in the manufacturing process. I wonder why. The Honeywell block we showed Lemercier had smooth edges."

"Different manufacturing technique, I suppose."

Tiny serrations were cut into all edges of the cube.

I glanced at Hereford. "This roughness might have punctured wire insulation near the contacts."

Hereford wrinkled his nose. "That's a different theory from the one presented by the cracks in the Poly-X wire insulation, isn't it, Joe? I mean, you are looking at two potential flaws now."

"I'm interested in how an electric spark could've entered the fuel tank via the probes in the central fuel tank's terminal block, how a surge got into a low-voltage wire. Maybe it has something to do with the Poly-X cracks or maybe with these serrated block edges, or some combination. I don't know."

"Or maybe your theory is all vapor," Hereford commented. "The FBI thinks so. They are hot on the trail of a bomber."

I rubbed my temple with a latex-covered finger, trying not to grimace at myself. "It's a feeble construct, Bruce, my theory about an overcharge. A whiff of fact from the FBI, and it'll topple."

He smiled at me. "That's why Rich Shrader took you on. So you'd chase down goofy theories like you always do." He moved away, toward his carrel near the fuselage, high-stepping over wing parts, leaving me with the block. "Keep at it, Joe."

SEVENTEEN

The Branding Iron was a cowboy bar, and I don't like cowboy bars because too many of them feature country bands, and I'd rather have a colonoscopy than listen to country music. It is little known that early in his career Gene Autry sang the blues, but then something went wrong in his head and out came "Rudolph the Red-Nosed Reindeer."

The bar had an open microphone on Wednesday nights. On the small stage was a lady, somewhere in her fifties, wearing a denim skirt with tassels, playing a solid metal National guitar and torturing us with a Lovin' Spoonful song. Reflections from the shiny guitar hit us in the face again and again. Once in a while her nose would hit the microphone, and we'd hear the amplified bumps. Nobody was listening to her.

I asked Linda Dillon, "What were your FBI peers yanking you about, referring to the mouse?"

She had checked herself out of St. Luke's once again, and this time no one saw any profit in taking her back. Her wrap and drain were under her jacket.

"I taught a class on interrogation at the academy for a while."

Sarah leaned forward to hear Linda, the singer having

cranked up her amplifier, so that what she lacked in talent she would make up for in volume. "The FBI academy?"

Linda didn't respond. She was taking the prescription painkiller Percodan, and was sometimes here in the tavern and sometimes on the moon.

"The mouse," I prompted.

"I would have a student sit at the interview table, the rest of the class watching. I would pull out a mouse from my pocket. A little thing, brown and cute. I'd put it on the table, and give that student and class just long enough to realize what it was. The mouse would sniff around."

Other than visiting Linda at the hospital earlier, I had spent the entire day staring at a computer screen, and my eyes were stinging. The document I had been preparing—actually, half document, half spreadsheet—carried the mild-mannered title "Electric and Fuel Systems Repair Trends." I added it to my database as the translations came in, e-mailed to me by the translators on a template document I had created. My computer program could generate graphs and pie charts in many snappy colors, and I was focusing on twenty-two different parts of the plane, out of an estimated 200,000 parts on any given ATF 94, looking for patterns of maintenance and repair. Translation of these French documents was tedious, and so distilling the records for even this small number of airplane parts was slow.

I admit now to being a partisan to my spark theory. NTSB investigators are professionally open-minded, but they are also human, and they begin to feel parental about their own ideas. I wanted the truth to come out about *Sacajawea*—all of us NTSB and FBI investigators did—but I would be happier if it turned out to be my truth.

So I was disappointed when early returns did not show a pattern of failure in the ATF 94 systems I was examining. Repairs to gauges and switches had been made to ATF 94s around the world by many airlines, but nothing seemed unduly worrisome. Nothing leaped out as being higher than standard repair rates on these systems in all commercial planes.

Because I was the NTSB's pipeline to the FBI, Rich Shrader also assigned me to freight and luggage analysis, which—unlike some of the more arcane aircraft systems examinations—was of major concern to both organizations. *Sacajawea*'s passengers and crew had checked in 340 items. We were unaware of the number of carry-on items, but pegged it at 1.8 pieces per passenger, the industry average on short-haul destination-resort flights. The plane also carried 85 pieces of freight and 44 packages sent by U.S. mail or Federal Express or United Parcel Service and other package shippers. Our count was becoming more accurate daily as intended recipients of freight or mail discovered and reported the losses. My examination, particularly in trying to find some odd package or some peculiar method of delivering a package to the Hailey airport, might be critical to the investigation. I had made more than eighty phone calls that day regarding luggage and packages.

Fifteen straight hours I had worked, and now I was rummy, though not as much as Linda.

My daughter asked, "So what did you do, Linda? With the mouse on the table?"

"I slapped my hand down on it, squishing it, then lifted it by the tail and put it into my mouth."

Sarah's hand flew to her mouth.

"I chewed it up and swallowed it, skull and all."

"No," my daughter exclaimed. "What would your class do?"

Linda hesitated. "When?" The drug was working on her.

"When you ate the mouse."

"The student across the table usually puked, and some of the rest of the class did, too. But it told them that I would do anything, absolutely anything, to get at the truth. That was the lesson."

"I could never, ever do that," Sarah said.

"Mice taste a little like buffalo wings, by the way," Linda said. "Where am I?"

"At the Branding Iron tavern," I said.

"Why am I here?"

"You asked to come here. You said I must be having a terrible effect on you, because you wanted to listen to some live music. This is the only place in Ketchum that has live music tonight."

She nodded. A diet Seven-Up was on the table in front of her, next to her bottle of painkillers. She had just taken another one. The Branding Iron was filled with dead animals. A stuffed cougar was above the backbar, its fangs bared, its coat a little tattered. A bear's pelt was spread on a wall next to two Chinese pheasants, their wings spread, their wild coloring glorious even in the dusky tavern. On the bar was some other awful animal, looking like a stunted bear, but meaner, maybe a wolverine. On a shelf over the door to the rest room were a cobra and a mongoose, the snake wrapped in diminishing spirals around the mongoose, the mongoose's teeth sunk into the reptile's neck, one of those taxidermal nightmares sailors brought back from the Philippines after World War II. From another wall hung the head of a moose, wavy lips and droopy snout, looking rather forlorn in its predicament. Next to it was an antique display case from the National Ammunition Company, showing its lethal products in precise rows, from .50-caliber buffalo gun ammunition down to .22-caliber varmint ammo. Another glass case, this one from the Chicago Steel Foundry, displayed two dozen different styles of barbed wire. The tavern smelled of old cigarettes and Pine Sol.

I asked, "What does your husband do, Linda?"

"He drinks."

The tavern's customers were a mix of vacationing skiers, most bent over the Branding Iron's famous baked potatoes, and locals, most at the bar throwing back well drinks. The Branding Iron's owner was behind the bar, pulling spigots and dipping a scoop into an ice bucket. The backbar was a labored assemblage of fluted walnut columns, intricate moldings, and beveled mirrors that had been carved in San Francisco and barged up the Columbia and Snake Rivers a century ago.

After a moment, Sarah asked, all innocence, "What does he drink?"

"If he runs out of vodka, he'll drink vanilla. That's why I haven't made a vanilla cake in five years. My German chocolate is good, though."

"Why would he drink vanilla?" Sarah asked.

"Because it has alcohol in it, and he's a knee-walking drunk."

Percodan was doing her talking. Unlike with Versed, Linda would remember this conversation tomorrow. She wouldn't like it.

"I'm sorry, Linda," my daughter said. "I didn't know."

"I didn't know either, when I married him."

Sarah asked, "What's your husband's name?"

"Kevin. It's a weak name. I should have known."

"Do you have a picture of Kevin?"

Linda reached into her handbag for her wallet. Inside the bag, her pistol clunked against the table. I wondered whether someone on Percodan should be carrying around such firepower. She passed a snapshot to Sarah, using her good hand.

Sarah studied it. "Wow."

When she handed it to me, I said, "He looks a little too much like Tom Cruise for my taste."

"That picture was taken before the adipose tissue began collecting on his nose," Linda said.

When I passed the photo back, she missed it on her first attempt. She blinked, then tried again, opening her hand wide to snare it.

"Why don't you ditch him?" Sarah asked.

Linda said, "I took a vow before God and a few other witnesses. I'm married to Kevin. Plain and simple. Good times and bad."

The lady with the National guitar stepped down from the stage to a dusting of applause, mostly at her leaving. She was replaced by an accordion player, a gentleman in his sixties with a white walrus mustache that hid his lips. He was wearing a Tam o' Shanter with a feather in it and leather lederhosen. He bowed stiffly over his accordion, then lit into "Lady of Spain."

"He sticks by me, as well as he can." Linda reached for her Seven-Up. "And I stick by him."

"That's so cool, Linda." My daughter had begun to worship Linda Dillon. I don't think either of them realized it yet.

"Kevin doesn't lie. He doesn't cheat. He works hard when he can. He loves me. And he drinks." She put a finger to the corner of her eye. "Yes, sir, he drinks."

Sarah tentatively reached across the table to put her hand on the FBI agent's arm.

Linda looked at me. "Why are you playing an accordion? I thought you played a harmonica."

"That's not me up on the stage. I'm sitting right here."

She stared at me.

"When are you going to be finished with the painkillers, Linda?" I asked. "You're killing me all the time with those pills."

"I'll try to go without them tomorrow." Sarah helped Linda into her jacket. "When is that?"

"It's the day after today." I left a tip on the table and started toward the door. Linda's white FBI Monte Carlo glowed blue from a Rolling Rock neon sign in the tavern's window.

"Do you want me to drive?" Linda asked.

My daughter took Linda's arm and squeezed it, then maybe thinking that insufficient, put an arm around her shoulders, half guiding her and half hugging her toward the door.

Sarah said sweetly, "With you driving, Linda, we'll end up in Australia or somewhere."

EIGHTEEN

The house was packed for the big screening. Investigators from a dozen agencies and representatives of the plane manufacturer and engine maker and the pilots' union were arrayed in chairs facing the screen. Behind them loomed *Sacajawea*, still with pieces missing, still looking shot-through, but more complete than in any previous day. To the FBI, the plane was a scarred, mute, unceasing reminder that the murderers of its passengers were still at large. To many NTSB investigators, the hulk was a reminder that no single theory of its destruction had as yet been agreed upon. To me, it said that I hadn't yet figured out how a spark entered the fuel tank.

Linda took a seat next to me. She glanced at me, then looked at the head table, then looked back. "That stuff I said about my husband."

"Yeah?"

"I shouldn't have inflicted it on you and Sarah."

"I didn't mind."

"Sarah is too young to suffer stories about my husband's . . . health problems."

"If she can take her mother ditching us, she can take that."

"It's a lot to dump on a fifteen-year-old. Sorry."

The IIC, Rich Shrader, said, "All right, let's put it up."

Jeff Rose bent over his projector. The white wall of the hangar was the screen. Lights in the building dimmed, and blue sky appeared on the wall, bluer at the top, and a few clouds high and to the left.

"This is our best-estimate re-creation." The hangar did not have a public address system, so Shrader was almost yelling. "Everything we know about the downing of *Sacajawea* that would be visible from a hundred yards off its left wing is in this computer animation."

An airplane, an ATF 94 turboprop wingover, appeared on the wall, coming into the field of sky from our right. Emerald Airlines's dark green logo—an airplane superimposed on a flashy emerald—was painted on the tail, and *Emerald Air* was on the fuselage and *Sacajawea* was below the pilot's windscreen. The port propeller was a blur. Sunlight glinted off the pilot's windshield. The plane gained slightly on the background clouds. A thin contrail streamed from the wing. When it was centered in the square of sky, it stopped gaining on the left-frame edge.

"*Sacajawea* is descending to eleven thousand feet, at five-ten in the afternoon. The plane has been picked up by Seattle Center. At this moment, this is a routine flight, and there is nothing untoward occurring inside or outside the plane."

Someone said, "Except maybe there's a Redeye missile headed toward it."

"We have found no evidence of warhead penetration," said Bruce Hereford.

"You've got an eyewitness who swears he saw a missile trail, a witness who passes a lie detector test," an FBI agent argued.

"Put a cork in it, Greg," Linda said. "Let's get on with this."

"You still on drugs, Linda?" the FBI agent named Greg countered. "But then, who'd know?"

The FBI agents in the hangar would deny it if asked, but they were desperate to pin *Sacajawea* on Ed Fahey, whose booby trap had brought down one of their own. A spring gun killing might only result in a prison term, but those convicted of bringing down *Sacajawea* would likely have an appointment with an executioner.

"Here it goes," Shrader said.

The plane's fuselage behind the cockpit abruptly looked as if it had been smattered with black paint, holes opening in metal.

"High-speed particle damage," Shrader said.

Strips of the fuselage immediately peeled back, some blowing off, some hanging from the fuselage like errant pieces of tape. The plane's left wing dipped, and the right wing lifted into sight. Loose objects shot out of the gaps, too fast to be recognizable, maybe blankets and pillows and purses. Then out came a human body, sucked from the plane, catching on something and flapping like a rag doll, then ripping loose and soaring out of sight.

Shrader said, "That was Robert Pendergrast, who had been in seat 3B. The medical examiner reports that he was already dead, shot through with shrapnel or debris before he left his seat."

Then another person, this one still strapped to a chair, was pulled out of the cabin. The chair remained wedged for an instant. The person's head wiggled violently, and then the seat broke through the fuselage, and it and its occupant streamed aft.

"That was Melissa Bradford and seat 1D. She was probably alive when she went through the gap, but the wind snapped her head and broke her neck when she was stuck there, so the medical examiner says."

An ATF agent asked, "How can you tell who went out first? By where they landed?"

"Where they landed, right," Shrader replied. "We know exactly the route of the plane, its altitude, and the time of day, so it's just a matter of geometry figuring out what passenger left the plane when."

Bruce Hereford cut in, "Says the fellow who had almost nothing to do with that so-called geometry." He was smiling, but narrowly. "We had to take into consideration many other factors, including variables we could only estimate, such as the wind. Even though the hydraulics and most of the electric system cut out, the flight data recorder was saving readings on engine power, flight control positions, and the like, in one-second intervals. It was a newer, solid-state FDR, and so is extremely reliable. Putting this sequence together was a mammoth job of mapping and mathematics. It was not done on a handheld calculator, Rich."

"I am suitably contrite," Shrader said, sounding anything but contrite.

Neither Hereford nor Shrader mentioned that a flight data recorder is like a tombstone. When you read the results, people are already dead.

The aircraft righted itself, but only for a few seconds, then the left wing lifted too high, and we could see the underside of the wings and fuselage.

"Here Captain Pritchard and First Officer Lopez are fighting to control the plane. They are working the wheel and pedals. But the hydraulics are already gone."

More of the fuselage peeled away. Items spilled from the plane in a steady flow.

"Now begins the spiral," Shrader said. "The first of three."

This time when the wing came up, it kept coming up until

it was vertical to the ground and we could see the undercarriage. The nose sank toward the ground.

"The FDR indicates the left aileron has been lowered, and it stays in that position for twenty-eight seconds. And the rudder is in right hard-over, and stays there for those same twenty-eight seconds. So the plane must spiral, and you can see, that's just what it does."

Sacajawea rolled over, its vertical fin pointing at the ground. An emergency hatch had been flung open and items streamed out.

"Those are snack trays," Jeff Rose said. "Pretzels and cheese sticks and apple juice on that flight."

When the turboprop came out of the spiral it was plummeting at a forty-five-degree angle. Much of the metal skin behind the cockpit had peeled back, giving the plane a ruff like a lion. The aircraft's nose came up ten degrees, then lowered, then came up again, then down again.

"The bucking you see is caused by the irregular aerodynamics of the jutting metal. Nothing is happening to the control surfaces to cause this, so says the recorder."

The left wing swung up again. The plane rolled over, graceful and slow, almost peacefully, except for the detritus coming from the hatch and the gaps in the fuselage.

"Depressurization was almost instantaneous, of course, but now the slipstream is blowing things out of the cabin."

Susan Halsey said, "We think about a third of the passengers died before impact with the ground because projectiles hit them in the cabin. Winds inside the passenger area were three hundred miles an hour, so it was like a tornado in there."

A person appeared at the hatch, head and shoulders clearly visible. He appeared to wrestle himself out, and he cartwheeled down and away.

Shrader referred to notes in his hand. "That was Emery Davis. He may have jumped out, or he may have been blown out."

"I made it look like he jumped, for dramatic effect," Jeff Rose said.

The plane rolled upright again, then yawed left and right. Terrain became visible at the bottom of the screen, jagged mountain peaks in the distance and forested slopes in the foreground. More skin peeled away.

"It pulls out of its last spiral, and its nose comes up fifteen degrees. For a few seconds here, the plane is once again flying within its design parameters, almost as if it's coming in for a landing, if you don't count the additional hundred fifty miles an hour."

The ground rose with sickening speed. Treetops fluttered by, then the aircraft banked a few degrees, lowering the left wing, and that's when a tree trunk sheared off the wing. Panels burst from the frame. The wing was there, and then it was gone, exposing for an instant the mechanics around the wing root. *Sacajawea* began a lateral acceleration, the tail coming around, the plane's heading changing even though the course remained true.

Jeff Rose said, "I've omitted trees in the foreground, so our view can follow the plane down."

Another tree sliced *Sacajawea*'s belly open, front to back, like filleting a fish.

Shrader said, "*Sacajawea*'s ground speed when it hit this tree is two hundred forty-eight miles an hour."

Luggage spilled out as if a bomb bay had opened. The plane careened sideways, its tail coming around, and another tree sliced through the fuselage behind the cockpit, severing the flight deck from the rest of the aircraft. Other trees ripped into the fuselage, churning the passengers like a food mixer. Pieces of the plane hit the hillside, rendered in white and brown. The animation froze when the last of the *Sacajawea*'s pieces came to rest on the snow.

"Anybody want to see it in slow motion?" Jeff Rose asked.

A deputy U.S. attorney said, "We'll show that to a jury, maybe wait for the penalty phase."

"That's our best estimate," the IIC said. "We'll continue to tweak it as new information comes in, but at this time we don't have any new flight path or weather or wreckage distribution information coming in, so I don't think this computer account of *Sacajawea*'s last seconds is going to change." He rubbed his hands together. "All right, let's break up."

Susan Halsey signaled me, and Linda and I walked back along *Sacajawea*'s carcass to join her. Dick Dahlberg was already at Dr. Halsey's desk. FBI Assistant Director Frederick Yamashita approached her desk, also at her signal. Sitting next to Halsey was Dr. Thomas French, the aviation pathologist from Cal Berkeley. I had worked with him before, and I shook his hand. He was a slight man, skinny everywhere, with the look of a long-distance runner. He wore a diamond stud in his ear—but never before a jury—and a tuft of a ponytail secured by a rubber band at the back of his head. He was this country's leading authority on identification of air crash victims. He took a day off when Jerry Garcia died.

Several documents were spread out on the desk top in front of Susan Halsey. She waited until we were gathered around. "We've run into a stone wall on three Emerald 37 bodies."

"What does that mean?" Linda asked.

French picked up a document from the desk. "Three males, sitting in seats 4A and B, and 5B, are shown on the passenger manifest as Abraham Mahalick, Edward Johnson, and Curtis Mahmoud." He tossed the paper back onto the desk, a gesture of dismissal. "The names were aliases, all of them."

"Their Emerald tickets were purchased with cash," Yamashita said.

"Isn't that unusual?" Linda asked.

I replied, "Four, five, six people on every flight pay with bills pulled from their wallets or purses. Some people just don't use credit cards, preferring wads of money. It's common enough so that ticket agents don't even look up from their computer screens."

Yamashita said, "We took photographs of their faces—the two that had faces when their bodies were found, Mahalick and Johnson—and altered the photos slightly by computer to make them look less beat up and a little more alive, and showed the photos all over Ketchum and Hailey. My agents took the photos to the ski-lift operators, to hotel clerks, to shuttle-bus drivers, car rental agents, restaurant employees, the works. Nobody recognizes any of them except for the Emerald ticket agent in Hailey."

"They were in Ketchum and Sun Valley, and nobody recognizes them, nobody at all?" Linda asked. "How does that happen?"

Yamashita shook his head.

"We've had Ellen Bever, the Duke forensic anthropologist, look at the bodies," Dr. Halsey said. "She bases her conclusion on DNA typing. She concludes all three were of the Semitic peoples."

"Semitic?" Linda asked. "From Israel?"

"From somewhere in the Middle East and maybe from northern Africa, not just Israel. At least that's their genetic heritage," Susan Halsey said. "But at least one of them—

Abraham Mahalick in 4A—lived in North America, or at least he was a visitor here at one point. Some time ago Mahalick suffered a both-bone forearm fracture. The radius and ulna were snapped. To make the repair, a surgeon bolted a metal plate to the bones over the fracture, a permanent plate, which allowed the bones to knit back together."

Thomas French said, "The fracture occurred at least five years ago, judging from development of bone near the plate."

"Holding the plate to the bone were cruciate-head screws," Susan said. "They look like regular carpenter's screws, and the surgeon installs them with an instrument that resembles a flathead screwdriver. Such screws are used almost exclusively by American surgeons. European and Middle Eastern doctors use a hexagonal-head screw, using a tool like an Allen wrench."

"So Abraham Mahalick could be from the Middle East, or he could be a fifth-generation American of Middle Eastern heritage," Linda said. "That's not too helpful."

Yamashita cracked a knuckle. He was good at it, and it sounded like a gunshot. He said, "Three guys on the same plane, all with Middle Eastern–Northern African DNA, all flying under aliases."

I asked Yamashita, "You've tried for a fingerprint match?"

"The prints were lifted off their cold dead fingers. Our computers show no matches. We've also had our odontologists from the dental identification team examine them. Nothing there, either."

"Did you send the prints overseas?" Linda asked.

"The Mossad had nothing, nor did Turkey's MIT, nor Egypt's State Security Service, nor Russia's Federal Security Service. We haven't heard from the Saudis or Jordanians, but they'll come through."

"They must have said something to the ticket agent," Linda said. "Any accents?"

"The agent said no, but then admits to having only heard a few words," Yamashita replied, "and might not have caught an accent."

"Maybe they were just changing planes in Hailey," Linda suggested. "And that's why nobody in the area recognizes them."

"Hailey—Sun Valley—is a destination airport," I said. "You change planes in Boise or Twin Falls or Salt Lake City or Seattle en route to or from Sun Valley. Nobody changes planes in Hailey."

"Well, these three didn't just spring from the ground like Topsy."

"Yes, they did." Yamashita smiled. "At least, judging from the current state of our information, these three just materialized at the airport and got onto *Sacajawea* headed for Seattle."

"These three guys," I said. "Could they have had anything to do with the Idaho Resisters, with Ed Fahey and his cronies?"

"Ed Fahey likes vanilla people," Yamashita said. "These three—rather, the two for whom we had faces—looked Middle Eastern. Dark hair, olive skin, brown eyes. Right out of biblical lands. Fahey wouldn't be caught dead with them."

Linda Dillon gingerly touched the bandage around her wrist. She was taking nothing stronger than aspirin.

"Maybe these three John Does were just on a ski vacation," Linda suggested. "Getting away from their wives, smoking some cigars and getting tight, making fools of themselves in singles' bars. From the little we know, that's as likely a scenario as anything mysterious involving the Middle East."

"I doubt it, because nobody at Sun Valley recognizes their photos." Yamashita masterfully cracked another knuckle. I wondered how he did it. "It's my guess these fellows went to such great lengths to hide their travels because they were up to something."

Susan Halsey and Tom French went back to looking at X-rays, so we left them at the desk.

Stepping quickly, his excitement visible on his face, Yamashita led us back toward *Sacajawea's* remains. "It's my hunch that these three are the best lead we've got right now, better than the Idaho Resisters, better than the poacher's claimed surface-to-air missile. Better than your convict who sends you an anonymous e-mail, Joe. And certainly better than your vapor theory."

"I call it my spark theory, not my vapor theory."

Yamashita wasn't listening. "I'm going to bring a lot of resources to this ID job, a ton of resources. And nobody who works for me is going to rest until we find out who these three guys are."

NINETEEN

The Grand Summit trailer park was neither grand nor at the summit, but it was indeed a trailer park, and a dog the color of tobacco spit charged us as we got out of the car. The animal skidded to a stop a dozen yards from us, its yellow fangs showing and its tail low, making sounds at the back of its throat, hair stiff along its spine.

"Beat it, cur," Linda said, not even looking at the animal.

The dog turned tail and slunk away, toward a stack of rain-sodden mattresses near a trailer. The animal slipped behind the mattresses, then under the trailer, next to a Yamaha dirt bike that was missing its rear wheel, the frame supported by short four-by-six pieces of lumber. We passed that trailer, then by six plastic barrels filled with empty brown and green beer bottles, then between trailers that had been laid out with Communist Bloc precision. A few had flowerpots hanging from brackets near the doors, the plants beaten down by the mountain winter. We walked carefully, avoiding ruts filled with brown water. Iridescent oil sheens floated atop muddy potholes. The driveway had once been gravel, but the stones had been packed into the dirt over the years, and most of the drive's surface was sodden crabgrass and cigarette butts and tin cans smashed flat. We picked our way along.

"There's no law against paying cash for a car," I observed.

"Stacks of hundred-dollar bills with rubber bands around them?" Linda was wearing a belted Burberry trench coat over jeans and boots, and a Wallace tartan scarf. Her arm was in a sling under the coat. The injury at her neck was now covered with a small dressing that did not show under her sweater and scarf. "So the car dealer thinks it's dope money and calls us."

"What kind of car dealer turns down stacks of hundred-dollar bills?" I asked. "First time in history."

"The woman changed her mind, the dealer said, when she looked out the dealership window and saw a Harley-Davidson sign across the street. She scooped up her money and left, jay-walked across four lanes of Aurora Avenue traffic, suitcase of cash under her arm."

"You think there's anything to this?"

"There's eight FBI and ATF agents surrounding her trailer right now, waiting for the result of our little talk with her."

I looked around. "I don't see anybody."

She smiled and glanced sideways at me. "You don't see a lot."

"I see the Harley-Davidson." I gestured at the last trailer in the lot. "Fire-engine red with blue stripes, all dressed out. Big saddlebags and chromed everything."

Linda had drawn the assignment because she was a priest, the FBI nickname for agents who for one reason or another excel at getting people to talk to them. We passed several more trailers, most up on cinder blocks. A few had lattice over the breezeways below the trailers, others had chicken wire. A sticker on one trailer announced PROTECTED BY SMITH AND WESSON. A wheelbarrow contained firewood, just claimed from the national forest that bordered the trailer park. Aluminum siding hung by one screw from the front of one trailer, exposing a tissue-thin layer of pink insulation. Gray wisps of smoke drifted away from several chimney pipes. A rusted-out exercise bicycle was near the rear of one trailer.

Mountains rose in all directions, snow still at the peaks. The low murmur of highway traffic came from the nearby interstate. Douglas firs girded the lot. These trailers were used by ski-area workers, full in the winter and mostly empty the rest of the year. Some were boarded up, with plywood over the windows.

"This one's hers, all right," Linda said. "Look at the boxes."

Outside the last trailer's door were seven or eight cardboard boxes with brand names stamped on them. On top of the trailer was a pizza-size satellite dish, but it was lying facedown on the roof, its installation apparently abandoned. Chained to a two-by-four that served as a banister up to the trailer's door was a Grimaldi mountain bicycle, the rear wheel still in the carton, and bubble wrap around the frame. The big Harley was parked next to it. The sound of electro-rock was coming from the trailer. The bass was all the way up, making it sound like the bass player was kicking his guitar with army boots. Another sound was mixed in with the music, something from the jungle, a peculiar screech. Then a dog barked. The strange sounds might have been from the CD—anything was possible with that music—but I doubted it.

"That bike cost about two thousand dollars," I said loudly, over the pulsating bass. "Sarah was lobbying me for one a while back."

Linda climbed to the porch and knocked lightly on the door, nothing like the standard police knock. We waited a moment, until it was clear that the person inside hadn't heard a thing over the music. Linda leaned over the railing and rapped a window with her wedding ring, timing her tattoo between the bass riffs. On her third try, the music abruptly stopped.

After a moment the door opened, just a slit at first, then more when Linda offered a glassy smile, full of her perfect teeth. "May we speak with you, Jennifer?"

"Why? Who are you? The police?"

"Sort of, but we're nicer than the police." She held up her ID. "FBI."

"I haven't done anything wrong." Her tone mixed both relief that the knock had finally come, and defiance that anyone might suggest that she had acted improperly.

"May we come in?" Linda tossed and caught her FBI badge as if it were a slight thing, then slid it into her coat pocket.

Jennifer Daily shrugged, the spaghetti strap of her black dress elegantly rising and falling. She was in pointy shoes with four-inch spike heels, and she tottered as she stepped back to open the door. "Sure. Come in."

Her hair was piled high, a complicated mass of loose curls and pins, done up for a big night, and tinted in honey tones. Her black dress was short and tight, hiding little. Around her neck was a slender silver chain on which hung a diamond much larger than any I had ever given my wife. Her earrings were rubies set in gold circles. Cosmetics were heavy on her face, not a pore showing, nothing uncolored, her lips red and livid.

Despite the makeup, visible through the powder were purple bruises, one under each eye, resembling dark oysters. And taped along the length of her nose was a surgeon's splint.

Linda asked, "Someone rough you up, Jennifer? Something we should know about, maybe help you out?"

The young lady grinned shyly. "I had my nose done two days ago. The doctor took the knob out of it. I told him I wanted it to look like Sheryl Crow's. I'm still a bit woozy."

"You look like you've got a date tonight," I said. "All dressed up. Maybe you should stay at home, with you still woozy."

"I'm not going anywhere. The dress and shoes are new and I wanted to try them on." She gestured dismissively. "My face hurts too much to go anywhere. The plastic surgeon warned me I'd get black eyes, but I sure didn't expect these shiners. I just wanted to take the clothes out of their bags. Who are you?"

I introduced myself. Bracing herself with a palm on the small table, her heels trembling, Jennifer lowered herself into a booth. Linda slid into the other side, her back against a refrigerator. I looked around for a chair, but found none, under all the packaging and electronics, so remained standing, hoping my posture suggested a benevolent readiness to hear whatever Jennifer might want to confide. The table's linoleum was hidden under instruction booklets.

"With all this stuff, your trailer is a bit tight," I said.

"Yeah." She brought down a plastic coffee cup from a ledge under the window behind her. "I went a little crazy, maybe. But you wouldn't have believed my beat-up TV. And my stereo had been given to me by my brother when he went into the army. One of the speakers was blown, so I had to do something."

On the bed at the back of the trailer, so heavy that the mattress was buckled under it, was a thirty-five-inch television set, and next to it was a computer monitor, the protective plastic sheet still plastered to the screen and the cord still bound tightly by plastic twists. A six-piece stereo system, including a sub-woofer the size of a suitcase, was arrayed along the narrow floor to the bedroom. Jennifer had plugged it in before finding a place for it. A miniature television, still in its box stamped SONY, was on top of the refrigerator. On the seat between Linda and the girl was a laptop computer, only partly out of its box. Styrofoam packing pellets were on the table, on the seat, the floor, clinging to the thin curtains, everywhere.

An electric space heater labored away, and Jennifer must have been wearing a pint of perfume—an expensive scent, it smelled like, but a shower of it—and the trailer had the atmosphere of an orchid hothouse. On the small kitchen counter were a dozen bottles of perfume, many of the containers crystal, most of them open. A damp and wadded dishrag lay next to them, probably used for wiping away the scent after each test. The light fixture above the stove was missing, leaving a bare bulb hanging from the ceiling.

I glanced into the tiny bathroom. On the shag throw rug in front of the toilet was a camcorder and a cell phone, out of their boxes, and a boom box and portable CD player and a cordless phone, still in their boxes. On top of the closed toilet was a cage in which was a blue and red and gold macaw, silent so far, and preening its feathers one by one, its head dipping and rising, one wing held open. Under the cage, staring balefully up at the bird was a black miniature poodle. The dog had been recently groomed, with puffs of hair divided by patches of nearly shaved gray skin. He whimpered up at the bird. A red rhinestone collar circled the poodle's neck.

Jennifer caught me looking at her animals. "I always wanted a parrot."

"I think it's a macaw," I said.

"A macaw, then."

A press of shopping bags kept her closet doors open. Nordstrom and Saks and Gap bags, most with twine handles, most with tissue still wrapped around the contents. More shopping bags were on the floor below the huge television set.

"I'd offer you coffee," Jennifer said, "but I took my old microwave to the dump and haven't taken the new one out of the box. I just heat the water in the microwave, mix in some Maxwell House with a spoon. I've never gotten into the espresso thing."

Linda didn't say anything, just tapped her fingers on the table. Jennifer stared at her own hands. Her nails were scarlet ovals, out of a package. She glanced into her bathroom, and then looked at me for help. I was impassive, so she glanced up and down the trailer's hall, not knowing what to do with her eyes. I tried smiling reassuringly. The macaw shrieked once, the dog yapped, then the bird ran his bill back and forth across the cage bars, sounding like a playing card stuck in bicycle spokes.

Finally Jennifer said, in almost a whisper, "It was drug money, wasn't it?"

"'Was'?" I asked. "You are using the past tense."

She shrugged. "It wasn't that much."

"How much?" Linda asked.

"I don't know," she said in a tone of attempted indifference. "Oh, probably eighty or ninety thousand, something around there."

Linda put a touch of officialdom into her voice. "How much exactly?"

"Ninety-five thousand, two hundred and twenty dollars," she answered miserably. "All bills, no coins."

"That's some Harley you've got outside," I said. "Same colors as your macaw. Sort of a theme there."

"I bought the motorcycle for my boyfriend," Jennifer said, smiling at my deflection of the conversation away from the money. "He works in the lodge kitchen when he's not attending the U-Dub. He's gone back to school, but I thought I'd stay around here, maybe take another quarter off, try out some of my new things."

"What's his name?" I asked.

"Travis McKinley. Like the mountain. He's not really my boyfriend, but I'll bet he thinks about it when he sees the motorcycle." She smiled knowingly.

"What was the money in, Jennifer? A box of some sort?" Linda's tone indicated she was quite bored with talk of money, but had to ask a few more questions, just to get them out of the way.

"In a cardboard box."

"I mean, was it a shipper's box, like Fed Ex or UPS?"

"Yeah, I guess. But not them. Some sort of company's box. It looked like an official box of some sort."

"Do you still have the box?" I asked.

"I tossed it into the Dumpster."

Linda asked, "Where's the Dumpster?"

"They change Dumpsters every Tuesday, so it wouldn't be out there." Linda pulled gently at an earring. "The driver usually has trouble telling the Dumpster from some of the trailers around here."

When I glanced at the minuscule kitchen countertop, Jennifer said, "Those're Beer Nuts." She pointed to a plastic grocery store bag. "Six cans. Travis loves Beer Nuts. So I'll get him to my trailer with the Harley, then get him inside with the Beer Nuts."

"How much of the money do you have left?" I asked, but the macaw's shriek, followed by a bark from the poodle, obliterated the last half of my question, so I tried again. "Any money left?"

Her face clouded. "Only about fifteen or twenty thousand, I suppose. I was going to take a big cruise, maybe through the Panama Canal. There's a Carnival ship that has a seven-story neon and brass atrium."

"How'd you find the box?" Linda asked.

The bird sounded again, and so did the dog.

"I was just out in the forest, walking along a path with Gooey."

"That's your dog?" I asked. "Gooey?"

"Her real name is Anastasia, but I've never been able to house-train her, so I call her Gooey. Sometimes I get her out the door in time, sometimes I don't."

"So you are walking along the path," Linda prompted, "and you just come upon this shipping box?"

"I don't know if Gooey or I spotted it first. Just lying there, beside a tree."

"Anything else nearby?" I asked.

She sighed heavily. "A coat, or maybe part of a coat, was dangling from the branch of a bush a couple steps away. Looked like a ski parka. Red."

"Do you have that?" I asked.

The parrot squawked. Gooey barked, a peculiar, piercing, strangled sound.

"I was more interested in the package, so I left the parka there. It didn't look like it fit me, anyway."

Linda leaned back, pressing against the refrigerator. Her jaw was set, and one hand gripped the table edge. Yet she still presented a smile, locked into place, her eyes eating Jennifer Daily. I could tell Linda was trying to control herself.

She asked, "Did it occur to you that the box might have fallen from the airplane that had crashed a couple miles away?"

Jennifer gestured despairingly. "Not for a while."

"I mean, you'd seen the crash coverage on TV, hadn't you?"

"My TV had only a ten-inch screen. That's why I needed a new one."

Linda bit down in rage. The tendons of her neck stood out. The knuckles on her hand around the table ledge were white. After a moment and a long breath she asked in an admirably toneless voice, "Was the package intact? Or was some of the cash lying about?"

"It was still in the carton. You can see what I mean about the TV, though, can't you? Ten-inchers don't pack it these days." Jennifer put a finger to the corner of her eye, and brought away a tear. "And my VCR only had two heads. My brother gave it to me when he bought a new one. A hand-me-down, just like his beat-up bicycles when I was a kid." She hesitated. "Am I going to jail?"

The bird cried out. The poodle barked.

"I don't know," Linda answered.

"I thought maybe it was finders-keepers."

Linda's eyebrows approached each other a trifle.

"Well, for a while I did, for sure. Finders-keepers, I thought." Jennifer nodded vigorously. "For sure."

Linda rose from the booth, the packing pebbles squeaking under her shoes. "You need to come with us, Jennifer."

"I've got all the receipts, if that's what you're wondering."

"Where's the rest of the money?" I asked.

"Hidden in an empty carton near my closet there, under the bags. Should I get it?"

"Leave it for now. We'll post a guard around your trailer."

"Should I bring the note?"

Linda spun to the girl. "A note?"

Perhaps sensing a reprieve, Jennifer smiled. "A note was in the box with the money. No signatures or name on it or anything. Just a few words about the weather and the roads, something like that."

"Where's the note?" I asked.

"With what's left of the money. Under a rubber band on top of some bills. Should I get it?"

"We'll have evidence guys here shortly," Linda said. "Let's leave the note and the remaining money where it is. Let's go."

She rose from the nook and crossed between us to the closet, sorting through the shopping bags, and finally bringing out a black leather coat, still with the tags hanging from a sleeve. The bird loosed a sound much like a table saw biting into a board. The dog barked.

Jennifer found scissors in a drawer. She clipped off the tags and then slid the coat over her shoulders. She brought up her arm to sniff the leather. "Maybe I should wear pants with this jacket, you think? Instead of a dress?" She looked up. "Will I be back by tonight?"

"Hard to say," Linda said, tightening the belt around her coat.

"I mean, who'll look after Gooey and the parrot?" the girl asked.

I said, "I'll make sure someone does, if you aren't back."

We led her from the trailer. The macaw screamed and the dog barked. Jennifer was startled to see that six other FBI agents had gathered around her door, waiting for her. When Linda handed her off to them, Jennifer smiled demurely up at a tall agent. Jennifer wiggled her head so her ruby earrings caught the light, and grinned at him again. He guided her toward a car.

Linda went to Seattle with the girl, and I spent the next two hours at a workstation in the command center at Snoqualmie Pass. Just as I was about to leave my phone rang, and I put it to my ear.

"Joe, it's Bruce Hereford. I'm down at the reconstruction hangar. I've got some news."

"What'd you find?"

"After you left, Ardis Thomas and I continued an examination of the left wing fuel tank. We took a cutting torch to it, and we looked around on the interior surfaces. We found a chemical deposit, a buildup of some sort. At first, we didn't know what it was. So we ran tests."

No chemicals should normally be found inside an empty fuel tank. Bruce Hereford would know of my rising excitement.

He made me ask. "What was it?"

"Copper sulfide."

I inhaled sharply.

Hereford said, "The fuel tank has a marked residue of copper sulfide near the terminal block port, probably a product of corrosion."

"Copper sulfide is an energy conductor, Bruce."

"You are talking to a chemistry major, you forget."

"So we have an electricity conductor inside the tank." I could feel the pulse in my temples.

"You still don't have me convinced, Joe. Your spark theory has big gaps. And I ran the copper sulfide discovery by Fred Yamashita, and he didn't even break step."

"But maybe this copper sulfide is a link in the chain."

"Maybe. And maybe it's nothing. Most peculiar things found in a crash reconstruction turn out to mean absolutely nothing."

A few minutes later I was crossing the gravel lot to my rig—thinking about copper sulfide, of course—when a gray and black Mercedes pulled into the parking lane near mine. The car stopped, and the driver's door opened. One of the largest human beings I had ever seen emerged. He kept coming out of that car and coming out of that car. He smiled at me in what he may have thought was a pleasant way, but it only hardened his face. I fought an urge to flee. The side windows were tinted, and I couldn't see if anybody was in the backseat. He opened a back door for me, and gestured like an usher.

When I hesitated, he said, "It's important."

So I stepped closer and bent to peer inside.

The woman with the big hat at the Thorpe funeral was waiting for me, the woman who had worn all the jewelry and who had stood apart from the other mourners. I got into the car, sliding into the backseat.

She was leaning against the far door, sunk into the black pleated leather, legs crossed. The driver returned to the front seat, where he pushed the rearview mirror to one side so he could not see behind him. Then he turned on the radio to a sports talk show, probably to give us privacy in the backseat.

She stared at me. Her eyes were enormous. So was her nose, but in an exotic, pleasing way. Her lips were full and painted rose red. She was dressed in black slacks and wore a diamond the size of a dime on a pendant.

"Mr. Durant." She offered a smile. "You are with your NTSB, are you not? I have seen you on television. And you are investigating *Sacajawea?*"

I nodded.

"I have information about *Sacajawea.*"

"Why go to the trouble of cornering me in a parking lot? I've got a telephone and a fax line and an e-mail address."

"I am watched all the time," she said. "My telephone calls are listened to."

"Who watches you?" I asked.

"My . . ." She searched for a word. "My enemies. Rather, my husband's enemies."

I asked, "What has that to do with *Sacajawea?*"

"My husband died on *Sacajawea.*"

"What was his name?" I knew them all by heart.

"Prince Khalid bin Abdallah."

But not that one. "Was he traveling anonymously? With two bodyguards?" That would explain the three nameless bodies found in the field.

"I don't know whether he was traveling anonymously," she replied. "But he always had personal guards."

"Why was he in Ketchum or Sun Valley? To ski?"

"He doesn't ski. I don't know why he was there. I don't even know why he was in the United States." She pulled lightly at the hem of her skirt. She wore a silver bracelet with inset rubies. "He does not consult me about his travels."

I asked the lady, "Who are your husband's enemies?"

"The Saudi Hizballah, among others."

"I thought the Hizballah was in Lebanon," I said.

When she shook her head, her silver earrings tapped against her neck. "After the Khobar Towers bombing near Dhahran, our security services discovered that the Hizballah is also in Saudi Arabia."

The Dhahran bombing in June 1996 took the lives of nineteen U.S. airmen. Forty suspects—all members of the kingdom's Shiite minority—had been arrested. Many had been executed. The Saudis suspected the Hizballah was funded by Iran, part of Iran's long-standing effort to subvert the kingdom.

I knew that the FBI and the State Department should be in on this conversation, that they would have questions I wouldn't know to ask. "Will you meet with other investigators?"

She moved her lips without speaking.

I said, "You travel with a bodyguard, so I know you must think you are in danger."

"Mr. Durant, I am afraid. You have no idea . . ." Her words trailed off.

"I can arrange as much security as you'd like. You can even bring your driver."

She hesitated. The driver, who had been listening despite the radio, turned to nod at her. She must have trusted his judgment, because the woman told me she was staying at the Olympic in downtown Seattle, and we set a time and place to meet the following morning.

As I was getting out of the car, she said, "My husband's enemies, Mr. Durant. To kill him, they would also kill all the other *Sacajawea* passengers. They would not hesitate, not an instant."

TWENTY

"There's more to this picture than meets the eye," Jeff Rose said.

I replied, "Isn't that like saying the music is better than it sounds?"

Rose was fairly rocking back and forth with excitement. We were in a corner of the reconstruction hangar. Behind us, *Sacajawea* was dark and stricken. Rose had rounded us up, and arrayed us in front of a twenty-five-inch monitor. His fingers were on a keyboard. "This photograph is worthy of a Hallmark calendar. It shows Elvin's Ridge in the foreground and the ridges and notches and crests of Quilcote Mountain on the left and Martens Peak to the right."

"Where is this?" Fred Yamashita asked.

"Three miles from Snoqualmie summit. The camera's point of view is the poacher Thad Wilson's point of view. This isn't an actual photograph. It's a digital re-creation of the moment Wilson claims he saw a missile shooting up into the sky. The sun is in the same location, even the clouds are where they were that moment, as best we can re-create them. Same with the color and density of the haze. Same with the snow line, which we dropped to make up for the time between when Wilson says he saw the missile and when we took these images. We've even made leaves and needles a little less green, taking away their spring colors."

"How do you know this is where Wilson was standing?" Jamie Suarez asked. He was sitting between Rich Shrader and Dick Dahlberg.

"We carted him into the mountains, and he took us right to the spot. He knows the woods because he's been working them illegally most of his life." Rose fiddled with the keyboard, then the mouse. A small black square appeared on the screen, framing about a sixteenth of the image. "This is what we call a deep photo. There's more here than you can see. Each one-degree angle—both horizontally and vertically—has been photographed at a much higher resolution than on this current screen. So I open this box on the screen, drag the box anywhere I want with the mouse, then click."

The image in that square frame instantly magnified to fill the monitor's screen. Now instead of just a distant green smudge that had been the wooded side of a mountain, we could see the components of that smudge: trees, a rock precipice, a ravine, and a narrow stream of snowmelt rushing down the incline.

"How'd you get rid of the heat waves?" Linda was slowly squeezing a ball of plastic-covered dough that her physical therapist had given her.

"We did it with help from the U.S. Navy Electronic Systems Command." He added sourly, "It has to do with cruise missile targeting systems, they said, and they said I didn't need to know more about it than that."

Another empty square appeared. Rose moved it around on the screen.

"I can do it yet again," he said, "I can pick anywhere on

the magnified image I want, move the empty square over it, then click, and the magnified image is magnified again."

The image inside the square enlarged to cover the entire screen. Now we could see individual boughs of trees and the stones of a scree slope that bordered the trees.

He said, "Now we return to our first image. I begin our motion sequence."

The view of the distant slopes moved slightly, but a pine tree a few yards from the camera quickly crossed the screen.

"This represents Poacher Wilson's view as he is walking. We've even programmed in the slight lurch of his footsteps. We are viewing the image at his eye level. Now watch closely."

Snow was still near the peaks of the distant mountains. The sky was cornflower blue.

"Did you program *Sacajawea* up in the sky?" Bridget Thompson asked.

"We believe the plane was above Wilson's field of vision at this moment. Watch."

A stab of yellow light began at ground level near the end of an alpine meadow.

Linda gasped and so did I. Fred Yamashita coughed to hide his yip of surprise.

The light shot skyward, not quite at a vertical angle, gaining speed as it rose, then disappearing near the top of the screen, there and gone in a few seconds.

Yamashita demanded, "What was that?"

"I'll be goddamned," Dahlberg said. "That looks like missile backblast."

"We have not found one goddamn scintilla of evidence that a missile hit *Sacajawea*," Rich Shrader said angrily, half rising from his chair. "The explosive device was planted inside *Sacajawea*. Nobody is going to tell me otherwise."

"I wouldn't dream of it," Jeff Rose said with immense satisfaction. "Let's close up on the source of the light."

A square frame appeared again on the screen. Jeff moved it down to the alpine meadow. The image switched to a magnification of the meadow. Now the screen showed large steel structures.

"Power towers?" Yamashita asked. "Utility power towers? I don't get it."

The towers were connected to each other by eight lines, each carrying electricity to Seattle from the hydroelectric dams on the Columbia River. The towers—five-story structures resembling Erector set men—were arrayed on the steep slope as if marching toward the sky. The power lines rose almost straight up the mountain.

"I'll run it again in close-up mode," Rose said. "And I'm going to slow it down."

This time the sense of motion was less pronounced. The steel towers and the ground underneath jiggled a bit. A yellow spike of light appeared near a lower tower, then crawled up the power line.

"It's a reflection of sunlight," Rose said. "As Thad Wilson walked, his angle to the power line changed, and the power line's reflecting surface changed with him, and the reflection perceived at the poacher's moving angle climbed quickly." Rose entered keystrokes. "If the poacher had stopped, then taken three steps backwards on his trail, the reflection would have fallen from the sky. Watch."

The screen froze, then the point of view began retreating, as if the camera were being walked back down the trail. The flash of light began at the top of the slope and slid quickly down to the base, following the power line. It seemed to fall from the sky.

"Pass my compliments to the sailors." Yamashita wearily rubbed the back of his neck. "Well, that's one theory we can cross off."

"That was never a theory," Shrader said, only partially mollified. "One ex-con poacher passing a lie detector test doesn't make a theory."

Yamashita turned to Linda. "Your phone call last night sure grabbed our attention."

"Have you figured out who Khalid bin Abdallah was?" she asked.

At that morning's interview, the Woman-in-the-Hat, as she was known to all the investigators, had told Yamashita and Linda and me that her dead husband, Khalid bin Abdallah, had worked for the Saudi government, but she knew little else, not even in which Riyadh building he reported to each day.

"He was the son of a second cousin of the monarch," Yamashita told us, "and was director of the Eastern Division of their security service, which meant that he headed Saudi intelligence efforts regarding Iran."

Yamashita continued, saying that the identification of Khalid bin Abdallah as a passenger on *Sacajawea* had abruptly given the investigation an international cast and had added urgency to our work. Instead of a plea-bargaining poacher saying he saw a missile, and instead of paranoid Ed Fahey and the other Idaho Resisters, and instead of a runaway spark due to faulty wiring—my theory that was gaining credence with NTSB investigators but was still dismissed by the FBI and ATF—now a truly menacing component had been discovered. Now the Mossad and the Saudi Security Service—which didn't like to advertise that they frequently worked together— were sending delegations to Seattle, and the State Department's Office of Combating Terrorism and its Division of Intelligence and Research were multiplying their personnel commitment to the investigation. The CIA had begun doing whatever it does, much of it inside Iran and Iraq and Syria. We weren't privy to its work, but Yamashita assured us it had begun in earnest. Our meeting with Yamashita lasted another twenty minutes.

Linda Dillon and I were in her car, leaving the hangar lot, slowly passing a security gate, when someone tapped on her window, knocking loudly. A woman, bent low to the window, was walking quickly to keep up with our car, wearing a gray raincoat. Linda stopped the car and rolled down the window.

"Mr. Durant?"

I leaned across the seat to look out. "I'm Joe Durant."

"Mr. Durant, I've seen you on TV. I'm Elizabeth Shorter."

I knew the name. She was the widow of a *Sacajawea* passenger, and deserved more than a discussion through a car window. I climbed out and walked around to her. "Can I help you, Mrs. Shorter?"

"My husband, Jerry, died on . . ." She couldn't even get this small sentence out. Her voice broke off and her hands came up to her face and she half turned away. "I'm . . . I'm sorry. I have been trying . . ."

I gently put my hand on her elbow. Linda Dillon joined us.

Elizabeth Shorter struggled for a moment. Then she said, "I heard that some of the passengers on *Sacajawea* died slowly, some of the passengers in the forward area. I know that's where Jerry was sitting."

"He was in seat 3D." I have a good memory for passenger locations.

"I heard a rumor that some of the passengers may have suffered a horrible death, may have been in agony for many minutes." She wiped tears from her face. "I loved Jerry so much, and I'm trying to deal with his death, and I'm trying . . ." She heaved with the effort to control herself, but had to turn away again.

Linda reached for her other arm, squeezing it gently. "You don't want to think of his last moments as being bad ones, I know."

She nodded. Her face had slightly magnified features, with large slate-colored eyes and a broad mouth. Tears had smeared her makeup. She was wearing jeans and tennis shoes.

"Your husband, Jerry, was killed instantly," I said. "He never knew a thing, and suffered absolutely no pain."

She smiled weakly at me. "Mr. Durant, I suspect you are a kind man."

"I suppose I am."

"And you'd tell me that just to make me feel better, wouldn't you?" She sniffed mightily.

"Well, I'm not kind." Linda's warm tone betrayed her fib. "And I wouldn't stretch the truth an inch to make you feel better."

She pulled her laptop computer from the backseat and placed it on the automobile's hood, then opened the cloth case and flipped up the screen. She pressed the power button. She rolled the track ball and pressed several keys. "This is an alphabetic list of *Sacajawea*'s passengers and the medical examiner's conclusion as to how each passenger died. We call it the *Death List*. I'll scroll down to your husband's name and cause of death." Linda turned away from the screen to look at Mrs. Shorter. "It's right here. Do you want to see it? I warn you that it's graphic."

Mrs. Shorter answered without hesitation. "I want to see it."

She bent down and squinted at the screen and read aloud,

"'Gerald Shorter; decapitation by seat-back tray propelled by blast force.'"

She slowly stood upright, her gaze on a distant hill. After a moment she said, "He did die instantly, didn't he? Just as you said, Mr. Durant." She turned to us. "I never thought learning Jerry had his head cut off would make me feel better, but it does."

"I understand," I said.

She wiped away a tear. "Thank you so much. I can't tell you how relieved I am. I hadn't been able to think of Jerry— to remember all our good times together—without thinking about the agony of his death. Now I can just remember our good times together." She gripped Linda's hand, then mine, and walked away, toward the parking lot across the street.

When she was out of earshot, Linda said fiercely, "Jerry Shorter was a son of a bitch."

I rubbed the corner of my eye.

She said it again, as if I were arguing. "He was a son of a bitch."

I said, "For a minute I was afraid Mrs. Shorter was going to ask about the passenger sitting next to her husband."

Jerry Shorter owned three automobile parts stores in north Seattle. He had met his brother in Sun Valley for seven days of skiing, or so he had told his wife. The FBI had determined he was there with an auto parts rep, Cheryl Cutler, staying together at the Eldorado Condominium. This was their second ski vacation together, two winters in a row, and Shorter's brother had covered for Jerry both times.

"I'd kill Jerry Shorter if he weren't already dead," Linda said, her chin chopping in syncopation with her words.

She got back into the car. "Now a nice woman is going to grieve over a philandering piece of crap who spent his last week on earth skiing all day and boinking some tramp all night."

"It's better Mrs. Shorter never learn of it and you know it." I returned to the passenger seat.

She started the car's engine. "The Hizballah should have exploded just Jerry Shorter. I would have helped them, goddamn him."

I looked at her. "There's air between Jerry Shorter's head and his shoulders, permanently. He's dead. So is Cheryl Cutler." She had been returning to Seattle on the same plane. "You don't need to worry about it. They're both dead. Cut them some slack."

"I don't cut assholes slack." She looked at me. "Remember that."

She was smiling a little as she said it, I think.

The testing ground belonging to Western Explosives Research was in the desert northeast of Las Vegas near the Nellis Air Force Base. I had flown in that morning to help set up the experiment, but Wayne Ray, Fred Yamashita, Jamie Suarez, and Rich Shrader had come down on an FBI plane, while Pierre Lemercier and his minions had arrived on an ATF corporate jet.

We stood inside a cinder-block building, staring out across the desert. Fifty yards from us was the cradle, the Western term for the detonation site. Most of Western's clients were mine operators, for which the company supplied drilling and blasting designs. It also performed Department of Transportation classification tests and munitions tests for a number of military organizations, both U.S. and foreign.

The cradle was nothing more than a steel bench, with its horizontal surface three feet above the ground. On it was a fuel tank of the type used by Aero Transport France, manufactured by Tenvik, the Dutch metal fabrication firm. The NTSB had purchased this particular tank from Rio Bravo Reclaimers, located in Ciudad Juárez, across the border from El Paso, a firm that specialized in refurbishing aircraft fuel tanks, above-ground aviation fuel tanks, and other flammable liquid containers.

A bundle of wires lay next to the tank, some of the wires attached to the connectors on the tank's terminal block. The wires trailed away from the bench onto the iron platform at ground level. The bundle was held together by plastic harnesses. The wires led to a technicians' shed fifty yards west of the cradle. The shed was made of reinforced concrete, with no windows facing the cradle. Inside the shed were several batteries, voltage regulators, a bank of gauges, and a telephone.

"This is a setup," Wayne Ray declared. He was standing next to Lemercier at our bulletproof window. "This so-called experiment has no value whatever."

"It is a stunt," Lemercier said. "Nothing but an artificial construct designed to impress."

At four locations near the cradle were air pressure monitors manufactured by Western, each of which could sample air pressure 16,000 times a second, and later produce waveform charts.

"This is a demonstration, no more and no less," I said.

Video cameras were mounted in five places, at various distances and angles from the cradle.

Aero Transport France had retained the Seattle law firm Wallace and Anderson. Sweating in his suit and tie, Daryl Wallace intoned, "There's nothing going on here that is admissible in a court of law."

The low summits of the Meadow Valley Range were purple

in the distance, and there was only baked and flat ground between us and those hills. The sky was pale blue above clear yellow.

"You've rigged it," Ray said.

"I want to understand what is possible," I argued. "I am not preparing for a trial. This is a demonstration, nothing more."

Linda Dillon stood beside me, and next to her was a Western Explosives Research technician with a telephone to his ear. He was connected to the windowless blockhouse.

Lemercier said, "The scientific community insists on controls, and this has none."

"It's no better than a fourth-grade science experiment," Ray accused. "You've shaved off the insulation on low-voltage wires and high-voltage wires, than taped the exposed conducting cores together. You've deliberately frayed the wires attached to the terminal block. You are deliberately using a tank that has buildups of copper sulfide. This is a setup."

"I've created the worst-case scenario," I said.

Ray added, "And you are going to shoot a bolt of electricity into a tank filled with flammable fuel vapor. It doesn't take a scientist to predict what's going to happen."

I said, "The amount of electricity that will enter the low-voltage system will be a quarter of the smallest spark you feel when scuffing your foot on a rug."

The desert sun beat down on us. Sweat had formed on my every surface. Even Pierre Lemercier—the embodiment of Continental *savoir-vivre*—was seen wiping perspiration from his forehead with a linen handkerchief.

"I was until now unclear as to the nature and purpose of this demonstration," the lawyer said. "This foolishness—and your video recordings of it—will play directly into the hands of the plaintiffs' bar. On behalf of my client Aero Transport France, I now demand that you stop this so-called experiment."

"Too late." I nodded at the Western technician.

He spoke one word into the telephone.

Fifty yards in front of us, the fuel tank was instantly replaced by an orange and black ball of flame, violently expanding outward, roiling and churning, competing with the Nevada sun in intensity. It blew out and up, enveloping the cradle, washing over the nearby ground and reaching toward the blockhouse. The sound felt like a blow. A pulse of air rammed our building, shaking the viewing windows. Small pieces of the fuel tank bit into the building.

The center of the fireball disappeared first, extinguished by its own fury, leaving at its perimeter tongues of yellow and red flame curling around nothing. Then they too flickered out, until nothing was left but shimmering heat waves and black smoke. The dark cloud of smoke was dispersed by the desert's mild wind. Pieces of the fuel tank lay all around, dappling the ground. The cradle was empty entirely, as if it had been wiped off with a towel.

It would have been unprofessional for me to goad Lemercier and his lawyer and Wayne Ray about the showy success of my experiment.

So Linda did it for me. She said sweetly, "I like explosions, and this was a nice big one."

His spine ramrod straight, Lemercier turned away from us, and led his lawyer and aides away.

Wayne Ray scowled at me. "Joe, you managed to create a blast, and destroy a fuel tank. But nothing—utterly nothing—proves that you replicated conditions on board *Saca-jawea*. You just as well could've used a stick of dynamite on that tank. It would have proved about as much." He left the building, following Lemercier.

Rich Shrader waited until they were out of earshot. "Well, so an explosion of fuel vapor was possible. You've scored a point, I suppose, Joe."

I stood there, looking out at the desert.

"But Wayne Ray is right," he went on. "You created an explosion. You didn't necessarily create conditions identical to those aboard *Sacajawea.*"

"Rich, I proved everything I set out to."

All of us down from Seattle left the building, walking across the parched ground toward the cradle. Western technicians were already plugging laptop computers into the vibration sensors to obtain readouts, and removing tape from the video cameras. Shattered fragments of the fuel tank crackled under my shoes. The sun was merciless, pressing down on us.

"Lemercier's lawyer knows lawsuits are coming," Rich Shrader said, "and he'll be lying in wait to suppress any evidence about this demonstration. He'll show that you haven't proved the trail of the electric charge. Junk science, he'll call it."

"The evidence is still coming in." I looked at him. "And I'm not done yet."

TWENTY-ONE

I stood near the door to the men's lavatory, watching Idaho Resister Runny Smith carry the bomb toward the Emerald Airlines counter. His walk was peculiar, as much up and down as forward. The folds of his shirt hid most of the bomb. Smith had tucked the package tightly against his stomach, as if he hoped to make it disappear.

Special Agent Jamie Suarez had told me that a gait is as distinctive as a face. Smith walked as I imagined a Neanderthal would, his shoulders hunched, with a peculiar rolling, as if he were trying to keep his center of gravity low. His eyes were on the ground a few feet in front of him, so perhaps he didn't trust the airport lobby's floor to be smooth.

The package wasn't a real bomb, of course, but a mock-up of the explosive device that had destroyed *Sacajawea*. Same estimated size and weight, wrapped in brown paper.

Smith had been told to ignore onlookers and cameras, not to glance at the six U.S. deputy marshals who were his escorts, to act naturally. One of the marshals still had Smith's handcuffs in his hand, and was flicking them open and closed. Smith had been arrested as an accomplice to the murder of Special Agent Bill Fitzpatrick, and had not made bail. A

7-Eleven clerk had recognized Smith when he tried to purchase an economy bag of pretzels and an air freshener.

Smith's court-appointed lawyer had moved that the charge be dismissed. The hearing was the next day, and Smith was going to walk from the hearing into the streets of Boise, a free man. Not enough evidence—not any evidence, the truth be known, the U.S. attorney had told me—connecting Smith to the spring gun in Ed Fahey's closet, other than beer talk about rifles and the oppressive United States government.

This event was testament to how little effect my investigation into a fuel vapor detonation was having on the FBI. They had an explosion and they had a threatening letter and they had some suspects and were busily looking for more. And while they would tell anyone who asked that all leads—even something as fragile and quick as a spark—needed to be investigated to the very end, FBI agents generally thought my inquiry into the possibility of a spark was as pointless as an NBA all-star game. They would deny it to my face, but I felt it. My puerile response—admitted to nobody and hardly to myself—was that I would show them.

IIC Rich Shrader and his superiors at the NTSB insisted on receiving intelligence on FBI progress. Although the bureau recognized that the *Sacajawea* investigation was at this stage still both a criminal and an engineering investigation, and that the NTSB should be kept posted on progress on the criminal side, it was not the FBI's history nor inclination to easily share its hard-won information. So I was observing their operation at the Hailey airport and elsewhere. Each evening I sent Shrader e-mail regarding the FBI's progress. I was a known spy, just as Linda Dillon was a known spy.

"Don't look at me, Smith," barked the marshal with the handcuffs. "Eyes straight ahead."

The prisoner's gaze turned back to the ticket counter. "Where do I go? I don't know what to do." His voice was fogged with self-pity. His skin had a jailbird's sallow tinge. The base of his nose was almost as wide as his mouth. Broad face, vapid eyes, bangs down to his eyebrows.

"Damn it," Fred Yamashita yelled, waving his hands. "Start again. Do it over."

The marshal with the handcuffs said, "You blow it this next time, Smith, and I'm going to be upset."

Smith stared blankly at the marshal, like he might at a crossword puzzle.

"My client won't be intimidated by jailer talk." Smith's lawyer, Max Whitten, stood near the stainless-steel baggage rack at the back wall. He wore a tie decorated with tiny rainbow trout. His blond hair was receding, and he had a lofty forehead. He held his briefcase in front of him with both hands, leaning against a wall. "Even a fellow with a pistol on his belt should be polite."

Runny Smith returned to his starting position, near the glass door to the parking lot. The Hailey airport lobby was a small one, a stone's throw in length. Baggage carts pulled up outside the back and suitcases were slid through flaps onto the racks, with no moving parts other than men's arms and backs. The lobby was cheery, done in light colors with many windows.

The weight of this event was fully on the Emerald Air employees behind the counter, and their faces and gestures were carefully composed. Marcie Olsen, an Emerald counter agent for eight years, even went through the motions of writing tickets, her gaze going between Runny Smith and Wayne Ray, her boss's boss. Marcie Olsen's hair was bleached to straw, and her grin was fixed and street smart. She wore beaded earrings two inches long. Wayne Ray had told me what

I would otherwise have quickly gathered; Marcie Olsen missed little. She had worked so long at the Emerald counter that she knew the rhythm of the place, and might have sensed peculiarities the day *Sacajawea* went down, slight things that she could not now remember. This reenactment was to prod her memory.

And perhaps it might prompt Robin Crawford's memory, if such a thing existed, what with all the other odd notions up there in her head. Crawford had been working alongside Marcie Olsen that day, and the transcript of her FBI interview revealed she believed in pyramid power and that people had colored auras surrounding them, visible only to a few, including herself. Earlier that day I had asked her—my face as straight as my shinbone—what my color was, and she had squinted at me and replied, "Puce. With nice orange accents. It means you are uptight." Which wasn't news to me, frankly. Robin Crawford's hair was the red of a road flare, and combed in a style that made it appear wind was blowing in her face. She had freckles across her nose, looking like they'd been tossed there.

The Port of Hailey director, Louise Champion, was directing this re-creation. She stood between Fred Yamashita and me. She held a clipboard on which was a computer-generated timeline, indicating to the best of her knowledge, and to the compiled recollections of all others who worked at the Hailey airport, the times of arrivals and departures of visitors to the airport that day. Also worked into the timeline were reports from UPS, Federal Express, Central Idaho Forwarders, Intermountain Lines, and other package and freight handlers regarding their employees who had visited the airport. Same with car rental agencies, airlines, the USPS, Coke and Frito Lay drivers, Idaho Power—which had had a crew at the airport—the hotels that had sent courtesy-van drivers, a real estate agency that had sent someone to replenish its supply of brochures, and others.

Louise Champion apparently thought her smile too thin, because she had a quarter-inch ring of red lipstick beyond the edges of her lips, making her mouth resemble a bull's-eye. She rocked back and forth on low heels, agitated that her entire domain, the Hailey airport, had come to a halt. She said something under her breath, something I didn't quite catch, something about the electric chair for morons.

Runny Smith walked in again, this time taking the short steps of a bride on the aisle. He didn't get far.

"Do it again, goddamn it," yelled Yamashita.

"What?" Smith yelped. "What'd I do?"

"You're walking like you've got shackles on."

"Well, I had them on a few minute ago," Smith said. "My ankles still hurt."

"Do it again."

Smith glanced at his lawyer, who dipped his chin.

"And this time don't hunch over when you walk, like you've got a bellyache," Yamashita ordered. "Carry the package like it's schoolbooks."

"How do you carry schoolbooks?" Smith asked.

Yamashita rubbed his forehead. "Carry it like a lunch pail."

Smith retreated, then came in again, at first backlit by watery sunshine coming through the glass doors, then gaining color and form as he stepped deeper into the lobby. Still tentative, he walked toward the Emerald counter, the package at his side.

Marcie Olsen shook her head.

"Take your time," Yamashita suggested. "Don't rush yourself, Marcie."

"How much time does she need?" Max Whitten asked. "If she doesn't recognize him, she doesn't recognize him."

"This isn't a lineup," a deputy U.S. attorney countered.

Jamie Suarez said, "We're trying to rule people out, not rule them in."

"Yeah, yeah, so you've said." Whitten's gaze swept the FBI agents in the lobby, about ten of them. "My client wants off your list."

"Do it again, Smith." Yamashita removed his spectacles to pinch the bridge of his nose.

Other suspects wanted off the FBI's list, too. They stood in line behind me, cheek by jowl, each one of them recomposing his face again and again, trying to look innocent. Acting as the usher, Linda Dillon answered their questions and smiled to reassure them. She was wearing a flowered skirt and light blouse with a pearl brooch near her collar. She looked more like a ticket agent than an FBI agent. She kept her damaged arm across her chest, moving it little.

They weren't suspects, really, Yamashita had explained, but people of interest who had been requested to appear at the airport so the FBI could "proceed with our investigation of the *Sacajawea* without giving your file another thought," as Yamashita's letter to these folks had put it, more elegantly than the usual bureau correspondence.

Linda had called it the kook round-up. She walked over to me. "See what I mean?"

I scratched at the corner of my eye. "They don't look too bad to me."

The first man in line ran his hands through his swan-white hair, and he repeatedly licked his lips and shifted his weight back and forth, as edgy as a whippet. He smiled nervously at Linda. His hair was whiter than his teeth. He wore a plaid shirt, and his pants were tucked into the tops of his logger boots.

"His name is Leo Ballard," she said. "You know those directions on cans of spray paint, 'Point nozzle away from face'? Those were put there for Leo Ballard."

On his shirt was a button that read FREE THE SECAUCUS SEVEN. He wore an earring embossed with a tiny have-a-happy-day face. His faded blue eyes swept left and right. He raked his hair with his fingers again.

"For thirty years Leo has tried to make a living and still be a hippie," Linda said. "He has tried bead-making, tie-dyeing, and manufacturing sandals made of car tires. He's failed at them all."

"Why's he here?" I asked.

"Three years ago Leo wrapped electrician's tape around three dozen sixpenny nails, and mailed them to the governor of Idaho."

"Just the nails? No explosives?"

"No crime in mailing someone some nails, but it was sufficiently goofy so that Leo entered our database, and goofy enough to ask him to appear here today. Leo whined about having to be away from his dream catcher business."

"A dream catcher?"

"Feathers and string and beads all tied together. You hang it over your bed."

"That's enough times, Smith," Frederick Yamashita called. When he looked at the counter, Robin Crawford and Marcie Olsen shook their heads. They didn't recognize anything about Smith, not his face, not his walk.

So Yamashita said to the marshals, "You can have him back." Then he turned to Leo Ballard. "Next."

Leo Ballard walked slowly to the door, stooped, not daring

to raise his eyes from the floor, seeming to shrink under the close scrutiny. A marshal retrieved the package from Runny Smith and passed it to Ballard, who handled it with the tips of his fingers as if it were hot. Ballard stood at the door, waiting for his cue. Cuffs were placed around Smith's wrists, and he was led away, bracketed by marshals.

"Now the next fellow in line is Keith Wright. He's here because of his web page, which he calls 'Anarchist Central.'"

"Why don't anarchists ever comb their hair?" I asked.

Wright's brown hair looked like a grenade had gone off in it, with tufts sticking out at random and the rest of it matted in clumps. He wore round tortoiseshell spectacles and a homespun khaki shirt. One of the rear pockets on his jeans was fabric from a farmer's red scarf.

Linda said, "His web site has a map of Haymarket Square, a biography of Mikhail Bakunin, and treatises on how to incite uprisings among the oppressed working masses."

Wright's eyes were hostile and his mouth a snarl. I suspected this was his professional presentation, his vision of how an anarchist should look in public. His thumbs were hooked on his belt, his posture one of contempt.

"But what got our attention," Linda continued, "was his page of hot links to bomb-making sites, to how-to-beat-the-metal-detector sites, and to sites on locating hidden cameras at airports. He lives just up the road in Ketchum."

"How'd you get him to come to the airport today?" I asked.

"We've been following him since the day after *Sacajawea* was destroyed. We promised we'd take the tail off him if he'd show up today."

"That'd make me show up, too."

Linda laughed. "Not if you knew we were lying to you."

Once again Robin Crawford and Marcie Olsen indicated that no memories had been nudged.

Yamashita said in crabbed tones, "Next."

Leo Ballard tossed the package to Yamashita and dashed through the door into the sunlight, double-pumping an arm like he'd caught a touchdown. All eyes turned to Keith Wright, who walked forward with pump-and-roll insolence. When Yamashita passed him the package, Wright tossed it into the air several times. He made his way slowly to the starting spot.

"Next in line we have Kurt Cheney." Linda gently touched the wrap around her wrist. "All you need to know about Cheney you can tell from looking at him."

Cheney was stitched taut with anger. As he stepped forward, his movements were constricted, as if he were fighting against cords that bound him. He rubbed his wrists, one after the other, using exaggerated hand motions and making a production of it. He glanced around, his gaze locking onto one person after another, staring at each until each looked away. Cheney was an ax-faced man, with a jutting jaw and a nose that had been broken and was now bent out of true. The skin of his face was sunken around wide cheekbones, and his brows were knobby shelves over coffee-black eyes. He had a convict's haircut, brown stubble that hid little of his scalp. His wore a jail-issue blue khaki shirt and jeans. He glowered at Linda, then at me, then at the counter agents, trying to staple us to the walls with his menace.

Next to him was an Idaho State patrolman, in boots and hat and Sam Browne, keeping an arm's length away from Cheney, and watching Cheney's hands. I guessed that Cheney was rubbing cuff burns on his wrists.

"No?" Yamashita asked.

The two ticket agents again indicated they hadn't seen anything in Wright that prompted a memory. Others in the room who had been at the airport that day shook their heads.

"Next." Yamashita again removed his spectacles, this time to shine them on his tie.

Anarchist Wright exhaled loudly. Despite his studied disdain for the proceeding, a grin of relief split his face. He rushed out of the lobby.

Kurt Cheney moved forward, more a prowl than a walk. At the counter, Marcie Olsen brought her hand up to her mouth.

His guard, the patrolman, said, "Easy, Cheney."

The guard followed Cheney until midway into the lobby, then dropped back. Cheney wore a black scowl; his gaze moved back and forth. He refused to take the package until his guard loudly unsnapped and snapped his holster flap. The lobby was so still—all attention on Cheney—that the snapping could be heard from one end of the lobby to the other. Cheney glared evilly at the patrolman, but accepted the package, held it against his belly, and walked from the doors toward the counter.

Marcie Olsen's eyes were white all around as she watched Cheney draw close, and the tips of her fingers covered her mouth. When Yamashita glanced at her, she nodded, almost imperceptibly. Standing next to her, Robin Crawford didn't appear to share Marcie Olsen's alarm. Wayne Ray did, though, and he walked to the counter to stand near her, reassuring Marcie with his presence.

"Next," Yamashita called.

Kurt Cheney was led away, and was replaced by Lee Dunstan, there because he had served two years on an explosives charge a decade ago, and who was in turn replaced by George Seadon, there because he had gained some knowledge about explosives working on a highway construction crew and had also spent four years at Western State Hospital in Washington State, some of the time in a padded cell.

Marcie Olsen hardly watched the last two. She rocked back and forth on her heels, repeatedly nodding at Yamashita, and working her mouth as if she could barely prevent herself from shouting out to him. Wayne Ray raised his eyebrows at her, silently inquiring.

The kook round-up was over. The lobby began to empty. Yamashita crossed the floor to the Emerald ticket counter. Linda and I met him there.

Marcie Olsen blurted, "I've seen him before."

"The fourth one?" Yamashita asked. "The fellow named Kurt Cheney?"

She nodded so vigorously her earrings bounced against her neck. "At first I wasn't sure, but then when he started to walk, it came back to me. I've seen him before, right here in this lobby."

"Did you talk to him?" I asked.

She hesitated. "I'm not sure. I'm not sure whether he came to the counter, or whether he just passed by."

"Was it the day *Sacajawea* came down, can you remember?" Wayne Ray asked.

She paused again. "I think so." She squinted nicely, straining her memory. "But I can't say for sure. A lot of people come through here."

Robin Crawford added, "He has a black aura around him, especially around his hands."

Yamashita ignored her, asking Marcie Olsen, "And you don't have any doubt you've seen Kurt Cheney before, in this airport lobby?"

She vigorously shook her head. "No doubt. He's pretty memorable, you have to admit. He looks tough, looks like he beats on his head with a plank. I'm sure, never more sure of anything."

Yamashita thanked them both and said he'd get back to them. Wayne Ray left for the Emerald office at the airport. Yamashita led Linda and me from the lobby onto the sidewalk. A row of courtesy vans were lined up, ready for the airport to open again.

"Damn it to hell," Yamashita exclaimed.

"What'd you expect, Fred?" Linda asked. "Memory is fallible."

Yamashita asked bitterly, "Now what the hell do we do? We've come to another dead end."

"We were just trolling for something, anything," Linda said.

Yamashita kicked a pebble out of his way. "I'm going to hit my own head with a plank."

"What's going on?" I asked.

"Kurt Cheney—who Marcie Olsen swears she has seen before—is an FBI agent," Yamashita said.

Linda said, "He was in the lineup as a plant."

"A plant?"

"To test reliability of witnesses," Linda replied. "He's an FBI agent. He's never been in Idaho before this morning."

Kurt Cheney was waiting for us at Yamashita's car. He was grinning, and he still looked tough. He asked around a laugh, "She picked me out, didn't she?"

Linda nodded.

"I make a living ruining lineups." He laughed again. "-That's probably the main reason the FBI pays me, so I can weed out mistaken witnesses before the defendants' lawyers destroy them on cross-examination."

Yamashita reached for the car door handle and yanked it angrily. "Another damned brick wall."

TWENTY-TWO

"You look like hell," Linda said, lowering herself into the chair across from me. She plunked her handbag on the table, rattling the knife and spoon.

"I was saving that line for you," I replied, "but you actually look better." Her arm was still in a wrap, but the sling was gone.

She asked, "When's the last time you slept?"

I looked down at my bacon and scrambled eggs. "I thought I was more hungry than tired. Now I'm not so sure."

"How long were you at it?"

"Do these eggs look heavier than normal?" I asked. "I don't think I can lift them."

She waited.

I looked at my watch. "Twenty-two hours, give or take, ever since the Hailey airport walk-through."

"Find anything?"

I pinched the bridge of my nose, as if that would pump revitalizing blood into my brain. "Not one damned thing." I sighed loudly, something I didn't like to be heard doing. "So far the *Sacajawea* investigation has generated 1.2 million distinct facts, and more are coming in every day."

"So you spent most of the day yesterday and all last night going through them?"

"Only those involving ATF 94 repair records, the translations." I stabbed at the eggs. I was so tired the eggs felt like they were resisting my fork.

She reached across the table for a slice of my toast. "So you've been squinting at the screen since I last saw you? No wonder your eyes are baggy."

"My eyes are always baggy." I shoved aside my plate and put both hands around my cup of tea, hoping the warmth would flow into my fingers and calm me. It didn't. "I'm convinced the ATF 94 is a faulty plane, that there's a deadly flaw in the plane's wiring—maybe in the wiring of every single ATF 94 flying, all sixteen hundred of them around the world—but damn it, I'm not finding a pattern of user complaints or manufacturer repairs that supports me."

She slid my plate over to her, and placed a napkin across her lap. She said around a mouthful of eggs, "Do you think the repair and maintenance records you are examining have been doctored, maybe by someone at ATF, before they were sent to you?"

"Pierre Lemercier would never do such a thing, and never allow such a thing."

"Joe, the fact he was good at shooting down Messerschmitts doesn't mean he wouldn't lie and cheat to protect his company."

"Lemercier would never risk ruining his reputation, and he just wouldn't stoop to criminal activity."

"I'm hearing a case of hero worship, Joe."

I slapped the table. "And I'm telling you he is a great man and he would never cover up a dangerous situation that could imperil many lives."

I bit off my words. My old man had taught me that anger revealed weakness. I didn't want my FBI agent to think I was weak. I looked away, looked at the wall. It was mid-morning.

Sally D's restaurant in Ketchum was mostly empty, one fellow sitting at the counter, hunched over his coffee, and the waitress setting out the lunch service.

Often when I had worked late into the night on an NTSB investigation, my wife, Janie, would be waiting for me at home with a cup of tea and brandy. I'd sit there in our breakfast nook with her, exhausted, yet too wound up to sleep. She'd listen to me, nodding and encouraging, and then she'd talk me down out of my agitated state, rubbing the back of my hand, and when all the words were out, she'd walk me to bed, make sure the blinds were tight against the coming sun, then switch out the bedroom light. I had no one to do those things now, those little acts of kindness that made coming home worthwhile and getting up the next day bearable. I missed my wife. I missed Janie so much. Goddamn her.

Linda waited, maybe reading my face.

Finally I said, "There's been an awful mistake on the ATF production line, something that allows an ignition source into the fuel tank. But it isn't Pierre Lemercier's fault. It's a design flaw, or a repair flaw. Something."

Linda stared at me fully, until I brought my gaze back to her. "So you received the letter from ATF's lawyers, and it's like your hero Pierre Lemercier has turned on you."

"Yeah, maybe something like that." I turned the cup in my hands. "It was some letter. I suppose you all got copies."

"Sent to Fred Yamashita, but he showed it around."

The letter had been written by Daryl Wallace, ATF's Seattle lawyer, and it threatened me with legal action for libel and slander and intentional interference with business expectancy and outrage should I allow word of my spark theory to reach the public. The severest legal consequences in the swiftest manner possible were promised.

"Rich Shrader ran the letter by the NTSB's legal counsel," I said. "Our lawyer reports that the letter is malarkey, every word in it. There are no credible legal grounds with which to threaten me and my part of the investigation, the NTSB lawyer says."

"But you are still upset that your hero sicced his dogs on you."

"This legal posturing is part of every investigation. I'm not upset about the letter."

"Sure, you are. It's there on your face."

"No, I'm not and no it isn't."

"Don't argue with me, Joe. It'll lead to disgrace and ruin."

I laughed, sort of.

She chewed a moment. "I thought you engineers were dispassionate sorts. Electronic calculators, T-squares, pocket protectors filled with number two pencils, haircuts about two decades behind the times, dull as this toast I'm eating. But here you were a minute ago, actually showing some emotion."

"We engineers know more about the last five minutes than do you FBI agents. Maybe that's why I show a little emotion sometimes."

She reached for more toast. "The last five minutes?"

"For a major, the NTSB drafts a 'Victims' Post-Incident Cabin Record.' That's the official title, but we all call it the Horror Report. It's a second-by-second, blow-by-blow account of what the passengers endured in the time between the initial incident and when the plane hits the ground."

"Why does the NTSB bother?" She opened one of those little squares of jelly and dug it out with her knife.

"Sometimes things can be learned regarding cabin safety. But it's terrible reading. Many passengers on *Sacajawea* were tortured before they died."

She stopped chewing. "What do you mean?"

"Many of *Sacajawea*'s passengers knew what was happening. The plane was open to the air, bucking and yawing, the horizon upside down or vertical. Debris was flying through the cabin just like in a hurricane. Passengers were watching people next to them being decapitated or pierced through with debris, or sucked out of their seats and thrown around the cabin like so much chaff. The screaming and moaning, the hanging on to loved ones in the next seat. Those people knew they were going to die."

My words were a torrent, and I checked myself. She only looked at me.

I gripped my teacup too hard. "Parents on *Sacajawea* had time to know their children at home were about to become orphans. Isn't that being tortured? Husbands on the plane had time to know their wives at home would never see them again. Passengers sitting next to their children had time to hug them, knowing it was the last time, the last time ever, and that their child was about to be torn apart by impact. That's torture."

"Take it easy, Joe."

I spread my hands on the table, a broad gesture to allow me to get a breath. "I can't stand the gore at a wreck site. It chased me away from my profession. But worse than the carnage is the certain knowledge that those people were tortured and tortured, and then killed. And there's a chance it's going to happen again, on another ATF 94."

"You need some sleep, Joe."

"I can't get Pierre Lemercier and his damned ATF and the FAA and you FBIers to pay attention. These are dangerous planes. Lives are in danger, right now, right as we sit here."

The waitress looked at me.

"Joe, you are shouting," Linda said.

I leaned back in my seat and took a long breath.

"Your gauge is in the red zone, partner." She tapped the

back of my hand. "You want me to drive you to your room?"

I stared at my teacup, seeing nothing.

"Joe?"

"I've got a car out in the lot."

"You okay, Joe? I've got a meeting with Fred Yamashita and Jamie Suarez, but I can put it off, and I'll stick around, if you want. Keep you company."

I looked up. "I'm okay."

"You aren't going back to your computer, not before getting some sleep, are you?"

"I'm going to sit here and have another cup of tea." I managed a weak smile. "Then I'll go straight to bed. You go to your meeting."

She lifted her handbag, then grabbed the last piece of toast to take with her. She walked toward the restaurant's door, glancing back at me once. Her hands were full with handbag and toast, so she turned around to push open the door with her tush. Little bells on the door rang brightly. I watched through the restaurant's windows as she walked quickly back to the parking lot. She moved with the fluid grace of an athlete, something that registered on me, even in my dopey state.

"You the guy on TV?"

The words came from my right, a voice full of the Idaho backwoods, and vaguely familiar. I turned to see a mug shot come to life, Doug Dietz, his face an assortment of bony angles, with the scar across his forehead, his chin way out in front of him. His eyes were narrowed, as if staring into a strong wind, like a dog with its head out the car window. His nose was bent out of true. His sweatshirt was stretched tightly across his pectorals, and his shoulders sloped up to his neck. His arms were like hawsers. I had heard his voice before, courtesy of the FBI bug at Ed Fahey's house.

I said the wrong thing. "You are shorter than your mug shot led me to believe."

He tightened like a twisted rope, from ears to calves, I could see it under his clothes, a rippling of all those muscles, the beginning of one of his 'roid rages. He snorted something unintelligible, glaring at me like a bull at a matador, his hands balled. Then with an effort that contorted his face, he calmed some, and lowered himself to the chair opposite me, the chair probably still warm from Linda.

I was too tired to be frightened by Doug Dietz. "What do you want?"

"You the crash investigator we see on TV?"

"Joe Durant, the NTSB. What do you want?"

Dietz glanced around the café. Maybe he didn't know what he wanted. He said, "The cops are looking for me and Ed Fahey."

"You and Fahey must be smarter than you look, to have evaded the FBI this long."

Dietz rubbed his big jaw, a handful of bone, then said, "I didn't have nothing to do with Ed Fahey's closet gun. It was his house and his idea and his shotgun."

"Why are you telling me this?"

"Anybody else we could tell would arrest us." He nodded at his own logic. "You don't even got a gun or a badge."

I resisted the impulse to say that I did indeed carry a badge.

Dietz added, "I mean, Ed showed us the shotgun trap a while back, sure, but we thought it was just his way of keeping his wife away from his gun collection."

Dietz's face was the color of a walnut, a deep tan being a requirement for bodybuilding contests. And, except for the blond bristle on his head and his short goatee, he was hairless, with even the back of his wrists shaved, also done for his contests, where the bodybuilder must glisten like oilskin. His ears were tight to his head, so small they looked useless. He had a brawler's presence, ready to charge.

"I want you to tell your FBI friends that I didn't know anything about Ed Fahey's spring gun being loaded and ready, nothing at all."

"Where is Ed Fahey?" I thought I'd give it a shot.

Dietz smacked his lips and blew wind, a scoff on steroids. "Fahey would kill me."

Doug Dietz looked like he'd take a lot of killing. I fingered the spoon next to my teacup. "The FBI isn't after you for Agent Fitzpatrick's death. They want Fahey for that, but not you."

Dietz's face opened a fraction. "No? Then why do they have our houses staked out? The feds sit in their cars a hundred yards away, looking through binoculars, as if we couldn't spot them. And at my job. And at my mother's house."

"The FBI wants to chat with you about *Sacajawea*."

He shot back in his chair as if he'd taken a blow to his sternum. "The plane? The goddamn airplane? What for?"

Dietz was convincing.

I suggested, "A couple minutes with an FBI lie detector could clear up any confusion."

"*Sacajawea?*" He rose from his chair, using his arms rather than his legs, like doing a push-up, his face right in mine. "A lie detector? The hell you talking about?" He turned away, then glanced back. "I wanted to talk to you about Ed Fahey's shotgun, and you're bringing up that Emerald plane and all those people killed."

Dietz was halfway to the door when he turned back. "Don't get near me. You or any of your FBI buddies. You got that?"

I got it, exhausted as I was. A steroid-bloated Idaho hillbilly with a hair-trigger temper was threatening me. I vowed to stay closer to my armed personal FBI agent.

TWENTY-THREE

Our view was in black and white, and obscured by cheap technology, as if we were peering through a misted window. But we could see the bar's occupants well enough, two men sitting on stools, leaning so they could look at a third fellow, this one at the end of the bar, also on a stool. The two were nodding and laughing, as the man at the end of the bar told a story or some joke, the sound too indistinct to be sure.

A bartender poured a drink from a bottle lifted off the backbar, not a drink from the well. Gin, I guessed, because he followed with a vermouth bottle. He added an olive, and passed it to the man telling the story, clearing away the dead glass. The bartender looked warily at the man, who gestured widely as his tale progressed.

"Can't these joints get better video equipment?" Linda asked, leaning toward the screen, as if that might make the image clearer.

We were watching the tape on a thirty-three-inch television. The bar's lights were low, and everything on the screen was gray and grainy. Fred Yamashita had not told us why we were watching this tape, had said he wanted our impressions fresh from viewing it. The tape had been turned over to the FBI by the restaurant that morning.

"The video camera is there mostly to keep the bartenders from stealing," Yamashita said. "But also for evidence should a robbery occur, or if someone sued for an imagined personal injury."

I asked, "The camera is always rolling?"

"So the owner tells me." Yamashita pushed back the spectacles on his nose. "He recycles the tapes in the machine over and over, but he kept this one because of what happens next."

The story at the bar must have been hilarious, because the two listeners rocked back and laughed, one applauding by picking up his glass and tapping it on the bar, his cigarette bouncing up and down as he laughed. The storyteller signaled the bartender to pour another round for his friends.

"The bartender has told us that the two listeners drank on the storyteller's dime all night," Jamie Suarez said. "The storyteller insisted on it. Wouldn't let the others reach for their wallets at all."

"How much did they drink?" I asked.

"Six or seven each. One is pouring down beer from bottles, you can see. He's a peeler, the bartender called him. Peeled the labels off his beer bottles with his thumb all night."

The bartender served new drinks to all three customers at the bar. The storyteller lifted a bill from a sloppy pile of them next to his glass and passed it to the bartender, and when the bartender tried to hand back change, he was waved away. The storyteller then continued with his tale, moving his hands in a pantomime of climbing a rope, an invitation to laugh. A cash register was at one end of the bar, with a screen that the bartender poked with a finger as he rang up the purchases. On the wall was a framed print of a high-climber topping a tree.

"Those are courtesy laughs he's getting from the drinkers."

Linda was wearing a ponytail that made her look like a schoolgirl. "He buys the drinks, they listen and laugh. It's a well-understood deal."

We could only hear broken pieces of the story, something about climbing down from an air force fighter cockpit onto a runway. Voices off-camera in a nearby dining room and the bartender's work—washing glasses, filling the nut basket, moving the bin of empties to a back room—punctuated the storyteller's patter. Above the rows of bottles on the backbar was a Budweiser diorama encased in plastic, showing a team of horses pulling a beer sleigh.

Prompted by a half-heard accent from the storyteller, I leaned forward abruptly. "That's the Arabian, isn't it? The Arabian who died on *Sacajawea*."

Yamashita smiled. "It's the Lady-in-the-Hat's husband, Khalid bin Abdallah. Went down with *Sacajawea*."

"Where's this bar?" I asked.

"In Ketchum," Yamashita replied. "It's the Pines Bar and Grill on the Warm Springs road just off State 75."

"It doesn't look like a celebrity hangout," Linda said. "No fur and jewels, no after-ski fashions."

"It's a local joint," Yamashita confirmed. "Loggers and mechanics and truck drivers come in after work to loosen up, have a few before they go home. Mostly regulars. Khalid bin Abdallah was a real oddity in the place. Cultured accent, nothing less than hundred-dollar bills and a lot of them, overly polite but talking and talking, going on and on as he threw back the martinis."

Khalid was mid-sentence, laughing at something he had just said, martini glass in one hand and paper napkin in another, waving the napkin around like a flag of surrender, when his gaze snapped left.

"He's looking at the door to the dining room," Yamashita said.

A man in a dark jacket moved into the bar, holding a hand out toward Khalid, with the palm up, a gesture of appeasement and understanding. Another fellow followed the first, and both approached Khalid slowly, the first still with his hand out, and then his hands came together as he laced his fingers, resembling a position of prayer, a gesture of utter deference. The sound was only of low murmurs. The two newcomers positioned themselves at Khalid's sides, as if to escort him from the room. The bartender sidled down the bar, perhaps toward a weapon or a phone. Khalid's two listeners became still, the peeler with his beer bottle halfway to his mouth.

Yamashita said, "Those're the two other Saudis who were on *Sacajawea*, who had given their names as Edward Johnson and Curtis Mahmoud to the Emerald ticket agent. They are bodyguards, the Lady-in-the-Hat tells us. They were well known to her."

When one of the bodyguards put his hand on Khalid's arm, gently and respectfully, Khalid bin Abdallah spun to the man, shouted something in Arabic, and then viciously swung the back of his hand into the bodyguard's cheek. A wide and powerful blow that would have staggered most people, and would have enraged them. But the bodyguard was tough, and controlled, and didn't even take a half step backward. He said something to Khalid in low, placating tones. Khalid screamed at him. One of the fellows at the bar, the beer drinker, held up both hands in a conciliatory gesture.

Yamashita said, "Those two bodyguards are also baby-sitters, looks like."

The second bodyguard tried to intercede, trying to insert himself between the two men. Khalid grabbed a beer bottle from the bar and smashed it into the second bodyguard's forehead. Glass shattered and spilled onto the bodyguard's shoulders, and blood instantly flowed from his forehead, spilling over his chin. The bodyguard lurched back, but caught himself. He didn't raise a hand, didn't wipe away the blood, and didn't move to defend himself when Khalid grabbed him by the hair and yanked his head toward the edge of the bar, slamming the man's head onto the flat surface, once, then again.

The first bodyguard put both hands on Khalid's arms. The second guard righted himself, and then carefully and respectfully placed a hand on Khalid's back to guide him away from the bar. Blood flowed down his face, black and gushing on our screen.

"That would've blacked out most people," Suarez breathed. "Getting your head banged like that. Those two guys are tough, and I mean tough."

"And professionally patient," Linda added. "Look at them coddle Khalid, nudging him toward the door, sort of moving him between them."

"Help me," Khalid yelled at his new friends at the bar. "These bastards are kidnapping me." Good English, with a touch of Oxford in it.

The beer drinker made one small motion, a shift of his buttocks on the bar stool, two inches toward his Arabian drinking pal. The first bodyguard lifted a finger and pointed it right between the beer drinker's eyes, keeping it there three inches from his face for several seconds, gluing the beer drinker to his stool.

"Freeze one with a look and deal with the other," Suarez said. "A pro move."

The second bodyguard's face was a mask of blood, entirely unattended as he and his partner herded Khalid away from

the bar, talking all the while, politely but firmly pushing, their
charge squeezed between them. Khalid howled and cuffed the
first bodyguard, and lunged toward the bar to grab an ashtray.
He smashed it into the first bodyguard's cheek, then at his ear,
blows that sounded clearly from our speakers.

Khalid might have been using a pillow for all the apparent
effect the strikes had. The bodyguards continued their job of
ushering Khalid from the bar. Khalid screamed something
more in Arabic, and then all three disappeared from our view
as they passed into the Pines's dining room, the Arab's yells
fading quickly.

"This isn't the first time those two bodyguards have done
this, I'll bet," Yamashita commented. "Probably part of their
job is to get beat up once in a while by their drunk boss, and
they have to take it, no matter how tough they are, because
that's how the world works for them."

"Why is this our only record of Khalid and his guards?" I
asked. "Until this video showed up, they were invisible in
Ketchum."

"The bartender quit his job a couple of days after this happened. Left Idaho for Alaska, so he wasn't there when we can-
vassed Ketchum with the photos of the Saudis. And we
must've never found the two drinking pals, or maybe we did
and they didn't want to admit they were at the Pines for some
reason."

The tape ended and the screen went to blue. Jamie Suarez
leaned forward to punch off the television. Yamashita gathered his notes and tapped them on his lap to square them.

"But what's a director of security for the Saudi government
doing in central Idaho?" I asked again.

"He's drinking himself into a stupor," Linda said under her
breath, more to me than the others.

I looked at her.

"I've seen it done many times," she said, now to the wall. "I'm sort of an expert on it."

"Are you ready for this?" Sarah was standing at my elbow.

"I'm the father," I replied, trying to insert the key into the lock. "I should be asking you that question."

"What if we find something awful in there?"

"Like what?" I turned the key upside down and tried again. The number on the door was 12.

"Well, maybe a hookah pipe."

"No way, not in your mom's apartment."

"Or maybe some . . . I don't know . . . some dirty videos or something else totally disgusting."

"Sarah, I knew your mother, and there's nothing like that in her apartment."

"Turns out you didn't know her that well."

I fiddled with the key more than necessary. Sarah was afraid of what we would discover behind the door, and so was I. The place my wife had found in Sun Valley was at Elkhorn, a development in the shadow of Dollar Mountain. Janie had leased the condominium from its absentee owner. None of our furniture in Seattle had disappeared, so maybe the condominium had come furnished.

Sarah added, "Or maybe something dead in there, like fish in a tank. Or a bunch of crummy stinking pizza boxes."

The lock turned over, and I took a nervous breath and pushed open the door.

Sarah followed me in. The room had been closed for many days, and the air was musty. A television set, a couch with a small table at the end on which was a telephone, an eating nook in an area formed by bay windows, and not much else.

Sarah said flatly, "This isn't Mom's place."

"Sure it is."

"Mom never watched television, you know that. Never bought a *TV Guide* in her life." She indicated the table. "But there's a stack of them."

"Well, there's not much to do in Sun Valley at night, so she watched television." It sounded weak even as I said it.

"And you know how tidy Mom was. She'd never leave those *TV Guide*s in that sloppy mound on the table. And she wouldn't have left those glasses on the counter. She would have put them into the dishwasher. She was a neat freak, you know that."

I did know that. The thought occurred, not for the first anguished time, that Janie had been living with a man here.

The condominium had only one bedroom. A kitchenette was adjacent to the living room. The carpet was sand-colored. A piece of resort art—a cheaply framed pastel painting of Mount Baldy—hung over the sofa. The windows had blinds, but no curtains. Janie had been a reader—sometimes a novel every two days—but the bookshelf against the wall near the living room window contained only a ceramic cat in a ceramic basket, and a folded sweater.

"Daddy, do you think she was living with someone?"

"After me? No way. I'm an act that can't be followed." But my voice broke as I said it, and Sarah glanced at me.

I opened the coat closet near the front door. A scarf hung over a dry-cleaner's hanger, and two coats were suspended from pegs on the back wall. I recognized both coats as Janie's; no man's coats in there. Her ski outfit—a one-piece crimson jumpsuit with silver piping at the seams—was also in the closet. It hung low, so I pushed it aside looking for her boots, but they weren't in the closet.

"What kind of boots did Mom have?" I asked.

Sarah was in the tiny space the developer had termed a kitchen. She opened the refrigerator and bent to peer inside. "Nordicas. Red with blue trim."

I walked across the room into the bedroom. The bed was made, but not neatly like Janie always did, not the boot camp tuck that would bounce a coin. I opened the closet. No men's clothes here, either, thank God, just some of Janie's clothes, most of which I knew well enough. I looked down at the floor. Some flats, a pair of running shoes, and a pair of hiking boots.

"Where are her ski boots?" I asked.

"Hey, there's cat food in the cupboard here," Sarah called from the kitchen. "Did Mom have a cat? She told me after Blackie died that we'd never get another cat, that their lives were too short and she couldn't stand putting them into graves."

"Your mom was always the sensitive type." Except about the effects of ditching her husband and daughter.

I walked into the bathroom. Janie's scent still lingered, maybe on the towels. I took a long breath, filling myself with the smell. Then I noticed a yellow piece of paper on the toilet's tank lid. I brought the paper up.

It was a form, looking as if it had been torn from a pad. I felt my neck tighten as I scanned it. My voice was a low growl. "Damn them."

I hurried out of the bathroom, the receipt in my hand, Sarah staring at me. I lifted the phone on the table, but it was dead so I pulled the cell phone from my pocket. After punching in a number, I waited a few seconds, anger making my breath shallow.

Over the line came, "Suarez, FBI."

"This is Durant. You bastards searched my wife's condominium."

Suarez hesitated only a fraction. "Of course."

I was sputtering. "You went through her stuff."

"Sure."

"You didn't ask me."

He said, "You and your wife were legally separated. We didn't have to, and we thought it might be stressful for you if we told you."

"Why'd you do it?"

"We are examining the possessions of everybody who died on *Sacajawea*."

"Why?"

"Joe, we are desperate, is why. If we can gather five million items into our data bank, maybe one of them will offer us a clue, and maybe we'll find some tiny connection."

He might have been inventing on the spot, about not having to get my permission, but he was smooth, and I liked Jamie Suarez. I slowed myself. "Your people left a receipt, an FBI form. It says you took four prescription medicine bottles."

I could hear him tap a keyboard. After a few seconds Suarez said, "That's right."

"Janie didn't take any prescription drugs."

"Looks like she did. Her fingerprints were on the bottles."

"You dusted the place for fingerprints, for God's sake?"

"We want five million pieces of information, Joe."

I rubbed my forehead, the cell phone uncomfortable against my ear. "What were they, the medicines?"

"We don't know yet for sure. The lab hasn't reported."

"Come on, damn it, Jamie. Just read me the labels on the bottles."

"They were all for Effexor."

"What's that?"

"Prescription antidepressant. Potent stuff."

I said cautiously, "Janie wasn't depressed, didn't have that history."

Suarez said nothing.

"Well, I wonder . . ." My words trailed off. I closed the phone without saying anything more. I returned it to my pocket. My face was knotted, I could feel it.

Then I heard Sarah sobbing, a sudden gulp and a big wail and then a hiccup and another wail. I moved quickly back into the bedroom. She was sitting on the edge of the bed, hunched over, a hand to her cheek and the other holding a framed photograph. I slid between the wall and the bed to lower myself next to her and put my arm around her.

In the frame was a photograph of herself, taken about a year ago. Sarah in her high school letter sweater she had earned on the basketball team, big smile, a little lift to an eyebrow, wearing a sugary expression, but a mock one for the camera.

Her shoulders lurched under my arm. She brought her hand across her mouth to stop the sound, but she burbled and yipped and then wiped away tears with the tips of her fingers.

She managed to say, "Mom had a photo of me on her bedside table."

I closed my eyes, squeezing them tight. "We'll figure it out, Sarah. Don't worry now. We'll help each other and we'll figure it all out."

TWENTY-FOUR

"This is no ordinary drunk tank," I said, wishing I were driving. I dislike being a passenger in an automobile, sitting there fiddling with my kneecaps.

"Don't call it a drunk tank, you insensitive boor." Linda should have smiled, but she had the wistful look of someone returning home after a long absence. One of her hands was on the wheel and the other around a paper coffee cup with a lid and straw. She was letting the coffee go cold, too intent to sip from the cup, or maybe her arm hurt too much to lift it. She glanced left and right, maybe seeing if the grounds matched her memory.

The driveway was long and winding, bordered by azaleas not yet in bloom and a few white birch. Two gardeners were turning the soil with hoes, near a green and yellow John Deere garden tractor. Its trailer was loaded with plants in plastic containers.

"The center has its own greenhouses, couple hundred yards down a service road toward the hills," Linda said. "Plants not hardy enough for Idaho winters are plucked from the ground in the autumn, and protected in the greenhouses during the winter."

"So you had this hunch about Khalid bin Abdallah while we watched the video of him banging up his bodyguards?"

"North Star is world renowned." She slowed the car for a squirrel that sprinted across the driveway. "Their motto is something like, 'We'll dry you out, but bring your wallet.' My husband tried the place. It worked, for a while."

"I've never heard of North Star."

"Most people in Ketchum—five miles down the road behind us—have never heard of it either."

We had already been stopped at the gatehouse, then waved through after the guard's phone call to the security office. We rounded a curve, with a wall of two-man boulders on both sides of the drive. Dusty gray stonecrop grew in the gaps between the boulders. Yellow daffodils and red and purple tulips were arrayed in raised gardens, probably hothouse flowers as the season was still too cool for even early bulbs. We approached the registration building, which resembled a ski lodge, made of lodgepole pine and river rock, with a porte cochere wide enough for three automobiles. Iron urns at the entrance were filled with red geraniums.

Behind the main structure was the pool building, condensation on the skylights. It, too, was made of lodgepole pine, like Lincoln Logs, but with vast windows, with long trails of water running down the glass on the inside. Several people dozed on recliners in the sun, blankets lying over them, for it was still cool in the mountains. Cottages could be seen through larch and hemlock trees. In another direction were a garage and maintenance shop and a garden equipment storehouse, partly hidden by ivy-covered walls.

The columns holding up the roof over the car porch were carved as totems, and painted deep red and turquoise and apricot. One of the totem faces looked like a schnauzer, and another like a ferret with a trout in its mouth. Something that resembled the symbol for yin and yang was under a beaver with buck teeth. A real Indian would have requested a chainsaw.

I looked over my shoulder. "Are your pals behind us?" The gatehouse had disappeared behind a grass slope.

"Jamie Suarez and Kurt Cheney and a big truck on loan from a Boise station."

"How're they going to get by the gate?"

"Kurt Cheney stopped by a gate?" She made a scoffing noise, sounding like she needed the Heimlich maneuver. "Be serious."

When two fellows emerged from the reception building, I asked Linda, "North Star has a golf course?" One man shouldered a tan golf bag. His shoes clicked across the drive.

"Nine holes and a putting green and a pro." Linda stopped our car in front of the reception building's doors, which were heavy glass with brass handles. "The caddy carries the clubs, but his main job is to make sure there's no bourbon bottle in the bag." She stepped on the parking brake. "In the winter these guys are called 'ski buddies,' and they ski with the client all day, just to make sure the client hasn't stashed a hip flask somewhere. Kevin says it's like being handcuffed to an evil twin."

I laughed politely. "That's clever."

She hesitated. Then her words were clipped. "For a drunk? He's clever for a drunk, is what you're implying?"

I felt as if I had been caught arguing my case. I opened the door and replied lamely, "No, of course not."

"Kevin can be funny." Linda had been thinking about her husband, and now I was going to pay for it. "He makes me laugh a lot."

"I'm sure he does." I stepped toward North Star's door, wanting away from this conversation.

She said in a pavement voice, "And before you add something like 'when he trips over a sofa,' let me remind you . . ." She caught herself. Her jaw worked on nothing a moment.

"Yeah?"

"Let me remind you that you are an insensitive boor." She smiled wanly. "Have I said that before?"

Sensing a reprieve, I made a production of glancing at my wristwatch. "Not for ninety seconds at least."

From a small cubicle to one side of the entrance, a valet stepped to our car. He looked amused without a smile at our dusty FBI Chevrolet, but was kind enough to take the keys from Linda. The glass doors opened automatically, sending forth a wall of scented air, and I followed her into North Star's lobby, which was lit by skylights overhead. Fan palms sat in ceramic pots all around, providing areas of privacy. The floor was moss green marble set off by patterns of black granite tile at the edges. A blaze worked away in a stone fireplace the size of an automobile, the gas jets hissing. Three people were huddled on leather chairs, speaking urgently to a fourth, a fellow rubbing his chin and scratching one wrist then the other and taking quick breaths, and who looked like he needed a drink, as we used to say. A curving wall of glass block was behind a black pearl wood reception desk, on which was a leaded glass lamp that dappled the nearby wall in amber and blue.

Linda introduced us to the receptionist, a young woman in a tailored suit but whose lower lip—pierced with a stainless-steel brad—gave her away. We were offered a vacant smile. She lifted her telephone. I looked around. I prefer blues clubs, a linoleum counter with a beer on it, rather than a faux Tiffany lamp on a black pearl wood table. My sports coat felt scratchy.

"This way, please," she said somehow, around the metal in her lip.

We were led down a hall toward the executive offices. One door was marked ENTERTAINMENT DIRECTOR and another EMPOWERMENT CENTER. We passed a worker dressed like a French maid—black dress, white apron, fluffs at the sleeves and a little hat—which must have been the help's uniform, at least, the female help. The worker averted her eyes, as if she wasn't supposed to remember faces. We came to DIRECTOR, and the receptionist opened the door and stepped aside.

"Mrs. Dillon. Linda." The director rose from her mahogany desk to approach us, hand extended. She looked at me, then added in a surprised tone, "This isn't Mr. Dillon."

Linda said, "Proof God exists and is merciful."

She had taken to doing that, roughing me up some, with an affectionate tone. When I'd bounce one back at her, she'd laugh and say something like, "Joe, who would have guessed you were so quick?" So I didn't do it often.

"I'm terribly sorry, Linda," the director said under her breath, I suppose apologizing for having revealed she knew Kevin Dillon, or that he might have a problem that required the clinic's services.

Linda made the introduction. The director's name was Fay Herwin. She stepped a little too close to shake my hand, maybe to smell my breath. Spangles on her bracelet tapped my wrist.

"I'm not here about Kevin," Linda said, helping herself to a chair.

I lowered myself into a sofa covered with tan chenille upholstery, sinking about a foot, which put my head lower than the director's. She had returned to her chair behind her S-shaped desk, which was made of military steel and must have weighed two thousand pounds. Two walls of the office were covered with fifteen-inch-wide distressed Douglas fir paneling. A third wall contained a bookshelf, holding family photographs, mementos, and a few leather-bound volumes, nothing anybody would ever read. Wood beams crossed the ceiling. Only a leather-framed blotter and an antique brass letter opener were on her desk. A computer monitor and keyboard and a telephone were on a back table.

Fay Herwin smiled at me, still sizing me up, maybe trying to see if my nostrils had been eaten away with cocaine. She was so thin the skin on her face appeared to be sprayed on, tight against the bones beneath. Above the neckline of her dress, her clavicle stood out like coyote ribs. Her head was peculiarly narrow, and seemed over-featured, with large hazel eyes and full lips and a nose that flared at the base. She was wearing a maroon wool crepe jacket over a striped silk shirt with pointed collars.

She asked, "Then how may I help you?"

"Fay, it's been a while since I visited you," Linda said.

"Yes, it has."

"And those visits were times of stress, with me putting Kevin in your charge." Linda was wearing a three-button tan wool jacket over a cotton shirt, and cuffed black wool twill trousers. Her handbag was on her lap. I could see the outline of her pistol grip on the handbag's fabric.

"Sometimes stress can be productive," Fay Herwin said.

"I'm sure. But it has affected my memory. The stress has, maybe." Linda matched Fay Herwin's smile, two professionals going at it.

I'm sure Fay Herwin wondered where the conversation was going.

Linda said, "I can't remember whether I told you I'm an FBI agent." She reached into her jacket pocket and tinned her.

The director's eyes opened as if someone had thrown water

at her. She recovered by drawing her palm across her blotter, as if it needed to be smoothed. "No, you didn't tell me." A touch of reproach.

"Joe Durant and I are here on business. FBI business."

"With this clinic?" She cast the smallest of glances at a mahogany frame containing a stack of computer disks.

"About the last flight of *Sacajawea*," I said.

"Dreadful, just dreadful," she said in a mortician's practiced tones.

"We need to know if you lost any patients on *Sacajawea*."

The director leaned back in her chair. It didn't squeak, unlike any chair I've ever used. She said, "As you know, Linda, our first service is hope, and our second is confidentiality, and we—"

"I'm sure," Linda interrupted.

"Just in the past twelve months our clients have included senators, ambassadors, some of the biggest stars in Hollywood—"

"Of course," Linda said.

"—prominent industrialists from around the world, and a smattering of royalty. When patients enter our program, they are assured of absolute discretion and confidentiality."

Linda pulled a photograph from her jacket pocket. She laid it on the director's desk, then scooted it across to her, holding the director with her eyes. "This is Khalid bin Abdallah. All we need to know is whether he was a patient at North Star. If you answer that, we won't ask anything else. That'll be our deal."

Fay Herwin didn't look down at the photo. "What you ask is impossible, Linda. I cannot betray the confidence invested in me."

I said, "We have a threat from the person or persons who

brought down *Sacajawea*. It's going to happen again, in the next few days. This is important."

She looked at me as if she were at an auction, judging a horse's musculature. "Everything is important to someone, Mr. Durant. My clients know their visits here will remain secret. Confidentiality is critical to them."

"We are talking about different levels here," I said. "You are talking about privacy, while I'm talking about saving lives."

Her phone rang, but she ignored it. She sniffed. "I do no advertising. Clients come here through word of mouth and through their doctors' recommendations. People who come here are not the type who later go on the talk show circuit to confess their substance abuse."

"Sixty-three people—"

"We even have the Gold Plan, where, for an additional fee, not even other patients will be aware you are visiting North Star." She spread her hands to encompass her office and the grounds beyond, her entire domain, and adopted the voice and look of a spoiled servant. "Complete and utter discretion."

"Can you just tell us whether Khalid was a patient here?" I asked.

Someone knocked on her office door, lightly at first, then more insistently.

"I can't confirm anything." She still refused to even glance at the photograph. "My business depends on the utter secrecy I offer. A whiff of publicity would ruin North Star."

Linda rose from her chair to step to the window. She nodded toward the driveway. "Then you aren't going to like this."

The door opened, just a fraction, by someone who hesitated to be meddlesome. A woman said, "Ms. Herwin, we've got a bit of a problem outside. A big problem, actually."

"Can it wait a moment, Lucinda?" More a command than a question.

"No, it can't, actually," Lucinda replied tremulously, still out of my sight behind the door. "Take a look out your window, Ms. Herwin."

She looked at us, measuring, then rose from her desk and crossed to the windows. She peered out, then bent forward a fraction as if that slight movement might bring things closer.

Then red rose in her face, from her neck through her cheeks as high as her eyes, like a waxing tide.

"You see your problem, Fay?" Linda asked.

The director's voice gained a metallic note, sounding like a spinning pistol cylinder. "I do, indeed."

Linda explained needlessly, "Coming up your driveway is the mobile unit for KLRY, the CBS television affiliate in Boise. I'll bet that big satellite dish on top connects right to a CBS feed, seen all around the world."

"What do they want?"

"They know an FBI agent—me—and an NTSB investigator, him"—she jerked her thumb at me—"are in your office, and those reporters are hoping for a juicy story, maybe about some of your clients."

Fay Herwin breathed in deep rasps that rattled her chest. She had the thousand-yard stare of the weary infantryman. She carefully touched her chin, as one might explore a bruise, then slowly turned away from the window. Her mouth worked once, then again, without saying anything. Finally, "I'm being blackmailed, aren't I?"

I said, "I prefer to think of it as a lesson on the relative importance of competing issues."

"A lesson?" She looked at me as if I were a bug, then crossed to her desk to lift the photo, but barely glanced at it.

The sound of the television truck could now be heard in the office as it drew near. Kurt Cheney was winding the engine up in its lowest gear, on purpose, I'd bet.

She said, "Khalid bin Abdallah was a patient here."

"More than once?" I asked.

"Was he visited by anybody during his stay?" Linda pulled out a notepad and returned to her chair.

The director looked at Linda with cold surmise. "You said you would only ask whether Khalid was a patient here. That was all."

Linda said, "Your second lesson, Fay, is to never make a deal with a blackmailer."

The director sat heavily on her chair.

"And when we are finished with our questions, why don't you download Khalid bin Abdallah's file onto a disk, and we'll take it with us," I said. "That won't be a problem, will it?"

The television station's truck rolled up and parked outside the director's window. The letters KLRY were in vibrant green and gold above a red logo YOUR NEWS NOW. I could see Kurt Cheney behind the wheel. He was grinning like a fiend. Jamie Suarez was on the passenger side, and he held up a big video camera, a well-used professional model, with electricians tape around the handle and with KLRY on its side.

With more force than I had used, Linda repeated my question, "That won't be a problem, will it?"

Her voice dark with resentment, Fay Herwin replied, "No, I guess it won't be a problem."

TWENTY-FIVE

Tromping around Idaho and Washington with my personal FBI agent, my view of the *Sacajawea* investigation suffered from a short horizon. It was easy for me—making telephone calls, participating in interviews, staring at a computer screen, mostly focusing on ATF 94 wiring and fuel systems—to lose sight of the massive effort underway to discover and capture the villain or villains the FBI believed placed a bomb on *Sacajawea*.

The FBI was not slowed at all by my "spark theory, an interesting notion," as Director William Henley had written in a progress memo to NTSB Board Chairman Hugh Clifton. I was winning converts at the NTSB, though. My fiery demonstration in the Nevada desert had impressed. But the FBI was on a blood trail, and no scientific theory about igniting vapors was going to give them the slightest pause.

This was the Normandy invasion of police investigations. More than 200 FBI agents were working the case, and another 100 from an alphabet of United States organizations: ATF, CIA, DEA, DIA, NTSB, and FAA. Investigators were on loan from the U.S. Army's Military Intelligence Brigade and from the Air Force's National Air Intelligence Center and the 497th Intelligence Group. The Royal Canadian Mounted Police and France's *Gendarmerie Nationale* had sent specialists. Because four people from New South Wales had been aboard *Sacajawea*, Australia's Federal Police had sent help. The wealthy founder of Shinsha Fabrication Ltd. and his wife had died on the plane, so two counterterrorism agents from Hong Kong Police's Criminal Intelligence Division were in Idaho. Because of their specialized knowledge in terrorist affairs, Germany's *Bundeskriminalamt* and the Republic of Georgia's Internal Forces—heir to much of the KGB's files—had sent database specialists.

Antiterrorist organizations from around the world had a stake in showing that their particular nemeses might have been involved. So the Greek Internal Security Agency had sent an investigator, believing the Revolutionary 17 November Organization, whose principal goal is the removal of the Turkish military from Cyprus, might have had a hand in *Sacajawea*, based on a letter from 17 November claiming responsibility. On similar evidence, investigators had arrived from Scotland Yard, the Royal Ulster Constabulary, the National Policy Agency of Japan, the South African Police Service, and the Philippine National Police. Interpol sent technicians to run its famous ASF (Automated Search Facility), containing computerized files on 200,000 potential suspects.

Two dozen intelligence officers and counterterrorism specialists from the Middle East were in Seattle and Ketchum and Hailey, most from Israel but also from Lebanon, Saudi Arabia, and Kuwait. Their list of suspects included Al-Fatah, the Palestine Liberation Front, Abu Nidal Organization, Force 17, the Secret Army for the Liberation of Armenia, Democratic Front for the Liberation of Palestine, Hawari

Group, Hizballah, Kurdish Worker's Party, Palestinian Islamic Jihad, and many others.

I asked one of the Israeli agents—a fellow with a knife scar from the corner of his mouth to an ear—why Middle Eastern terrorists would want to bring down a plane full of Sun Valley skiers, and he looked at me like I was in diapers, and said with a smile made crooked by the scar, "You Americans are so sweet."

A reward of four million dollars was being funded by the Airline Pilots' Association and the Air Transport Association, available to anyone who would provide information leading to the arrest and conviction of those responsible for the bombing.

The press was making a living off the mad bomber. Electronic and print news organizations from around the world had sent teams to the Pacific Northwest. The FBI director knew that the bomber's letter would become public one way or another, and so at a press conference he had revealed that the FBI had received a message, that the letter had contained a signature that may only have been known by the bomber, and that the bomber had threatened to bring down another plane six days from the day of the press conference.

Around the world, television newscasts began with Voice of Time announcers intoning, "Five days left on the Sky Bomber's calendar," or "The bomber's grim countdown continues." Tabloid television shows breathlessly broke story after story, seizing on inconsequential items, magnifying them wildly out of proportion and feeding them to the gullible. My favorite was the interview with Sallandro the Psychic, proprietor Sallandro's of Seattle—ALL YOUR METAPHYSICAL NEEDS UNDER ONE ROOF—who claimed that the *Sacajawea* bomber had once been married to a redhead, and that any future plane with redheads as passengers was a target. Air Lingus reported an immediate flood of cancellations.

The citizens of Hailey and Ketchum and Sun Valley were being hit hard. Despite Greyhound and Trailways adding more bus service into the area, it was simply easier for folks to travel elsewhere—Park City, Vail, Whistler, Aspen—for their spring skiing than to take a bus or car to the mountains of Idaho. Nobody was flying into the Hailey airport, not on Emerald, not on Horizon or Idaho Air, not on chartered planes. The ski area at Sun Valley has the world's most elaborate snow-making machinery—computers, brass nozzles up and down the mountain, pumps and generators, automated weather stations—and the area was known for fine spring skiing, often late into April when few other resorts were operating. So even this late in the season Sun Valley's Bald and Dollar Mountains had perfect snow, but few skiers. The ski operation was laying off employees, and so were restaurants, hotels, shuttle services, sporting goods stores, and many other businesses. Idaho's governor had declared a state of emergency, making loans available to suffering Blaine County businesses. Ketchum's streets were mostly empty, except for Mossad agents, and there were plenty of them; they couldn't be mistaken for your usual skier from Chicago.

Fear of flying wasn't limited to folks in Sun Valley. Flights into nearby Boise and Idaho Falls and Pocatello were still running on their pre-*Sacajawea* schedules, but the planes were almost empty. And as the bomber's target date drew closer, passenger loads declined to twenty and thirty percent of normal on flights in and out of Spokane, Great Falls, Missoula, Portland, Seattle, and Salt Lake City. The public figured, maybe correctly, that the FBI and NTSB were going to make sure no bomb was placed on a Hailey to Seattle flight, so the bomber would simply pick another route. As the days ticked off, planes serving the Mountain and Pacific Northwest were becoming emptier and emptier.

That the perpetrator of the *Sacajawea* disaster might have a Middle East connection—now that Khalid bin Abdallah, director of Saudi Arabia's Eastern Security Bureau, had been identified—was only one of many possibilities for the FBI, but the State Department and CIA acted from the moment Khalid was IDed as if *Sacajawea* were a political assassination.

I was not privy to CIA maneuvering, of course, but Fred Yamashita had assured me there was plenty of it. And the State Department had begun a series of briefings with our European and Middle Eastern allies designed to gauge the strength of a potential coalition against Iraq—the main beneficiary of instability in Saudi Arabia—should the evidence eventually point to Baghdad. The State Department had hopes of reconstructing the Gulf war partnership. The French were already objecting. The Secretary of State had promised "swift and sure" justice should a foreign nation be implicated, which in the language of diplomats meant the navy had already been ordered to prepare a carrier group to enter the Persian Gulf.

As the FBI's investigation gained momentum, the importance of my liaison work grew larger. More and more, I was the NTSB's eyes and ears on the FBI's investigation. I attended the bureau's briefings and I did some legwork, though at times I felt I was only tagging along. I was tolerated by FBI agents because the Woman-in-the-Hat had contacted me, a valuable lead they might not otherwise have obtained, so the FBI thought perhaps I might shake something else loose, by accident if not by skill. I was also a handy reference for questions relating to airplanes in general and *Sacajawea* in particular.

Henley and Yamashita and the rest of the FBI were working in a pressure cooker. A small but vocal group of representatives in Congress were suggesting that *Sacajawea* should never have happened, given advances in airport security. These congresspersons were threatening to convene hearings "to hold the FBI accountable for once," one congressman told CNN. *The Wall Street Journal* pointed out that these particular congressmen and women were police-haters from way back in their student demonstration days, but some of the press had seized on this theme, saying the FBI's investigation of *Sacajawea* was moving at a glacial pace. The NTSB and FAA were criticized for failing to recommend security apparatus that would have prevented *Sacajawea*.

We were all professionals working in an area that drew intense scrutiny. Pressure was part of our job. But a new element had been added to that pressure on the FBI: the bomber's letter. The bureau had only a few days remaining, and then the bomber would strike again, so he had promised.

A touch of hysteria had come to the upper-left-hand quarter of the United States. The public was afraid, and was demanding that we do our job: find the person or persons responsible for *Sacajawea*. The bomber had brought down a plane, and television commentators and newspaper letter writers and folks interviewed on the street had no doubt he could bring down another.

I had told Pierre Lemercier that the NTSB would not go public with the possibility that *Sacajawea* was destroyed by an ignition of fuel vapor. I should have known that such a thing cannot be kept secret. Newspaper and magazine articles about the *Sacajawea* bomb now often had sidebars titled "An Alternative Explanation" or something similar, with cutaway drawings of the plane and close-ups of terminal blocks.

Judging from the reaction of the French press, America had declared war on its oldest ally. The French were outraged that Americans were trying to divert attention from a mad bomber—doubtless a Yankee, given their proclivity toward expressing their eccentricities through violence—by accusing a French hero and a leading French manufacturer of producing a shoddy product. *Le Monde* ran an article about me, suggesting that grief over the death of my wife had given me a taste for revenge against the French or had made me delusional. The French had not guillotined me in effigy yet, but it was probably coming.

I was losing weight, and Sarah noticed that my face had "gone sort of slack, except your eyes, which have gotten sort of puffy," as she nicely put it. I needed sleep. I needed a vacation. I needed to jam with the band. I needed to spend time with Sarah.

But more than all this, I needed to find out how a spark got into a fuel tank.

"You think they'll go for it?" I asked.

"Anybody who deals in hundred-dollar bills," Jamie Suarez said, "tightly bound in rubber bands and shipped in a plane's cargo hold, rather than using wire transfers like normal people, would kill his mother to get those stacks of money back. They'll go for it."

"And you're sure it's drug money?" I squinted through my hole in the wall, standing next to Suarez, who had his own portal. Kurt Cheney and another agent named Glen Rosenbloom were watching the proceedings on a monitor on a desk behind us. They were wearing flak jackets and FBI baseball caps. Rosenbloom's handgun and a two-way radio were on the table next to the monitor. The action would take place in the room next to ours, and it had been outfitted with a video camera.

Suarez said, "Traces of cocaine or heroin can be found on most hundred-dollar bills in circulation, but the *Sacajawea* bills had much more than traces. Somebody was handling coke one minute and these bills the next."

To my mind, I had shown the possibility that *Sacajawea*'s fuel tank had detonated due to an electrical surge, but my delicate engineering construct had not convinced many law enforcement investigators. I had created a test in the Nevada desert that assumed all the facts my way. Pierre Lemercier and his lawyers were correct: *Sacajawea* had destroyed much of the evidence itself. None of the wiring near *Sacajawea*'s center fuel tank terminal block had been found, or perhaps it had been found but not identified. In all likelihood those pieces of wire critical to my theory would never be found because they had been vaporized in the blast, and so whether *Sacajawea*'s wiring resembled my desert test was forever unknowable.

I needed supporting evidence from other sources. I had just spent most of a day poring over disaster reports from national aviation authorities from around the world, with the help of translators of many languages. And I had found a lead: a pilot with a tale to tell. He was traveling a long distance to Seattle, and would be wearing handcuffs the entire journey. Until he arrived, I was back on the FBI beat, doing my liaising.

Suarez peered through his viewing port. "It looks good in there." He added, more to himself, "They'll go for it."

We were in a strip mall on Highway 99 near SeaTac airport, not far from the NTSB's regional office. The FBI had rented two rooms which, judging from the smell, had once been a Korean restaurant selling kimchi. The mall also contained a mini-mart and a chiropractor's office.

Visible through my small hole in the wall was the FBI's second room, containing wall shelves and a counter with a computer monitor on it. To one side of the counter were a row of suitcases, lined up like dominoes. Most of the suitcases looked battered, and some were held together with duct tape. All had blue tags hanging from their handles. Shelves behind the counter held purses, several briefcases, a laptop computer bag, and a dozen Fed Ex, UPS, and other shippers' packages. Four ski bags were in the corner.

Linda Dillon stood behind the counter, staring at a clipboard, a pencil in one hand. Across the counter from her was a woman dressed in a green raincoat, inspecting a handbag. The third person in the room, an elderly fellow, bald except for a horseshoe of white hair, was sitting in a chair at the end of the counter, studying a printout. The man's cane was across his lap. The rubber traction knob was well worn.

"The old guy is the clincher," Suarez said. "Nobody associates police action with the elderly."

"He's an agent?" I asked.

"Retired. His name is McGraw, and even J. Edgar called him Quick Draw."

"And the lady in there?"

"Another agent. Fifty-five years old, wearing flats and an old scarf. Somebody is going to peer through the plate-glass window into our claims room here, and see no threat at all."

"Have any legitimate claimants shown up today?" I asked.

"None will." Suarez moved away from his peephole to rub his eye. "We made sure that every little scrap of personal property that came down with *Sacajawea*, and that could be identified, went to next of kin. Families of the dead have already visited our stowage area, viewing personal items that were found in the plane and on the mountainside." He sat at the table next to Cheney. "Anybody who shows up here is a suspect."

A speaker on the table broadcast Linda Dillon's voice. She was chatting with the female FBI agent at the counter. They had worked together before, it sounded like. Linda laughed at something.

Bells rang softly from the claims room, heard over the speaker on the table. I returned to my hole in the wall. Cheney and Rosenbloom leaned toward the screen.

Jamie Suarez adjusted the monitor's color tint. "Seen this guy before, Kurt? Glen?"

Cheney shook his head. "He looks like a puke, doesn't he?"

Through the hole in the wall, I saw Linda look up from her clipboard. She smiled in the manner of a bureaucrat, long suffering but willing to push some papers for you, at least until the coffee break. "May I help you?"

"This the claims center?" The voice was rough, and intentionally careless, as if the speaker were trying to sound like he didn't care one way or another.

Linda nodded. "*Sacajawea* claim center. May I help you?"

"I never got a package sent to me."

"Many packages broke open. I have lists of recovered items we think were blown out of ruined packages. And we have some unopened boxes. What was in yours?"

"Fishing lures."

Linda entered several keystrokes. After a moment she said, "Well, we never found fishing lures loose on the ground. So maybe they're in one of our boxes that weren't breached." Linda sounded bored and officious. "Was it a Fed Ex package? We have quite a few left unclaimed. And two UPS."

"Well, I dunno."

Jamie Suarez whispered, "He's a runner, not a player. He's

being paid a couple bills or a couple of lines to come here to try to retrieve that package."

Linda's customer was in his early twenties, with long brown hair that looked like it hadn't seen shampoo in a month. He wore a stubble goatee and a ring in one ear. His jeans were torn at a knee, but his Nike high-tops were new and white. Quick Draw McGraw appeared to be ignoring him, searching his own ear with a finger then earnestly studying his find. The lady in the flats examined a shelf of items.

"I got a shipper's receipt." The runner dug into his jeans pocket.

"That'll help," Linda said dryly.

The FBI had placed notices in the *Seattle Times* and *Post-Intelligencer* and all the alternative papers, even *The Rocket* for rock and rollers, announcing that a claims center would open for intended recipients of shipping parcels. If the recipients suspected they had not received all the personal property or packages, they could appear at this strip mall address and look over the remaining articles. The FBI used similar scams, sometimes sending letters offering prizes, the way Ed McMahon did, if fugitives will appear at such and such a place. These ruses almost always resulted in a dozen or more arrests, guys walking in thinking they're going to score a TV and ending up in the clink.

"These traps prove it doesn't take brains to be a crook," Fred Yamashita had said. And when I told Fred that the people dealing in this amount of money—$100,000—aren't likely to be that stupid, he replied perhaps not, but that it would make them take a risk. He had added, "Some drug dealer's life may depend on getting that money back. His supplier isn't going to believe he lost it when *Sacajawea* went down. Who'd believe that story? Some druggie is a hundred grand in the hole, and he has to find that money."

"Here it is," the runner said, holding out a pink slip of paper.

"It's an Air Idaho parcel." Linda scratched her chin. "I don't remember one of those."

"She's playing him like a fish," Kurt Cheney said to the monitor.

"Give me a second," Linda said, then made a notation on the document on her clipboard, pursed her lips, and added another note, apparently lost in thought.

The runner rocked on his feet and chewed his lower lip.

"He's been told to be cool," Suarez said, "but look at him. He's on a spring. He's about ready to bolt."

"Let me see," Linda said idly, bringing up the receipt to study it. "You say the package was on *Sacajawea?*"

"Yeah." The guy pulled at his earring.

Linda stepped to the shelves, out of my sight through the port, so I turned to the monitor. She moved one box at a time, sliding them along the shelf to peer at the labels, then held up the shipping bill to study it again. "I'm not seeing it."

"Oscar time for Linda," Rosenbloom added. "She'll be up onstage, thanking all the little people."

The runner was about to flee, but Linda said, "Wait. This might be it. Let's see." She held the bill next to the Air Idaho parcel. "Here it is." She lifted the box down from the shelf and placed it on the counter. "Lots of these boxes blew open. You're one of the lucky ones."

"Yeah."

Linda playfully shook the package. "Must be some of those new soft fishing lures that don't make a sound when you shake them."

"For God's sake, Linda," Suarez said under his breath. "Give him the package."

"Yeah. New lures."

"You'll have to sign a receipt," Linda instructed, back to being the bureaucrat.

"Is there real money in that box?" I asked. "A hundred thousand?"

Suarez nodded. "Just in case the runner has been told to peek inside before he gets too close to the player. So we put a hundred thousand in stacks into the package. Dirty money seized from raids."

"We've got that package tricked out," Rosenbloom said.

"There's a microphone and a homing beacon and a transmitter, all hidden in the cardboard," Cheney explained.

"It's my bet we're not going to need any of that technology," Suarez said. "The dealer is caught between two fears. First, he's afraid his runner will bolt with all the money, will just disappear with it the minute he leaves our building. But, second, he's also afraid this is an FBI or ATF setup."

"I'm guessing the cash makes him careless," Cheney said.

"That's my guess too," Suarez said. "I'm thinking the dealer is within eyesight of us right now. He doesn't want to let his gofer out of his sight, not with a hundred thousand on the line."

On the screen, the runner was bent over the counter signing his name. It took him a while. Linda looked at the ceiling for our benefit.

"Here you go then." She pushed the box to him.

"Yeah." He tucked it under an arm and turned for the door.

"He's on foot," Linda said from the neighboring room, her voice broadcast over a speaker. "At least, I didn't see a car."

Rosenbloom grabbed his handgun and said into his radio, "You see the guy with the box, Ted?"

From Rosenbloom's radio came the voice of an FBI agent

who was posted a block north in an automobile. "I've got him through my binoculars. He's walking my way, and the box is under his arm."

"You spotted his boss?" Rosenbloom asked.

"Just the runner. I don't see anybody waiting to relieve him of the box yet." The voice paused. "Wait a minute. The kid just looked left and right and left again, and now he's popping open the end of the box, seeing what's inside."

Jamie Suarez leaned toward the radio.

The next words over the radio were clipped. "He's making a run for it, taking off across 99."

Suarez barked, "Ted, stay put. Don't follow him. See how it plays."

From the radio: "He's running like he's on fire, really moving." A slight hesitation. "Man, he almost got hit by a car. . . . Now he's sprinting across a mini-mart parking lot, and now he has disappeared between the store and a Dumpster, still running. We'd better do something, Jamie."

A new voice came from the speaker, another agent in another position. "A blue Ford pickup has just shot out of the liquor store parking lot, Jamie. Rubber burning, really winding up through the gears."

"Where's he headed, Allen?"

"Toward the mini-mart, just jumped the curb. You'd better let us loose, Jamie."

"Go now," Suarez ordered.

He rushed out the back door, and Linda and the others were right behind him.

I'm an engineer. I'm not a cop or a soldier. I'm not a sprinter on the starting blocks. Long ago my fast-twitch muscles atrophied, to be replaced by inertia muscles.

So I hesitated, just a second or two, just long enough to

wonder whether I should have taken navy pistol training more seriously, to wonder what I might add to the chase, what skill I might bring to it. And by the time I had gathered myself to join in, the FBI agents had vanished out the door and were throwing themselves into their vehicles.

Two FBI cars roared onto 99, Suarez and Linda Dillon in the lead and Cheney and Rosenbloom right behind. On the way out, one of them had grabbed the two-way radio, so I couldn't even listen in.

I lowered myself into a metal chair, feeling heavy and useless, feeling like an academic. Like an actuary. Like a soft and pulpy cantaloupe, ready to be tossed into the garbage can under the sink.

They made short work of it.

Jamie Suarez returned, carrying an automatic shotgun in one hand, the shipping box of cash in another—one end torn partly open and green bills visible—and wearing a grin under his mustache. He was strutting. "Pure FBI. The pure stuff." He mouthed a whistle. "I love this job. And I love the world and all its people."

Next into the building came the runner, his face slack with bafflement. Somehow his earring had been ripped off, and blood spotted his earlobe. He was bleeding from his nose, and his forehead had suffered a gash from his eyebrow to his hairline. The plastic cuffs were high and tight behind his back, and his thin shoulders were hunched protectively. His shirt was torn and hanging, exposing some of his belly. He was pushed along by Rosenbloom, who was also smiling, and who shoved the runner into a chair.

Then through the door came Kurt Cheney. "Joe, you should've seen me. An open field tackle. It'll make ESPN's replay show."

He turned to grab the arm of the captured dealer, a man in his mid-thirties wearing a golf shirt and jeans and hiking boots, walking in a stoop, his hands behind his back. He wore three days' beard and a Mariners baseball cap. His face was red and shiny, and he was breathing hard, his chest going in and out.

He snarled, "Maybe we'll be in the same prison, asshole." His eyes were locked on the runner, who trembled under it.

Linda entered the room. Everybody was grinning but me. She said, "Joe, meet Sonny Berquist, a big-time destroyer of our American way of life."

"We've been looking for something on this guy for a year," Suarez said. "We knew he was dirty, but we could never prove it."

Cheney laughed. "Joe, by the time we got to Sonny here, he had leaped out of his pickup and had wrestled the gofer to the ground. What's your name, Skateboard?"

"Nicholas Lawson," the runner said. "Nick." He brought his gaze up, but it fell back to the linoleum under the weight of Sonny's stare.

"So Sonny is beating the crap out of Nick, using this box of cash to do so." Linda laughed. "Yelling at him about trying to steal his money, and just banging away at him."

Suarez said, "Sonny was so intent on beating up Nick here, he didn't even see us come at him. Sonny had my pistol in his face before it registered on him that, well, this might be his last breath of freedom for what, Sonny, maybe fifteen years, twenty? This'll be your second time, won't it?"

"I'm going to kill your ass, Nick, kill it dead, goddamn you. Going to steal my money, goddamn you." Even in a rage, Sonny Berquist knew better than to take a step toward the runner, with Kurt Cheney standing there, coiled and looking for an excuse.

I felt like I was shrinking, getting smaller in front of Linda and Jamie and the others, withered by all this law enforcement competence and jubilation, all these congratulations among team members for a superb job.

I tried to rally. I looked at Berquist and then at Lawson. "We want to talk to you about *Sacajawea*."

Both turned to me, seeing me for the first time. Their faces showed they had utterly no idea why I might be asking them about the plane. These guys had yet to determine that the downing of a plane—not a routine drug arrest—had been our primary concern.

Their blank faces told me all I needed to know. A drug dealer had used the plane to ship cash.

They would have nothing to offer about *Sacajawea*'s destruction. Not one damned thing.

TWENTY-SIX

A man sat across the table from Linda and me, and some of him was there, and some of him was not. He stared at me, his scarred face resembling a gnawed bone.

His left arm ended just below his shoulder, and his shirt sleeve was tucked into his belt. On that same side, his leg from the knee down was missing. Visible below his pants cuff was a wood prosthesis, and it appeared to have been carved from a bough, exhibiting none of the high-tech plastics and alloys of a modern artificial limb. A rubber knob, maybe taken from a crutch, was at the end of the wooden leg.

I asked, "What was your altitude when the detonation occurred?"

"I had just taken off." His accent was Australian, plain in just those few words. "Fifty feet, maybe a hundred."

"Your cargo?"

"Rifles. AK-47s."

His name was Brian Maxwell, and he had been flown to Seattle from Malaysia, where he had spent the last six years at Penang Prison, convicted of smuggling. Penang Prison is almost 150 years old, and has been the home of many notorious criminals, including See Bah Seng, the Gulf of Thailand pirate. It is a harsh place filled with desperate men. I'm sure Maxwell viewed this trip to Seattle as a vacation, even though his one hand was cuffed to his belt the entire time.

"What was the disabling sequence?" I asked.

"Hardly a sequence. Everything happened at once. Suddenly I had no elevators, no rudder, no ailerons, no flaps, no throttle."

The skin under Maxwell's chin was a purple crepe, a burn scar that began at his chin and disappeared under his shirt. His left ear was missing, and the short prison haircut did not quite cover the hole in his head. I tried not to look there.

"Some of my gauges still had power, I remember, but I can't be sure about which ones. There was suddenly fire everywhere."

Maxwell had been flying automatic rifles from Kelang, a Malaysian waterfront town, to Chiang Rai in northern Thailand, with a planned refueling stop at a grass strip west of Bangkok. Mae Hong Sing was a warlord who controlled five hundred square miles of mountainous Thailand, and his soldiers required modern weapons, and the warlord paid handsomely for anyone who could find a way to get them to him, all this from the Malay prosecutor who put Brian Maxwell in prison for ten years, once Maxwell left the hospital. Rather, after what was left of Maxwell left the hospital. He had been flying without a copilot.

Sitting to Maxwell's right was one of his Malay escorts, one of three prison guards who had brought him to Seattle, along with a Malay consular official. The guard was wearing a coat and tie, and nodded at each of my questions. The Malaysians had been cooperative, immediately granting my request to interview Maxwell, asking only that they be allowed to tape the interview. A recorder was on the table between us.

"And you are confident the detonation occurred immediately behind you, not maybe one of the engines?"

"Right enough, though when the 94 slid into the ground, I was pretty much concerned with getting out, not doing a damage inventory."

The impact with the ground had pushed back the plane's nose, crumpling the cockpit and jamming the hatch, trapping Maxwell in the pilot's seat. The blaze enveloped the cockpit and began eating at him. He managed to free himself from the chair, some of him on fire, then smashed a side window with a tool box and squeezed through and dropped to the ground. He crawled away from the plane. Shells detonated, hundreds of them, making the field sound like it was hosting a war. Maxwell lay in the field until soldiers of the Malay Defense Force found him. His arm and leg had been so badly burned doctors were unable to save them, and of his ear there was no trace. The field had been littered with AK-47s, so the prosecutor had no difficulty gathering evidence, and the judge had no difficulty sentencing Maxwell to a decade in Penang Prison.

Linda asked, "Are you sure the explosion wasn't caused by ammunition in your cargo bay?"

"It's unlikely a shell would have gone off on its own, much less a box or a crate of them. No, it wasn't shells. It was the plane."

"Had your ATF 94 experienced fuel gauge problems?" I asked.

"It wasn't my plane. I had chartered it from Rayong Leasing in Bangkok. Told them I was going to ferry machine parts all around the peninsula. This was only my second flight on the plane. I wasn't aware of any problem with fuel gauges."

"I've looked at the documents from the Malaysian investigation of the crash," I said. "The investigators didn't assign a probable cause."

"There wasn't much of the plane left to investigate. It was still burning when I was found and put into an ambulance. And the Malays don't have the resources for a big investigation, not like you Yanks."

"Could the location of the blast have been the center fuel tank?"

"That was its general direction," Maxwell answered. "I can't be more precise."

Linda and I questioned Brian Maxwell for another hour. At the end of the interview he was led away, headed to SeaTac, then to Malaysia to serve the rest of his sentence.

"He didn't offer much," Linda said when she and I were alone in the room. "Nothing specific."

Incredulous, I looked at her. "An otherwise unexplainable explosion from the direction of the center fuel tank? That's not much?"

"Joe, he was a pilot who was on fire and frantically fled a burning plane, and who almost died. He didn't have the time or inclination to take notes or photos. All you've got is a six-year-old vague impression."

"All I've got," I said with conviction, "is another ATF 94 center fuel tank explosion. Just like *Sacajawea*'s."

"He's not a suspect because of that, is he?" Wayne Ray asked. "I mean, just because he's building a kit plane?"

Fred Yamashita replied, "A suspect, no. But it's a trace of a shadow of an insubstantial lead. How's that?"

Ray said, "Thin as tissue."

We all knew it, too. Yamashita, Linda Dillon, Jamie Suarez, and Kurt Cheney were on one side of the conference table, with IIC Rich Shrader and Dick Dahlberg and me on the other. Wayne Ray sat on our side, closest to the screen. He was the only one in a business suit. When he had entered the room, seeing the others in sports clothes, Ray had told me that putting on a tie every day reminded him of going to work, of running an airline, something he wasn't doing much of now that Emerald couldn't sell a seat, couldn't even give them away.

Emerald's human resources director, Alice Miranda, had accompanied Ray. She wore a dove gray jacket over a red blouse, with a string of pearls at her neck. Her hair was bayonet gray and her eyes were the color of concrete. Only her red lipstick gave her face any color, so much that her mouth looked sticky. She sat next to her boss. Her son was at Stanford, which she worked into any conversation lasting more than sixty seconds.

Yamashita said, "We think whoever brought down *Sacajawea* knew something about airplanes."

Suarez added, "The bomb was placed right where it would sever controls for most of the plane's systems."

I had presented my new evidence: a plane going down in Malaysia under circumstances similar to *Sacajawea*'s destruction, arguing that it pointed to a flaw in the plane's mechanics. Yamashita had countered that until a probable cause was assigned to *Sacajawea,* he was proceeding with all vigor on the criminal side of the investigation, still presuming the detonation was caused by a bomb. I found some satisfaction that while I was closing in on proving my theory, this meeting showed that the FBI was getting further and further away from theirs.

"So you pick on a guy just because he's building a plane?" Ray asked.

I didn't blame Wayne Ray for being indignant on behalf of his employee.

"We're picking on everybody," Yamashita answered, not for the first time during this session. "What can you tell me about him?"

"Ben Cook has worked for Emerald for seven years, rising to reservations manager," Alice Miranda said.

Ray added, "He celebrated his new job back then, seven years ago, by buying a kit airplane."

"A Swan," Suarez said. "We checked the Swan Company's records, which is how we focused on Ben Cook."

"And Ben has purchased a Rotax engine for it." Ray turned to look at Ben Cook's image on the screen. "The plane has a three-blade propeller, a tricycle landing gear with a nose wheel. It'll cruise at one hundred fifty miles an hour, he told me."

"You ever see the plane?" Yamashita asked.

"I visited his house, two or so years ago, when he was recovering from a bad skiing accident, a both-bone break in his right leg. I pushed him in his wheelchair to his garage so he could show me the plane. Swan, the manufacturer, promised it'd take Cook seven hundred twenty hours to assemble it, and Cook laughed and said seven hundred twenty hours was about three hundred hours ago. The plane was in parts, all over his garage."

Ben Cook's face was carefully deadpan for the company photo. He was as bald as a peeled egg. His eyeglasses had caught some of the photographer's flash, and one of Cook's eyes was washed out.

"Has he ever said anything odd to you, maybe something against Emerald?" Linda asked.

Ray and Alice Miranda had endured these questions for the past ninety minutes.

"Ben Cook is a deacon at my church, runs one of the church's charity teams. Sometimes he and his wife and me and Charlotte sit together . . ." Ray caught himself. His wife, Charlotte, had died on *Sacajawea*. He cleared his throat to give himself a second, then changed tenses. "We sat together sometimes, same pew, me and Charlotte and Ben and his wife."

"Ben's a perfect employee," Alice Miranda said, "and he's a plain-vanilla kind of guy."

Fred Yamashita pressed a button on the remote. "All right, how about this Emerald employee?"

Up came a new face. Black hair in tight curls, big and glorious teeth, a pert, upturned nose, and permanently amused eyes. She wore a thick bow at her neck. She had one of those pert, crinkly, sunny faces, everybody's friend.

"My lord, what's Grace Justin doing up there on the screen?" Ray's eyebrows were back on his head. "She's my SeaTac ramp manager, and as nice a person as you'll ever meet."

Yamashita squared his pencil to his notepad, looking a touch embarrassed. "Well, we've found a videotape of her at an anti-government rally."

"I didn't think there were anti-government rallies anymore, not since Vietnam."

Yamashita hesitated. "Well, this is from the Vietnam era."

Wayne Ray stared at him. Then he burst out laughing, not an unkind laugh, a real laugh.

I couldn't help smiling, and neither could Dahlberg and Shrader. The faces of the FBI agents remained set in stone.

"Grace Justin must have been fifteen years old when that war ended," Ray could finally say.

"Fourteen," Yamashita said with starched dignity.

"And—what?—she was with a bunch of protestors outside a federal building somewhere, in Seattle? And you found her on a grainy old FBI tape of the event? A fourteen-year-old girl carrying a placard that said something like 'Stop the war'?"

"Precisely."

"That's really scraping the bottom, isn't it, Fred?"

Yamashita replied dully, "The slightest thing could lead somewhere important."

Wayne Ray admitted with a long breath, "Yeah, I know." Ray also knew that Yamashita and the others had been putting in hundred-hour weeks trying to—among other things—save Ray's airline. "Grace Justin is a sweet woman, a terrific employee. She actually says 'shucks' once in a while."

"Have you heard her say anything that was different or peculiar, could be construed as aggressive? Anything against Emerald?"

"Grace is about to be a grandmother," Ray said. "Her daughter is due in the next couple of days. Grace is a good employee, a smile for everybody. I wish I had a dozen like her."

Grace Justin was the last of twenty-two Emerald employees we had discussed at this meeting, each brought to the FBI's attention by some minuscule curiosity in his or her past. One employee had a brother who had spent time in the King County jail for burgling a Radio Shack. Another employee had washed out of the army's Ranger training, and had then quickly left the army. Another had been cited by the police for setting off cherry bombs—illegal in Seattle—on Independence Day. Piddling things, all of them, and they showed how desperate the FBI was.

Wayne Ray and Alice Miranda excused themselves, and Yamashita rubbed his face with his hands as if he had a towel. Next into our conference room came three deputy assistant

U.S. attorneys general—already building their prosecution against unidentified and unapprehended felons—and they remained just long enough for the FBI to tell them of its progress, less than five minutes.

Yamashita told them that the Saudi angle had so far come to nothing, and he told them that the drug-runners, Sonny Berquist and Nicholas Lawson, had been given an array of lie-detecting tests, and had been cleared of involvement with the detonation aboard *Sacajawea,* not that they were going to escape a visit to prison.

Then we spent ten minutes with the deputy director of the Federal Aviation Administration, filling him in. Discussions with the FAA were sometimes testy because the NTSB is concerned only with air safety, and need not consider the cost of any of its recommendations, which the FAA frequently likes to point out by way of criticism. The FAA's principal role is the promotion of the air industry, which might sometimes be viewed as being at cross purposes with the NTSB. This brief meeting was civil, and lasted less than ten minutes.

Though I was going back to my computer in the same building as this conference room at the Hailey airport, I walked Linda Dillon to her car. I told her it was to stretch my legs but I just wanted a few moments of her company. The sun at this high elevation was white and close, and I squinted against it. The parking lot was half full, mostly rental cars, and also a well-known red Hummer I'd seen around, owned by a Sun Valley Realtor. The sound of a small jet came from the north, drawing near. I didn't look up, but knew from the noise that it was a late-model Lear, probably a corporate plane.

We arrived at Linda's car. She fished in her bag for her keys. "I'm going to come back at six o'clock tonight, and wrestle you away from your computer."

"Make it eight," I said. "Then I'll buy you dinner."

"You say that, but you'll just expense account me."

"Somewhere nice, like the Pioneer Saloon. A baked potato with chives and minced olives and cilantro, all the stuff you rich people like, all in one potato. It'll be great."

"It's clear you didn't get enough sleep, Joe." Her chin came up. "You hear that?"

I shook my head.

She moved her head slowly, trying to pick up a sound. "Something . . ."

Then I heard it too, a soft soughing, like wind through the trees, though there weren't trees nearby. Then it came again. Something human, sort of.

Linda stepped quickly to the front of her car, which was parked in a row of other vehicles against a vacant lot covered with cheat grass and Jim Hill mustard and dandelions. Two legs stuck out from the weeds onto the asphalt. Wool suit pants and black wing tips. One of the legs twitched. We heard the noise again, and this time we knew it was a moan.

We rushed past four automobiles to the body, me following Linda, she digging into her bag for her pistol. I stepped over the man's legs, then brushed aside the tall grass.

"Ah hell," I breathed. "It's Wayne Ray."

I knelt to him, my knee sinking into the soft soil. I put my hand on his neck. His pulse was strong, but irregular. He tried to raise a hand, but it fell back. His mouth opened. Two of his front teeth were broken off at the gum, leaving ragged stumps. His nose was flat against his face. On his forehead and on his left cheek were abrasions, as if his face had been scraped against the asphalt. The knot of his tie was tight against his Adam's apple. I loosened it, then lightly gripped his arm. With another groan, he tried to get his elbows under himself to rise.

"Stay there, Wayne." I gently held him down. "It's me, Joe Durant. We'll get help."

Linda was already on her cell phone, telling a 911 dispatcher our location.

Blood flowed from a cut on Ray's lip. A piece of fractured tooth was stuck at the corner of his mouth. He moaned again, and I shifted to block the sun from his eyes.

Linda snapped her phone closed, then lowered herself to us. She was more cop than caregiver. "Who did this, Wayne?"

His eyes closed slowly, then reopened. With the slightest of movements of his head, he conveyed that he didn't know.

We waited for the ambulance, and Linda held Wayne Ray's hand.

Maybe this had nothing to do with *Sacajawea,* maybe this was a random mugging, but with a glance Linda told me she knew better, and so did I.

"I don't have any money." I opened my wallet to show her. "You'll have to pay for dinner."

"Use a credit card." Linda had ordered a twelve-ounce New York steak instead of a potato, and nothing was left on her plate, not a scrap.

"My daughter Sarah's counselor at Ballard High School called me into his office six months ago."

She sipped her water. "What's that got to do with you trying to chisel out of your deal to buy me dinner?"

"The counselor told me that Sarah had a good chance to get into Princeton. So I cut up all my credit cards in an attempt to start saving more money for her college tuition. You'll have to buy dinner. I'll pay you back."

She said, "You're a lot of fun, you know that, Joe?"

"It's not like I didn't try. I went to the cash machine around the corner, and the screen said it was temporarily out of service, and to come back in an hour."

"And the dog ate your homework." She reached into her purse for her wallet.

We had just spent two hours at the Wood River Medical Center, until the emergency room physician could give us a report on Wayne Ray. In addition to those injuries evident to us as he lay on the weeds next to the parking lot, Ray was suffering a concussion and a broken thumb and a fractured foot. The doctor had said, "Looks like somebody snapped his thumb back, and it broke like a candle. Then stomped on his foot, hard."

The physician had refused to let us speak with Ray, who was still rummy, but Linda had pushed the doctor aside like a gate and entered his room. I followed her. She asked Ray again if he could identify the person who had assaulted him. Ray's lower face was numb from the local anesthesia used when his lip was sutured, and he spoke as if he had a mouthful of marbles. He said he had been about to get into his car when he saw a blur at the edge of his vision, and the next thing he knew he was on the ground.

The blow to his head must have come first, and from behind—the doctor found a contusion at the rear of the skull, too sizable to be made with a fist, maybe a rock, the doctor guessed—because Ray couldn't remember his thumb being broken or his lip being split open, or his face being scraped along the asphalt. The doctor found small pebbles in the wounds.

Over dinner, Linda and I had speculated about who would want to rough up Wayne Ray. He had been a University of Washington lineman, and was a big fellow who still looked fit. Few muggers would dare to go one-on-one with him. Linda suggested that two people might have committed the assault. The muggers didn't take Ray's wallet or his car, and so were only interested in hurting him.

The list of folks who might have generated reasons to despise the Emerald Airline CEO was a long one: relatives of all *Sacajawea* victims. But that a relative would assault Wayne Ray ran against my understanding of how one heals after such a blow. These poor folks were mostly interested in trying to recover, were trying to throw off their terrible grief.

Or perhaps one of the Idaho Resisters—Ed Fahey or Doug Dietz or Runny Smith—had decided that sending the Emerald chief to the hospital would make some point. Smith was out of jail. Fahey enjoyed his fearsome reputation. And though the Resisters were dumber than gravel, it didn't seem likely they would compound their troubles by viciously assaulting the Emerald CEO. A team of FBI agents and a Blaine County deputy sheriff were going to question Wayne Ray after he got a night's sleep.

So Linda and I were clueless, not for the first time on the *Sacajawea* investigation. Still, I enjoyed sitting across from her, watching her eat, and catching other men glancing at her. The Pioneer Saloon was dimly lit, and the table's candle threw soft colors across her face, accenting her high cheekbones and the graceful lines of her jaw and chin. She was feeling better, and she sat across from me and talked away, delighted that she did not have to accommodate so much pain. Her lipstick was darker than usual, maybe applied for the evening, and her hair was swept back into a gay ponytail that made her look like she was just off the slopes, rather than packing firepower in her purse. She was wearing a fairly tight-fitting knit ski sweater that was the particular focus of several guys at the bar.

She calculated the tip, then left the money next to her

plate. When I helped Linda into her coat, it required her to reach back and push her chest out, and it took me a while to help her, with her arm still in a wrap. The gaze of every male in the place snapped around, damn them, as if some Marine Corps DI had just barked, "Eyes right." Linda knew what was going on, probably accepted it as her due, and smiled to herself in a small way. I followed her down the narrow aisle and out of the tavern, two dozen pairs of eyes watching us.

A spring wind was blowing down Ketchum's main street, as cold as any other place's winter wind. I held my coat against myself as we walked along. "I'm going to pay you back for dinner."

"Who cares whether the FBI or the NTSB buys it? I'll just add it to my account."

"Then I'll buy you a post-dinner sherry," I offered. "A really good twenty-year-old sherry. Sarah doesn't need to go to college."

"I still can't drink alcohol, the doctor said, not until I'm entirely clear of the painkiller."

"Then I'll buy you a Dr. Pepper." I was trying to tell her I didn't want the evening to end yet, but she wasn't getting it.

The cash machine was half a block away and around a corner. I entered my card and my number, hoping the machine was back on line.

Linda nodded down the street and said, "This guy wants to talk to one of us."

I followed her gaze. The snow was gone but the street was still lined with rows of gravel thrown down for traction during the last storm. It was eleven o'clock at night, yet the fellow who approached us was wearing a business suit and black wing tips. Behind him at the curb, the rear door of a Lincoln was open, so this fellow had a driver.

The man grinned at us in a practiced way. He slowed as he approached, and half extended his hand. There was an unmistakable urbanity, a silkiness, in his motions.

"May I speak with you, Ms. Dillon?"

"You already are." She shifted her bag so her gun hand was near the zipper.

"Mr. Durant?"

"That's me." The cash machine whirred faintly. "Can we help you?"

"My name is Hamed Ibn Mahtab."

"Something to do with the Lady-in-the-Hat?" I took the eighty dollars from the machine, then moved my hand to wait for the receipt and my card.

He was too polished to act puzzled by my remark. "I am the third deputy ambassador to the United States from the Kingdom of Saudi Arabia."

Linda eyed him. "At Russian embassies, the third guy on the chart is always the intelligence chief, more powerful than the ambassador. Is that how it works in Saudi Arabia?"

His smile was as thin as a razor cut. "I normally try a little charm at first, but with you"—he dipped his chin at Linda—"I don't think it will work."

She smiled, charmed.

Hamed Ibn Mahtab wore a mustache the color of his shoes, and a ruby ring on his left pinky. His tie was maroon silk with no pattern. His eyes were set narrowly, and not even his suave presentation could remove the cunning from them. His lips were compressed and bloodless. His hands were elegant, with long fingers and well-manicured nails, a pianist's hands.

"I am here on a matter of some urgency," he said. "It's a matter of security for my country, a grave matter."

"Fay Herwin at North Star contacted you?" Linda asked.

"It was a service, yes." He stroked his chin. "We've come upon a bit of a difficulty regarding the gentleman from Saudi Arabia who was in North Star's care."

"Khalid bin Abdallah," Linda said. "Go ahead, you can say his name. We all know it."

"Yes, well, that would point to our problem, wouldn't it?" The diplomat had no accent that I could detect. He said, "Khalid was in a delicate position within the kingdom's administration."

"He oversaw intelligence operations against Iraq and Iran," I said.

He inhaled through his teeth, a sharp reptilian sound. "You have excellent sources, yes."

"So what are you suggesting?" Linda's hand moved slightly away from her bag.

"It would do the kingdom significant harm were Khalid's difficulties to be known."

"That he was a drunk and a bully?"

"Irreparable harm," the Saudi said smoothly. "It would create a host of grave problems."

"Yeah, I know how that works," she said tonelessly.

"No, you don't, I assure you." The man was exquisitely polite, an art, really. Sincere, entirely convincing, yet with a touch of diffidence, and as smooth as river stone. He wore a tuxedo most of the time, you could bet. "I'm speaking of damage to a large security apparatus. The spread of this knowledge could cause a wide breach. Many of our people would be vulnerable were this to become known."

"Mostly, though," I said, "you just don't want your ruling family—in a rigidly teetotaling country—to be embarrassed by word getting out about Khalid's alcohol problems."

He nodded in a way that complimented me on my wisdom. "There is also an element of that, to be sure."

"You're too late," Linda said. "Even if we were to agree to your suggestion that we sit on it, our conversation with Fay Herwin at North Star is already in the system."

"Of course it is." The diplomat renewed his skillful smile. "But judicious requests here and there can make an enormous difference, we have found. And we must begin with those who made the discovery, which is to say, you both."

Linda said, "Yeah, well, it sounds like you are trying to squelch an aspect of the *Sacajawea* investigation, trying to hinder the FBI and NTSB in their investigation. Is that it?"

"Nothing of the sort." He spread his hands in a gesture of utter reason.

"Impeding an FBI investigation is a felony." Her voice was flinty.

"Nothing could be further from my intent. I just want to suggest that intelligence is a fragile thing, susceptible to many influences, including scandal."

"We'll keep it in mind," Linda said.

The Saudi waited until three fellows passed us, smelling of beer and singing the Michigan fight song.

Then he said, "The more delicate an aspect of intelligence is, the more value we put on it."

He was making a suggestion, but it was yet too veiled for me to see it. I looked over his shoulder at the Lincoln. In the darkness I couldn't see the fellow sitting behind the wheel, but he'd be plenty tough.

Hamed Ibn Mahtab went on, "The more we know, the better our choices."

"Is there a point here?" Linda asked, still miffed.

He shrugged, but not like I shrug, just a ripple of his suit

at the shoulder. "For example, yesterday Coach Benson telephoned Coach Upton asking to see Jason's game films."

So full of Americana was this piece of news, and so familiar to me were the names, that for a moment it seemed the
Arab had switched languages.

"What did you say?" I asked.

"Jason's got a good chance for a scholarship to the University of Washington, it would appear."

Jason was my daughter's boyfriend. Doug Benson was the
men's basketball coach at the University of Washington, and
Cal Upton was the men's basketball coach at Ballard High
School, where Sarah and her boyfriend Jason went to school.

I tried not to gape at the man. "How can you possibly
know that?"

He bowed his head slightly, taking my question as a com-
pliment. "Intelligence means we know our enemies"—he
paused significantly—"and we know our friends. I feel as if
I've come to know you both."

Linda put a charge into her voice. "There's nothing we can
do. We already told you that."

"You use this automatic teller frequently, Mr. Durant,
whenever you are in Ketchum." He turned his head to look at
the cash machine. "You always take eighty dollars from it. But
sometimes it doesn't work as well as it should. Ninety minutes
ago this machine wasn't working."

Linda was about to say something more, but I shook my
head at her. I was both bewildered and curious. The Arab was
leading me down a road, and I wanted to know where it went.

"I cannot ask to look inside your wallet, of course." These
words were said more slowly, as if he already knew this ven-
ture was going to be successful. And the diplomat was a man
who took pleasure in listening to himself. "But if you just

removed your usual eighty dollars from the machine, you now have three hundred twenty dollars remaining in your checking account."

I flushed with anger, and was about to sputter some response, but he cut me off.

"And twelve hundred seven dollars in your savings account." He allowed himself a larger smile. "But, you see, sometimes even our intelligence services can give us a faulty report, and we make a mistake."

"The hell you doing snooping around my bank account?"

He asked, "Will you do me the kindness of inspecting the receipt this automatic teller machine just gave you?"

It was still in my hand, waiting transfer to my wallet. I glanced at Linda. Then I stepped closer to the cash machine's light and brought up the slip of paper. Under the THANK YOU FOR USING A MARTEL AUTOMATIC TELLER was the line showing my $80 withdrawal, and below that my ending balance.

One million three hundred twenty dollars.

I played trombone with the paper, adjusting the receipt to the light and my eyes. The new million dollars stubbornly remained attached to my $320.

I turned to the Arab, holding the receipt like it was a piece of the true cross.

"Something amiss?" he asked sweetly, all innocence.

Linda took the receipt from my hand to peer at it. "You've put a million dollars into Joe's account." She whistled. "That's about six different felonies."

"A million dollars," I said to myself.

"A million three twenty," he corrected.

"You're a goddamn crook, no better than a bank robber," Linda exclaimed, her voice a piping that could be heard down the block. "Trying to bribe us, for God's sake."

The diplomat said, "Ms. Dillon, you shouldn't keep so much money in your checking account. Over ten thousand dollars. But you should examine your account more often. You'd be surprised how money can grow, even in a low-interest checking account."

Linda was so angry she was vibrating, all of her, and my little receipt was shaking in her hand. "I'm going to bust you." She brought her handbag around.

Again he smiled. "After your first mention of American criminal law a moment ago—something about impeding an investigation—I should have pointed out that I have diplomatic immunity. I cannot be arrested for anything. Under any circumstance. At any time."

She had opened her bag, but now her hand stilled.

The Saudi said, "It's one of my job's nicer benefits."

"There's ways to take care of pissant diplomats, ways that aren't in the manuals," she said in a stainless-steel voice. "Publicity, for one. The FBI will go public with this."

"With what? If Mr. Durant were to check his account again right now, he would find the same old boring three hundred twenty dollars."

I studied the receipt. I liked all those zeros.

He said, "Perhaps that one million dollars was just a typographical error, something wrong with the automatic teller's printer, or a little glitch at the bank."

"Goddamn you," she said.

The diplomat took a half step toward his car. "What do you Americans say? Easy come, easy go?"

"I still ought to run you in. It'll take your government a day or two to find you and spring you."

The Arab clucked his teeth. "We help our friends and punish our enemies. If we decide you've been helpful keeping this little secret, who knows what might again happen to your bank account." He dipped his head in a vaguely French way. "Ms. Dillon. Mr. Durant. Something to think about, wouldn't you say?"

He retreated to his automobile. A fellow the size of a sofa—tight blue suit, granite jaw, a veteran of some war or another—leaped out of the driver's side door and ran around the back of the car to shut the door.

I took the receipt from her and looked forlornly at it. The Lincoln pulled away from the curb, did a U-turn, and headed east toward the Sun Valley Lodge.

She stared at it until it disappeared, then said, "We've just learned something important, Joe."

"Like what?"

"Something, and it's big. I just don't know what."

"That guy went to a lot of trouble to trick out a cash machine," I said.

"So it was important to them. Other than that, I don't know. Fred Yamashita's head is going to explode when he hears this. He hates this kind of stuff, trying to taint one of his jobs. And he'll also dislike that it's going to give the State Department and CIA a bigger role in the investigation. It suggests that the three Arabs on the plane might have had something to do with a bomb on the plane."

"There was no bomb on the plane," I said equably. "I am in the middle of proving that it was a bit of electricity finding its way to the center fuel tank."

"So you keep saying."

"A million dollars, you just cost me," I said.

"I should've slammed that Arab diplomat against the cash machine and put cuffs on him."

"My daughter's education at Princeton, my bills all paid

for the first time ever, a nice summer home up in the San Juan Islands."

She grabbed my arm and dragged me away from the cash machine and toward our car, which was down the block behind Louis's Pizza. "Joe, you're yanking my chain, and I know it, and you know I know it."

"I'd buy a Jaguar," I said dreamily. "Some nice cigars. Look into a cruise to the Azores."

When she squeezed my arm, I could feel her fingernails. "Joe, if I thought you'd have taken that silky bastard's money, I'd give you one to the groin and leave you curled up in a fetal position along this Ketchum curb, you retching and gasping, and I'd never give you another thought."

"You say the most romantic things, Linda."

We walked a few paces, then she smiled widely at me.

TWENTY-SEVEN

To the employees of Central Idaho Forwarders, it must have seemed that the dam broke.

One minute they were sitting there in their carrels and offices near the Boise airport, working their keyboards and telephones, thinking about lunch, and the next minute their offices were filled to the walls with IRS and FBI agents, who had rushed in from three doors, waving subpoenas.

The agents shouted, "Hands off the keyboards," and "Get away from your computers," and "Don't touch anything."

They didn't want hard drives erased or disks slipped out of sight. Some of the agents carried empty cardboard file boxes. Within seconds, every Central Forwarder employee had an IRS or FBI agent at his or her elbow.

"What's going on here?" A fellow wearing a rumpled white shirt and a tie four inches too short emerged from his office at the corner of the work area. Several other Central Forwarder executives had offices along the wall. All the offices had windows to the main work area so they could monitor the employees at their workstations.

He had been eating a Hostess cupcake, and still had half of it in his hand. He wiped the corners of his mouth with his hand, and tossed the remaining pastry into a wastebasket as he looked around, trying to determine which of us was in charge. He no longer was, that was for sure.

He said brusquely, "Someone tell me what's going on."

Linda Dillon had entered the office just ahead of me. When she held up her badge, the man involuntarily back-stepped.

She said, "FBI. We are seizing your records as per a sub-poena duces tecum issued by the federal district court an hour ago. Please remain where you are, and do not return to your office." She had a manila envelope in her other hand.

"The hell?" Still chewing, he tucked in an errant shirttail. "The hell the FBI doing here? A subpoena? For what?"

His name was Bob Arneson, and I had read the file the FBI had just compiled on him. Arneson was the founder of Central Idaho Forwarders, a man who credited gallstones for his success. Twenty years ago the stones hurt so much he could no longer drive his eighteen-wheeler, so he took out a Small Business Association loan and purchased two more trucks, and hired his friends to drive all three, Arneson acting as dispatcher. Arneson's trucking line was a success because he worked harder than his competitors, which he happily ad-mitted to anyone who would listen, and because he fudged the paperwork here and there, which he had also admitted in a plea bargain before an Idaho Superior Court five years ago after being indicted for cheating employees out of over-time wages. He was sentenced to community service and restitution.

"The FBI visited you a week ago," Linda said. "You remem-ber?"

He wet his lower lip. "Yeah, sure. They didn't talk to me though, just our hiring guy."

"He played dumb for us. Said he didn't recognize anybody in the photos we showed him."

"Well, he answered as best he could." Arneson tried to sound indignant.

"We're here for your records," Linda said. "All your files, all your paperwork, hard drives, everything."

"What for, for God's sake?" he blustered. "You can't do this."

"I bet we can." Linda turned a full circle, inventorying the room, with all the federal suits hovering over the dispatchers and salespeople. "Looks like we already have."

"You'll shut me down." Arneson flapped his arms like a bird. "I can't do business, you take away all my records. All my trucks'll go idle."

Bob Arneson's face was full, almost bloated, maybe from years of cupcakes. There were no angles to it, just smooth curves. His pink nose was a network of burst capillaries, and his small eyes were set far back in his skull. Maybe wondering whether he should be offended or afraid, Arneson continued to wave his arms, stirring the air.

Linda said, "We've got credible evidence that you've been paying cash to some of your temp drivers, not bothering with pesky formalities like income tax and Social Security deductions."

He gave her a black scowl. "Well, that's all crapola, and I can prove it."

"You'll get your chance," she replied. "Under oath, before a jury."

Central Idaho Forwarders ran almost eighty trucks, mostly out of its warehouse at the edge of the Boise airport. The company owned cargo vans, flatbeds, low boys, boom trucks, an air ride van, tilt beds, curtain side trucks, and pole trailers, and it hauled freight as far east as Idaho Falls and as far west as Payette and Fruitland in Idaho and Ontario in eastern Oregon. Much of its territory was in the Sawtooths, serving the small communities north and east of Boise.

"I can't be shut down," he tried again. "I've got six thousand live chicks sitting in one of my trucks waiting to be taken to Nampa. I've got two thousand gallons of ice cream on its way to Mountain Home Air Force Base, and it's broke down and waiting for one of my mechanics." He searched his memory, rubbing the back of his hand across his mouth. "I've got a shipment of tetanus vaccine headed to Twin Falls. You don't want a bunch of kids getting lockjaw, do you?" Arneson's tie was a green field covered with tiny semitractors. "What could be worse? You shut me down, there could be an outbreak of lockjaw. Live with that."

Linda stared at him. "An outbreak of lockjaw?"

He nodded vigorously, his second chin going in and out.

"Follow me," Linda ordered. "Maybe we can talk."

It sounded like an offer to bargain. Arneson almost walked on her heels toward a corner of the office. All eyes were on her. Some of the FBI agents were wearing mean grins. This was Jamie Suarez and Linda Dillon's operation, and they had recruited the IRS. Suarez and several other agents were in the next room, keeping folks away from the IBM AS-400 computer, which ran Varipro software, monitoring each shipment from point of order through dispatch to delivery. The AS-400 also controlled the payroll and billing systems.

Some of Arneson's employees, many wearing telephone headsets, half rose from their carrels to watch their boss. A punch clock was near a row of gray lockers. The office contained not one decoration, nothing on the walls, no plants on desks, not even framed photographs of family members. The large calendar near the water cooler didn't have the standard Idaho wildlife print attached to it. People worked here, nothing else.

I followed Arneson. Linda hadn't introduced me, wanting to blindside him. He reached the corner and turned to face us, his mouth working silently, ready to agree to almost anything.

She said, "We know you've been giving some of your temps envelopes of cash, instead of doing the proper payroll deductions, and nothing I can do is going to make that headache go away for you. The IRS will see to that."

Arneson shrugged. "Hey, I've been—"

She didn't let him continue. "The IRS has been investigating you for eight months. They have you cold. But maybe you can keep your stock rolling today and tomorrow and next month, and you can deal with the IRS in the courts, and maybe your company will survive and maybe it won't. But at least you can deliver those chicks and the vaccine, and continue on day to day."

"Yeah, well—"

"But if you don't talk to me right now about one of your employees, I'm going to shut your doors. And I'm going to confiscate all your records, everything right down to your vehicles' hand tags, haul logs, and daily inspection books."

"Which employee?" Arneson asked eagerly, ready to rat on anybody.

"I don't want any hemming or hawing because you might've been paying this driver cash, and you don't want to fess up to cheating the government and the Idaho Department of Revenue. This is bigger than that. Got it?"

"Which one?" He was fairly panting.

Linda pulled out three eight-by-eleven photographs from

the envelope. The Idaho Resisters. Ed Fahey, Doug Dietz, and Runny Smith.

Arneson took two of the photos, and took a step to one side to gather better light from an overhead fixture. Linda held up the third photo for him. His gaze went back and forth.

Finally he shook his head. "I don't know any of these guys."

"You sure?" Linda's voice was metallic, like a padlock snapping shut on the gate to Arneson's truck lot.

"I got over a hundred drivers. I don't know them all, never even seen some of them, for God's sake." He turned toward the row of glass-paneled offices, and yelled, "Ted, get over here."

An executive emerged from a glass-paneled office, where he had been watched over by an FBI agent. He approached us tentatively.

"This is Ted Sessions, my hiring guy," Arneson said without looking at him. "Ted, the FBI is back, and this time they aren't kidding."

"My title is human resources manager," Sessions replied with the slightly pained expression of one wearing tight shoes.

"Take a look at these three, Ted. They work for us? We ever hire any of them?"

"Well," he looked at Linda, "one of your agents already asked me about these photos, last week, and—"

Arneson cut him off. "Ted, now I'm telling you to remember better. Last time, you may not have known what was on the line here. They're going to shut us down unless your memory improves."

Sessions gathered the photographs, then spread them in his hands like he was fanning cards. He was no taller than Linda, and wore a pager on his belt, and spectacles that flashed on and off with reflected light as he moved his head. On his lip was an over-clipped, prissy mustache. His mouth twitched as he studied the photos. Then his gaze shifted to one wall, then another, as if he were looking for an escape route.

When he finally looked at his boss, Arneson said, "Better tell it all, Ted."

Sessions cleared his throat. "I hired this fellow, and he worked for us for about three weeks, I think." He paused. "That's right, about three weeks."

I leaned forward. He was pointing at the photo of Runny Smith.

"When did he work for you?" I asked.

Sessions turned to me, seeing me for the first time. "Well, it was—"

"Do you have a record of his employment?" I asked. "Did you get a federal ID or a Social Security number, or a current medical card? His licenses? Do you have results of a drug screen?"

Bob Arneson scratched his nose with a finger. "Well, sometimes we don't keep good records on our temp drivers. You know, with all the paperwork and stuff."

"You don't do the paperwork so you don't have to pay overtime and Social Security," Linda said. "Keeps your overhead down, lets you give lowball pricing that J.B. Hunt and Consolidated and the other big shippers can't match."

"I may have some record of him." Sessions squirmed. "What was his name again?"

"Gerald Smith," Linda replied. "Goes by Runny Smith."

During the earlier interview—done by an FBI agent as part of a canvass of every freight handling firm in Idaho—the Central Idaho Forwarders' HR manager Ted Sessions had apparently lied, saying he didn't recognize Smith, to avoid implicating himself and his company on federal and state wage and tax charges.

But this morning the FBI had received a break. An agent carrying copies of the three Idaho Resisters' photos door to door in Hailey came across a tavern owner who thought—he couldn't be sure, but he just thought—that the fellow with the long bangs might have delivered a new Foosball table to his place of business. The tavern owner couldn't remember the Central Idaho Forwarder driver saying anything other than, "Got a delivery for you. Need some help getting it off the rig." The tavern owner had assisted him in unloading the table. The driver hadn't said anything else, had just held out the receipt for signature, climbed back into the cab of his truck, and off he went.

"You're sure?" I pointed at the photo of Smith. "This fellow, the guy with the bangs?"

"Yeah, I'm positive. He was a big guy, sort of a lump. Didn't say much. But he could drive a truck well enough."

"Did he have a State of Idaho truck permit?"

"Well, I didn't ask him," Sessions replied, stiff with embarrassment. "I hired him first as a package handler at our warehouse, but then a couple days later we let him behind the wheel, as we were short of drivers."

"Was he working for you last April, in early April? Driving?"

"Yeah, he was, I'm sure," Sessions said. "He left here in April, sometime in the middle of the month. One Monday he didn't show up for work, and we never saw him again."

"As part of his job did he deliver parcels to the Hailey airport?" I asked.

"All our drivers do, every one of them."

Arneson added, "Most of our business is shipping to and from airports."

"Do you have any record of the parcels he delivered?" I asked.

"That's a while ago." Sessions chewed on his lip. "Maybe."

"You still going to close us down?" Arneson asked nervously.

"All I want are the records you have about Runny Smith and his deliveries," Linda said. "I don't control the IRS. They're going to dig around."

"But my trucks can still roll?"

"As far as the FBI is concerned."

He exhaled hugely, a man with a pardon. "Everything we've got, Ted. Give'm the works."

I looked at Linda, and she was staring right back at me, her eyes bright with this victory. The FBI had something solid. At last.

My spark theory was about to be destroyed—dismantled, plowed under, and the ground salted—and I should have known as much when I walked into the reconstruction hangar, and saw Pierre Lemercier standing next to a fuel tank mock-up identical to the one I had prepared in the Nevada desert. He was in a crowd, but he was up on his toes, his gaze on the door, waiting my entrance. When he saw me, his eyes lit with the pleasure of imminent revenge and his mouth took on a wintry grin.

The knot of investigators was near *Sacajawea*'s nose cone. Rich Shrader and Dick Dahlberg and others, and Hugh Clifton, the board chairman, were there. William Henley, the FBI director, was speaking with Fred Yamashita and Linda Dillon. People from the FAA and State Department were also gathered around.

A fuel tank was propped up on sawhorses, the same-style

Tenvik tank. A nozzle was attached to an intake valve, and a hose went between the fuel tank and a white pressurized container, resembling a propane tank. Wires ran from a terminal block to a panel of instruments. All eyes turned to me. ATF's lawyer Daryl Wallace wasn't so professional that he wasn't wearing a huge victory grin.

"Joe, I am delighted you could make time to visit us here," Lemercier boomed.

As if I had a choice, when asked by NTSB Chairman Clifton.

The ATF founder introduced me to two scientists from the California Institute of Technology, but I was trying to anticipate what awful thing was coming, and I didn't catch their names.

Lemercier said, "At my request, Cal Tech performed a few tests on fuel vapor. We precisely replicated your Nevada test, right down to the buildup of copper sulfide on the interior of the tank, to the frayed wires, and all the other fiddling you did to get your explosion." He clapped his hands twice, like a maître d'hôtel summoning a waiter. "Are we ready?"

"You are going to put electricity into the tank?" I asked. "With fuel vapors in there?"

"Precisely." The Frenchman offered an indulgent smile.

I asked, "We're standing a little close, don't you think?"

"We are perfectly safe. Let's start with the same one-quarter millijoule that detonated the Nevada tank." Lemercier nodded at one of the scientists, who had assumed a position behind the instrument panel.

I rubbed my hands together. A completely unnecessary showy red light—resembling a cop car's bubble—had been placed on the instrument panel. It flashed on then off.

"Do you see?" Lemercier said. "Nothing."

Linda Dillon joined me.

"Let's quadruple the charge, to a millijoule," Lemercier said.

The scientist made an adjustment, then said, "Ready."

The red light blinked on and off again. The tank remained undisturbed on the sawhorses.

"Joe, your error was in ignoring ambient temperature," Lemercier said magisterially. "Now let's turn it up to ten millijoules."

It was done. Other than the red light briefly doing its work, nothing happened.

Lemercier said, "The Cal Tech study, which I must admit to having funded, has shown that there exists a huge difference between the electric energy required to detonate fuel vapors in a cool tank and in a tank just a few degrees warmer, even if the vapors inside the tank are sufficiently hot to make them flammable. Let's go to a hundred millijoules."

Another flash of light from the bubble, painting all of our faces red for an instant. Mine didn't need any more red.

"You see, Joe, it gets hot in the desert." He glanced at me. "The Nevada sun, beating down on the flat metal of the tank, radiating up from the hot ground, had warmed your tank at Western Explosives Research to perhaps a hundred twenty degrees."

Linda shifted her weight my way, a tiny indication of support.

"Yet, *Sacajawea* was flying on a cool spring day at eleven thousand feet over the mountains. Temperature at that altitude on that date was perhaps ten degrees."

I countered weakly, "What about heat from the heating and air-conditioning units near *Sacajawea*'s tank?"

"Our studies show they could not possibly have raised the temperature around *Sacajawea*'s fuel tanks more than a few degrees." Lemercier again addressed the Cal Tech scientist at the panel. "Now let's try, for the fun of it, a thousand milli-joules."

The splash of red light again came and went. The fuel tank obdurately remained intact. Director Henley looked at me. I give him credit: he kept this victory off his face.

Which was more than Lemercier could do. He grinned broadly and said, "Cal Tech has shown that it would take a spark a hundred thousand times stronger to ignite fuel in a tank at seventy degrees—and *Sacajawea*'s tank vapors could not possibly have been that warm—than at your hundred twenty degrees in the Nevada desert."

I felt like a cable was around my chest. Each of Lemercier's words cinched it tighter. I had to work to breathe.

"So what we have found," Lemercier announced in a princely manner, "is that your vapor ignition simply could not have happened, not at those temperatures, not with *Sacajawea*'s wiring, even if that wiring were faulty."

Linda brushed me with her shoulder.

Might as well drive that nail all the way home. He said, "A vapor explosion aboard *Sacajawea* was a physical impossibility, rather like a perpetual motion machine."

I was petulant. "You don't have evidence of a bomb."

He said, "When you eliminate all other possibilities, you must examine closely whatever remains. Only a bomb remains, Joe."

After a moment I could say, "Yeah, well, I'm not done."

I turned away from Lemercier, and walked away from the group of investigators, walked away from *Sacajawea*'s hulk, toward the hangar door. Linda was beside me.

I knew then, and all of my friends at the NTSB whose opinion I valued so highly, Dick Dahlberg and Rich Shrader and the others, also knew, that I had committed the egregious error of becoming a partisan for a probable cause. I had made up my mind before all the evidence was in, and had been pressing my opinion on others in an unprofessional way. I had fallen victim to human nature, but NTSB investigators are required to overcome that nature, to be as dispassionate and as neutral as possible. I had failed, and so looked like a ridiculous amateur. I beat my retreat across the hangar to the white light of the door, and it was an act of will that kept me from sprinting.

Linda said, "You can start on another angle right away, Joe."

I didn't bother to reply. I felt like I'd been beaten up in a school-yard fight. So complete was this humiliation that I ached in my joints.

Just as I reached the door, I was astonished when Pierre Lemercier—his cane in his hand and not touching the floor—caught up with Linda and me.

"Joe, a moment, please."

I turned to him, wincing.

He peered at me. "Joe, I've been shot out of the sky, too."

I hesitated, then replied, "Those were Messerschmitts doing the shooting."

"I suspect the feeling is the same."

"Yes, sir."

He gripped my arm tightly, like I imagined he had gripped the stick of his Spitfire. "Every time it happened, I just started over again."

My eyes were locked on his. I felt his strength pour into me, so intensely and fiercely I was suddenly giddy.

"The poacher's missile and the drug hit have already been

eliminated. Now we must turn to whatever is left. You have the expertise and the reputation. I need your help, Joe." His words were slow, and said with an iron cadence, "I need you to help find the bastards who did this to *Sacajawea*."

I nodded.

"So you dust yourself off, and begin again."

I felt like I had just regained the twelve or eighteen inches that had been chopped off me a few minutes before in the hangar.

"Thank you, sir." I was so grateful I was about to shed tears.

He smiled knowingly, winked at Linda in the way only the French can wink, and turned to rejoin the investigators.

Large with renewed confidence and energy, I stepped into the light. Linda walked next to me.

She teased, "You're a little old for hero worship, aren't you, Joe?"

"Not at all," I replied adamantly. "Not at all."

Not that my spark theory needed another nail in its coffin, but it got one anyway. Later that afternoon Fred Yamashita received a phone call from Susan Halsey, who was on her way from Ellensburg to Seattle. She said she had something, and it was important.

We met her in Yamashita's office in the federal building. She had been in such a hurry she had not removed her examining-room apron. She brushed back her hair with the back of her hand. Her forehead glistened with sweat. She had been moving fast, maybe too impatient to take the elevator. She carried a briefcase.

She said, "Yesterday the remains of Matthew Palmer were found, almost two miles from the crash site. Now we are missing only two other bodies. Much of Matthew Palmer had been eaten by vultures and coyotes, but I examined what remained of his body."

Palmer had been sitting in 2A. Yamashita worked his mouth, anticipating the news.

Dr. Halsey said, "I almost missed it, because it was lodged behind the ischium, which is the name of the bone at the lower part of the pelvis."

"Missed what?" Yamashita demanded.

She opened her briefcase and pulled out an evidence Baggie. She passed it to Yamashita.

"It's a nail," she said needlessly. "And I'll bet your tests show it is a double-zinc shingle nail."

Yamashita held the bag carefully, reverentially. "And I'll bet it was manufactured by the Sure-Secure Company of Leeds, England, the same kind of nail sent to us in the envelope."

TWENTY-EIGHT

The next day we were at 10,000 feet over eastern Washington, heading southeast toward the Hailey airport. The sun was still high, but most of the window slats were down. This was a State Department Fokker. The forward third of the cabin consisted of two meeting rooms, where I suspected DCI Alexander Barrow was taking a nap. In the row ahead of me, Rich Shrader had nodded off. Across the aisle Fred Yamashita dozed, his chin on his tie. His eyeglasses were folded across a spiral binder on his lap. Other investigators in the cabin also dozed. Kurt Cheney was in the seat behind me.

I removed my laptop from its case. This Fokker had both power and access links for every seat on the plane. The plane's electronics were connected to the State Department's server, I don't know how. I plugged in the computer, opened it, and pressed the power button.

Linda Dillon slept in the seat next to me, a brown wool blanket over her and a small aircraft-issue pillow behind her neck. Her head wagged when the plane dipped in an air current. I leaned slightly her way, and turned my head. Her hair smelled of lilacs. I breathed the scent a moment, not too long, then turned back to the computer, feeling like a thief.

Logging on took a moment, and then I found the usual fifty new messages, give or take, most from the *Sacajawea* team, routed through the NTSB Seattle field office. One e-mail was marked PRIORITY. Only a few people had that code. I brought it up. It was from my daughter Sarah, saying she had decided to forgo college, and instead take a correspondence course in aromatherapy from a school based in Nepal.

She was giving me the business. I typed, *You already smell great, so save your money. I love you.* I never knew whether she thought I was funny or corny, whether she would laugh or roll her eyes to the ceiling, a gesture learned from her mother. I moved the cursor to the send button on the tool bar and tapped a key.

Then I brought up the latest medical report on Wayne Ray. He had checked out of the hospital, wearing a walking foot cast, and was spending much of the day at a dentist's office to have temporary caps put on his front teeth. The permanent caps would be ready in a week. A cast was on his hand, holding his fractured thumb in place. A butterfly bandage was holding a splint on the bridge of his nose. The clinic had given him motor and memory tests, and he seemed fine, though Ray could still remember nothing of the incident, except the blur at the corner of his vision before he was brought low.

I checked a message from ANG—Aviation National Guarantee—a leading American insurer of private aircraft. For a year they had been trying to hire me as an accident investigator. This message increased their offer by $10,000 a year. ANG was becoming hard to ignore. I filed it to my hard drive.

Linda shifted in her seat, leaning a little closer, a soft sound escaping her, not a snore, more a purr. She was exhausted—we all were—working on just a few hours' sleep each night. *Sacajawea* investigators had been reduced to snatching catnaps here and there. Most of us on the State Department plane were using this short journey to try to catch up on our shut-eye, insulated however briefly from the tension and the grind.

Eighteen-hour days had filled my head with cotton, and I had trouble concentrating. My eyes were grainy. Words on the screen floated together. Yet I couldn't sleep, frustration was seeing to that. I had been hired for this job, yet didn't feel like I was adding much to the investigation, except a flawed and distracting theory.

I pulled up another e-mail, one with an odd origin, the Elko County, Nevada, sheriff, distributed to me and five hundred other *Sacajawea* investigators by the FBI. One of his deputy sheriffs had pulled over a 1998 Caprice heading south on U.S. 93, between Twin Falls, Idaho, and Wells, Nevada, near H-D Summit. The Caprice had registered ninety-eight miles an hour on the deputy's radar gun. The officer knew from the plate that the Caprice was a rental, and with his onboard computer had checked the Caprice with the Nevada State Patrol's central records—the inquiry came back negative—then left his prowl car to approach the Caprice.

The Caprice's driver emerged from his car, his right hand trailing behind him and hidden for that instant, and took one step toward the deputy and swung at him, a roundhouse arc that landed a heavy metal bar square on the deputy's cap and head, sending the officer to the ground. A crowbar, the deputy later guessed from his hospital room. The driver then used the bar on the prowl car's radios and computer. The deputy awoke a few minutes later when a passing motorist stopped and sprinkled water on the officer's forehead. The Caprice was gone.

The rental car was later found in Wells, wiped clean of prints. Four days before the battery on the deputy sheriff, the car had been rented in Reno from the airport Budget counter by a Greg

Johnson, who had produced a Nevada driver's license that the sheriff had now determined had been altered. The license's number, recorded by the Budget agent, led nowhere.

The Elko County sheriff had notified the FBI because of the similarity between Wayne Ray's and the deputy's beating, done with a heavy length of metal, maybe a crowbar. The deputy had had only a fleeting glance of the Caprice driver. About six feet three or four, thick chest, no neck, dark hair swept back on his head, a blue or gray sports jacket, in his mid or late thirties. In his hospital bed, the deputy had been shown photographs of the Idaho Resisters, and was confident that none of them was the Caprice driver. The FBI was preparing to show the deputy photographs of all male adult relatives of the *Sacajawea* victims, and anybody else they could think of.

Fred Yamashita had awoken, and had reapplied his spectacles to his face, and was trying to read the notebook on his lap, but his head dipped down, then jerked up again, then down again, like one of those toy birds at a water glass. The plane's wing lifted a fraction. I opened the window slat several inches, saw only blue sky and green fields, which merged seamlessly in the hazy distance. The light fell across Linda, and she half said something, so I lowered the blind. She shifted, her hair touching my shoulder. I opened and closed my mouth, trying to relieve the pressure in my ears.

"You think there's any weight to this, Joe?" Fred Yamashita had woken fully, and was looking at me. He tapped his notebook.

"The Saudis think so." I spoke softly, just over the engine noise, so as not to awaken Linda. "They know more about their enemies than we do, I suppose."

"Yeah, but these damned people come through the U.S. all the time, more than most people would believe. These sightings may be pure coincidence."

Perhaps abashed at one of their diplomats dangling a fortune in front of Linda and me—or abashed at our swatting it aside and reporting it to Linda's superiors—the Saudis had allowed the State Department limited access to a few of their intelligence files. Director Henley had told us that the amount of information the Saudis had produced had been the subject of much debate and negotiation within the Saudi government. He also had said that the Saudis knew more than they were revealing—they always did—perhaps not directly about *Sacajawea,* but certainly about the man they identified to us, and his suspected mission and itinerary.

This is what the Saudis told us: Eleven days before *Sacajawea* was destroyed, a Shiite Saudi named Ibrahim Sinani was seen in Toronto, and then three days later was spotted in Vancouver. He stayed in an apartment in Vancouver, with a Saudi Shiite who was not under suspicion, but was rather a friend of Sinani's. The friend had been questioned when he had returned to Saudi Arabia. The friend had said that Ibrahim Sinani had said he was leaving Vancouver to travel south to the United States. The Saudis assured us Ibrahim Sinani would not be up to any good. Given the chance to kill the Saudi director of the eastern division of their security service, the Lady-in-the-Hat's husband, Khalid bin Abdallah, Sinani would certainly do so.

Sinani was a member of the Saudi Hizballah, which was dedicated to overthrowing the kingdom's monarchy, and which, Saudi intelligence believed, was funded by Iran. He had trained at a Hizballah camp in Lebanon's Bekáa Valley, and was believed to have participated in the November 1995 bombing of an American-run training center in Riyadh. Seven people were killed, including five Americans.

The Saudis would not say how Sinani was involved in the

training-center bombing, or how they had determined that he was. They did not know Sinani's current location, but he was believed to still be in the United States. They gave us his fingerprints and several photographs.

"It's a mess, Joe." Yamashita was leaning conspiratorially toward me, the aisle separating us. He removed his glasses and rubbed his face from his forehead to chin, as if to wipe the slate clean. "Nothing adds up. None of it."

I knew this well enough, but I asked, "Like what?"

"No part of the investigation adds up. Like this: no Lebanese Hizballah ever uses a pipe bomb with nails in it."

"What if that's all he could find, not being able to get explosives into the United States?"

"And the goddamn Idaho Resisters. Given that their thought processes may not track with normal humans, I still can't fathom why they would bomb an airplane and threaten to blow up another one. Something is screwy there. Thirty years as an FBI agent makes me think so. I can't put my finger on it better than that."

Linda's hand brushed my knee as she turned in her sleep.

Yamashita added, "But the bomber is either the Saudi terrorist or the Idaho Resisters."

"Maybe it's someone else or some other organization we haven't tripped upon yet."

He looked at me like I might be the Grim Reaper at his front door. "Joe, we don't have anything else."

Yamashita turned to the window, maybe to hide a scowl he couldn't remove from his face. After a moment he looked back. "Nobody—*nobody*—brings down a plane without leaving a single piece of evidence that points to himself. Lockerbie—a skilled, professional job with an entire government behind it—proved that. The perpetrator or perpetrators for *Sacajawea* can be found in one of our two scenarios. The Resisters or a Saudi terrorist. Got to be." He wrapped the glasses back around his face, then sighed heavily. "I just don't know which one, and we don't have enough evidence to convict, even if I did know which one."

Yamashita smiled briefly at me, perhaps to thank me for listening to his confession of confusion. "But I've got something going in Idaho that may help us out." He opened his notebook again.

Just as I returned to my computer, Linda moved in her seat, adjusting her elbow on the armrest, not quite awake. She shifted yet again, then raised a hand to pat the pillow into place, then rested against it, pressing on my shoulder. She looked uncomfortable.

I looked down at my computer.

This time she rotated in her seat, pushed the pillow against me high on my chest, shoving me back in my seat. She must have been awake, at least sort of. She adjusted the pillow against the outer curve of my shoulder. She put her head on the pillow and breathed once or twice, her eyes closed.

Then she groaned sweetly and whispered, "Damned airplane travel," and still leaning toward me, she reached for my nearest arm and brought it up and over her head so my arm was around her shoulders. Then she leaned into me, put her head under my chin, her arm across my lap, and soon was back to sleep, her hair against my neck and chin and cheek.

Had she been my wife or daughter, I would have instinctively kissed the top of her head, and I had to restrain myself. But I held her, feeling her breathe, feeling her shift beneath me, my computer forgotten. I lightly stroked the back of her neck most of the while.

I didn't give the *Sacajawea* investigation another thought until we reached the Hailey airport.

• • •

I was raised in wheat country, so I like dirt, but not enough to lie in it for any length of time. For ten minutes I had been down on the ground, the giddy reek of Idaho topsoil filling my nose, and my chin and nose being scratched red by wheat stubble. The field was fallow this season, letting the ground recuperate, and so had no winter wheat coming up. Linda Dillon was on one side of me, and Jamie Suarez on the other. Suarez was sneezing every few seconds, maybe allergic to wheat straw.

My eyes were a foot off the dirt so I couldn't see much beyond the two FBI bomb techs forty yards farther along the furrow. Both were wearing armor, including steel-lined gloves. Shields over their faces resembled welder's helmets. They were leaning over a hole in the ground, shovels and probes to one side. A portable generator and an industrial vacuum cleaner were on the back of a nearby pickup truck, and the vacuum hose snaked across the ground into the hole. One of the bomb techs was loosening dirt and the other was sucking it away.

Fred Yamashita had invited me along, back to Idaho and out into this field, I thought at first as a courtesy, as a way of making up for being made the fool with my spark theory. It gave me something to do after having been publicly drawn and quartered. Then I learned that my remaining on the investigation had been agreed to by the NTSB and FBI, not without some kicking by the latter.

ICC Rich Shrader had tired of hosting press briefings, so he had given me the task. I was as good at handling relentless reporters as he was, he had said. It might've been his way of keeping me employed.

When one organization has done its work in an air-disaster probe, it is expected to step aside. The FBI now expected the

National Transportation Safety Board to gracefully step aside on *Sacajawea*. The entire world knew a bomb had brought down the turboprop. The FBI could now reasonably conclude that the NTSB—all us engineers and retired pilots and theoreticians, anybody who didn't wear a holster—should get the hell away from the business of finding the perpetrators.

It wasn't that simple, as Dick Dahlberg stressed to FBI Director Henley and Executive Assistant Director Yamashita. The more evidence gained—the more complete was the reconstruction of the event, including the rebuilding of *Sacajawea*—the easier it would be to bring the perpetrators to justice, and the more complete would be the NTSB's eventual recommendations regarding future airplane and airport security. The NTSB was not ready to announce a probable cause and so end its investigation. It sounded lame, and Director Henley actually rolled his eyes when he heard it, Yamashita reported gleefully to me.

The truth was that *Sacajawea*—with the credible threat to bring down another plane—presented "a serial bomber, and so the major of all majors," as Dahlberg had told me. NTSB investigators just weren't ready to relinquish the investigation, not while some parts of the puzzle remained unsolved, even if those portions of the puzzle belonged to the FBI. But there was less and less for the NTSB to do. Director Henley complained that the pieces of *Sacajawea*'s skin now being reapplied to the plane were the size of children's bandages, and called it "make-work," not without some justification.

Suarez said, "We've been running our truck-mounted metal detector over Ed Fahey's fields for two hours, aiming those rays right into the ground. It's slow, with the furrows bouncing around the delicate equipment."

I shifted on my belly to push aside a dirt clod that had been pressing on my sternum.

Linda noticed. "Too tough for you NTSB guys out here,

looks like." She threw a wide grin at me. Her hair was the color of the wheat stubble. She had picked a piece of the straw, and was chewing it like a toothpick.

Suarez said, "We've found harness buckles and an old silvered plate and a hoe blade. Now this." Suarez sneezed into his hand, then wiped his hand on wheat straw. "You see how Fahey knew how to find the spot again?"

"Marking off paces from somewhere at the edge of the field?" I guessed.

"He dug the hole where two imaginary lines cross, those lines between two sets of fence posts."

The field had once been a pasture. Old fence posts, grayed by the sun, lined the boundaries. Some posts were missing and others were canted with age. A few posts still had strands of barbed wire connecting them.

Suarez went on, "Crisscross the field with imaginary lines between the four posts nearest the corners of the field. Fahey's spot isn't exactly in the center of the field because of several missing posts near the corners. He put a rock—small enough so that it wouldn't draw attention to itself unless the searcher were within a couple feet—right on the hole."

"So how did you notice the rock?" I asked.

"We didn't, not until we had already found the location with the detector truck."

Linda asked, "So you ran the metal detector over everything? Every inch of ground Ed Fahey owns?"

"Just like mowing a lawn. Back and forth, back and forth with the truck. This field and another field, his front lawn, and around his garage and toolshed."

The bomb tech to our left slithered into the hole, his arms and head disappearing. The generator hummed. Then the vacuum nozzle and hose were tossed aside, and the bomb tech inched his way backward out of the hole, a difficult maneuver in all his padding. Still on his stomach, he held up a cardboard box, no larger than a shoe box. The contents must have been heavy, as he used both hands. He held it aloft like a trophy.

The bomb tech lifted the edge of his face shield to make it easier to be heard. "It's all clear. The box has a tear in it. I can see the contents."

We rose from the field, brushing ourselves off and stepping along furrows toward the bomb specialists, who stood and removed their helmets. The soil sank under my feet. A gauzy horizon hid the foothills. Mountains rose above the haze.

The FBI bomb technicians were grinning widely, as if they had just caught their man. We gathered around the box.

Jamie Suarez announced the obvious, "Nails."

A few nails had spilled out of the box. More were visible through an opening in the cardboard. The box was about a quarter full.

"I'll be damned," Linda Dillon said.

"They look like those same shingle nails to you?" a tech asked. "Same as the signature nail?"

"We'll test them," Suarez replied. "But it's my guess they are one-and-seven-eighths-inch asphalt shingle nails with seven-sixteenths-inch heads that have been double-dipped in zinc."

Linda added, "And manufactured in Leeds, England, by the Sure-Secure Company."

Suarez brushed his pants as he led us away from the hole, leaving the nails to the bomb techs. "Ed Fahey will have a lot to talk about with his lawyer, like sixty-three counts of aggravated first-degree murder for *Sacajawea*."

"You haven't caught him yet," I pointed out.

Suarez scowled at me. "We always catch them."

I was about to mention D.B. Cooper, but Linda shot me a glance, and I zipped it up.

TWENTY-NINE

We were again staring at the Lady-in-the-Hat, Khalid bin Abdallah's wife. She was frozen on the screen, standing apart from the other mourners. Her necklace threw back shafts of sunlight. She said something to herself.

"Can you make it out?" I asked, sitting on a folding chair in front of the screen, the remote control in my hand.

"I'm not sure," Donna Lawrence replied. "Something about a carrot."

"A carrot? You sure?" Linda Dillon rubbed the back of her neck. "Run it again, Joe."

I backed up the tape. "Would slowing it down help? I can do that."

Donna Lawrence shook her head. "I need to see her mouth in real time."

I backed up the tape and let it run again. The Lady-in-the-Hat said her words once more.

"She is saying something about a carrot, maybe a green carrot." Donna looked at me. "Wait a minute. Is this woman an American?"

"A Saudi. But she speaks English."

"Joe, for Pete's sake, she's speaking Arabic, whispering

something to herself. I can't help you with her." She laughed. "And here I thought she was talking about a green carrot."

I chewed on my lower lip. I had approached Donna Lawrence that morning at church, where she sat each Sunday below the pulpit, rendering the pastor's words into sign language for a number of hearing-impaired folks sitting in the front pews. The pastor was giving his annual recruitment sermon, the gist of it being that Presbyterians no longer believe in predestination, most of us, anyway, and that John Calvin couldn't have been as stern as his portraits might lead us to believe, and probably actually laughed once or twice in his life. I had asked Donna Lawrence if she could read lips, and she had assured me she was excellent at it.

An hour later found us at the FBI's Seattle office. I had called in Linda and Fred Yamashita and Special Agent Bridget Thompson from the FBI's Terrorism Research Analytical Center, who was still in Seattle. Fred claimed I was grasping at straws, but then added he wished he would have thought of it. I reversed the tape, stopping closer to the beginning of the funeral. On the screen, data boxes were next to most attendees.

Donna Lawrence was a grandmother, with a doughy face and a ready smile, with what looked like her own teeth. Her gray hair was tucked in at her neck. Her purse was on the floor. She studied the screen. "The mayor is whispering to his aide, out of the side of his mouth, but I can read it anyway"—her words slowed, matching the pace of the mayor's lips—"'Christ-on-a-crutch, the minister is reading the entire Bible. Can't he shut up and let me get back to work?'" She looked at me, an impish cast to her face. "Does that help?"

"Tons." I fiddled with the remote, moving the scene forward about ninety seconds and left ten degrees. In my other hand was a laser pointer, and I centered a red dot just above a young man in a scruffy herringbone jacket and no tie. He was standing next to another male, in his early twenties, this one wearing jeans, a striped shirt, and a narrow black tie.

Yamashita said, "These are two of the three people at the Pritchard funeral who remain unidentified. They are talking to each other, while watching the proceedings, and they don't really look like they belong there. Can you catch what they're saying?"

I let the tape roll. The fellow in the herringbone coat moved his mouth while peering at the minister.

With the busy concentration of a wasp, Donna Lawrence shifted forward in her chair, her eyes narrowed at the screen. " 'I went back to monkey—' I lost it. Will you back it up?"

I punched the remote's buttons. The scene flickered, then began again.

" 'I went back to Monkey Lube when they started offering free vacuuming after they changed the oil.' "

In unison we slumped back in our chairs. Yamashita bunched his hands and cursed. Linda grimaced and rubbed her temple with her knuckles.

Donna continued, "Then the other guy replies, 'Yeah, but do you pay more than at Quick Lube?'" The camera mercifully panned left.

"Damn it," Yamashita exclaimed.

I moved the scene forward again and stabbed the laser pointer at a woman in a black wool coat. "This is Carla Devona, Emerald's corporate purchasing manager. She says something to her husband, Jack. Donna?"

" 'I feel so sorry for Gwen. What's she going to do?' " Donna's voice roughened with sympathy. " 'And those beautiful children.' "

Then we examined the snippets of twenty-six other graveside conversations. Relayed by Donna, we heard grief, anger, and boredom. We heard bits of a carpool arrangement and of plans to travel to Arizona for Mariners spring training.

When I put the red dot over Charles Ray, Emerald's founder, whose lips were moving as he stared down at the casket, Donna said, "He's not saying anything."

"Well, his mouth is moving," Bridget Thompson pointed out. "Maybe he's talking to his son Wayne next to him."

Donna shook her head. "He's weeping. His mouth is just moving, probably trying to keep himself from bawling out loud."

I was embarrassed, feeling like a voyeur. I moved the dot. "This is Wayne Ray, Emerald's CEO. He lost his wife, Charlotte, on *Sacajawea*."

"His head is half turned away," Donna said. "I can't make it out."

I ran the tape back and forth, then again.

"Still can't."

"Standing next to Wayne is Charlotte's brother, Dwight Vaughn," Fred informed her.

"That's easy. He's spitting out his words, and whispering at the same time. 'So you've got no Emerald Airlines left, do you? All of it turned to nothing, goddamn you.'" Here Vaughn turned back to fully face the casket. "'And my poor dead sister . . .' That's all he says."

Yamashita said, "Dwight Vaughn isn't the only person angry at Wayne Ray. Emerald Airlines has virtually shut down, after *Sacajawea* and word getting out about the threatening letter. Stockholders have seen their shares quickly fall to half their pre-crash value, and now the shares are even lower."

I said, "Wayne told me Emerald has hired Chapter 11 lawyers. The decision hasn't been made, but they are getting ready."

"Emerald is closely held," Yamashita said, "but even so, Dwight Vaughn owned six thousand Emerald shares. He's blaming Wayne Ray for incompetence, probably thinking something should have been done that could have prevented *Sacajawea*."

Over the next hour we found another twelve fragments of mourners' conversations, and similarly parsed them, looking for something, anything. At the end of it, Fred Yamashita's head was in his hands. Then he remembered himself, and levered himself out of his chair, despair slowing him, about to thank Donna Lawrence.

The phone rang. Linda Dillon put the receiver to her ear. She leaped up from her chair, propelled by excitement.

"It's Wayne Ray," she exclaimed. "He has something for us. Says it's important. At Emerald headquarters."

Linda and Fred and I rushed toward the door. I tossed a thanks to Donna Lawrence. She said, "Joe, we sign-language folks don't say, 'Break a leg,' like actors."

Still headed for the door, I glanced at her.

She laughed. "So break an arm, Joe."

Wayne Ray introduced us to Ben Cook, the Emerald reservations manager, and he in turn introduced Anne Shipley, Emerald's reservations auditor. Cook was the fellow who was spending a lifetime building the Swan airplane in his basement.

When Linda asked what a reservations auditor did, Anne Shipley replied, "A better title would be yield manager. I look for ways to increase yield, to fill seats. It's sort of a new area, because with computers and modern communications, we know exactly how much we need to discount seats for each flight to fill it. The closer in time the flight's departure, the deeper the discount. Or if a flight isn't full, we open up more seats for travel packages, or we open up seats to frequent travelers, trying to use up our inventory of miles we've given out over the years. And finally we open it up to standbys."

"An empty seat earns Emerald nothing," Ray said. "It's Anne's job to make sure we fly as full as possible. Every plane, every leg, every day."

Ben Cook smiled and graciously gave his subordinate her due. "Anne was responsible for adding a real-time searchable database for consolidators and wholesalers."

We were in a windowless room at the Emerald building near SeaTac airport. The room was filled with cubicles for the reservations personnel, most of whom had been laid off, with the promise of a recall when the bomber was found, and when the traveling public again began using Emerald Airlines.

Fluorescent lights overhead made Cook's bald head gleam. Seen through his bottle-bottom spectacles, his eyes appeared so small as to be useless. His mouth was damp and eager. "Our direct connect is run on a Stratus computer under VOS. Our total access runs on VAX computers under VMS, and . . ."

He sputtered to a stop when Wayne Ray smiled and held up a hand. "Ben, just tell us what Anne discovered."

Ray had not shaved for several days and his dark hair was oily. He had apologized for his appearance when we arrived at Emerald's office. He said that he hadn't figured out how to shave or shower with much effect, what with wearing two casts, one on his hand, another on his foot. He was no longer wearing a dressing on his nose, and the tissue under his eyes was losing its green hue. He had said he was getting light-headed after standing for more than a few minutes, but the doctor assured him those conditions would abate in the next few days. The sutures on his lip were so small as to be invisible to my eye, but the lip itself was purple and brown. The temporary caps on his front teeth were too yellow. His face was speckled with scabs where it had been rubbed on the asphalt.

Ray had slit open the leg of his trousers, up the inseam several inches, so the pant leg would fit over the cast. The cast on his hand was ungainly, with the thumb sticking out. He was wearing a rumpled golf shirt, and I gathered that his wife, Charlotte, used to do the laundry in his house, and Wayne hadn't yet figured out how to do it himself. He looked like hell. Linda had given him a big—but careful—hug when we had arrived, saying it was wonderful to see him out of the hospital, and that he looked great. He smiled ruefully and said, "You lie, but thanks."

Anne Shipley said, "Part of my job is to look for patterns, and I was trying to figure out how to make it less attractive for customers to double book just to keep their options open, and then cancel one booking at the last minute."

"Double booking means we have less seat inventory in the weeks leading up to a given flight," Cook explained.

Shipley was in her mid-twenties, and was wearing a tight leather skirt and so much rose-red lipstick that her mouth reflected light. Her ears were pierced once on her right side and three times on her left. Her hair was short—not quite punk short, but almost—and colored white. She was made up for the evening, with broad strokes of eyeliner. The girl would be fun at a dance joint, no question about that, not that anybody my age would be able to keep up with her. She had a master's degree in information systems, and was headed higher in the Emerald organization, Ray had told me on the way into the room.

She said, "Corporate travel planners are notorious for double booking, and I was looking for those companies that reserve a lot of seats, then use only a few, canceling the rest at the last minute."

"We allow some of it, because otherwise they'll just give their business to Horizon or Alaska or United Express," Ray said. "But our goal has been to pare back some of the abuse."

Cook said, "Anne and I were going to maybe ask Wayne to write letters to the chronic double and triple and quadruple bookers, asking them not to operate like that, as a first step."

Wayne Ray smiled, stretching the sutures on his lip. "So Anne here was searching for patterns of cancellations, and she tripped on something peculiar."

"Really peculiar." A lock of white hair fell over her forehead, and she pushed it back. "I was generating timeline graphs, and a single cancellation popped up where it shouldn't be."

"Where it shouldn't be?" Linda asked. She and Fred were leaning on Anne Shipley's cubicle, peering down at her and her monitor. Wayne and I were behind Anne. She was good at twisting back and forth, including all of us in her conversation.

"Look at this." She indicated her monitor, where a chart was displayed. "This shows the number of cancellations for Emerald Airlines for each of the prior five years, broken down by month." Her fingers flashed over the keyboard. "Now I break it out, showing the cancellations by year for only the Hailey-Seattle run."

The monitor blinked out a new chart.

"And now I show cancellations for only one flight, *Sacajawea*, for that day and the route it was on when it went down."

Zigzagging blue lines remade themselves on a white field, with data fields at the bottom and left edges of the screen.

"You can see that in the month prior to the flight, the total number of cancellations for this one flight—Emerald 37, Hailey to SeaTac on *Sacajawea*—was forty-eight, which is typical for any given flight. Some cancellations occurred fifteen minutes before the flight. We quickly resold all the seats, even the late cancels, as it is our busy time on that route, during the ski season. *Sacajawea* flew full that day, as you know."

Ray nodded at Yamashita and Linda, letting them know the hook was coming.

"But look at this." Anne Shipley pointed at the screen. "One cancellation occurs outside the main body of my chart."

I leaned forward to better view the screen. "What's that mean?"

Wayne Ray looked at me with purpose. "It means the reservation was canceled after *Sacajawea* left the Hailey airport, *after* the plane went down."

Ben Cook said, "The next day."

"Why would your reservation agents cancel a reservation for a flight that has already flown?" Linda asked.

"They wouldn't," Ray replied, satisfaction large on his bruised face. "It would be nonsensical to do so."

I asked, "So why did they?"

"They didn't," he said. "No reservations agent of mine would do such a thing."

His words hung in the air, their import growing and growing.

Ray said, "Someone canceled this reservation—deleted the name of the reservation holder—after the plane flew, perhaps to hide the identity of someone who had planned to be aboard *Sacajawea*." He gestured at his reservations auditor in a small way. "Anne discovered this, and that's her conclusion, and Ben and I agree."

"Any way to get the name back?" Linda asked quickly. "A backup tape?"

Anne Shipley shook her head. "We run a daily backup on such data, but our cycle is two weeks. An earlier-used backup tape is used again for another backup two weeks later, and the earlier information is erased as it is overridden. We have no record of the name on the canceled reservation."

Yamashita's mind was racing. I could see it on his face. His words spilled out. "Who possesses the technical capacity and knowledge to make a post-flight cancellation?"

"Anybody who works at the Emerald ticket counter or in the reservations room," Cook answered. "And anyone with access to our system . . ."—his voice lost some of its force and pleasure as he added, "which includes all the nation's ticket agents and wholesalers and consolidators, if they have a little programming skill."

"Any kid with a computer and a modem and an inclination to hack," Shipley said. "We've tried to build firewalls. Sometimes they work. Sometimes they don't."

Yamashita asked Anne Shipley and Ben Cook twice more if there was a chance that any evidence remained, anywhere, of the name on the reservation that had been canceled after the *Saca-jawea* crash, and they affirmed that the name had been erased.

"Absolutely, entirely, and permanently," Anne Shipley said. "Gone."

On the way to the parking lot, Yamashita said, "This canceled reservation on *Sacajawea* is important. I don't know yet how we can proceed with it, but my gut tells me it'll break something loose for us. At least it'll narrow things down."

The sun had set, and I volunteered to drive Linda home. The wipers swatted away a light rain as we crossed the Evergreen Point Bridge—a floating bridge built on concrete pontoons—and turned north into her neighborhood, one where homes aren't visible from the road, hidden behind ten-foot laurel hedges and impenetrable banks of rhododendrons, up long driveways. When we reached her mailbox, she clicked a remote on her key chain. An iron picket gate opened.

"Sometimes Kevin forgets to close the gate." She added under her breath, more a prayer, "Not today, so maybe it's a good day."

But it wasn't a good day. We drove past beds of purple heather, still in winter bloom, and paper birch trees, with their dappled white trunks. The lower boughs of the birch and several pine trees were illuminated by can lights at the base of their trunks. Cast-iron light fixtures resembling tiny pagodas lined the driveway, marking our way up and over a rise to the house. The view seen between Linda's home and the neighboring house was of Seattle's university district, the dormitories with their even rows of lights. Husky Stadium lights were on, so maybe the football team was having a spring workout.

The house was a remodel of a home built in the late 1950s, recently given an upper story and a new façade, including one of those ubiquitous half moon windows above the front door. The other windows were huge, and I glimpsed a large and bold modern painting—mostly red squares—over a stone fireplace.

Porch lights illuminated Kevin Dillon, lying on the welcome mat, a small smile on his face, his keys in one hand. He had almost made it. His knees were tucked up, just as if he were in bed. His black Lexus was in front of the three-car garage, the car's door still open and the dome light on. I stopped my car.

As Linda climbed out, she said dully, "Two months ago, in the dead of winter, he almost froze to death out here." She blinked away tears. "Help me get him into the house, will you, Joe?"

I got out of the car. While she unlocked the house and deactivated the alarm, I lifted Kevin Dillon by his shoulders, and half dragged, half carried him through the door into the living room. He nodded pleasantly, the little smile still on his mouth. His eyes opened, then closed. His brown hair was damp where it had lain on the welcome mat.

"Put him on the sofa," she said, turning on recessed lights in the ceiling and a lamp near the couch.

The room smelled of leather and gift-shop potpourri. The

rug was a cream berber. A stainless-steel sculpture—a passing resemblance to a Giacometti—was on a stand in one corner, lit by low-voltage lights in the ceiling. Kevin mumbled something as I hauled him onto the sofa.

"He'll be hurting tomorrow, headaches and stuff, then he'll be fine for a while, for four or five days." Linda turned away to busy herself with straightening magazines in a wrought-iron rack. She was weeping silently, rubbing away tears with the back of her hand. I pulled off Kevin's shoes and placed them on the rug, squaring them perfectly. I had never owned a pair of shoes that weighed so little.

"I'll call you tomorrow," I said. "Bright and early. If I know Fred, he'll have people working on this post-crash cancellation all night."

Linda walked me to the door, sniffing and bubbling and looking anywhere but at me, a witness to her profound troubles. She opened the door for me.

I was about to take my leave, but her hand caught my arm. She smiled weakly, her cheeks damp. "Joe, on the plane ride to Hailey yesterday, you thought I was asleep, but I wasn't."

"You were awake?"

She whispered, "I wanted that time with you, with your arm around me, and me against you."

I looked at her.

Maybe that was too much, would lead to a misimpression, so she added quickly, "I needed some strength from somewhere, and some comfort." Her smile gained a little. "You were handy, sitting right there next to me on that plane."

She went to her toes to peck me on the cheek. Her mouth still near my ear, she said, "Your wife, Janie, was an idiot, leaving you, Joe. A complete brain-dead idiot." She turned back into her house.

I drove west across the floating bridge toward home, not really seeing anything, wishing I could undo some things in my life. And wishing beyond reason that I could undo some things in Linda Dillon's life.

"Why do we have to screw around with them?" Linda was lying on the ground, and wearing black Kevlar body armor, making her resemble a turtle.

"You know the answer as well as I do," Suarez replied. "This is a softer, gentler era."

"Those are killers in there," Linda countered.

"We aren't going to have another Ruby Ridge." Yamashita's tone was one of finality.

Tones of finality didn't work with Linda. "Damn it, you've got the killers of an FBI agent in there, Fred. Do something."

Yamashita shook his head, then placed binoculars to his eyes.

We were back in Idaho. Yamashita had called me two hours after I left Linda, and had called the others, and we had boarded the FBI plane to Boise, then north into the hills in automobiles. The Boise sheriff had done the cornering, and Yamashita and his team had taken over when we arrived.

Linda looked at Suarez, lying beside her. Her voice rose, and she spoke as if Fred Yamashita couldn't hear her. "Fred is mostly a scientist. We can't expect anything from him, but Jamie, you're a Vietnam combat vet and you're in charge of the *Sacajawea* field operations. Do something. Get those killers out of there."

Suarez ran his black-gloved hand across his upper lip. He was dressed in full SWAT team regalia, including a black hood under a coal-scuttle helmet and body armor. A megaphone, a two-way radio, and an M16 were on the ground in front of him.

"Fred is my superior, Linda," he said, embarrassment in his voice.

"Give me that." She grabbed the megaphone and put the speaker to her mouth and depressed the trigger. "You in the cabin. Ed Fahey and Doug Dietz." Her voice bounced between the hills. "You think we're going to try to talk you out of there, use a little psychology, try to wait you out. But that touchy-feely Jimmy Carter United Nations I'm okay–You're okay–type negotiations is a bunch of crap, and I don't negotiate with cop-killers as a matter of principle."

Yamashita reached for the megaphone, getting his fingers around the metal cone, but Linda jerked it back to her mouth. She barked into it, "Five minutes. You hear me, you cop killers? Five minutes, then you get the Iwo Jima treatment, you hear me?" She lowered the microphone and returned her hand to her rifle's grip. "This isn't goddamn beach volleyball we're doing here."

Yamashita said, "You're cool, Linda. You know that? You're history at the FBI, but you're still cool."

Ed Fahey and Doug Dietz were inside a foreman's shed a hundred yards west of us. We were in the middle of a quarry owned by Cottonwood Sand and Gravel, northwest of Boise, where the plains turned to mountains. A mile west of the yard was an Idaho National Guard lot. We had passed their equipment—tanks and trucks and armored personnel carriers, in even rows—on the county road on our way here.

The Boise mountains were north and east of us, but nearer and all around were hillocks of gravel and stone and sand. A crushing plant was at the north end of the lot, backed up against a half-eaten hill. Feeders led to a jaw crusher and an impactor and a hammer mill. Conveyor belts led away from a screening plant in five directions, where gravel in different grades was deposited on the ground, forming upside-down cones, all perfectly symmetrical and smooth, giving the yard the look of a geometry text.

Nearby was a wash plant. In a Quonset hut were five dump trucks and a Caterpillar D-6 with a blade mounted on the front. A Euclid rock truck with wheels taller than me was parked just inside the yard's front gate.

The gravel pit's buildings—made of metal sheets and clapboard, seemingly randomly tacked together—had concrete blocks for foundations. Crawl spaces under the structures were open. A tool shop and vehicle maintenance shed were at the corner of the yard opposite the hillside. A sales office was near the front gate, the only structure carrying any paint. A bare flagpole rose in front of the building. A misty three-quarter moon was overhead, drifting in and out of leaden clouds.

Forty or more FBI agents were in the yard, all in combat gear, peering down from the gravel mounds and from the backs of buildings. The foreman's shop was being viewed through dozens of crosshairs. FBI vehicles were parked along the road that served the gravel lot. The low growl of a heavy truck came from the west, from along the road, the driver working it through the gears as the truck climbed the hill toward the lot.

"What do you think Fahey and Dietz were doing here?" I asked, determined to contribute to the proceeding, if only with a question. I was out of my element.

"Sand and gravel companies usually have explosives around," Jamie Suarez answered, "and maybe that's what they were after. Or maybe they were looking to appropriate a car."

Yamashita added, "Or maybe they just wanted a place to hide until morning. We've been an hour or two behind them for days. They were looking for somewhere to sack out for a few hours, is my guess."

Cottonwood Sand and Gravel's manager had been working late at his computer, and had heard the scrape of a gate on gravel. The manager's office had been lit only by a small desk lamp and the glow of a computer monitor, and so perhaps Fahey and Dietz believed no one was around. The yard's front entrance was illuminated by a lamp on a pole, and when the manager saw two men slip through the gate, running in a crouch and looking furtive, he called the sheriff. He knew—everyone in Idaho knew—that the FBI was looking for these two men.

Yard lamps had been doused, and high-powered spotlights had been brought in and were casting a pitiless white light at the foreman's shed from three directions. We had seen a flicker of movement from the front window, and then nothing more. Lying on the gravel mound with us was Kurt Cheney. He was flicking the safety of a grenade launcher on which was mounted a tear gas bomb. He fidgeted like a terrier at the end of its leash.

The sound of a diesel engine grew louder, and then the driver applied the compression brakes, and the roar sped along the hills and came back to us in a long serrated echo.

Jamie Suarez said, "Linda, you don't think I'm upset about Bill Fitzpatrick's death."

She rose on her arms a fraction, the gravel sounding under her. "What brings that on?"

"You like to think the FBI is run by unfeeling bureaucrats." He was wearing a baiting grin. "And you like to think that we have lost our humanness, that we have lost certain desires felt by the layman. Such as vengeance."

Alert to this whiff of irregularity, Fred Yamashita lowered his binoculars. "What are you talking about, Jamie?"

"You are being more obscure than usual," Linda said.

The truck engine quieted, but the sound was immediately replaced by an even louder growl, this engine less tamed, the pounding of each cylinder audible. The source of the raw noise was lost in the blackness.

"I was raised in Boise, I ever tell you that?" Jamie asked Linda. "I know a lot of folks around here."

She looked at me. "Jamie is suffering from random synapse firing, and not for the first time."

"Including Colonel Burt Winsor, who runs the National Guard armory west of here."

"Jamie, you aren't paying attention to this process," Yamashita said. "We've got Fahey and Dietz cornered, now we set up the communications network, the triage station, the press holding area, call in the negotiators . . ."

Suarez ignored him. "So, Linda, you think for one minute I'm going to let those bastards sit over there in that hut, fat and happy, and create a spectacle, picked up by the international press vultures, distributed by CNN to every corner of the world?" Suarez's voice had gained an edge. "So Fahey and Dietz can become celebrities? So they can become heroes to weird pukes? You think you're the only person in the world pissed off at Bill's death?"

"I didn't say any of that," Linda protested.

"Well, watch this."

The rumble of the hidden engine abruptly rose an octave, then came the grind of shifting gears, then a repeated metallic clanking that drew closer and closer. I smelled diesel exhaust. The gravel under my belly trembled. A harsh laugh came from the direction of the machine.

A barrel suspended eight feet in the air formed out of the night. Ten feet wide, with heavy chains hanging from it, held above the ground by steel arms. The arms resembled a bulldozer's push arms. Then came the tank that was holding the contraption in the air, growling and huffing, its treads clattering loudly.

"It's a mine flail," Suarez said with grim satisfaction.

"A mine flail?" Linda asked.

"A spinning drum mounted in front of an old M60 tank. Lengths of heavy chain attached to the drum beat the ground out in front of the tank, setting off mines that the enemy has laid there. The drum is driven by a sprocket chain run off the main engine."

Armor extensions had been welded to the tank's front mud shields and side bazooka plates. The gun and hull machine gun were missing, as were the turret machine gun and the smoke bomb discharger. The M60 was wearing light shades of brown and green, desert camouflage. The push arms were attached by trunnions to the track frame. Hydraulic lift cylinders were mounted on the tank's glacis plate.

Smoke blew from exhaust pipes, and the thing lurched forward, then turned on one tread, pushing dirt to the side as it maneuvered toward the rear of the foreman's shack.

"What's it going to do?" Yamashita's voice was tight.

"It's going to blenderize that shack."

"Blenderize?" Yamashita asked.

"It's going to start at the back of the shed. If Fahey and Dietz want to stay in there, fine," Suarez said, louder now, above the tank's engine. "But I doubt they will."

The tank was now partly hidden from us by the shed. Light glinted off the driver's periscope. Another gear was engaged, clattering loudly, and the drum began to turn, slowly at first, the chains draping over the steel drum then sliding off toward the ground. The driver revved the engine, and the drum turned more and more quickly, so that the lengths of chain became rigid with centrifugal force, and the mechanism resembled an enormous bottle brush. The sound was a piercing mechanical howl. I'd heard more pleasant cat fights.

The M60 crept forward in its lowest gear. The chains were blurred, a ripple in the air framing our view of the tank. The driver lowered the push arms so that the end chain links were just above the ground. The tank inched forward, and the chains bit into the back of the foreman's shed.

Wood cracked and splintered and flew away from the shed. Shattered glass was thrown into the night, refracting and opalescing, and casting tiny shafts of blue and red in all directions. Wiring spun out and up, and hung in the air before drifting down. Shingles burst apart and were whipped skyward by the churning chains. When the M60 moved forward again, just a fraction, more of the building was fed into the chains, disintegrating and flying away.

Linda squeezed Suarez's arm. "You're my big hero, Jamie."

Suarez balled his gloved hand. "I'll give them another ten seconds."

They didn't last that long. The shack's door was flung open, and Ed Fahey and Doug Dietz sprinted out, their legs digging wildly, their hands empty and pumping, Dietz looking over his shoulder as if he were being chased by something from the grave. They ran out of the light, heading in our direction.

Linda rose from our gravel pile, Suarez and Kurt Cheney at her elbow. Fahey and Dietz, who had been peering out into the hot spotlights, never saw them. Jamie Suarez grabbed Dietz by the lapels, stuck out his hip, and whipped Dietz over his body and onto the ground, where he landed loudly and lay still, his arms out, Suarez's fist under his chin, pinning him to the dirt. Cheney covered him with a pistol.

At the same instant, Linda stuck her rifle between Ed

Fahey's legs, and the big man spilled forward, his arms out instinctively. He landed heavily on all fours, skidding, but catching himself. Linda kicked an arm away, then sent her boot into his head.

Fahey shuddered with the blow, grunted and collapsed, rolling onto his side. Linda used her foot to push him onto his back. He stared into the black sky, his eyes perfect circles. The mine flail was still chewing away at the shack.

Fahey lifted a leg as if to rise. Linda roughly poked the muzzle of her rifle at Fahey's forehead.

"Bill Fitzpatrick was a friend of mine," she said, almost a whisper. "A close, close friend."

"No, don't," Fahey said tremulously, looking up the long length of the barrel.

"If my boss over there—" she dipped her head at Yamashita— "weren't such a nitpicker..." She put some weight behind the rifle. The flash suppressor ground into the Resister's forehead.

"No, please." Fahey was begging.

"Special Agent Dillon," Yamashita said sternly as he approached.

He and Suarez shouldered her away from him, and began their pat down. Suarez reached for the cuffs on his belt dump. Other agents climbed down from the gravel hillocks.

A dark scowl on her face, she walked back to me, the rifle pointed in the air. "I almost did it, shot that piece of dirt."

"You wouldn't do that, just kill a guy lying in front of you helpless," I said. "Ever."

"At least I kept him guessing for a few seconds." She glanced at me. Her frown broke to a smile. "Just like I keep you guessing, Joe."

THIRTY

Two eighteen-foot Bekins vans hid much of Wayne Ray's house. Linda was driving our FBI car, and she parked in a paved turnaround at one side of the house, near a five-car garage. The fifth garage slot was larger than the rest, I suppose for a boat or an RV.

The home was made of stone and heavy timbers with steep gray slate roofs on its many gables. Glass in the windows was leaded, and in diamond-shaped panes. This was a new house built to look old and Kentish, where in response to the contractor's inquiries during the building, the owner would invariably have replied, "I'll take a dozen of the European ones." Everything would be leaded or coppered or timbered. There would be a white pergola out back, if the place held true to form. The home was in a gated neighborhood called the Highlands, just north of Seattle's city limits.

"Where's Wayne moving to?" Linda asked, stepping on the parking brake.

"It's news to me if he is."

The driveway was made of square cobblestones set in a parquet pattern. I followed Linda to the front door, which was recessed under an arced stone lintel. The door was open, and we stepped out of the way to allow two white-coated Bekins loaders carrying a leather couch to pass. When Linda pressed the doorbell, Westminster chimes sounded from deep within.

Hidden in the foyer's darkness, Wayne Ray saw us before we saw him. "Yeah, hi, Joe. Linda." He hesitated. "Come in." His voice was soft, as if in the presence of the dead.

We stepped inside, onto limestone tiles in a foyer. A Persian rug was rolled up to one side.

He cleared his throat. "Nice of you to come." His words faded as he turned away. Ray was embarrassed.

"You moving somewhere, Wayne?" I asked.

His chest rose and fell. "Not far. To an apartment a couple miles from here, in Shoreline."

The loaders returned, and this time each lifted a cardboard box with BEKINS stamped in green on the sides. The foyer contained two dozen other such boxes. We followed Ray into the living room.

Three picture windows revealed views of Puget Sound and the Great Peninsula six miles distant. The gray sky lay close, hiding the Olympic Mountains. Two other movers were taking the legs off a black Bösendorfer piano that was next to a large fireplace framed in antique copper. The handles of the fireplace implements were boars' heads carved from ivory, looking two centuries old. Two piano dollies were near these Bekins workers. A pile of green pads was nearby, ready to be wrapped around the Bösendorfer. All other furniture had been removed except eight lamps, which stood around the room like sentinels, and seven identical Sony television sets, brought down from other rooms.

"I've lost the house," Ray said miserably. He faced the view, and wouldn't look at us.

"What do you mean?"

He pinched the bridge of his nose, his eyes closed. "After

Sacajawea went down, and after the flying public learned about the threat to blow up another plane, Emerald Airlines has had few bookings, little revenue. The company needed an infusion of cash. I didn't want to sell off the stock my dad had been giving me over the years—he wouldn't have liked that and either would I, because it's our family business—so I put this house on the market. I've sold it for a little under three million, but I'll only clear a quarter of that after the mortgage is covered."

"And you've put the money into Emerald's operating fund?" Linda asked. She was wearing a bold blue fleece jacket with stylized trees on it, and jeans. Over her shoulder was a beaded bag just big enough to contain her weaponry. She carried a manila envelope in one hand. Her hair was pulled back into a ponytail, secured with a blue ribbon that matched her eyes.

"Emerald has a lot of goodwill in the Northwest and Mountain West. The airline may still recover from *Sacajawea*. Maybe it's just a matter of time, but right now it needs ready cash to make payroll and other expenses."

He finally turned to us. His face was clouded with worry. "All this wouldn't bother me so much, Joe, if I had founded Emerald, and built it up over the years. But I didn't. My father did. I was born into the airline business. My first job was at Emerald—Dad insisted I start out in the hangar, as an apprentice mechanic, did you know that?—and I've never worked anywhere else."

"Yeah, I know," I said.

"I rose higher at Emerald, one level to the next. Sure, my dad made that possible, but I worked damned hard, all the same. And I proved myself, and so for the past ten years, Dad has been handing over the airline to me in increments, not only the stock, but also the responsibilities of running the company." He grabbed his own head, as if suddenly in vast pain. "It's been given to me by my father, and I've lost it." His voice was dark with sorrow. "I've lost it."

One of the piano movers said, "This picture was on the piano." He pronounced it *pianer*. "You want us to pack it with the other stuff?" He held up a photograph framed in silver filigree.

A ferocious scowl twisted Ray's face into a knot. "That's my wife. Goddamn it, give me that." He limped toward the mover, his good hand out. "Give me that."

He snatched it away from the mover, but hesitated, then opened his hand in a gesture of apology. "She was my wife," he said emptily. "She's dead. I was going to take this picture of her with me in my car. That's why I left it out. Sorry."

He came back to us, carrying the framed photograph, his cast making him walk as if he were on the deck of a rolling ship. His lip was still colored with the wound.

His gaze found Linda. "You and your bosses could've stopped this." He was instantly angry again. "You could've announced that the Idaho Resisters or whatever the hell their name is have all been caught."

"We're going to give Fahey a few tests, if his lawyer lets us, and then we can—"

"The FBI could announce that shingle nails had been found in Ed Fahey's field, even if there weren't a formal arrest yet." His voice was bitter. "The public would understand that the bomber had been caught, and they'd come back to Emerald."

"The tests will—"

"That's just crap," he exploded, waving his wife's photo. "That's just a damned delay until the FBI gets every perfect little fact in perfect little rows, and you and they don't give a damn whether Emerald folds and all my employees get pink slips and . . . and whether I go down with everybody else."

"Wayne," I said. "Listen, we can—"

"Joe," he shouted. "I'm being ruined by the FBI's dragging their feet." He suddenly grabbed my arm with his good hand. He lowered his voice and said fiercely, "Joe, listen, you at the NTSB can make announcements regarding *Sacajawea*, can't you? You can announce the perpetrators have been arrested, can't you? It'd be just as good as the FBI doing it. The traveling public will realize Emerald is safe again."

I could only look at him. He knew better. Such an announcement was entirely out of the NTSB's domain. He released my arm.

The storm blew out as quickly as it had risen. He shut his eyes a moment, then gripped my arm again, this time an apology. "I'm under some pressure."

"Yeah, we know," Linda said.

"You FBI agents like guns, Linda. I had a gun collection, worth more than a hundred thousand dollars. I sold it two weeks ago, put the money into Emerald, made that week's payroll. But I kept one pistol, a Colt Derringer, a .22-caliber replica. My father had a silversmith engrave the barrels, and he gave it to me a couple years ago, presentation case and all, on the anniversary of my twentieth year at the airline. I couldn't sell it along with the others. Maybe I'll use it on myself. Then I won't have to think about my company anymore."

"That's a joke, right, Wayne?" I asked.

"Yeah." His shoulders sagged, an attitude of utter defeat. "Yeah, a joke."

"You sure?" Linda asked. "We don't need to post a guard on you, do we, Wayne? Make sure you don't do something stupid and fatal?"

His thoughts seemed to focus. He smiled quickly. "No, no. It's a joke. I'm too much of a coward to do that." He made an attempt at a laugh. "Why'd you folks come out here? Not to help me move out, I'll bet." He chuckled, but it was feeble.

Linda opened the envelope and pulled out a photograph. "This is the last unidentified person who attended Captain Pritchard's funeral. This photo was taken off a videotape, and wasn't too clear. So we've had a computer artist enhance it. Some of it is guesswork—the enhancement—but this is what we think the person looks like." She passed him the five-by-seven print.

He held it up to the gray daylight coming through the window. "It looks like Peggy Straub's husband. Peggy is Emerald's food service manager." He brought the photo closer to his face. "At least I think it is. Hard to tell. His name is Stan, if this is him."

We already knew that Peggy Straub had attended the funeral. Somehow we had missed that her husband went with her. Linda glanced at me. This photo now had the dusty scent of a dead end, yet another one. The two fellows talking about oil-change prices had turned out to be second cousins of Captain Pritchard. They had attended the funeral and had not bothered to introduce themselves to the other relatives. All the attendees at Captain Pritchard's funeral had now been identified. We had—with this computer-enhanced photograph—at last learned that thousands of hours of work had produced nothing. My mouth was sour with the wasted effort.

Linda looked quickly at me again, perhaps to see if we were thinking of the same thing. We weren't. She was ahead of me.

"Wayne, Ed Fahey is being questioned at our office downtown"—she looked at her wristwatch—"in about an hour. He's agreed to cooperate. We are going go find out once and for all whether he or any of the other Idaho Resisters had anything to do with bringing down *Sacajawea*."

"They found the goddamn nails in his pasture," Ray said bitterly.

"Well, we're going to be giving him a few tests. We'll know for sure whether he's involved. And if he is, we'll bring the charges and make the announcement to the press that the bomber has been caught."

"This'll all happen this afternoon," I said.

"Why don't you come with us?" Linda asked. "You can sit in on it. See for yourself. Maybe we'll have it all wrapped up by dinnertime—the arrest, the press conference announcing the arrest—and you can put on a coat and tie and tell the press that Emerald is resuming its full schedule now that the bomber has been apprehended."

He brightened. "You think?"

"Only if Ed Fahey is shown to have been involved in bringing down *Sacajawea*, Wayne. And, as you say, the shingle nails were in his field."

He smiled gently. "This is a suicide watch, isn't it? Keep me with you so I won't be tempted to actually use my gun on myself."

I said, "Wayne, you've lost your wife and your house, you may be about to lose your airline, and you've had some bones broken and teeth knocked out. You're depressed, and you've got a right to be. But why don't you come with us? We'll keep you too busy to think about your pistol."

"And Joe here is a bunch of laughs," Linda said. "Mostly inadvertent."

She sure liked to stick me once in a while.

"I'll get my coat and come along." He grinned again, perhaps heartened that he had something to do other than watch his belongings being moved out of his family home. "But the Colt was a joke, believe me."

"There's often a seed of truth in a joke, Wayne," I said.

• • • •

"What's in the bags?" I resisted the urge to press my nose against the one-way window to get closer to the action.

Yamashita said, "Saline in one, and sodium thiopental in the other. It's a barbiturate, comes and goes in the system quickly. Makes people talky and less discreet."

"A truth serum?"

"Exactly."

"Fahey's lawyer allowed this?"

"For the spring gun killing of Bill Fitzpatrick, we offered Fahey a manslaughter charge instead of murder of a federal officer, a conviction for which gets you a syringe and a gurney. In return, Fahey talks to us about *Sacajawea*. When his lawyer objected, Fahey fired him on the spot. So here the Resister is, gabbing away."

Ed Fahey was inside a room resembling a library, with a wall lined with bookshelves, and a settee behind a coffee table. Drawn curtains hid a bare wall, for the room had no windows to the outside. One corner was occupied by a gray leather wingback chair and a matching ottoman. Except for the drug dispenser, there was nothing high tech in the room: no computer or obvious recording devices, not even a telephone. Even the speakers, which were broadcasting Mancini into the room, were hidden. The room was designed to relax its occupants. We were in the federal building in downtown Seattle.

Fahey sat in a lounge chair, his feet up, his arms on the rests, each arm with a needle in it. The bag stands were behind him, out of his sight. Around his right biceps was a blood pressure cuff, slack at the moment. He filled the chair, his beer belly its own horizon, higher than his chin or his knees. His steel gray hair was longer than in the photographs I had seen, and it seemed to be growing in patches, longer in some areas than in others, giving him an abandoned look. His face rested on his double chin. His eyes were open but seemed unfocused. His flat nose didn't stick out much farther than his lips. His chest rose and fell slowly. He even blinked slowly. He wore a small smile. Fahey seemed blissful.

Jamie Suarez sat on a straight-back chair to Fahey's right, nearby but out of sight, unless Fahey turned his head, and the Idaho Resister looked too comfortable to attempt any motion at all. Behind Fahey was an anesthesiologist employed by the FBI. The doctor was wearing street clothes, and he monitored the instruments in front of him.

"Can't Jamie keep him on the subject?" Wayne Ray whispered.

Perhaps the one-way glass was sufficiently thick so we didn't need to keep our voices down, but we weren't risking it.

"Part of it is the drug, which makes the mind wander," Yamashita said. "And part of it is Jamie's technique."

Linda explained, "Jamie comes at a pertinent question obliquely, not so much to catch Fahey off guard, but to reinforce the notion that they're just having a nice little chat."

We had been in front of the window for an hour. Fahey had told Suarez of his dear old mom and her sixteen cats, of his pilfering a box of Bazooka bubble gum from the Stanley general store when he was nine years old, of him paying his little brother to enter the Ketchum Rexall to buy a three-pack of condoms when Fahey was sixteen, not that he had any girl to try them out on, he just wanted to show them around to his friends. He and his pals ended up blowing them up like balloons and leaving them in the girls' gym at school, "funniest thing I ever did, I guarantee you that, and I still get a laugh out of it now and then."

"Is he simpleminded?" Ray asked.

"Some of it is the barbiturate," Yamashita replied. "And some of it is Ed."

A stenographer's notebook was on Suarez's lap, and he consulted it once in a while, not taking notes because the conversation was being taped, but to keep his questions in line. He finally worked around to Emerald Airlines, beginning with nonincriminating queries such as whether Fahey had ever taken an Emerald flight, and asking the questions in an offhand manner.

The Idaho Resister's voice came to us from speakers above the window. "Nah, I drive places I want to go. What kind of name is Jamie, Jamie?"

"It's short for James," Suarez replied.

"I'd kill myself if my name were Jamie. Or I'd start wearing skirts." Fahey's voice was avuncular, and he wasn't intending to give offense.

"The names they give these days," Fahey added. "What's the country coming to?"

"Have you ever been to the airport in Hailey?" Suarez asked.

"Sure. Who hasn't?"

"Have you ever delivered a package of any sort to the Hailey airport?"

"I saw Dick Clark there once, I ever tell you? He was going skiing. I hollered over to him, 'Dick, I give it a seventy-eight because I like the beat and you can dance to it.' " Fahey laughed, a wet gurgle. "He gave me a wave, and sort of rushed away with his skis. But he looked as young as ever, I couldn't get over it, not a day older than when I used to watch him in black and white."

Suarez tried again. "Ed, have you ever done any business at the Hailey airport, like taking a package there?"

"Nah. I've picked up my wife there couple times. She visits her sister in California, a woman who has the sense of humor of a dead mule."

"Tell me about the last time you took an Emerald Airlines flight?"

"I've never been on an Emerald flight."

"Ever been inside one of their planes? They're pretty nice inside. Nice colors."

"Nah. Never been inside an Emerald plane. When I was a kid, maybe seven, I told my older brother his jockey shorts were brown, and he grabbed my hair and held my head in a rain barrel until I almost drowned."

Suarez glanced at the one-way mirror. He raised his eyebrows for our benefit. The anesthesiologist twirled a finger, indicating Jamie should hurry.

Yamashita whispered, "The length of sodium thiopental's effectiveness varies. Fahey may clam up entirely in a moment, or he may nod off."

"You know about *Sacajawea*, don't you, Ed?"

"Who doesn't?"

"What do you know about it?"

"It's a plane that came down."

"Do you know how it came down?" Suarez asked.

"A bomb. Everybody knows that."

"Is there anything about that bomb you know, that others don't?"

"What'd you say?" Fahey ran his tongue along his lower lip.

"The drug dries you out some," Yamashita whispered.

"Can you help me with that bomb, Ed?" Suarez asked, his tone of someone asking the time of day. "What do you know about it?"

Fahey tried to shake his head, but it was too much effort, so he lay there, sunk into the lounger, his gaze on the ceiling. "I don't know anything about the bomb. You and I ought to go have a few beers some time, Jamie. You ain't bad, for a blood-sucking federal bureaucrat."

"It must have been a kick putting it together," Suarez tried.

"Just the right amount of nails, just the right amount of explosives. Where do you learn to do that?"

"I never put together a bomb."

I could see Suarez struggling to keep his face impassive, to keep the frustration from showing.

He asked, "Do you know anything about the bombing of *Sacajawea,* Ed?"

"Nah. I read about it. That's all."

Suarez looked again at the mirror. "Ed, when did you bury that box of nails in your wheat field?"

"I never did that."

"Do you know who did?"

"Nah. I don't know anything about them nails."

"Runny Smith, maybe?"

Fahey burbled a laugh. "That goddamn Runny can't figure out which end of a nail you put the hammer to. He didn't bury nothing in my field. I'd've smacked him upside the head, I found him in my field with a shovel and a box of nails." He laughed again.

I looked along the window. Linda's mouth was a thin line as she witnessed our most promising lead vanish. Wayne Ray's forehead was resting against the glass and his eyes were closed. There would be no FBI press conference saving Emerald Airlines today, it was becoming increasingly clear.

"What about Doug Dietz?" came from the speakers.

"Doug's a good guy. He's just short. I don't hold that against him, much."

"You didn't bury a box of nails in your field, Ed?"

"No, hell no. Why would I do that?"

"Do you know who did?"

"Nah. No idea. Stupid thing to do. Nails don't grow like wheat seed." He coughed out a laugh.

Suarez began another line of questions, but we knew it was all over.

Yamashita said tonelessly, "The Idaho Resisters and their box of double-zinced shingle nails manufactured by the Sure-Secure Manufacturing Company in Leeds, England, has turned to nothing. Just crumpled to nothing right in front of us."

"Ed Fahey had to bury that box of nails in his field." Linda was adamant. "Who else could have? It doesn't make sense that someone else did."

"Nobody can beat that drug, Linda." Yamashita turned away from the window.

Suarez asked questions, his voice above us like God's, and Ed Fahey replied, "Nah," again and again.

Yamashita removed his spectacles to wipe them on his tie. "You got here just before Jamie started the interrogation, so you don't yet know that the wiz, Eric Thorberg, gave Fahey a lie detector test this morning."

"Yeah?" Linda said.

"Fahey had nothing to do with *Sacajawea*, Thorberg assures us. Doesn't know a thing about it." He exhaled loudly. "And though Thorberg can't be beaten at a lie detector, we gave Fahey the serum anyway, just to double check."

"Well, nuts," Linda said.

"Ed Fahey is going to do five to eight for manslaughter, but he and the other Idaho Resisters are off our *Sacajawea* list."

I asked, "What about Runny Smith getting a temp job with the Idaho Freight Forwarders?"

"Smith was only wanted on an avoiding process warrant," Yamashita said, "and we told him we'll drop the charge if he'll take these tests. He is eager to be cleared, so I suspect we'll discover that Smith needed the money, and Idaho Forwarders hired him, and it's pure, unadulterated coincidence, damn it to hell. Dietz has also said he'll take the tests if we drop the avoidance warrant." Yamashita started toward a door down the hallway. The door had a keypad above the handle. "I'm going back to work. On what, I don't know."

I turned to see Wayne Ray, slumped in a swivel chair near a water cooler. His shoulders were low, and he stared at the floor in front of his feet.

Linda and I approached him.

"I guess it's gone, then. Is it?" he asked, more to himself. "Emerald Airlines. Gone."

"Wayne, it's not gone until the bank hauls away your planes. There's still a chance."

Ray's voice was a ghost of a whisper. "Emerald Airlines. Founded by Charles Ray. Destroyed by his loving son, Wayne Ray. May it rest in peace."

Linda said softly, "Wayne, you need some help."

He said nothing, studying the floor.

"Do we need to worry about you, Wayne?" I asked.

He might have shaken his head.

"You and your dumb little Derringer replica?" Linda clarified.

This time he looked up. "No. I wouldn't do that."

"So you keep telling us," Linda said.

"I wasn't kidding about being a coward," he said. "Put a pistol barrel in my mouth? I couldn't do it, ever. Don't worry about me. Okay?"

"Well, we do worry about you," I said. "You've been through more than most people could bear."

"Can we drive you home?" Linda asked.

"I don't have a home. I have an apartment. The clothes washer is in the basement. Costs a dollar in quarters."

Linda said, "Wayne, look—"

"Please." He struggled to his feet, moving like a ninety-year-old man. "Please, Joe and Linda. I'm grieving, but I'm not suicidal. You won't have a body on your hands, I promise."

Linda took him by the arm and we started toward the elevator bank. He hobbled on his cast. The elevator door opened, and we stepped inside.

As the doors began to close, Ray said, "Besides, my father would kill me if I committed suicide."

THIRTY-ONE

NTSB investigators know that a singular truth can be plucked out of a dense thicket of other truths. Among all the discrete facts, now grown to about two million—most of them true, at least to the knowledge of the investigators who discovered and catalogued them—is a fact that, if turned over and over, if prodded and poked and tapped against the table's edge, will abruptly show itself to be critical to the case. An obscure, camouflaged bit of insignificance will suddenly shoot up and away like a flare against the night sky.

Seldom will such a glittering piece of evidence reveal itself during the first pass, because it requires the context of many other evidential odds and ends. It needs time, it needs curing, it needs the proper setting.

And in this case, it needed me, sitting in front of a computer monitor for endless hour upon endless hour. This tiny piece of information—nothing but a few jotted words on a slip of paper, later entered into the computer by a data processor—had been in front of me on the hard drive most of the time, but its significance had escaped me, and it was little solace that something lost is always in the last place you look for it.

Linda was asleep at her desk, her head on her arms. Her handbag was at her feet, and a half-eaten meal from Burrito Loco near an elbow. Jamie Suarez was on the phone at a desk against the wall. Bridget Thompson and Fred Yamashita were staring at a monitor on Yamashita's desk, consulting with each other. Wayne Ray was on a folding chair, leaning back against the wall, a biography of J. Edgar Hoover that Suarez had given him on his lap. He had left the building during the serum test on Ed Fahey, had had a drink or two, then had returned. Ray had been staring at the first page for an hour. He had the look of a man with nowhere to go and nothing to do.

I brought up the list of packages shipped from Hailey on *Sacajawea* that day. The FBI and NTSB believed they had determined the contents of all packages they had discovered, which was not to say they were certain they knew of all the packages.

We had just learned that Doug Dietz and Runny Smith had waltzed through the lie detector test and truth serum interrogations. Yamashita had been correct: Runny Smith had hired on at Idaho Freight Forwarders for no other reason than that he needed the money. He had not delivered a mysterious package to the Emerald freight counter at the Hailey airport.

We had also just learned, courtesy of the Malaysian government, that the Australian gun smuggler Brian Maxwell had admitted to a cellmate two years ago that in addition to the automatic rifles, he was also ferrying several World War II British Mark V antipersonnel mines, each containing seven ounces of explosives, and detonated by a pressure plate. With a laugh Maxwell had told the cellmate back then that perhaps he should have stowed the mines more securely. The Malays did not inform us how they had come across this bit of information from Maxwell's cellmate. So perhaps an antipersonnel mine had brought down Maxwell's leased ATF 94. I doubted I would ever know.

The hard fact that Idaho Resisters did not put a bomb aboard *Sacajawea* shook loose a notion in my brain, that perhaps the bomb had been loaded not in Hailey but in Seattle, where the flight originated.

I had not been the first *Sacajawea* investigator to give the idea credence, but the notion was usually dismissed because all packages shipped from Seattle to Hailey earlier on the day of the explosion had been taken off the plane, emptying *Sacajawea*'s hold. Further, bombs were almost always designed to detonate on the originating leg of the journey because the devices were usually pressure-activated or activated by a timer, often a kitchen timer, with its simple mechanism. These days, though, with computer chips running even kitchen clocks, a bomb could fairly easily be manufactured to detonate hours into a flight, or on the second or third or fourth leg of a plane's daily route. Still, *Sacajawea*'s eastbound—Seattle to Hailey—cargo and luggage had been accounted for, we believed. The bomb had, of course, gone off on the return route, Hailey to SeaTac.

Captain Pritchard and Co-captain Lopez's backgrounds had been examined closely, even though no one suspected them of anything untoward, and certainly not anything suicidal. Same with the *Sacajawea*'s flight attendants. But few controls existed on a flight crew to prevent them from bringing items aboard an aircraft.

I flipped through screen menus until I found the one I wanted. For purposes of determining the aircraft's loaded weight, before each flight crewmembers filled out a personal manifest, listing in boxes on a form their body weights, weight of clothing, and miscellaneous. At the beginning of the day, while he was still at SeaTac, Captain Barry Pritchard had listed his miscellaneous carry-on at twenty-three pounds, and Co-captain Aurelio Lopez listed his at eight pounds.

I stood to look over the carrel. "Wayne, do you keep back records of personal manifests, say for a year or so before *Sacajawea?*"

He looked up from the book and thought for a moment. "We'll probably have old personal manifests. Couple years' worth."

"Can you get them for the year before *Sacajawea?* For both Pritchard and Lopez?"

Ray walked to a phone on Suarez's table. "I'll have Ben Cook find them. He probably can e-mail them to your terminal. Won't take long." While he dialed the number, he asked, "Pritchard and Lopez? I didn't think they were suspects."

"They aren't. I'm just trying to get a feel for the load they usually brought on. What would Pritchard carry on a flight that originates and ends at SeaTac on the same day? A briefcase?"

"Probably an expansion briefcase, and maybe a case for his own headset. A sack lunch, sometimes. Same with Lopez. On a layover, they'd bring a small rolling suitcase, but our schedulers try to avoid layovers."

Ray got through to Ben Cook. Linda stretched and looked around at me, her expression sheepish at having fallen asleep. The buzzer on the door sounded, and she crossed to the door to unbolt it. She was handed a brown shipping parcel. Linda turned the package over, peering at the return address. Arabic script appeared in the corner of it, above English words.

"It's from the guy who tried to bribe us, Hamed Ibn Mahtab," Linda said. "Sent from Riyadh to here. It's addressed to you and me."

Only half joking, I asked, "You sure all parcels received in this building go through an X-ray machine?"

She pulled open the package. "It's a VCR tape."

"I've had enough of Hamed's games," I said warily.

She led me toward a conference room that contained a television set and a VCR. She signaled Jamie Suarez and Fred Yamashita. We gathered around the set. Linda inserted the tape and turned on the machine.

The video contained no introduction and no credits. The camera had been held in someone's hand, as the picture on the screen was jerky. The image was of a small area that was cordoned off by policemen, all in military-style uniforms, with pant legs tucked into boots like paratroopers. Several, standing back from the cordon, carried submachine guns, the barrels pointed at the ground. A green panel truck with black Arabic lettering on its door and a blue light on the roof was parked in the cleared area, next to an ambulance. The cobblestones were pink and tan, but near the ambulance, the stones were stained to a wine-red. Two men in the square wore traditional robes, one carrying a thick volume. The crowd was mannerly, and the police holding them back were not working hard. Shimmered and blurred by the heat, a slender minaret rose near a corner of the square.

The policeman pulled open the van's rear doors. Two green-clad guards stepped out, then turned to pull out a man dressed in white trousers and a loose shirt without a collar. The spectators cheered. The man's black beard was full in the Islamic fundamentalist way. His eyes were red-rimmed and watery. His hands were bound behind his back.

Hamed's stately, mocking voice came from the TV's speakers. "Greetings, Joe Durant and Linda Dillon. This poor fellow is Ibrahim Sinani, the member of the Lebanese Hizballah whom we identified to you as having crossed Canada, and as having perhaps entered the United States just prior to the destruction of *Sacajawea*."

The man was led in the direction of the camera, and the guards stopped him two yards from it. His mouth sagged open. A guard was at each of his shoulders. One guard held a leather cord in a hand, looped like a lariat.

"Ibrahim Sinani was apprehended as he tried to enter the Kingdom of Saudi Arabia last Wednesday," Hamed said through the speakers. "He had been on a flight from Tunis, and arrived at the Riyadh airport. We were unaware of his arrival, but we had a bit of luck. He was pulled over for speeding, and our thorough police found forty pounds of plastic explosives in the trunk of his automobile."

I had not seen the sheath on the belt of the soldier near the ambulance. He stepped forward. The man with the heavy volume—the Koran—opened it and began reading, his words lost in the clamor of the crowd.

The Saudi continued his voice-over. "We don't have your Bill of Rights, and your judicial activism in our kingdom, so our interviewers can be a bit more direct."

"He means they tortured the hell out of Ibrahim Sinani before they brought him to the square," Yamashita said.

"We learned what we have long suspected," Hamed said. "Sinani is a follower of Osam bin Saad, the self-styled *jihadi* who is suspected of masterminding the Khobar Towers bombing."

On the screen, the bomb-maker was forced to his knees.

The diplomat said, "But now Ibrahim Sinani finds himself in a bit of a bind. American tourists call this place Chop Chop Square."

The executioner drew a curved four-foot blade from the

sheath. A guard slipped the leather cord around Sinani's neck while another raised the bomb-maker's tied hands, forcing him to bend forward. The policeman drew on the cord, pulling the neck to a horizontal position, and stretching and steadying the condemned man.

I quickly turned away from the screen. A wimp, pure and simple.

My back to the screen, Linda gave me a play-by-play. "The executioner is measuring his sword against the man's neck. There goes the sword." Linda's voice was deliberately calm, almost indifferent. "And there goes the head, right to the cobblestones. Ouch. That must smart."

The crowd roared its approval.

Yamashita's voice was rough. "I could've lived my whole life and not seen that."

I was still facing the door to the conference room, not the television screen. My stomach was under control so far.

"Now the camera is getting closer to the body and the head." Linda might have been imitating Marlin Perkins. "A close-up of the head, the camera pointing down, blood leaking all around."

Jamie Suarez scratched his chin. "I don't like looking at severed heads, come to think of it."

"Joe, you can turn around now," Linda chided. "The camera is only showing his head."

Feeling ridiculous, I turned, squinting my eyes like a child entering a county fair spook house. Sinani's face filled the screen. His eyes were open, and had a mirthless shine. His beard was black and matted. His mouth was lifted in a rueful smile. The dead face matched the photographs the Saudi Interior Ministry had given us.

"Sinani told us that he had crossed Canada, as we suspected

and reported to you," Hamed went on. "He indeed entered the United States at Blaine, Washington. He was carrying ten forged Saudi passports. His purpose was to deliver them to a number of Saudis—all Hizballah members, we believe—so that they could attempt to return to Saudi Arabia."

Yamashita clucked at the spectacle of another lead vanishing.

"We are now confident," Hamed said, the screen still on the dead man's face, "that Ibrahim Sinani had nothing to do with your *Sacajawea*. My government still believes there is a chance that the director of the eastern division of our security service, Khalid bin Abdallah, was assassinated, an act which destroyed *Sacajawea*, but we must admit that we have no proof of it."

"They just believe it," Suarez said, "same way they just believe Tel Aviv controls our Congress."

Linda turned off the set. The lead provided by Lady-in-the-Hat had finally turned to nothing. Exhausted, Jamie Suarez remained in the conference room, staring at the black screen. I passed Wayne Ray on my way back to my desk. He had managed to turn a page in the Hoover biography. An e-mail from Emerald's reservations manager, Ben Cook, had arrived at my machine while I was giving Chop Chop Square the back of my head.

The e-mail contained a copy of all the records Captain Pritchard had personally filed at Emerald flight office for the year preceding his death on *Sacajawea*. The information was not on a spreadsheet, so I had to break it out myself, copying what I wanted on a pad of paper next to the monitor. It took me two hours. In that year, Pritchard had made 165 first legs, for which he had filed personal manifests. Emerald required pilots to enter their weight and the weight of any carry-on items so that it could maximize revenue-generating load—packages and mail in the hold—without exceeding the ATF 94's gross load limits.

Wayne Ray came over to say good night. Linda offered to drive him to his new apartment, but he declined, and before we could add anything, he protested that he was fine—that he was over his funk—and that he would be at his office tomorrow morning, if only to stall bankers who might be looking for Emerald's aircraft.

In two columns, I wrote down the date and the declared carry-on weight for each of Pritchard's flights. The least he ever carried on a flight originating at SeaTac was six pounds. The weight he carried on to the planes averaged between ten and twelve pounds. The most he carried aboard was twenty-three pounds, which had been the last day of his life.

I stared at the columns a moment, and at that figure, twenty-three pounds.

"Linda," I called out. "I've got something. Maybe."

THIRTY-TWO

A few minutes later another tape came in, sent to Fred Yamashita. He watched it first, then called us into his office. We arranged ourselves around the television set and VCR. He glanced at the report that had accompanied the tape.

Yamashita said, "This was taken with a Canon eight millimeter video recorder. The camera was sitting on top of Russ Tyler's television set, with a bunch of tapes, and so I suppose the big guy didn't see it."

"Who is Russ Tyler?" Linda asked.

Overhead lights in the room were off, and we were illuminated only by the screen's glare, which cast our faces in an ethereal blue.

Yamashita pointed. "The fellow you see there on the screen is Russ Tyler, twisting his hands together and pacing and looking at his front door." Yamashita hit the PAUSE button and glanced at his documents. "He's a lawyer who lives in Sacramento. Has a one-man firm. Siren goes by, he leaps from his chair and runs to the door. He's thirty-one, never been married. Lives in a small house four blocks from the capitol building."

"And who is the big guy?" I said. "I don't see a big guy."

"You will. His appearance is rather sudden, and unwelcome. The Sacramento police department sent us this tape, for a reason you'll see in just a second."

"How did the Sacramento police get the tape?" Suarez asked.

"Well, it wasn't Russ Tyler's doing. A neighbor heard the ruckus and called the police. The police found the Canon and the tape inside when their prowl cars arrived."

"Who started the Canon's tape rolling, sitting there on Russ Tyler's TV?" Linda asked.

"Tyler himself. He knew—or at least he suspected—what was about to happen, and he wanted a record of it. He's a lawyer. He likes to build a record. But he won't talk to the police. Won't say a word. Says it's his own business. So we haven't identified the big guy yet."

"Says what's his own business?" I asked. "I'm half a beat behind the rest of the band here, Fred."

"You'll catch up in a minute."

"Why did Russ Tyler let the Sacramento police take the tape?" Linda asked.

"He was in no position to object, down at the emergency room," Yamashita replied. "Here we go."

When he pressed the button, the scene began to move again, Russ Tyler taking two steps then turning, his eyes never leaving the door as he paced, hands knotted in front of him. Next to the door were drawn drapes in a pale floral pattern.

A thump was heard, something off camera.

Russ Tyler started, his arms shooting up as if someone had tossed him a basketball. He squeaked, "Leave me alone."

Another thud, this one louder. Tyler turned to the camera. His mouth was pulled back in fear, and his eyes darted left and right, settling only for a second on the camera, perhaps to make sure the red light was blinking. Tyler was wearing jeans and a red Fresno State sweatshirt. His face was pinched and disillusioned, his eyes tight to the sides of his nose and his cheeks sunk deeply. His hair was black and wild above his face, as if he'd been tearing at it.

His mouth closed then opened again. He put a palm against his forehead, a pantomime of hard thinking. He clamped his eyes closed for two seconds. At yet another dull rap out of our sight, he spun back to the door.

A gash abruptly opened in the front door just above the lock. Splinters of wood shot outward, some falling to the floor, others hanging from the jagged new hole. A black length of metal appeared at the hole, then plunged back, ripping the door's wound wider. Tyler was rooted to the spot.

A gloved hand emerged from the ragged hole, a thick hand in black leather. It reached down and gripped the doorknob and twisted it, then withdrew. The door was pushed open from the outside.

The man standing there filled the door frame. His black hair was brushed back on his head, and gleamed with oil. His wintry smile didn't touch his eyes, which were veiled and remote. His large, knobby jaw looked like it had been hewn with an axe. He stepped into the living room, over the splinters. Without turning around, he closed the door, clicking it into place.

"Mind if I come in?" he asked.

"Leave me alone. Please, Harry." Tyler's voice wavered as if Yamashita were playing with the VCR's volume control. "This is my house."

The man looked left and right in an exaggerated way, grinning all the while. "And a pretty little thing it is, too."

"What'd he use to rip open the door?" I asked. "His hands are empty."

"He must've left it on the porch," Yamashita replied.

"I tried to call," Russ Tyler said in a beseeching voice. "I really did."

"Probably all the circuits were busy," Harry said. "That can happen, I know, what with all the cell phones and fax lines."

He walked to one side of the room, to a bookcase that held stereo equipment and a few books and picture frames. "This your CD system? Big bucks, I'll bet. Bang and Olufsen." He lifted the receiver from the bookcase, ripped the wires from the back, and dropped it to the floor. The front panel popped off and skidded along the floor.

The big man said, "They don't make them like they used to, do they?"

He turned back to the bookcase. Next to hit the floor was the CD player, then the tape player.

"You'd think they'd do crash tests on this high-tech stereo stuff," Harry said. "Sort of like the bumper tests Volvo does, you see them on TV." He lifted a picture frame. "Who's this? Nice-looking couple of senior citizens. Your mom and dad?" He blew a fist through the glass and photograph, punching it out the back of the frame. "Whoops. Hope they've got Medicare." Mom and Dad floated to the floor.

"There's no need to do all this," Tyler pleaded. "We can make some arrangement, can't we, Harry?"

The big man stepped around Tyler. He grew on our television screen as he moved toward the video camera that was recording him. His white shirt was pulled taut by his bulk. Over the shirt was a navy jacket with gold buttons that might have been decorated with nautical insignias. The cuffs were too short, up past his wrist bone. He wore slip-on deck shoes.

"These big TV sets. Sometimes they can be unreliable."

His size belied his speed. He half turned and snatched

Tyler by the scruff of his neck. "Maybe we can do our own little crash test. What do you say, Russ?"

He held Tyler by the hair and his belt, and he rammed the lawyer's head into the television screen, just below our camera. Our view lurched as the camera jumped. Tyler groaned.

Harry held him up. Blood flowed from cuts on Tyler's forehead.

"An arrangement, you say?" Harry asked.

Tyler could only hang there, so the big man grabbed his head and moved it up and down, as if Tyler were nodding. The Canon's view had been shifted slightly to our left.

"What kind of arrangement, Russ?"

Harry walked away from the video camera, toward the opposite wall. Tyler's legs dragged across his wrecked stereo equipment. The big man pulled open the drapes near the ruined door to reveal a window with nine panes. Only darkness was visible through the window. Still gripping Tyler by his hair and belt, he held him up to the window, as if allowing him to inspect it.

"You like tic-tac-toe, Russ? I do. I'll take O's. You take X's." Harry smashed a gloved fist into the upper right pane, which fractured instantly, the sparkling splinters falling away. "Your turn."

He jerked Tyler's head forward, smashing it into the lower left pane. The glass shattered and fell away.

"Good move," Harry said. "You've played before, I can tell."

The big man rammed his fist through another window, the upper left. "My boss is upset, Russ."

"Please." Tyler somehow formed the word. "I can't . . ."

"Russ, you talking to me is like Charles Manson talking to his parole board. It don't do a lot of good. You should've talked to the boss when he called."

He moved Tyler's head to the top center, and slammed it into the glass. "Good block. My boss says any lawyer like you should understand the rules, but you don't seem to get them."

Tyler made some sound, a sputtering cough, followed by a low groan.

Harry shattered the lower right pane. "Your turn, Russ."

The lawyer's head was shot forward into the center middle pane.

"Ooh, a strategist," Harry exclaimed. "You blocked me again."

Russ Tyler hung there like an empty gunnysack, held almost off the ground by the big man, who said, "I'm tired of tic-tac-toe. How about you?" When Tyler moaned, Harry said, "I'll take that as a yes. You've got one week, Russ. You understand?"

Harry grabbed the lawyer's head again, and moved it up and down, then said, "I'll take that as another yes." His voice was entirely conciliatory. "My next visit isn't going to be this pleasant."

Blood from Tyler's forehead ran down Harry's shirt sleeve and onto the floor. The big man turned, surveying the room, and revealing Tyler's face to our view. The forehead was a pulp of cuts and bruises. Blood covered his face like a mask, dripping off his chin. Shards of glass stuck out from his forehead.

"Instead of tic-tac-toe, next time you and I are going to play eyeball ping-pong," Harry said pleasantly. "You won't like it, Russ. Not a moment of it."

The big man lifted Russ Tyler up to horizontal, as if he were about to do a military press. "As much fun as this visit has been, Russ, I hope we don't see each other again. Truly."

Harry tossed Tyler toward the remains of the window, head first, a smooth javelin toss, not even a grunt coming from the big man. The panes and remaining glass billowed out, and

Tyler's shoulders then legs then shoes disappeared out into the night. Only fragments of glass stuck to putty at the edges remained of the window. Harry closed the drapes.

He dusted his hands together, squared the shoulders of his jacket, then stepped to the door. He pulled it open, looked around once more at his handiwork, then exited the house, closing the door behind him.

Fred Yamashita punched off the television screen, and pushed his chair away from the set. "The Sacramento police realized this Harry does this kind of thing for a living. It's an art, really. Not a lot of folks know how to do it, giving the victim just the right amount of pain."

"And just the right lesson," Jamie Suarez said. He was wearing a green University of Idaho cap.

"So they sent us a copy of Russ Tyler's tape," Yamashita went on, "which they found when they answered Tyler's neighbor's 911 call. Tyler was taken to the local emergency room, and the police searched Tyler's house."

"All right, I give up," Linda said. "Who is Big Harry, and what does he have to do with *Sacajawea?*"

Yamashita replied, "I don't know the answers to either of those questions."

"Then why are we here," I asked, "watching this hapless fellow get beat up?"

Yamashita backed up the tape, then jumped it forward and back in split-second intervals until he found the frame he wanted. It was of the door being punctured by the metal rod.

He let us look at the frozen image a moment, savoring superior knowledge, looking meaningfully at each of us. "It's hard to tell what Harry used to puncture the door, but it looked enough like the curve of a crowbar that I sent a photo of Harry—taken from this tape—to Wells, Nevada."

"The deputy?" Linda asked.

Yamashita nodded. "Big Harry is the fellow who kayoed the Elko County deputy with a crowbar."

An hour later we walked into the manager's office at the Store More Warehouse on North Aurora. Store More was a regional chain, with fourteen self-service storage warehouses from Olympia to Bellingham, all in the state of Washington. Spaces for rent ranged from Winnebago-size to an area that would accommodate no more than six stacked apple boxes.

The night manager was in a secure area behind bulletproof glass that had a slot through which he could shove a key. He was sitting on a swivel chair reading that evening's *Seattle Times*'s sports section. On his metal desk was the *Times*'s front page, the headline reading EMERALD BOMBER'S COUNTDOWN ENDS TOMORROW. The sub headline added INVESTIGATORS NO CLOSER TO ARREST.

A thermos bottle and a computer screen and keyboard were on his desk. The CPU was to one side on the floor. A truck-parts calendar was taped to the wall above the desk, a buxom young lady dressed as Carmen Miranda standing between two engine blocks and holding a distributor cap as if it were a glass of champagne.

The manager stood slowly when he saw Linda and me, and his face tightened when Linda pressed her FBI identification against the window. He looked left and right, as if he had something to hide, his face hard with thought. Then he apparently decided he was clean. He stepped to the door to unlock it.

"The FBI? What do you want?" The night manager had a full, almost bloated face, with acne scars under his ears. The skin of his cheeks and forehead was pink, as bright as paint, as if he had been standing out in a cold wind. His nose was a rosy knob. He was wearing an Eddie Bauer hunting vest, which had worn out a bottom seam, with a patch of white insulation showing.

"We want to look into a storage room," I said.

"Can't do that." His voice as common as a mongrel. "Hey, aren't you the guy on TV, about the *Sacajawea?*"

"That's me." IIC Rich Shrader had still been passing off press updates to me, claiming it was part of my liaising. In truth, there had been nothing that could be said to the press for days, and I was better at saying nothing than he was, I suppose.

He stuck out his hand, instantly friendly, and introduced himself as Rod Norquist. He asked, "Does this have something to do with all those hundred-dollar bills that fell out of the sky? Man, I dream about that. Falling like snow. What I couldn't do with a wheelbarrow of money. Like winning the lottery. Is there tax on something like that, cash falling from the sky?"

After the drug distributors Sonny Berquist and Nicholas Lawson had been arrested, the NTSB released to the press that a box of money had fallen from the plane. The press had made Jennifer Daily, who had found the money and had spent most of it, the darling of the week. She was on the cover of *People*. The FBI had decided not to file charges against her. The citizenry would not have stood for it.

Linda said, "Yeah, it's got to do with that money."

"Drug money, wasn't it?"

I affirmed it was. "Traces of cocaine all over those bills. We've got a lead we want to check out in one of your storage lockers."

"Right from Colombia, I'll bet." Norquist's stare revealed

he was far away. "Those guys down there, those Colombians, they swim in money. They fill their pools with it."

"We want to look inside one of your lockers," I requested.

That brought the manager back. He pulled his mouth into a grimace. "Geez, I need a warrant, usually, you know."

We had been in too much of a hurry to seek a warrant.

I said, "Reward money is just like cash falling from the sky."

"Reward?"

"You've read about it," I tempted him. "The airline association and the pilots' association have put up big bucks. When the bomber is caught, that money is going to be split among the folks who helped the investigation."

"Split among those who helped the most and the quickest," Linda added.

The struggle was on his face. It lasted all of three seconds. He turned to a safe at the back of the office. "Which number?"

"We've got a name, not a number."

"Okay. The name."

I told him.

When he tapped a keyboard, customer names rolled bottom to top on the screen. Then he dialed the combination lock and pulled the handle. Keys hung from rows of pegs inside the safe. He brought out a steel key.

"Can we keep this between us, just the three of us?" He handed me the key. "My boss would burst an artery, he knew I let you into a locker without a warrant, even if you are FBI."

"Just the three of us," Linda promised. "Not a word to anyone else."

"I mean, this would get me fired faster than crap goes through a goose."

At the sound of footsteps we all turned. The entryway

quickly filled with FBI agents and crime scene specialists, a dozen of them, some carrying evidence kits, others cameras and laptops. Jamie Suarez was still in his Idaho cap.

Linda held up the key and said to Norquist, "Take us to this locker, will you?"

He protested, "You said it'd just be the three of us."

"Well, three of us and some friends." She smiled. "And don't worry, FBI agents can't collect the reward. Your split is still your split. My friends here can't take a portion."

He brightened. "I'll take you to the room."

He brushed by us out to the hallway where the FBI agents were waiting. He signaled the charge like George Custer, and led the way deeper into the building, everyone following.

So many leads had led nowhere. So much time trying to tease out evidence from nothing, all with the smug bomber's clock ticking.

The night manager marched along next to Jamie Suarez, and he asked, "What's my cut of the reward, do you think? Do I need an agent?"

My pulse was quick with excitement. I walked next to Linda and tried to keep my voice level as I asked her, "You think we've got something?"

"I do, Joe." Her eyes shone with emotion. "I think this is solid."

"We've thought that before, with the Resisters."

"Joe, if this turns to nothing, Wayne Ray isn't the only one who'll need a suicide watch," she said. "I'm going to jump off the Aurora Bridge, right alongside him."

THIRTY-THREE

"He's from Hawaii?" I asked, peering through the window at the prisoner. "How'd you find that out?"

"He has the look of some of the Hawaiians I used to play football with at USC," Jamie Suarez said. "Low center of gravity, huge arms and hands, blue-black hair and swarthy skin. But not Mexican."

"He could be Mexican," Linda said, standing at my elbow, her head next to mine as she tried to look through the portal.

"My great-grandfather invented the taco, so I know Mexican," Suarez countered. "And the Hawaiians were quick down at USC, especially for guys weighing three hundred pounds. Most of them are linemen, and they'd hit you so hard coming off the line they'd kill you and your parents."

"And he's been identified?" Linda asked. I moved aside so she could get a better view through the narrow window into the holding cell. "He doesn't weigh three hundred. Maybe only two seventy."

"We had sent the Hawaiian's photo—taken from the video—to all West Coast police departments," Suarez said. "A Kelso uniform spotted him at a burger drive-through. The arrest didn't go smoothly. The Hawaiian put an elbow into one Kelso policeman's nose and snapped it flat. And he had his hand around another Kelso cop's throat, the cop's tongue sticking out between his teeth and him turning blue, until the first one—with the smashed nose—blasted the Hawaiian with pepper spray. Took half a can, right up the Hawaiian's nostrils and right into his eyes. He still looks a little teary." Kelso is a town on the Washington side of the Columbia River north of Portland.

I moved back to the viewing portal. The Hawaiian's eyes were red and leaky. The skin over his cheekbone had purpled, so maybe the Kelso policeman had given him the toe of a boot when the Hawaiian was thrashing away on the ground, his face full of chemicals. His hair—greased back over the knobs of his temples in the Sacramento video—was sticking out at random angles, evidence of the struggle. His fleshy cheeks resembled half melons, and his mouth and nose seemed afterthoughts, stuck between his big cheeks. His eyes were far back in his head. His neck was a short stump. His arms were the size of hawsers, and his thighs strained the fabric of his pants.

"His name is Harry Soames," Suarez said. "He was a truck driver in the U.S. Army, where he was on the army's boxing team. Once he got as far as the army heavyweight championship quarterfinals before being eliminated."

"He left the army?" I asked.

"Soames was given a dishonorable discharge," Suarez explained. "Seems he was denied a three-day pass, so he stuffed his sergeant into the trunk of a car and went on leave anyway. The sergeant banged on the trunk for two hours before being rescued, and that was the end of Soames's army career."

"So how did he come to roughing up people for a living?" Linda asked.

"He's never held a job after the army," Suarez said. "At least, no job we can detect. He disappeared. We can't find records of him anywhere. No passport applications, no bank records, no tax returns or social security records, no credit card applications."

"So what was he doing?" I asked.

"He's a leg-breaker," Suarez replied. "He makes collections."

I asked, "For whom?"

"We don't know."

"Let's find out." Linda motioned to the jailer.

"He won't say a word," Suarez warned. "Not even his name. We only know it and his background because the Honolulu police recognized his photo. They got back to us even before we got a return from Washington on his prints."

"Jamie, you don't know how to interrogate a suspect," Linda taunted sweetly.

He smiled. "Yeah?"

"My technique is to lie and lie and lie. And when you are done, you lie some more."

We were at the Cowlitz County jail, hard by the Columbia. Kelso and neighboring Longview are pulp-mill towns, and the brown smell of sulfur often hangs in the air. The jailer opened the narrow door and the three of us walked single-file into the cell.

Almost invariably, a prisoner will rise when anyone enters his cell, but Harry Soames sat there, not even his eyes moving.

Linda leaned against the pale green wall. "We know who you are, Harry Soames."

He shifted his eyes to her, the smallest of movements.

"We also know what is going to happen to you."

He made a sound, maybe a grunt. He was one vast lump of immobility and recalcitrance.

"You remember that deputy you creamed with a tire iron, over in northern Nevada?" Linda said. "You left the deputy with a dent in his head, and you trashed his car."

Nothing from the huge Hawaiian.

"The Elko County sheriff has sent the Cowlitz County sheriff a special request. Turns out the sheriffs were friends in college." Linda's eyes dug into him. "The Elko County sheriff wants you returned to Nevada, to his custody—and get this—without any record of you being arrested here in Kelso."

Harry Soames curled his upper lip, the beginning of a snarl.

Linda went on, "The Elko County sheriff and the deputy you coldcocked want to be the arresting officers."

By now I knew what Linda was implying, but Soames was heavy and still on the concrete bench, his ham-hock fists on his lap. Next to him was a toilet with no seat. The room was lit by a single bulb recessed behind a screen.

"What they plan on doing, of course, is to arrest you after you attempt to escape. After you attempt to flee by falling down some stairs, three or four times."

Soames turned his head toward her, the mechanical motion of a tank turret.

"The Elko County sheriff has told his friend the Cowlitz County sheriff that he wants you arraigned for battery with a deadly weapon, but he doesn't want you arraigned until you've spent a month in a hospital."

Silence from the bench.

"You smacked one of his deputies with a crowbar, and the Elko County sheriff is waiting to get his hands on you. He wants your ass and he wants it in an emergency ward."

Soames looked at me, then Suarez, the slightest shift of his black eyes.

"We are going to let him have you," Linda lied. "What are you to us? A big gob of stupid muscle."

The Hawaiian took a long breath, his chest expanding like a bellows.

"You talk to us for five minutes, we'll keep you in federal custody," Linda promised. "You'll go to prison, sure, but you won't spend weeks in an iron lung, your head and brain too smashed from falling down those Elko County stairs to work your lungs."

Nothing from the muscle.

"So long, Harry," she said, turning to the door. "The Elko sheriff—his name is Lance, if you can believe it—is waiting out by the admissions desk. I'll sign the papers, and off you go to Nevada."

She left the cell, Jamie behind her.

I was last in line, and I was half through the door when Soames said, "I work for Guy Leaf. He runs an operation on Antigua. He told me . . ."

We hustled back into the cell. Linda shot me a victorious glance.

Harry Soames spoke without interruption for five minutes.

He knew nothing about *Sacajawea*. He knew nothing, but he told us a lot.

Ten calendars were on my desk. They were wall calendars, with spiral binding, and a little box for each day so appointments or reminders could be jotted down. A decade of a busy life. For the first years, the calendars had kittens and pony themes. Then the last four years before she died, the calendar were less cute, featuring photographs of the Pacific North west. The year she died, her calendar showed serene pho tographs of lighthouses, with waves crashing on rocks below

January was the Point Reyes lighthouse. February, the Lime Kiln lighthouse, and the month she died was the Alcatraz Island lighthouse.

"They went over to Sun Valley a lot," I said. "Five, six, seven times a year."

Linda sat on a chair next to me, squeezed into the carrel, while Jamie Suarez and Fred Yamashita hovered above us, leaning over the carrel walls. We turned to the squares beneath the Alcatraz Island photo.

Cold steel seemed to be pressed onto my back, along the spine, raising the hair at the base of my neck. My throat grew tight with the discovery. "He had a reservation for the flight. And he didn't get on the plane."

"Jesus." Yamashita sucked wind through his teeth, sounding like escaping steam. "Sweet Jesus."

We called the U.S. attorney for Western Washington, and he met us at the federal courthouse on Sixth Avenue in Seattle. We found District Judge Adrian Hardaway in her chambers, and she signed the warrant five sentences into the U.S. attorney's argument.

Suarez and Yamashita returned to the FBI office to coordinate the arrest. They would be quick and careful. The suspect must not know anything was amiss until a badge and many pistols were two feet away.

The brokerage offices were in the 1001 Fourth Avenue Plaza building, two blocks nearer Puget Sound than the federal courthouse. When the elevator doors opened on the fortieth floor, Linda showed her badge at the receptionist, and asked her to direct us to Walter Ponsonby's office. The startled receptionist moved her mouth silently, then said she would buzz him to tell him we were here.

"Just point us to his office," Linda ordered. "Now, if you please."

We were rushing by framed artwork on the walls and broadleaf potted plants, then down a hallway lined with glass-fronted offices, the junior brokers working their telephones, a few rising from their desks to follow us with their eyes as we sped by. Nobody usually moved this fast in these staid offices, not even on a triple-witching Friday.

Senior Vice President Walter Ponsonby was in his corner office, his windows looking out to gray Puget Sound and the ferry coming from Bremerton. West Seattle was in the near distance and Bainbridge Island in the far. He had been staring at a computer monitor, a telephone handset tucked between his shoulder and chin.

We charged into his office, and Linda put the warrant and her badge in his face before he could rise from his swivel chair.

"I'll call you back, Larry." Ponsonby lowered the phone.

"We need all the records of all the accounts," I demanded. "How long will that take?"

He scanned the warrant. "Couple minutes. Just as long as it takes a printer."

Ten minutes later we left the building, the damning documents in our hands.

Sarah and I sat in the den with the television on, me trying to wrest the remote control from her. I wanted to watch the local news, but she switched to MTV, where a singer with vacant eyes and a flannel shirt walked along a city street moaning about his girlfriend having an appendectomy and falling in love with a male nurse in the recovery room, something along those lines. Then Sarah flipped to the shopping network where a chirpy woman with her legs crossed perfectly was sell ing cubic zirconium napkin rings. Then to ESPN2, which was broadcasting a rerun of a coconut-tossing competition from the Cook Islands.

She was doing it to bug me, glancing at me sideways once in a while to detect my reaction. Then she found an Ethel Merman movie where Ethel was playing a singing cab driver.

I looked at my wristwatch. "Will you turn it back to the news, please?"

She found a Canadian station broadcasting news about a dispute between Wisconsin and Saskatchewan cheese-makers regarding tariffs. The shot was of a two-hundred-pound cheese rolling up a truck ramp.

"That's not what I want, and you know it."

She laughed and switched to one of the local independent news stations. Their top story was about a Skagit River bridge that was being imperiled by spring runoff from the mountains. Nothing about the *Sacajawea* bomber. No breaking news about an arrest. I was nervous. My chest was tight and my palms were wet with sweat. She switched the channel to another movie, this one a colorized version from the 1940s, where everything looked green and brown.

I had gone with Yamashita and Suarez and Linda and two dozen other FBI and ATF agents to make an arrest, and we had sat on our hands for three hours. No one was there. Nobody showed up.

The FBI staked out the place and asked the Seattle Police and King County Sheriff's Department to help in a search. Linda had gone to SeaTac to assist the Port of Seattle police and security personnel in the event an escape might be attempted on a scheduled flight. The FBI director and NTSB chairman and State and Justice had been alerted that an arrest was imminent, but so far the bomber hadn't cooperated.

There had been nothing for me to do, so I returned home.

The news station went to a commercial, so Sarah changed the channel to one showing Australian Rules football. She said, "Why do all the hunks live in Australia? Do I need a visa, or will my passport do?"

My work on *Sacajawea* was at an end. The prospect of returning to my computer at Boeing was weighing heavily on my mind. How would I sit there, my hand on a mouse, and call up structural blueprints to stare at little representations of steel rivets on an airplane wing, after having spent these past few weeks with Fred and Jamie and Linda and getting my old investigative juices flowing again?

Sure, my system might reissue a meal once in a while, but even exhausted, as we all were, I had been springing out of bed in the morning, rather than slapping the alarm clock and groaning and wondering what hellish commute on I-5 awaited me as I journeyed to the Boeing plant. I had been eating Cup-A-Soups with Linda, laughing and talking, often on the FBI or NTSB jet between Seattle and Hailey, rather than putting quarters into the sandwich vending machine at the Boeing plant, usually to eat by myself, where I'd read whatever had been left on the cafeteria table, often the *Little Nickel Want Ads*.

The coming news story wouldn't feature my work, of course, but I'd be able to brag a little to Sarah, and later Linda would help me do so. My spark-to-the-fuel-tank theory had been wildly wrong, and I had led investigators far astray. But then, working desperately to compensate for my distracting spark theory, and staring at computer monitors hour after hour, day after day, until my eyes felt like they were bleeding, I had come upon that one fact—that one fact in the NTSB and FBI's two million regarding *Sacajawea*: the disparity between Captain Pritchard's normal first-leg carry-on weight and the carry-on weight he brought onto *Sacajawea* the day of the disaster. It had been a slight thing, a statistic, an entry by a data-processing clerk, but once it was found, all the other damning evidence bubbled up. We had the perpetrator cold, or would shortly when the FBI made the arrest.

NTSB chairman Hugh Clifton had called an hour ago, congratulating me. Dick Dahlberg and Rich Shrader had also telephoned, delighted the villain had been identified, and ecstatic the NTSB—me—rather than the FBI had discovered the pivotal evidence. Pierre Lemercier had telephoned from Paris, and said he would send me one of his World War II medals, if he could find the box he kept them in. I was going to explain my feat to Sarah, and I wondered how I could make staring at a computer screen sound Homeric.

By way of an attempt at modesty, I had told Shrader that the idea of comparing weights was the result of an instant of serendipity, that it just popped into my head. He replied that to call it serendipity was to say that Christopher Columbus just discovered America, when in truth he had been sailing west for months. "Without all the preliminary work, much of it seeming to lead nowhere, there are no breakthrough moments," Shrader had said. I agreed with him.

But I wasn't going to say anything to Sarah until after the arrest. I leaned a little toward my daughter. I glanced at the clock on top of the television, then at the upright piano in the corner. The piano always made me think of my wife. Janie hadn't been a bad player, and she had had a lovely alto voice. Sometimes she would sit in this room and sing to herself, following along on the piano. She never understood the harmonica.

"Check the news again, will you, Sarah?" I asked. We were

sitting on the floor in front of the couch, where she had her homework spread out between us and the TV.

"I just did ninety seconds ago."

But she fingered the remote, and a news station appeared again. A weatherman was waving his arms in approximation of an incoming high-pressure zone.

Something had gone wrong.

Yamashita had said that once the perpetrator was identified, the arrest would be swift and clinical. "We'll have a hundred people on it," he had said. "Nothing to it." Yet there must have been something to it, because it hadn't occurred yet.

Sarah had a bowl of microwaved popcorn on her lap. She had arranged a study date with Jason, but I had told her the *Sacajawea* investigation was over, and that an arrest was imminent, and that an FBI and NTSB and ATF joint announcement would be break-in news around the world, so she had telephoned Jason to put off their date until the following evening. Jason hadn't liked it, and said he was coming over anyway, but Sarah was firm, and they argued for thirty seconds until Sarah said—I shouldn't have been listening—that she needed to spend the evening with her dad because it was a big night for him. Then she sent Jason a smooch over the phone and hung up.

The subtext of her conversation with Jason, I suppose, was that Sarah knew that I wanted her to watch the news of the arrest with me, so she could see the results of her old dad's work. Perhaps it was immature, but I suffered a need to be a hero in my daughter's eyes. Linda Dillon had said she would join us after the arrest, and we'd all go out for a late pizza to celebrate. So Sarah and I sat in front of the TV, waiting for news, and I sensed that something had gone terribly wrong.

Our doorbell rang, and I started, as it was late, after ten o'clock.

Sarah laughed and said, "Jason couldn't keep away." She put the popcorn bowl on the rug and rose to answer the door.

I said, "He's probably worried you ditched him tonight for some other date."

She handed me the remote control as she stepped over my legs and left the den. I punched up CNN, then the local ABC affiliate, then Fox News. Still nothing.

I heard Sarah say, "Hold your horses, Jason, and I'll get the bolt. Jeez, do you have some explaining to do, showing up here in the middle of the night." She laughed, delighted.

I reached for some popcorn.

The door opened, then I didn't hear anything for a moment. Sarah and Jason always whispered when I was near. But then I heard something heavy drop to the floor, a muffled sound, like a sack of flour hitting the deck, followed immediately by the shattering of glass, a jangling sound that quickly stilled.

"Sarah?" I called. "That you, Jason?"

No sound came from the foyer. I lay the remote on the rug and rose to leave the den, turning right into the foyer toward the front door.

Sarah lay on the rug on her side, her legs at unnatural angles. Blood seeped from her forehead. A candy dish that had been on a side table in the foyer was in pieces on the hardwood at the side of the rug.

"Oh, God. Sarah . . . what . . ." I saw only her, only my daughter, wounded and down. I sank to a knee before I realized someone was at the open door.

Wayne Ray stood there, a pistol in his hand pointed at me, the tiny Derringer that he had talked about.

The front door had three small leaded windows at eye level. Expecting Jason, Sarah must not have looked through them to see who had rung the bell.

"My broker, Walter Ponsonby, called me at work," Ray said. "Said you and the FBI woman had visited him. I couldn't go to my apartment. I could tell from two blocks away that cops were all around."

"Wayne . . . My girl here . . ."

He hobbled on his cast into the hallway and closed the door. "She opened the door, but wouldn't get out of my way."

"Wayne, let me get help."

He fired the pistol.

The sound instantly filled the hallway and fled just as quickly, and my right arm was yanked toward the floor. I slipped sideways, the pain in my arm rolling up to my shoulder then seeming to detonate in my head. I landed heavily on the floor next to Sarah. My eyes found my arm.

The sleeve of my shirt had a ragged hole in it. So did my arm, a hole clean through it. Blood bubbled out two sides of my arm. My head grew light, filling with the white cotton of shock.

"Sarah." My voice was broken and far away.

THIRTY-FOUR

"Missed." Wayne Ray leaned against the wall. "I was aiming at your head. I was never much of a shot, and now I'm even worse, now that my hand is in a cast. I've been holding this damned thing in my off hand, if you can imagine."

I groaned, and used my good arm to roll upright to a sitting position, my back against the wall. I reached for my daughter, putting my hand on her neck. Her pulse was strong, but her eyes were still closed. Blood from the gash on her head dripped to the floor.

"You figured out about my canceled trip," Ray said. His gaze was on a print on the wall, something Janie had purchased at an art fair, featuring what looked to be daffodils, or maybe hockey players, it was hard to tell.

He said, "You went to the storage warehouse where I was keeping my things after I moved out of the Highlands, and you found my wife's calendars. I have no idea why I didn't throw them away. Never crossed my mind, I guess."

I gasped, "My daughter needs a doctor. Help us, Wayne."

He might not have heard me. He pushed a new shell into the small pistol's empty barrel. "I had to have the money, Joe. It was as simple as that."

Studying Charlotte Ray's calendars, Linda and I had learned that Charlotte and Wayne usually took ski vacations together. Without exception, Charlotte marked down on her calendar—in advance of the event—"Wayne and I to Sun Valley," or "Wayne and I to Whistler." Then, she would write in another box, four or five days later, "Wayne and I return to Seattle." Linda and I concluded these calendar entries were always written in advance, because twice in the past five years a ski vacation had been canceled, once due to rain at Whistler, and another time because Charlotte had come down with the flu. On both these occasions, the original entries "Wayne and I to Sun Valley" and "Wayne and I to Whistler" had been struck through with a pencil. In the former calendar box, Charlotte had added, "Flu. Feel terrible," and in the latter, "Rain. Slushy snow. Canceled." In other words, these were primarily pre-event entries, in the manner of an appointments calendar, rather than post-event entries like a diary.

On Charlotte's calendar for last March's trip to Sun Valley was the standard, "Wayne and I to Sun Valley," and five little boxes to the right, the day *Sacajawea* was destroyed, appeared, "Wayne and I back from Sun Valley."

According to the calendar Wayne Ray had planned on going skiing with his wife that trip. According to the calendar, Wayne Ray should have died aboard *Sacajawea* with his wife.

I bent over my daughter and stroked her hair. "Sarah, it's Daddy. Sarah?" My voice was weak, and sounded strange to me.

My arm was on fire, everything below my shoulder, and it was pumping pain into the rest of me. I tried to move it, but a renewed flash of pain shot up my arm. My ears were ringing with the agony. I was vaguely aware of the new hole in our foyer wall, where the bullet had traveled after its passage through my arm. It was a diminutive hole, out of proportion with the pain in my arm.

I coughed. "So you didn't go . . . didn't go to Idaho on that trip."

To the extent I could concentrate on anything—useful thoughts being pierced and broken by pain—I was determined to keep him from thinking about the weapon in his hand, and my helpless daughter at his feet.

"We were meeting Charlotte's sister over there, and her parents live over there. So when I canceled the trip at the last minute, Charlotte went anyway. I knew she would. It was business, and I couldn't go. I told her I might be able to join her in Sun Valley in a day or two. I kept my return reservation, to convince her."

I stared at my girl's forehead, with its blackening bruise around the laceration where Ray had hit her.

"And then you discovered who beat me up, the crazy Hawaiian," he said. "The guy's a strong-arm man, a gorilla, you found out. He collects overdue debts. Scares the hell out of you on his first visit, then beats the hell out of you his second visit. I never knew the bastard's name. I owed his boss a lot of money. I told the FBI that I didn't recognize who nailed me in the Hailey parking lot, but hell yes I did. That's the whole point of the exercise. He beats you just this side of death, so you'll pay your debts. Only trouble is, I didn't have anything to pay them with. I've been broke, more or less, on and off, for years. And I mean, broke bad."

Sarah's eyes fluttered open, though she didn't appear to be focusing on anything.

"Sarah, it's me, Dad." I had to force my mouth to work. I was lost in the pain from my arm. "Can you hear me?"

Her eyes slowly closed. I dabbed at a new bead of blood on her forehead.

"Then this afternoon you subpoenaed my stockbroker," Ray said. "You found out that I had borrowed against all my Emerald stock several years ago, and you figured out that I didn't lose my shirt when the price of Emerald stock fell after *Sacajawea,* and then fell and fell when news of the threatening letter got out. I had nothing to lose when Emerald Airlines went into the tank."

I tried to cradle her head, but each motion rolled pain up my arm.

Ray said, "I had borrowed against my stock, and so it was worthless to me. I had sold my house. I told you I put the house sale money into Emerald, but I just paid off a couple of collectors and put the rest on some games, and lost it all. I even broke into my IRAs, emptying them out. I didn't have a penny, no equity in anything, and was living paycheck to paycheck, and they were coming after me, those collectors I still owed money to. The pressure you wouldn't believe."

I couldn't put weight down on my punctured arm. Shock was leaching away useful ideas. Maybe I could walk to the den, to the telephone there.

Wayne Ray was talking away, explaining and rationalizing and arguing to himself, maybe because he had no one else to hear his dreadful confession. Perhaps I was forgotten. I put a leg under me, staggered with the pain, and tried to rise.

He fired again. The bullet bit into my shoulder, through the meat above the collarbone, and I pitched forward onto the rug.

"Missed again," he said.

I panted against the burning in my shoulder. I rolled over to face him again. The pistol was again at rest against his leg.

Sarah's eyes opened again, but her face was slack. Tiny pieces of my shoulder were stuck to the hallway wall. The bullet had dug a trench on the top of my shoulder.

"I'm a player, Joe." He brought a hand to the side of his face. Had I not known him to have murdered his wife and sixty-two other people on *Sacajawea,* I would have sworn he was wiping away a tear. "It got away from me, is all." He reloaded the tiny pistol.

With the Hawaiian enforcer identified, the FBI had quickly pieced together Wayne Ray's economic demise. Ray had played college football, and shortly thereafter began wagering on football. Back then, Ray found action only through bookies or on an occasional trip to Las Vegas to visit the sports books. The FBI had someone on the payroll in the information systems office of a major Las Vegas casino, and she reported that the sports book's records showed Ray visited six or seven times a year, wagering on athletic events at the casino's sports book, often putting $10,000 on a single sporting event. On a big NFL Sunday or during the run to the NCAA Final Four, he might wager $100,000 in a single day.

Then several years ago Ray apparently stopped visiting Las Vegas, the casino informant reported. With sports gambling illegal in forty-nine states, Ray found the Internet. The FBI subpoenaed Ray's Internet service provider, and discovered that for the prior four years Ray had communicated almost daily with five Internet gambling services located in Antigua, in the Caribbean's Leeward Islands. Antigua licenses these Internet gambling concerns, and more than thirty of them have set up shops on the island, little more than rooms filled with modems and computers.

Wagering on sports through the Internet with these offshore shops is perfectly legal. Most Americans wager on the big four sports but bets can be placed on almost any contest worldwide. Nine will get you one that Tasmania will win cricket's Mercantile Cup.

Still studying the pattern on the wallpaper, his pistol dangling from his hand, Ray asked me, "It was all those television sets in my living room that tipped you off, wasn't it?"

I couldn't reply, could only breathe loudly and wince against the pain, which seemed to be coming from everywhere, rushing up and down me like an echo in a canyon.

Sarah's eyes remained open. Now she was looking at me. She mouthed the word *Dad*.

"All those TV sets you saw in my living room, about to be packed and stored," Ray said. "I had this frame built by a cabinetmaker, really nice, made of walnut. I could put eight TVs in it, up in my bedroom. I had two satellite dishes, a big one and one of those pizza-size dishes. I could follow a ton of games, with those eight TVs and a remote control, pounding a new wager into my keyboard anytime one occurred to me."

Once Ray's use of the Antigua gaming shops had been established by reviewing his ISP records, the FBI turned to the National Security Agency, which monitors satellite communications. The NSA closely examines offshore wagering because the Internet sports books are often used to launder money, typically drug money. Large bets will be made on both teams about to play, say, a professional football game. By properly structuring the wager, the bettor wins and loses on the same game, breaking about even. The money returned to his account is now clean. All the bettor pays is the vigorish of 4.5 percent.

Ray was still staring at the wall, lost in his recounting of a failed life. I shook my head at Sarah, a small movement, trying to tell her to lie absolutely still and not say anything.

She mouthed *Dad* again. Her eyelids lowered, then opened. Her pupils were too big. She was looking at me, now fully conscious, I thought, and she was asking me to help her, to end this, to get both of us out of here and away from the crazy man with the pistol. Awash in pain, still bleeding, I could think of nothing. I was helpless. I couldn't save my daughter, and she lay only three feet from me.

Wayne Ray's words fluttered in and out, though I'm sure it was my mind, rather than his voice. "I tried Gamblers Anonymous a couple of times. The twelve steps to recovery. But it always was five to one against me getting through the steps. I never did." He laughed in a woolly way.

Through data pulled off satellite relays, the NSA had been attempting to spot laundering by establishing the wagering patterns of the big bettors. When the FBI request came in, NSA turned to its Cray computers, and within an hour provided a breakdown of Wayne Ray's offshore gambling.

Ray had not been laundering money. He had been losing it, and in large amounts. He would wager modest sums—by his standards, anyway—at the beginning of a weekend, and if caught in a losing streak, he would engage in the notorious gambler's folly of chasing bad money with good by doubling, then quadrupling the size of his wagers as the weekend drew to a close. After a losing weekend of pro football bets, Ray would often have $200,000 riding on the Monday night game, hoping to recoup his weekend losses.

This work by the FBI and NSA had all occurred since identifying the Hawaiian collector and subpoenaing the stockbroker that afternoon. Most of the offshore gambling parlors insist on money up front. Using a credit card or a Western Union Quick Collect, an account is opened before any bets are placed. But Wayne Ray was a frequent customer of an outfit called All Sports World, and Ray was dealing in huge sums of money. Coveting a major player, All Sports World began allowing Ray to bet on credit.

Ray wasn't any better a bettor on credit than he was when wagering his own money. His losses mounted, year by year. After repeated attempts to get Ray to pay up, All Sports World sent Harry Soames to negotiate. The Hawaiian had found Ray in Hailey, Idaho. Soames was an independent contractor, and had toured the West Coast on assignments from several sports books. All Sports World wasn't the only operation that had given Ray credit, and it wasn't the only operation that had sent a collector.

His assets gone, the collectors after him, and his thirst for gambling still unquenched, the three-million-dollar policy on his wife's life must have floated in front of Wayne Ray like a life ring.

"Well, it's all over now, I suppose." He turned from the wall and looked down at Sarah.

He was making a decision, staring down at my girl. She sensed it, heard the change in his voice. She bit her lower lip, still lying without moving. She stared at me, pleading with her eyes to help her.

I tried to divert him. "The nails." My voice cracked with pain.

He smiled sadly. "A pretty good idea, I thought. Ed Fahey is found with AA missiles in his closet. What more did the goddamn FBI want? Those were his missiles, the stupid paranoid hillbilly. Still, the FBI dawdled and dawdled and didn't arrest him."

"So you put the nails in his field?" My words came slowly, my mouth not cooperating.

"I was flying back and forth between Hailey and SeaTac,

couple times a week, trying to keep Emerald running. So one night when I was over there I went out to his pasture and buried those nails, knowing full well the FBI would find them. Same batch I used on *Sacajawea*. I figured those shingle nails would send Ed Fahey to the executioner. What more did the FBI want?"

My breathing was in short gulps, each punctuated with a stab of pain.

Ray said, "And earlier I sent the threatening letter, with the shingle nail in it, hoping the FBI would be prompted to arrest Fahey and the other Idaho Resisters. The letter would pressure the FBI to round them up. But they still delayed."

He was still staring at Sarah. The murderer of sixty-three people was studying my daughter.

I tried again. "Why'd you report that Emerald's . . ." My mouth fished open uncontrollably as pain washed over me. "Why'd you report to us that Emerald's reservations computer had been tampered with, that someone had erased a reservation on *Sacajawea* after the plane had gone down?"

"Anne Shipley discovered it, and she told Ben Cook, and then they told me. That cat was out of the bag. No way I could stop the news getting out. Plus, I figured that if I quickly and enthusiastically relayed to you their discovery, it'd deflect suspicion from me."

I groaned. My shirt was damp with blood. I leaned against the wall, and streaked it with more blood.

Ray said, "I'd worked my way up at Emerald, job to job, and I knew the reservation system. I didn't break a sweat doing it. All evidence in our computer that I was to fly on *Sacajawea* just disappeared. Except for her calendar, which you found."

Sarah's eyes were wide. She was fully alert, and looking to

me. I was an utter supplicant, for my life and my daughter's. I could do nothing but keep Ray talking.

"The bomb." My voice was pinched, like an old man's. "*Sacajawea*'s pilot was carrying extra weight. You somehow got the pilots to carry it on."

"When I told you at the morgue that I stopped sending seafood to Charlotte's father, I was being a bit untruthful. Just before *Sacajawea* left SeaTac for Hailey, I asked Captain Pritchard to take a box of oysters to Hailey, and told him Charlotte's father would send someone down from Ketchum to pick them up."

I let another groan slip, some caused by pain, some from the realization of how he had done it.

"I told Barry Pritchard as I handed him the package that if for some reason nobody appeared to pick up the oysters, just bring them back and I would eat them. Dry ice and oysters, I told him. He put the box in the cargo bay. And, of course, nobody showed up at the Hailey airport—I never told Charlotte's father they were coming—so Pritchard flew the package back with him to Seattle. Well, almost to Seattle. I had a digital timer on the detonator, set to blow on the return leg."

That the bomb had been put aboard *Sacajawea* in Seattle on the originating flight, rather than in Hailey on the doomed return flight, was a singular fact that had misled us investigators.

"Why are you here?" I managed to ask.

"After you asked for the personal manifests, I knew that I was lost. I knew you'd discover how it happened, would find out that the bomb was put onboard in Seattle and made a round trip. I could've beaten you, if you hadn't tripped on that little fact. The insurance company was set to pay me the three million, once you and the FBI closed the *Sacajawea* investigation."

"You loved your wife." Iridescent colors danced at the

edges of my vision. I didn't have long. I had to keep him talking. "I could tell you loved your wife."

"I needed the insurance money on my wife's life more than I needed my wife."

I panted with pain, and didn't dare to even look again at Sarah.

He searched my face, perhaps seeking understanding and commiseration. "I needed the money, Joe. I had people after me. I'd pay them some now and then, but I'd lose more on the games, and they'd still be after me." He wiped his forehead with his gun hand. "I couldn't stop the wagering. I had lost everything. Everything my father had given me, gone. It was day to day with those people, coming after me with a crowbar."

My breath was ragged.

He said, "But I was almost clear, almost had the insurance money in my hands, and you ruined it. That's why I'm here, Joe. You ruined it for me, Joe, goddamn you."

A sound escaped my mouth, a low lament of pain and despair. Wayne Ray had started to blur in my sight. I reached for my daughter's hand, abruptly enraged that I could do nothing for her. When her mother had left, I could do nothing. And now, once again, I could do nothing but moan like a child. I was powerless. Tears of pain and rage and frustration formed at the corners of my eyes.

"And so I'm going to ruin it for you." Ray made a face of concentration, my daughter's and my fate in the balance. "And so what's the worst thing I can do, to ruin it for you?"

The pistol twitched, then slowly came up, an inch and then another inch, coming up. Ray's face held no expression. No anger, no fear, no revulsion for what he had done or what he was about to do, no look of victory that he was about to bring me low, not even resignation. Wayne Ray's was a blank face. A man who could kill sixty-three people to collect insurance proceeds on his wife would, of course, have a blank face.

He said in a low voice, "After sixty-three, what's two more, I suppose?"

The pistol rose and rose, and came to rest pointed at my daughter's head.

"Please," I begged. "Not my girl. Please, Wayne. . . ."

The words died in my throat as his finger drew back.

Perhaps the pain from my wounds and the loss of blood had finally addled me, because the physical world began to play games. One of the small panes of leaded glass on our front door shattered. It was there, solid and whole, and then it was in a thousand pieces, bursting, the tiny shards thrown into the foyer.

At the same instant a flower opened on Wayne Ray's shirt, under his clavicle. A rose that bloomed suddenly in glorious red. Ray bucked and staggered, then caught himself, his face still devoid of expression, just maybe a touch of curiosity.

He sagged, then caught himself again, the muzzle of his pistol now pointed at the floor. Blood pumped from his chest.

He dropped the pistol, and it bounced off my daughter's shoulder to the rug. The lovely blooming rose, I vaguely realized, was an exit wound.

Ray half turned toward the door, and I could see the entrance wound on his back, much smaller, just above his heart. Then his knees buckled and he fell back against the wall and slid to the floor next to my daughter.

Linda Dillon pushed open the door, a pizza carton in one hand and her pistol in the other.

She stepped into the crowded hallway.

Wayne Ray looked up at her.

"Drop the gun, Wayne," she ordered, her pistol pointed at him.

He had already dropped the gun. His hands were empty. The small pistol was nearer to me than to him.

"Drop the gun, now," she barked, still holding the pizza.

"Please," he gasped.

Her pistol roared, and a second hole opened on Wayne Ray's chest, this one right at the heart.

He spasmed once, then toppled sideways. Blood rushed from his chest for a few seconds, then quickly slowed to a dribble. His face was still blank, now for an eternity.

My daughter looked up. "Linda." She winced with the pain in her head.

Linda glanced at me, a quick inventory. Then to Sarah, "You okay, honey? You took one for the team, right on your head, looks like."

"I'm okay." She pushed herself to a sitting position. Her voice was just above a whisper. "Help Daddy, quick, Linda."

"He's all right," Linda said, lowering herself to sit next to Sarah.

"He's been shot. Twice."

"I've been hurt worse playing chess with my father." She grinned at me. "He's not even bleeding anymore."

I wanted to say something snappy, but my mouth had dried up. The pain from both directions had steadied to dull throbs. I hadn't passed out, a tiny victory. I could feel a strong pulse in my neck, magnified by the pain. I would live, I decided vaguely.

Linda returned her pistol to her purse and reached for her cell phone to call 911.

But before she punched in the numbers, she opened the pizza box. "Here, Sarah." Another smile at me. She was strutting her stuff for my daughter. "Pepperoni and extra cheese. Don't let it get cold."

THIRTY-FIVE

The psychiatrist was sitting stiffly across from me in one of North Star's green leather chairs, a file open on his lap. His name was Bernard Chatwin. He wore a prim mustache and a club tie and tassels on his shoes, and I suspected he had gone his whole life without anyone calling him Bernie. He consulted with a number of North Star patients, and agreed the lobby would be a convenient place to meet. And Linda Dillon and I had other business here, besides him.

Linda was in a chair next to me. She was wearing a leather car coat over a white fisherman's knit sweater, and black wool knit pants. Her hair was loose to her shoulders. A fan palm with its large serrated leaves was behind our chairs. The fireplace was roaring and the receptionist with the brad through her lip was fielding telephone calls at her desk.

I was in the hospital only three days, and when they pushed me toward the door I asked if I shouldn't stay longer, what with two holes in me. The discharging nurse said they needed my bed for someone who was really hurt. I spent two weeks in a chair in my den, some of it reading a biography of Wellington. My shoulder and arm felt like I had served in one of his squares at Waterloo. Then Linda had called, asking for help.

Dr. Chatwin said, "I treated your wife Jane over the course of nine months, and we made progress."

I had been working on *Sacajawea,* and had put aside determining the meaning of the prescription drugs I had found in Janie's apartment in Ketchum. But Linda had made telephone calls, and had found Janie's psychiatrist, which she said hadn't been hard because Ketchum had only two of them. When Dr. Chatwin had balked at discussing one of his patients, Linda had pointed out that a surviving spouse—me—could waive the doctor-patient privilege, and that she was an FBI agent and was going to fall on the doctor like a wall of bricks if he didn't cooperate. She assured me she had said it sweetly, smiling all the while. So the doctor had agreed to meet with us at North Star, just up the road from his office.

"Jane Durant suffered major depressive disorder."

"I know," I said. "At least, since I found the prescription drugs in her apartment. Jamie Suarez told me about the type of medicine she was taking."

"You don't know all of it. Her disorder was marked by feelings of hopelessness and pessimism and worthlessness. And irritability and restlessness."

"How could I have missed all of that, when she was still living with me?" Blood rose to my cheeks. I simply could not have been that blind. She was my wife. We shared the same breakfast table and bedroom. I couldn't have been blind to something like that.

The psychiatrist said, "It happens more frequently than you'd think. The spouse doesn't see it, doesn't see the signs."

I blinked, trying to think of a response.

"You should know, Mr. Durant, that the symptoms of major depressive disorder can be subtle, particularly in the early stages, and that it is common for a spouse to fail to detect it."

In his clinical, too-many-degrees way, he was trying to be kind. Maybe he had been called Bernie at some point, after all.

"Tell Joe about the medicines he found in her room," Linda asked.

"I had put Jane on a regimen of antidepressant medication and psychotherapy. I had prescribed a new-generation antidepressant, Effexor, a brand name for venlafaxine, which is a serotonin-norepinephrine reuptake inhibitor."

"English, if you please, Doc," Linda said.

"Linda tells me you are an engineer." The psychiatrist changed directions.

"Among other things," I replied, feeling I needed to be defensive.

"It is particularly difficult for some people—engineers are often among them—to realize that depression is not caused by a weakness of character. Someone with major depressive disorder cannot simply pull herself out of it, and be her normal cheery self if she'll just try hard."

I said, "Well, I never thought that . . ."

He said, "Linda told me about your daughter Sarah, and how devastated she had been by her mother leaving the family. It is important for you and Sarah to understand that depression is a biological disorder. Something is physically wrong in the brain, just like something is physically wrong when a bullet passes through an arm." He smiled. Bernie, for sure.

"It isn't a matter of willpower," Linda added.

"No. It is an imbalance of neurotransmitters, which are natural chemicals that allow brain cells to communicate with each other."

"Sure." I suppose I knew that, maybe read about it in *Time* or somewhere.

"The drug I prescribed for Janie increased the amount of neurotransmitters in the synapses. She was improving."

"Well, she's not improving any longer," I said.

"Mr. Durant, you must also know, and you must tell Sarah," the doctor said, "that an abandonment of family is not uncommon in cases of major depressive disorder. Jane's symptoms went even beyond that. She spent her days watching television. She liked to think of herself as a skier, but I don't think she skied at all while she was under my care. She didn't have the capacity to ski, or for most other activities you and I would consider normal. I had to make sure she had food in her apartment, because it didn't occur to her to shop."

I suppose this explained why there were no books in Janie's condominium, a woman who had once viewed books like I view food. And her missing ski boots, and the condo's general untidiness that Sarah had commented on.

"Tell Joe how bad it was," Linda said.

"I believed her to be suicidal," Dr. Chatwin said, "at least in the early stages of treatment."

I chewed on a lip.

"And tell him what you speculated on, what you told me," Linda said.

"Well, it's not something I can be sure of."

"Tell him anyway," she insisted.

"Jane had progressed, and was showing indications of increased energy and appetite, and she was sleeping a little better."

"And?" Linda prompted.

He glanced at her peevishly, not appreciating being led as if he were on a witness stand. "I cannot be sure, because she did not tell me directly, but she may have been leaving my care. She had asked about the procedure for transferring her prescriptions."

"Tell Joe what that means."

The psychiatrist looked at her again. Then he said, "Jane

wanted to know how she could continue her drug therapy in Seattle."

"Janie may have been returning to you and Sarah," Linda said. "She may have boarded *Sacajawea* to come home, Joe."

I tried to absorb the knowledge. Maybe there had been something more to Janie leaving than me being a boring engineer, as Janie's sister Eva had claimed. Maybe there was something more to her abandoning us than the forever unfathomable. Maybe when our family history is written a century hence, there will be more to Sarah losing her mother than a blank page. I inhaled long and slowly, my eyes on a spot on the far wall, my thoughts forming and re-forming.

Dr. Chatwin assembled his file, smiled professionally at me, and said he hoped our discussion had been of some help. I thanked him, my mind still on the revelations of the past ten minutes.

After he had disappeared through the lobby's glass doors, Linda asked, "Are you ready to give an assist, Joe?"

I smiled at her, a full smile.

She grinned back. "Learning Janie was depressed might sort of help un-depress you, maybe?"

"I've got something to tell Sarah, something solid and understandable about her mother, at least."

I followed her from the lobby into the high mountain sunshine. The Sawtooths were to the west, still snow clad, but the ski runs were no longer operating. The slopes were purple and gray, rising to a rinsed blue sky.

We walked from under the portico, past several gardeners to the parking lot. Her rental Mercury was there, not her FBI Chevrolet, because she wasn't on bureau business. The car was under branches of a canoe birch, swaying in a small wind. The lot was lined with pink heather. At the edge of the asphalt, wilderness began with wheatgrass and Idaho fescue in front of a stand of white-bark pine and Douglas fir. Hidden in the boughs, a Stellar's jay loosed its metallic clacking.

Linda opened the Mercury's front passenger door. "Still ready, Kevin?"

Her husband had unbuckled the belt but had gotten no further. His hands were in his lap, and he was gripping one in the other. He was wearing a Nordstrom shirt with a little stitched sail on the breast. The shirttails were out. He had cut himself shaving that morning, an angry gash under an ear.

Linda had told me that twelve months ago she had gotten her husband to this parking lot but had been unable to budge him farther. She had told me she didn't expect me to wrestle Kevin through North Star's door, but had thought that someone else nearby might make a difference, might prevent a last-second change of mind. I had flown over with them, Kevin sitting between us. She had paid for my air ticket and my rental car.

"Let's go, Kevin." I bent to put a hand on his shoulder. "They're waiting for you in there. Thumb screws, the rack, iron bars glowing red in the fire pit, the works."

He looked up at me, pleading in his eyes, but I couldn't tell whether he was silently begging me to push him harder toward the clinic's door, or to let him escape, let him back down into Ketchum, maybe to the Pioneer Saloon.

He said with false bonhomie, "I've been here before, Joe. You can't scare me."

"Please, Kevin," Linda said. "We're close. Couple of steps more."

He pursed his lips, then swung his legs out of the door, and slowly stood. I was going to get Kevin Dillon into North Star one way or another, I had promised myself, and I thought when he hesitated just then, his hand on the Mercury's roof, that I might have to resort to a half nelson. But he pushed himself off, and positioned himself between us, clearing his throat and running his palsied hands back through his hair. Linda took his arm.

"I'm all right," he whispered.

"I know you are," she said.

"This is going to be tough."

"I know, but no tougher than taking bullets through the body, which Joe here likes to do."

He managed to pull back the corners of his mouth. "No, it's probably not going to be as bad as that." His pace gained a little purpose.

We escorted him under the porte cochere, where out of the sun it was much cooler, then into the lobby. We crossed the green marble floor to the reception desk.

Fay Herwin was there to greet Kevin. She said warmly, "Welcome back. We're glad you're here."

Her offense at being roughed up during Linda and my last visit had evaporated at the prospect of Kevin's long stay, and the fees it would generate. North Star's director shook his hand, and presented him with an embossed leather folder containing the admission forms. She was entirely smooth and persuasive.

Kevin turned to me. "I'm on my way, Joe. Thanks." He lowered himself unsteadily to a chair across from Fay Herwin. She passed him a pen. An attendant in a ski sweater stood nearby, waiting to escort him to his room.

Linda told her husband she'd be right back, and she walked me out to my car, glancing once or twice over her shoulder, perhaps afraid Kevin still might bolt.

At my car, she said, "I'm taking some time off, a sabbatical. I'll be here in Ketchum for two months, maybe more, depending on Kevin. Got a sublease on a condo. I'm going to check in on Kevin every day, maybe make it a practice to have lunch with him."

I nodded.

She said, "Fay Herwin said two months might or might not do it, so I may be here longer."

"I couldn't afford two days at this place," I said.

She smiled. "Kevin Dillon didn't marry a wealthy woman for nothing."

I couldn't think of anything to say, nothing she would want me to say, anyway. I looked at her, then looked away, then rubbed my lip with the back of my hand, then glanced at her again. "Well, I'll be going."

"Sarah told me something, Joe."

"She can be a talker, I know that much."

"When we were at the hospital with you, waiting outside the operating room, Sarah said that after *Sacajawea* was finally over, and when you and I say good-bye, it was going to be tough for you."

"Yeah? Well, what does she know? She's a kid."

"She's a smart kid." Linda had me by the eyes, staring straight into me, and she wouldn't let go. "She didn't know about how difficult it would be for me, too. But now the time has come, and I'm telling you it is."

I smiled weakly. "I suppose I'm glad."

"You always search for symmetry, Joe. I've noticed that about you. Little things, like always squaring your pen to the lines of your desk."

"Sometimes it's a nuisance."

She put her hand on my arm. "I'm here with Kevin. He's my husband. I'm bound to be here."

I nodded.

"Sometimes there is no symmetry, Joe. Sometimes things just don't fit. They just hang there, loose and at odds." Her voice had been lowering, and now it was a whisper. "Doesn't matter how much I might wish it weren't so."

I breathed.

She went up on her toes, and kissed me at the corner of my mouth. "Good-bye, Joe."

She turned to reenter North Star. I watched her until the glass door swung back and she and Kevin and all that was inside were hidden by the glass's bright reflection.

I drove down the hill toward Ketchum, and then turned south on the road that would take me eleven miles to the Hailey airport. At the end of the flight, Sarah was going to pick me up at SeaTac in her new used Volvo, her freshly stamped driver's license in her pocket.

I spent the time of those eleven miles, and then the flight to Seattle, trying to compose the news I would give to Sarah about her mother's mental disorder and how it made her do things she wouldn't otherwise have done, but my mind drifted back to Linda again and again. I stared at the seat back in front of me the entire flight, my face stormy.

At one point—with the plane over Snoqualmie Pass, just where *Sacajawea* had gone down—the lady in the neighboring seat asked me if I was all right, and I said that I was.

My amp was in the trunk of Sarah's Volvo, and we traveled from SeaTac directly to the tavern. My shoulder still felt like it was filled with fishing hooks, but the Longliners didn't get enough gigs for me to sit one out.

You wouldn't think a harmonica, being so small, would require both hands, but it does, and though I could by then bring my wounded arm to my mouth, I didn't know if I could hold it there for three sets, or even one. When he was still working Jackson, Mississippi, street corners, Sonny Boy Williamson would sometimes play his harmonica with no hands. I tried that once in my basement, and Sarah threw me a dime.

The factory trawler *Bering Sea* was in, and its crew crowded the tavern, ready to drink beer and ignore the band. Cooks on factory trawlers always have missing teeth, and I don't know why that is. Sarah muscled my amp toward the stage, turning it sideways so she could squeeze between the chairs. The Longliners had a roadie, at last. Three leering fishermen offered to help her, one after another. She gave each a look that would have shattered granite, learned from Linda Dillon. Gray clouds of cigarette smoke obscured the ceiling. Johnny Moore aka Maloney was behind his kit, lightly tapping his hi-hat with a stick. Will Worthington was eating chowder at the bar, and Mike Dunham was tuning his guitar to one side of the stage.

I was hailed by a familiar voice, and turned to see Jamie Suarez and Fred Yamashita sitting at a table near the window. Suarez had a grin on his face and a half-empty pitcher of beer at his elbow. Yamashita's hand was around a glass of Seven-Up over ice. I left my harmonica case on the stage and went over to their table. Yamashita cast nervous glances at the rowdy fishermen.

Suarez announced, "Big news on all fronts." He lifted his glass. "Here's to me."

"Jamie has been promoted," Yamashita said. "He's headed down Interstate 5 to Portland as special-agent-in-charge."

I shook his hand. "You deserve it, after your work on *Sacajawea*, Jamie."

Suarez pushed a chair out for me. Sarah sat next to Will Worthington at the bar, and she laughed at something he said. The bartender put a Coke in front of her.

"How're you feeling?" Yamashita asked.

"Never better," I replied, "except for some bullet holes."

Suarez said, "Here's more good news. The Arab who tried to bribe Linda and you, Hamed Ibn Mahtab, has been recalled to Riyadh. The Saudi government has apologized to the FBI and the NTSB for the error in judgment of a lesser-ranking official, as they termed it."

Whistles and cheers came from the pool table, where a shooter had just sunk the eight ball on a bank shot.

"Just recalled?" I asked. "Hamed should have been fired."

"That doesn't happen over there," Yamashita said, "not when you are a member of the royal family, however distant. Hamed was reassigned from the diplomatic service to the agriculture ministry. Something to do with fig production subsidies."

Suarez laughed. "Joe, I'll bet you still check your bank balance, hoping maybe that million dollars will magically reappear."

I grinned. Even smiling seemed to pull the damaged tissue in my shoulder. "I'm still finding my usual three hundred dollars. Not a dime more, unfortunately. You've stayed around here to tie things up on *Sacajawea*, Fred. Now where to?"

"Back to D.C. I'm already executive assistant director." He smiled. "I can't get a promotion unless Director Henley dies. He has asked me not to think about that, and I don't, much."

Suarez said, "I received a phone call from Hawaii, from Dwight Vaughn, Charlotte Ray's brother. Remember in our video of the funeral, him snapping at Wayne Ray?"

I said, "Our lip-reader said Vaughn was saying something like, 'So you've got no Emerald Airlines left? Turned to nothing.'"

"Vaughn read in the Honolulu newspaper about his brother-in-law's death, and his culpability for *Sacajawea*, so he gave us a call. When he was barking at Wayne graveside, Dwight wasn't talking about Wayne's perceived mismanagement of Emerald after *Sacajawea* came down. Instead, Dwight knew of Wayne's gambling addiction, and knew that Wayne Ray had hocked all his Emerald holdings. Dwight was chewing on him because of his gambling."

"So why didn't he contact us earlier?" I asked.

Yamashita's expression was corrosive. "He didn't make the

connection. It simply didn't occur to Dwight Vaughn that his brother-in-law might be a murderer. And he knew nothing of Wayne being scheduled for the flight, and not being on it."

"Will the United Express deal go through?" I asked.

"Almost certainly." Yamashita sipped his soda. "United is negotiating with the Emerald board—mainly with Charles Ray—for the gates and planes, the hangars, the employment contracts, the works. Couple weeks from now, there won't be any planes with *Emerald* painted on them."

Johnny Moore aka Maloney gave himself a rimshot, the ending cymbal crash ringing nicely through the tavern.

"I'm getting phone calls and letters," Yamashita said, "from relatives of *Sacajawea*'s victims."

"Of Wayne Ray's victims," I corrected him. "*Sacajawea* had nothing to do with it. It was a victim, too."

He nodded. "The relatives still grieve, but now they feel they can rest. Letter after letter, and phone call after phone call, says the same thing, in different ways. Catching Wayne Ray has been a great relief for them. It'll help them put an end to it."

Charles Ray had agreed that his son should not have a headstone in a cemetery because it would leave a tormenting reminder. Ray's body had been cremated, and the ashes quietly disposed of.

"Some of the relatives say they're glad there'll be no trial of Wayne Ray," Suarez said. "They're happy and relieved it all ended in your hallway."

Both Yamashita and Suarez stared at me meaningfully, Yamashita's eyebrows up.

Did they suspect what Linda had done? Ray had been shot twice, once from the back and once from the front, which opened numerous scenarios.

Sarah and I had told the FBI and the King County coroner

that after the first bullet hit him, Ray turned to the door and started to raise his pistol, and so Special Agent Linda Dillon obliged him with a second shot. My daughter and I had no interest in revealing the truth: that Linda had hurried the judicial process with her second shot, that she had decided that life without parole was a possible and yet entirely unacceptable sentence for Wayne Ray.

"Well," Yamashita said finally, realizing they would never know, "we—Jamie and I—know *Sacajawea*'s crash was terrible for you, because of your wife." He glanced at Suarez, maybe looking for assistance finding the right words. "We can only suspect what you went through, working on the crash, and knowing your wife had been killed by it. But you can bring something good away from it all. We caught the bastard."

Janie was still too complicated a subject for me. I didn't want to be helped through anything at this stage, but I nodded my thanks.

Mike Dunham ran up and down a blues scale on his Fender, signaling me that we were on. I shook both men's hands again, and Fred took mine in both his hands for a moment before releasing it.

Will Worthington squeezed Sarah's arm then climbed onto the stage. He put the strap of his bass guitar around his neck. Moore aka Maloney's sticks were up, an expression of mad rapture on his face. He had forgotten to shave the right side of his face, making it appear out of focus.

Normally we kick in with something up-tempo, but I had told Sarah our first song was for her. I stamped the time, Dunham began with the crisp intro riff, and Will and I joined on the first bar. It was Duke Robillard's "You're the One I Adore." Three or four of the patrons turned their chairs to watch the band, one fellow beating time with his ashtray on the table. Most ignored us.

We were into the second verse—my arm and shoulder already aching, but my voice strong—before I looked over to Sarah.

She knew the song. She had to brush away a tear, but she was smiling at me, her old dad.

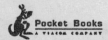
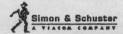